AVENGER OF ROME

www.transworldbooks.co.uk

Also by Douglas Jackson

CALIGULA
CLAUDIUS
HERO OF ROME
DEFENDER OF ROME

For more information on Douglas Jackson and his books,
see his website at www.douglas-jackson.net

AVENGER OF ROME

Douglas Jackson

BANTAM PRESS

LONDON · TORONTO · SYDNEY · AUCKLAND · JOHANNESBURG

TRANSWORLD PUBLISHERS
61–63 Uxbridge Road, London W5 5SA
A Random House Group Company
www.transworldbooks.co.uk

First published in Great Britain
in 2012 by Bantam Press
an imprint of Transworld Publishers

A CIP catalogue record for this book
is available from the British Library.

ISBNs 9780593065167 (cased)
9780593065174 (tpb)

Addresses for Random House Group Ltd companies outside the UK
can be found at: www.randomhouse.co.uk
The Random House Group Ltd Reg. No. 954009

The Random House Group Limited supports the Forest Stewardship Council (FSC®),
the leading international forest-certification organization. Our books carrying the FSC
label are printed on FSC®-certified paper. FSC is the only forest-certification scheme
endorsed by the leading environmental organizations, including Greenpeace. Our
paper procurement policy can be found at www.randomhouse.co.uk/environment.

Typeset in 11½/15¼pt Electra by
Kestrel Data, Exeter, Devon.
Printed and bound by
CPI Group (UK) Ltd, Croydon, CR0 4YY.

2 4 6 8 10 9 7 5 3 1

For Nikki

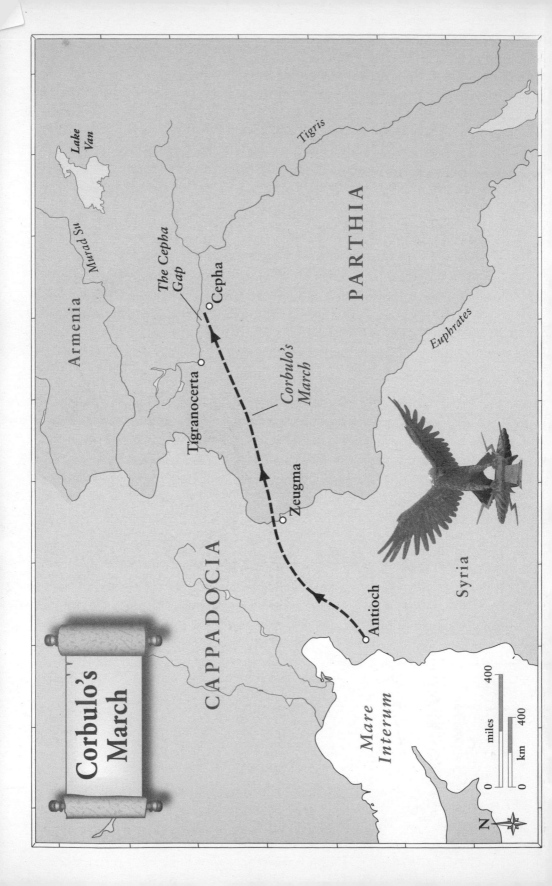

Corbulo's March

Lake Van

Murad Su

Armenia

The Cepha Gap

Cepha

Tigranocerta

Corbulo's March

Zeugma

Antioch

CAPPADOCIA

PARTHIA

Tigris

Euphrates

Syria

Mare Interum

N

miles 0 · · · 400

km 0 · · · 400

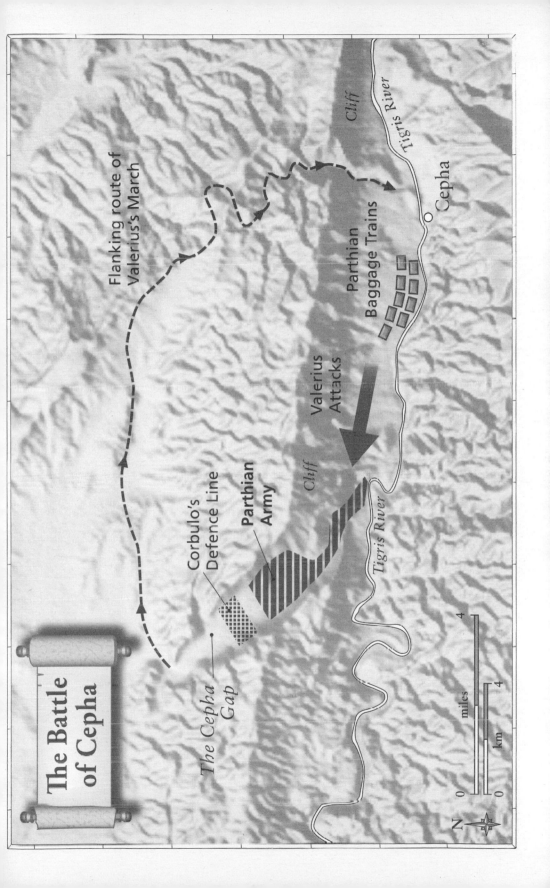

The Battle of Cepha

Flanking route of Valerius's March

The Cepha Gap

Corbulo's Defence Line

Parthian Army

Cliff

Valerius Attacks

Parthian Baggage Trains

Cliff

Tigris River

Tigris River

Tigris River

Cepha

N

miles

km

0   4

0   4

I

'Having restored their discipline, Domitius Corbulo held back
the Parthians with two logions and a very few auxilia'
Sextus Julius Frontinus, *Stratagems*

A man's sword could be his friend or his enemy. Every sword was subtly
different. A rich man's sword would be forged of the finest carbon-rich
iron and have the edge of a surgeon's scalpel. An auxiliary's sword would
be one of a thousand, crude and poorly finished in some provincial
armoury. A poor sword might bend or break. The best swords were like
the men who wielded them: tested to their very limits in the balefire
of battle. The sword Gaius Valerius Verrens held was a warrior's sword.

Valerius studied the blade in the light from the oil lamp. A simple
legionary *gladius*, twenty-two inches long, honed to the sharpness only
a veteran soldier could give it and with a leather hand-grip moulded
by use to the grasp of his fingers. The *gladius* was a killing weapon, no
more and no less. In the right hands it would harvest flesh as efficiently
as a scythe would harvest wheat. Only the decorated pommel, a gleaming silver bulb embossed with a snake-headed Medusa, differentiated
this sword from any other.

His fingers flexed on the grip and his mind sought to gauge the
approaching danger. He had felt the vibrations first: the almost

9

imperceptible shiver resonating through the heat-seasoned earth of the road to the family villa at Fidenae. Now the sensation was swiftly transformed into the muted thunder of galloping horses. There was no fear. If anything, he felt an odd serenity. He had always known they would come. It was only a matter of when. A rustling sound alerted him and he turned, ready to meet the new threat, only to find himself staring into the wide, liquid eyes of his sister Olivia. Of course, she would have heard them. In her own way, she had as much to fear as he. He smiled gently and shook his head. They had gone through this often. Nothing to be done. They would each meet what came in their own fashion. The pale, almost alabaster features turned resolute. She nodded farewell before retreating to make her peace with her God, and find comfort in the dagger that would save her the terrible end the Emperor had dictated for those who worshipped the man Christus. Valerius had debated long and hard whether to follow that route. He knew exactly where to place the point, the angle of penetration and the force required. He raised the sword in front of him, turning the blade into a bar of flickering gold. So beautiful. How many men had felt the sting of its cold metal? To use it on his own flesh would have a certain terrible symmetry. But would that make it his friend or his enemy? A smile flitted briefly across his scarred face as he made his decision.

Others might take that road, but Gaius Valerius Verrens, Hero of Rome and last survivor of the Temple of Claudius, would not.

He emerged into the grey softness of the pre-dawn. Nero would have sent his best. He would face them in the open, where his speed and his skill would give him the greatest advantage. The result was in no doubt, nor did he intend it to be, but he would give them a fight to remember. A soldier's end, because, whatever they said, he would always be a soldier.

The shrill sound of a horse's whinny cut the still air and the rhythmic thud of individual hoofbeats reverberated like the snap of a *ballista* volley. Twenty at least, but then they wouldn't have sent fewer. Soon. Valerius readied himself as the cavalry galloped into the broad courtyard with their red cloaks streaming behind them. His sudden appearance from the shadows gave him the element of surprise and there was a moment of confusion before the decurion in charge sawed his mount to a halt and gaped in disbelief at the tall, commanding figure with the sword in his left hand. It lasted all of a second before he heard the nerve-tingling hiss of twenty blades being unsheathed.

He waited unflinchingly for the command that would begin it and end it. But before it could be given a hooded figure emerged from the centre of the mass and drew back the cowl that hid his face.

'I see you still know how to wield a sword.' A tall man, spare and neat, with his prematurely white hair cropped short. The voice was soft, almost gentle, but it was belied by basilisk eyes that hinted at just how dangerous he could be. 'It is a fine weapon.'

Valerius attempted to hide his astonishment at his visitor's identity. 'As fine as the day you placed it in my hand.'

'But somewhat rash to bare it in the presence of a consul of Rome.'

He replaced the sword in its ornate sheath and bowed to Gaius Suetonius Paulinus, formerly Britain's governor and destroyer of Boudicca's rebel armies, later political outcast and now, against all reason, restored to high office by his Emperor. 'Welcome to my home.'

Paulinus looked around appreciatively at his rustic surroundings. 'A fine estate, but then you have had ample time to concentrate upon it this last year.'

Valerius smiled politely at the unsubtle hint. Of course Paulinus would be fully versed on his self-imposed exile since returning from Africa, where he had served as *quaestor* to the proconsul, Aulus Vitellius. But his heart pounded as he sought a reason for the consul's unlikely appearance. It was five years since they had last met and the then governor of Britain had recommended him for the honour that had changed his life. This was no social visit. Belatedly, he remembered his manners.

'I know it is early, but perhaps you would like to sample our wine?' he offered. 'I will have my slaves see to your horses and feed your men.'

Paulinus shook his head. 'A little water and whatever you normally break your fast with. We have matters to discuss, Gaius Valerius Verrens. Private matters.'

The words *private matters* rang a warning bell in Valerius's head. As he led Paulinus inside he felt as if a dozen arrows were aimed at the centre of his spine. He saw a flash of Olivia's pale features in the door-way of the *triclinium* and steered Paulinus past to the library, which was the most secluded room in the house. The consul pretended to admire a marble bust of Valerius's grandfather while they waited for the slaves to deliver food and leave. Valerius unbelted his sword and placed it on one of the two couches in the room. The other man gave a smile that asked permission to inspect the weapon and took Valerius's look of indecision for acceptance. He slid the sword from the ornate scabbard and weighed it in his hand, his eyes narrowing as he studied the blade. Just for a moment Valerius thought he had misjudged the situation and Paulinus had been sent to kill him, but eventually the consul nodded in satisfaction and slid it home.

'A fine sword, indeed. A sword worthy of the man who held the Temple of Claudius to the last man.' He reached beneath his cloak and withdrew a slim object which he handed to Valerius. 'You served your Emperor well at Colonia. Now you have your opportunity to serve him again.'

What Valerius held in his hand was a leather tube, dark brown and weathered with age, about twelve inches in length and with the scuffs and scrapes of long usage clear beneath the layers of constant waxing. The imperial seal, an image of the Emperor Nero as the Sun King, was embossed in wax across the join.

'Open it.'

He felt Paulinus's eyes on him as he wedged the tube in his right hand and worked at the stiff flap with his left. The contents were a single sheet of parchment.

'Read it, please. Aloud.'

Valerius was surprised at the power in his voice as he deciphered the neat clerkish hand. '*Gaius Valerius Verrens, Hero of Rome, is to assume the rank of senior military tribune and proceed to the headquarters of General Gnaeus Domitius Corbulo, there to take up the position of second in command, and to undertake whatever duties the general sees fit in the service of the Empire.*' There was more. Travel details and a list of personal equipment. A warrant for passage on a ship leaving from Ostia in one week.

His head spun. *Gaius Valerius Verrens, Hero of Rome, is to assume the rank of senior military tribune.* And with Corbulo, Rome's greatest general. The man who had outfought and outthought the tribes of Germania and whose feats of engineering had astounded the Empire. So why did he feel as if he held a squirming viper? He looked up and sensed the almost mocking glint in the granite-chip eyes that surveyed him from beneath Paulinus's heavy brows.

'The appointment does not please you?'

Valerius stared at the older man. 'It pleases me well enough, but the method of delivery surprises me. I ask myself why a serving consul of Rome should rise before dawn and ride six miles to convey a routine message from the Palatium that could have been delivered at any time by imperial courier.'

'Call it an old comrade's whim,' Paulinus suggested, the pale lips curving upwards in a parody of a smile.

'Call it a trap. If you are going to play games with me, consul, perhaps it would be better if you left now.' Valerius kept his tone unforgiving and he allowed his eyes to stray to the sword. 'I am no longer the boy you knew.'

Paulinus's rasping laugh surprised him. 'So the pup has not lost his fangs. Yes,' he admitted, 'there is more, but I doubt it will give you any greater pleasure. A direct order from the Emperor to his subject which must be delivered by someone trusted by both and conveyed by word of mouth only. It is this.' The consul's voice hardened, along with the eyes. 'Gnaeus Domitius Corbulo is suspected of overstepping the powers of *imperium* granted him in the east by his Emperor. While you are on his staff you will compile a report on his activities and those of his senior officers. That report will be thorough and objective and when it is completed you will find a way to get it into my hands.'

'You are asking me to spy?'

Paulinus sniffed. 'I am told you have some talents in that direction.'

'That was different.' Valerius remembered his pursuit of Petrus, the Christian leader, two years earlier. 'The man was an enemy of the state. General Corbulo is . . .'

'Successful, quite ruthless and utterly vain, and that vanity makes

13

him certain of his infallibility. So certain that he believes he can overrule the Emperor's advisers and follow his own policy in Armenia and Cappadocia. If that suggestion is confirmed it may be that Corbulo will be withdrawn, perhaps even retired.' The words contained a hint of satisfaction and Valerius was reminded of something else: that before his disgrace, Suetonius Paulinus had vied with Corbulo for the position of Rome's paramount general. 'It will not be an easy assignment. Corbulo has friends in the Palatium and at court. He may well hear of your mission and, if he does, he will try to delay you or stop you entirely.' Paulinus hesitated and the younger man noticed the unnecessary emphasis his visitor placed on the last three words. 'The task requires a man of resource and courage, but Gaius Valerius Verrens has proved himself to be such a man in the past. Your Emperor has every faith in you.'

If his situation hadn't been so perilous, Valerius would have laughed at the blatant flattery. Instead, he said: 'I am honoured by the Emperor's confidence in my abilities, but I do not believe I have the capacity to complete this mission successfully. I am a simple soldier, without the . . . subtlety required. He has other men, better qualified than I, he can call upon, I'm sure.' He stood, but Paulinus remained seated and fury flared like a flash of lightning in his eyes. Boudicca's conqueror might be a consul in name only, but he still had power and knew how to use it.

'You forget yourself, young man. I can think of a dozen others who would cut off their right arms for the chance to prove their faith to the Emperor.' He cast a contemptuous glance at the carved wooden fist that had replaced Valerius's right hand. 'They now lie in the depths of the Palatine awaiting his pleasure.' Paulinus had raised his voice and it must have been a signal because Valerius heard scuffling behind him. He turned to find Olivia held by two of Paulinus's bodyguards – a helpless, waif-like figure shivering with fear. 'It would take but a single word and the family of Verrens would join them. Do not think we are unaware of the conflicting loyalties within this house. You cannot hide from reality for ever, as you have hidden here from those who could have linked you to the traitor Piso's cause. Consuls, senators and knights have been imprisoned and tortured, their families forced to take poison. Your old mentor, Seneca. Did you believe your isolation freed you from his taint? Gaius Valerius Verrens should know better than most men that there are no innocents on the battlefield, and that in a fight to the death those who believe otherwise will be crushed.' For a moment, Valerius considered making a grab for the sword lying so conveniently at Paulinus's right hand, but he knew that even if he reached it Olivia would be dead before he could turn. Paulinus saw his glance and smiled. 'Think yourself fortunate that you have been given the luxury of choice.'

The reality was that there had never been any choice, and they both knew it. Paulinus nodded as Valerius acknowledged his defeat and Olivia protested as she was taken from the room.

'She will be safe under the Emperor's protection while you are in Antioch. You understand your orders?'

The answer was no, but the word that emerged from Valerius's mouth was 'Yes'.

Paulinus rose to his feet. 'You will visit the Palatium where they will be explained to you in more detail. Methods of communication. Friends you may depend on and those to avoid.' Valerius turned to go, but Paulinus wasn't finished with him. 'It is possible that your investigations may uncover something more than mere vanity and over-enthusiasm at Corbulo's headquarters.' He paused to allow the full significance of his words to register. 'Should that be the case, you may be required to take further, more direct, action.' He picked up the sword with the silver hilt and placed it in the younger man's left hand. 'Do we understand each other?'

Valerius nodded, because the words would have choked him.

Yes, they understood each other.

If he discovered any link between Rome's greatest general and the Piso conspiracy he would become Gnaeus Domitius Corbulo's executioner.

II

Valerius twitched the reins to steer the big gelding around a stationary cart. Portus, which Emperor Claudius had begun building at the Tiber mouth almost twenty years earlier and was still only half completed, must be the busiest port in the world, he thought. It was a bustling place of trade and commerce where wagons and packhorses thronged the streets and smaller boats scuttled like water beetles among the stately giants loading up for the grain convoys to the east. They had to ask twice before they were eventually directed to where their ship was docked.

'By Mars' sacred arse, will you look at that.'

Valerius reined the horse to a stop and followed his companion's eye towards the vessel that waited to carry them to Syria. He would have expected a well-worn cargo ship, or at best a fast military galley to transport General Corbulo's new second in command to his posting. This was anything but. It was larger than any normal merchant vessel, forty paces from elegant bow to angular stern, with a breadth of perhaps ten or twelve where the hull bellied out like a pregnant sow between them. Astonishingly, the ship was painted a bright gold, so that it shone like a jewel in the sunlight. The figure of a swan with wings outstretched was carved above the bowsprit. A substantial curtained awning had been set up behind the single central mast and a pair of twin steering oars projected from below a platform in the stern. As they watched, lines of slaves hurried up the gangplanks carrying assorted sacks and *amphorae*.

'An imperial ship?'

'Or a floating whorehouse?' Serpentius offered.

'Either way it can't be for us.'

But he was wrong.

An ancient sailor burned almost black by the sun ambled up and gave an awkward salute. 'Tribune Verrens?' Valerius nodded. 'My captain requests that you embark your horses and equipment within the hour. We sail as soon as our other passengers arrive.'

'Other passengers?'

The man's face took on the blank stare of a legionary on parade.

Valerius exchanged an amused glance with his companion. 'Curiouser and curiouser. In that case send some slaves to unload the mules and get our mounts aboard.' The two men supervised as the nervous animals were walked up the unfamiliar wooden gangplank and into the stifling darkness of the hold.

'I'll come down twice a day to make sure they're properly fed and watered,' Serpentius said as they returned to the deck. Valerius nodded. He wouldn't like to be whoever was responsible if Serpentius discovered that the horses were neglected. The former gladiator was the most capable fighter he had ever known and a slave in name only. Part companion, part bodyguard, the wiry Spaniard wore his manumission on a leather loop round his neck and swore he would use it when he elected and not when some Roman decided it was time. They had been together almost three years and the first time they'd met, on the dusty surface of a gladiatorial practice ground, Serpentius had tried to kill him. The resentful eyes and shaven head with its patchwork of half-healed scars made men wary of him, and they were right to be. There would come a time when the gladiator needed to be told the true nature of his mission. For the moment, all he knew was that Valerius was travelling to a new appointment in Antioch.

They emerged into the sunshine to the usual organized chaos of a ship being prepared for sail – with one peculiar difference. Amongst the sailors loading last-minute provisions Valerius saw one man sprinkling water on the planking: perfumed water, if his nose didn't mistake him, that masked but didn't quite overcome the stench from the bilges and the familiar scents of sea salt, male sweat and new laid pitch. Serpentius shook his head, muttered something about being right about the brothel, and went off to check their equipment was properly stored. Valerius noticed a heavily built man in conversation with a young legionary officer. The older man looked up and they both hurried across to greet him.

'Aelius Aurelius, *magister navis*,' the captain introduced himself in a voice that would be useful in a howling gale. His accent marked him as a southerner, as did his looks. Dark, soulful eyes shone from heavy-browed features weathered to the colour of polished teak and his hair was styled in long ringlets. A thick gold ring hung from the lobe of his right ear. 'My apologies for not welcoming you on board the *Golden Cygnet*, tribune. But if I take my eyes off these dogs they'll turn the deck into a latrine.'

Valerius smiled at the exaggeration. He doubted if a single rope's end was out of place in this ship. 'Unless my nose is mistaken your deck smells more like a lady's bedroom than a latrine, captain. I had expected a less elaborate transport.'

Aurelius's laugh sounded like a seal barking. 'She may look like a fat-bottomed old tart in her imperial livery, but she's the sweetest sailing ship in the Mare Nostrum and can lie closer to the wind than most. You may thank your fellow passenger for the Emperor's generosity.'

The young soldier noticed Valerius's look of surprise and shook his head. 'Please don't think I'm the cause of all this, sir. Tiberius Claudius Crescens, junior tribune, on the way to join General Corbulo's eastern forces, and may I venture to say that your fame precedes you.'

Valerius studied him for any hint of mockery. He'd seen the pink-cheeked soldier dart a glance at his sleeve, where the walnut-carved fist replaced his right hand, the only visible scar of his encounter with Boudicca. The boy was what the legionaries called 'frontier fodder', one of the young officers Rome sent to the farthest points of her Empire to learn fast or die fast. Tiberius had the plump, earnest face and bright eyes of a teenager, but he must be past twenty and well connected to have been given such a prestigious assignment. Eventually, to the younger man's relief, Valerius smiled acceptance of the compliment. 'Then who is responsible for our good fortune?'

His question was answered by a commotion on the far side of the harbour which alerted them to the arrival of a four-wheeled carriage escorted by a detachment of German auxiliary cavalry. The coach clattered over the cobbles and drew to a halt by the foremost gangplank.

'About time,' the *Golden Cygnet*'s master grumbled. 'I'd have preferred to wait until the next grain convoy east, but my sailing orders were specific. The only consolation is that we'll have a pair of galleys from the base at Misenum to keep us safe from any sea scum as far as Creta. The gods be thanked that she sent her baggage in advance. Still, we should make Neapolis by nightfall. Say a prayer to Poseidon and we'll be in Seleucia Pieria in twelve days.' He let out a roar. 'Ready the sails!'

The ship burst into life around them and Valerius watched as a slim figure in a blue veil dismounted from the coach and swept up the gangway accompanied by a pair of dark slave girls. The little procession was followed by another, older woman, and finally four of the cavalry escort relinquished their mounts and marched towards the ship. Tiberius Crescens laughed.

'I almost forgot. I'm supposed to take command of her guard.' He rushed for the top of the gangway, grinning over his shoulder. 'The lady Domitia Longina Corbulo, the general's daughter. It should certainly make the voyage interesting.'

III

With a favourable wind and light seas the *Cygnet* made good time on the first leg of her journey south, and as her captain had predicted she set anchor off Neapolis as dusk fell. There was just enough soft roseate light to show the bay in all its glory: the familiar sweeping curve of low grey cliff and white sand, washed by a gentle sea the colour of aged Niger wine. Above it, the rustic cloak of grey and green that garbed the great mountain which dominated the city shone gold in the dying embers of the day.

Valerius was relieved that he'd seen little of his fellow passengers during the sedate, timeless run down the coast from Ostia. The guilt he felt over his unwanted mission was more than enough without being confronted by Corbulo's daughter to remind him of it. He had spent his time trying to discover some kind of escape, but without success. For the moment, all he could do was carry on and make his decision when the moment came.

Makeshift accommodation had been created in the bow for Domitia and her women, and they'd stayed there all day, behind screens, amid rumours that the lady and her entourage were stricken by the usual first-time sailor's malady. Seasickness had never bothered Valerius and the same was obviously true for Tiberius Crescens, who had divided his time between his duties as guard commander and badgering his superior for stories of the British war. Valerius had told the tale a thousand times and had perfected a version that played down his own part in the defence of Colonia and gave credit to the real heroes: men like Falco, veteran centurion of the Twentieth legion and commander of the Colonia militia; brave Lunaris, who had stood at his side through the dark days of the temple; and the legionaries, Gracilis and Messor, who had given their lives so that he could fight on.

'So all you did was stand back and direct the battle?' The younger man didn't try to hide his doubt.

'That is what a commander must do,' Valerius said airily. 'As I am sure you will find out one day.'

Tiberius preened at the flattery, but he refused to be discouraged. 'Yet the Emperor awarded you the Corona Aurea, the Gold Crown of Valour?'

Valerius shrugged. 'Colonia was a disaster, but just one of many. When the last battle was won and Boudicca dead, the governor of Britain needed a hero – a live hero. As the only Roman survivor of the Temple of Claudius he had little choice but to honour me.'

Tiberius had stared out over the sea as it flowed beneath the wooden keel, endless and anonymous, barely rippling in the light breeze that carried them southwards. The land was just a faint presence on the far horizon. 'And the barbarians took your hand. I think I would rather die than not be able to hold a sword again.'

If the words hadn't been spoken so innocently – a little boy musing on whether the moon might be made of cheese – Valerius would have been tempted to throw the young man over the side. But Tiberius probably couldn't swim, and since he'd just come off duty his buoyancy was unlikely to be helped by the plate armour that covered his chest and shoulders. He sighed.

'We'll see how well I can hold a sword tomorrow, tribune. Exercise for you and your men at dawn. I'm sure they will have some wooden practice swords and a couple of shields aboard that we can borrow.'

Tiberius turned and saluted. Was there just the hint of mischief in his eye? 'Of course, sir. I will arrange it. Tomorrow at dawn. Exercise with sword and shield, sir.'

21

*

By the time Valerius woke, the *Golden Cygnet* was well under way and the sun came up between two hills on the eastern horizon, creating a spectacular bridge of light between ship and land. He took a deep breath of invigorating sea air and tasted the salt on his lips. Serpentius had already risen from his place on the deck, and the distinctive clash of two wooden swords, followed instantly by the boom of a blade against one of the big curved *scutum* shields, reminded Valerius how he had planned to start the day. His first action, as it was every morning, was to oil the mottled purple stump of his right arm and fit the wooden hand on its thick cowhide socket over the end. With his teeth and the fingers of his left hand, made nimble by habit, he tightened and knotted the leather bindings. The arm had been chopped off four inches above the wrist by a Celtic battle sword and the replacement was designed to exactly match the length of the original. Satisfied, he wrapped a short kilt round his waist and set out along the deck towards the small group of men gathered just behind the bow.

As he approached, Serpentius, tall and leopard lean, walked past and whispered: 'Beware of the puppy.'

Valerius raised an eyebrow and the Spaniard grinned, taking his seat on a coiled pile of rope. Tiberius looked relaxed as he stood among his men, dressed in a short white tunic.

'My apologies for keeping you and your men waiting, tribune.' Valerius took in the glances at the carved walnut fist, which, as always, ranged between amusement and contempt, either of which was better than pity.

'No apologies required, sir.' Tiberius smiled. 'We were eager to get started, and put on an exhibition of basic swordplay for your slave. He seemed most interested. Perhaps you should have him trained? He has the build for it and a slave who can fight might save your life one day.'

Valerius somehow kept his face straight. 'I will think on it, Tiberius, but a slave with a blade seems quite wrong. The Spanish rogue is as likely to slit my throat as protect me.'

A big, curve-edged shield of raw wood lay against the bowsprit and Valerius pushed his arm through the leather strap and fitted the walnut fist, which had been carved specifically to take a standard *scutum*, to the grip. One of the cavalrymen handed him a practice sword cut from seasoned oak and he weighed it in his left hand. It was the same length and design as the basic legionary *gladius*, but almost twice as heavy. It had no edge and a blunt point, but in the right hands it could still be dangerous. 'All right, who's first?'

The German cavalrymen eyed him warily, taking in the hard eyes and sharp-edged, angular features of a face that wore its trials like a badge of honour. One-handed or not, the scars he bore were evidence they faced a veteran fighter. Valerius had always been powerfully built, but daily practice with Serpentius had broadened his shoulders and toughened his arms and legs. The former gladiator had taught him the merits of speed and footwork as well as a useful assortment of dirty tricks from the arena. He looked confident because he was. He chose the most likely of the four. 'You.'

'Sir!' The man saluted and faced up to him three paces away on the wooden deck, crouching with his shield in his left hand and the sword in his right. His first moves were tentative because he had never faced a left-handed man. Valerius allowed him to take the initiative, meeting each attack as it came and leaving it until late to counter. Gradually, the cavalryman gained confidence and his attacks were launched with more venom. Valerius let him work up a sweat before calling a halt and ordering the next man forward. There was nothing to be gained by humiliating the soldier; bad feeling in the cramped confines of a ship, even one the size of the *Golden Cygnet*, would only fester and spread.

The bouts proved what he had expected. The *gladius* was an infantry-man's weapon, designed to be used in a shield line. Double-edged, and with a needle-sharp triangular point, it was a highly efficient, deadly weapon in the hands of a man who knew how to use it. In battle, each legionary braced his shield against the man on his right and, once they were in contact with the enemy, rammed the shield forward to create a narrow gap through which the point of his *gladius* could dart into an opponent's abdomen. They were taught never to inflict a wound more than three inches deep, but when combined with the classic ripping, twisting withdrawal such injuries were invariably fatal. Valerius had seen a legionary cohort cut down a force of attacking tribesmen twice their number, like farmers harvesting a field of corn.

These men were cavalry troopers, more used to wielding the longer and heavier *spatha* from the saddle. The *spatha* was a fearsome killer in the hands of a man who knew how to use it, but the technique, basically hacking and bludgeoning an opponent's head and neck, was entirely different from the *gladius*-wielder's. It meant the men were slow and awkward on their feet, lacked any feel for the sword and held the shield as if it was an encumbrance and not a weapon of both attack and defence. He resolved to repeat the exercise every morning, so that when they left the ship they were better equipped for battle than when they boarded. He felt an unaccustomed surge of joy overwhelm the melancholy that had settled over him since he'd left Fidenae. He was a soldier again.

'I suppose I must be next?' Tiberius smiled absently as he untied his tunic and pulled it over his head.

For some reason Valerius felt the hair rise on the back of his neck. It was exactly the feeling he'd had when he'd led patrols among the innocent woods and harmless rolling hills of southern Britain, right up to the moment the innocent woods had turned out not to be so innocent and the rolling hills had spewed out fifty blood-crazed Celtic champions.

IV

Beware of the puppy. Tiberius Crescens might have the face of a benign cherub and the bumbling awkwardness of a fledgling philosopher, but when he stripped to his loincloth Valerius immediately recognized what Serpentius had known by sheer instinct. He was facing a warrior. The young tribune had the stocky, muscular physique of a professional athlete and short, solid legs, but he balanced on his feet like a dancer. The boyish features were like the velvet glove that covered a boxer's brass knuckles: the disguise that made you underestimate the danger beneath. There was something else, too, a fierce concentration in the eyes and a tension in the body that reminded Valerius of a bear trap ready to snap shut. The last time he'd seen the combination was at the gladiator school in Rome where he'd found the Spaniard. All that was missing was hate.

Tiberius picked up a shield and moved into position, the wooden *gladius* steady in his right hand. At first Valerius wondered why the boy had revealed his true self. Why not maintain the disguise and take his opponent by surprise? A hint of a smile flickered on the younger man's face and gave Valerius his answer. It wasn't, as he'd half suspected, arrogance or conceit: quite the opposite. Tiberius wanted him to know, because, above all, Tiberius wanted his respect. A fair contest between the unblooded boy and the seasoned Hero of Rome. No subterfuge. No

25

tricks. Just warrior against warrior. Valerius felt a rush of energy as he realized he could be in the fight of his life.

Battle madness they called it, but there were different kinds of battle madness. He had seen British warriors drunk on blood charge into a wall of shields and try to tear out Roman throats with their teeth. He had felt it himself, in the final moments in the Temple of Claudius when the great double doors had smashed open in an explosion of fire and smoke. And there was the mechanical madness of the fighting machine that was the Roman legion, as it killed and killed again until there was nothing left to kill on the slope where Boudicca had fought her last battle. This was the white heat of war, when a man lost his mind and rose above the field of blood on a red-eyed wave of Elysian rapture.

Then there was the kind of madness Valerius needed now. The cold, detached madness of the true killer. A man had to seek this madness within. It took a different kind of courage to allow some inner power to rule heart and mind and body. To let speed and power and instinct be dictated by a force beyond understanding or design. Valerius never took his eyes off his opponent's and he saw the moment Tiberius found what *he* sought. He allowed his mind to clear and his body to empty of emotion. It was like being inside a flawless diamond. The coldness started at the centre before expanding to fill him from head to toe.

'Fight.'

To the watchers, the early movements were less a battle than a court-ship. A gentle collision of sword and shield. A ritual coming and going of bare feet on boards now hot from the morning sun. A seeking with-out finding. Probe and counter probe. Stroke and counter stroke.

In the cold core of his mind Valerius understood that Tiberius had watched and analysed every action of the earlier bouts, and from that briefest of scrutinies had formed a greater understanding of a left-handed fighter's strengths and weaknesses than any other man he had faced. But Valerius *was* a left-handed fighter and he *knew* what Tiberius had only seen. Each attack came from the angle he expected. When the young tribune's deft feet carried him to an impossible position of strength, Valerius was there to meet the blow before it began to fall. A moment of comedy, with each man so attuned to the other's movement that they appeared to be dancing.

Slowly, the tempo increased as they found each other's measure. Sword against sword, shield against shield. Feinting right and left, up and down, always seeking that elusive opening. The cavalrymen gasped at the speed of the attacks and even Serpentius's face wore a puzzled frown. By now the sweat was coursing over Valerius's eyes, but his unconscious mind saw beyond it. Tiberius was like a wraith in the distance. Where the spectators saw a halo of blurred movement, Valerius experienced everything as if the two men were fighting under water. It was as though he could read his opponent's every thought and intention, prepare for each attack and have the time to choose the exact manoeuvre that would nullify it. He wasn't aware of effort or tiredness or pain. He was what he was. Gaius Valerius Verrens, Hero of Rome.

A blade's length away, Tiberius barely noted his opponent's existence. He recognized the sweat-slick, muscled figure with the sword-scarred face only as a machine that countered his every move. Make one attack and three came back in reply. Find an opening and the body that had invited the sword was gone before the point could reach it. At times it was as if he was fighting two men. By now he understood they were equal in strength and speed and stamina. Their ability with the weapons matched as if they had emerged from the same womb. Still he knew that he would win, because this was what he had been born for.

The rattle of oak upon oak was a never-ending roll of thunder. The speed, which for ordinary men would have been impossible to maintain for a few minutes, had been kept up for more than fifteen. And still the swords flew and the noise grew to a climax. It could not last. Surely one of them had to give? No man was capable of sustaining such a tempo.

A snapping crash. A fracture in the rhythm. A scream of victory.

'No!'

Valerius felt an iron grip on his sword arm. His eyes focused on Serpentius standing beside him. Tiberius lay on his back with the splintered remains of his sword in his hand and the point of Valerius's wooden *gladius* an inch from his right eye. He was still smiling.

'I think we've given the ladies enough entertainment for today.' Serpentius nodded over Valerius's left shoulder and he turned his head to look towards the curtained pavilion ten feet away. The scene resembled a marble tableau he had once seen in Nero's private quarters in the Domus Transitoria: three young women in almost identical poses, but wearing different expressions. Domitia Longina's two slave girls had their hands to their mouths, one in horror and the other in delight. The general's daughter stood slightly behind them, tall, imperious and obviously fully recovered from her seasickness, wearing a red dress and a look of puzzled amusement. It was the first time Valerius had seen her face properly and something lurched inside him as he realized whom she resembled. Before the older woman emerged from the tent to shoo her charges inside he felt an almost physical pain as he remembered another momentous meeting, in the courtyard of the Temple of Claudius. A meeting that had changed his life and almost cost him it.

'I hope I didn't tire you, sir?' Tiberius stood at his shoulder, his eyes on the group disappearing behind the curtains.

'No. A pity it ended so quickly – I was just getting into my rhythm.'

Tiberius grinned at the lie. 'Do you have any suggestions for an honest journeyman?'

Now it was Valerius's turn to smile. It took him a few moments to remember the words of Marcus, the arena veteran who trained the gladiators, on the day he had met Serpentius. 'An old gladiator once told me: don't fight like a one-handed man, or a two-handed man. Fight like a killer.' The younger man nodded solemnly. 'But I think you already know that, Tiberius.'

The tribune's grin deepened and he turned to walk away.

'And Tiberius?'

'Yes, sir.'

'Never underestimate your opponent.'

V

The *Golden Cygnet* passed through the Strait of Messana on the morning of the fourth day, with the vast dusty bulk of Sicilia a mile to their right and, to their left, the province of Lucania, the most southern point of mainland Italia. Valerius stood beside the steering platform with captain Aurelius as they left the mainland behind.

'Make course due east,' the sailor ordered. The steersmen grunted as they hauled the massive oars against the force of the waters rushing below the hull and the sailmaster, a tall Nubian, trimmed the sails to make the best speed on their new course. Valerius watched as the two naval galleys kept station, sleek and narrow as a pair of dolphins, three ship-lengths off the bow. Aurelius reached up to touch the *tutela*, the carved talisman of Poseidon that protected the ship. 'If the wind gods favour us we'll make landfall on the Achaean coast two hours before dark. I have a mind to anchor up early today. The lady Domitia has graciously invited us to join her for dinner.'

Aurelius misinterpreted Valerius's look of alarm. 'Yes, it is unusual, but she is an unusual young woman. Her father's daughter, I would say. Her mother died in Antioch two months ago, after a long illness, and the Emperor offered the use of this ship as soon as he heard. She bears her grief like a soldier. Your companion the young tribune is also invited to attend, as well as the commanders of the two *classis* galleys.'

29

The master's entreaty to Poseidon must have been successful because the *Cygnet* and her two outriders cut an arrow-straight furrow across the cobalt waters of the Aegean and they anchored in a sheltered bay with the mountains of central Achaea a brown haze in the distance when the sun was still well above the western horizon. Valerius could make out a settlement on the far side of the bay. After consulting with their host's freedwoman, a widow called Tulia whose every disappointment was written in her curled lip and small, suspicious eyes, Aurelius sent a swimmer to organize fresh fruit and vegetables and anything else that would enhance the meal, while a rough table built by the ship's carpenter was set up in front of the lady Domitia's curtained tent. The arrival of an imperial ship had caused a sensation in the village, and within an hour small boats were ferrying back and forth with the produce of the land. Others, filled with spectators, simply anchored while the occupants stared in awe at the great gold-painted hull.

'Keep them away unless they have something to sell,' Aurelius roared as one boat came too close to his paintwork. 'I don't want any thieving Greek getting on board this ship.'

Valerius washed on deck in a bucket of sea water, and Serpentius erected a curtain to allow him to dress in privacy. Over his best tunic with the broad stripe of a senior tribune on the hem and sleeves he wore a moulded leather breastplate embossed with silver and the white cloak which differentiated him from any other officer in the legion. No sword or crested helmet, for this was a purely social occasion. He ran his hand through his hair and exchanged a glance with the Spaniard.

'You look like a scarred old tom leopard in a dress, but you'll do,' was Serpentius's opinion. 'I've seen you looking less nervous before a fight. Mind you, that Tulia's face is enough to scare a Scythian sword-swallower into an early grave. Or is there someone else who frightens you?'

Valerius decided not to hear the final sentence. Tiberius, scrubbed, polished and wearing armour buffed to a mirror shine, was waiting just the right distance from the table to be polite. Beside him stood the two captains of the escort galleys, who if anything appeared even younger than their companion. They saluted Valerius, warily eyeing the wooden hand and the vivid red line that scarred his face from below his left eye to the corner of his mouth, but Tiberius noticed his smile.

'I apologize if we have amused you, sir.'

'Never apologize for amusing someone, Tiberius; there is not enough amusement in the world. And never mistake jest for insult, or you may find that winning a battle costs more than you are willing to pay. I was just thinking that you fight as if you were born with a sword in your hand.'

The young man nodded, accepting the compliment as his due. 'Thank you, sir. And it's almost true. My father was legate of the Fifteenth Primigenia and later the Eighth Augusta, so my brother and I grew up in military headquarters on the Rhenus and in Moesia. We loved him, of course, but he was a man of little imagination and our education was limited to basics such as grammar and rhetoric. He was very insistent that we should be self-sufficient in every way, so we trained and exercised with the soldiers each day. The armourer first fashioned me a small sword when I was four years old, I believe, and apart from the occasional childhood illness I have held one every day from that to this.'

He was interrupted as the curtains of the tent fell back and the lady Domitia Longina Corbulo took her place at the head of the table. She had exchanged red for blue, a long flowing gown that bared the unblemished flesh of her shoulders and was low enough to give a hint of shadow between her bound breasts. Dark, piercing eyes took in each of the guests in turn. She could only have been seventeen at most, but the way she carried herself reminded Valerius of an Egyptian princess, slim and lithe and at one with herself and her destiny. Confident, but not arrogant. Clear of mind and clear of purpose. Tulia, the freedwoman, emerged to sit on a second small bench. The younger of Domitia's slave girls, a pretty dark-skinned child who looked about fourteen, led Aurelius to the longer bench on the hostess's left before returning for Tiberius and the two young naval commanders and finally Valerius, who ended up sitting closest to Domitia in the place of honour to her right.

The general's daughter waited until they were settled before she spoke.

'You must forgive me for the unorthodox seating arrangements, honoured guests, but this is an unorthodox occasion. I hope you will not find it too upsetting not to recline. I fear our couches are so narrow that we would all end up falling to the deck – that is what we call the floor of the ship, is it not, master Aurelius?' She said it with a smile and Aurelius answered with an embarrassed grunt which Domitia gracefully accepted as agreement. She clapped her hands twice and the slave girls appeared with silver cups and a jug of wine. 'I have taken the liberty of watering it, but only slightly, because it is very fine, and fine wine deserves not to be adulterated too much, do you not agree, tribune?'

The question was directed at Valerius, but the wine and the ability to answer seemed to stick in his throat. It was a few seconds before he was able to speak and when he did the banality of his words horrified him. 'I am afraid my acquaintance with wine of this quality is so fleeting as to deny me an opinion, my lady Domitia, but . . .'

Tiberius saved him. 'A Falernian, I think, brother Valerius,' he interrupted. 'And perhaps aged ten years, but I'm sure you would have outed it in the end. The sweetness is the key; nothing that came off those slopes could generate so much honey in less time.'

Valerius heard a snort of annoyance from the far end of the table.

'I am afraid Tulia disapproves of our gathering,' Domitia explained. 'As she disapproves of much that I do. But surely it is not right to be confined to our quarters on an adventure such as this? It will be the first time in two years that I shall have seen my father. In any case, I wished to congratulate you on the condition of your ship, captain Aurelius. I had heard sea voyages were arduous and dangerous, but apart from Tulia's constant complaining this has been most pleasant.' Aurelius bowed his shaggy head. 'May I ask how long it will be before we reach Antioch?'

'We are at the mercy of the sea gods, lady,' the sailor ventured. 'But with good fortune we will reach Syria in just over a week. In a few days we will call in at Creta to resupply and take on cargo.' He produced a rare smile. 'Timber, olive oil and cloth will offset the cost of the voyage. The Emperor is a generous man, but he likes his ships to turn a profit.'

The fare was surprisingly good. Domitia had brought on board a plentiful supply of preserved food, and a selection of fresh and pickled vegetables from the village was followed by shoulder of hare, cuts of salted pork and two whole chickens. Aurelius had supplied a sizeable tunny fish, cooked black on the outside and bloody in the middle as the crew of the *Golden Cygnet* preferred it. The taller of the two naval officers ate voraciously, as if he never expected to see food again, while the other held Valerius's attention with a lecture on shipboard fighting tactics.

'The key is to fight on your enemy's ground. If he outnumbers you, which he generally does in our case, once he has boarded you it is only a matter of time before he prevails. So you must board him. The first two or three over the side will probably die, of course' – his smile said it was regrettable but necessary – 'but once you have formed your shield line you will find your Roman soldier or even marine is a match for any pirate.'

Valerius thanked him. He kept his eyes on the table, but his attention was drawn to Domitia, who was discussing the uprising in Judaea with Tiberius. The war had begun so disastrously for the Roman commander of the province, Cestius Florus, that rumour said he was to be replaced by Titus Flavius Vespasian, one of the generals who had conquered Britain for Claudius almost a quarter of a century earlier. 'I had thought we might be diverted there, but it will be an honour to serve with your father,' the younger tribune said smoothly. 'His success in Armenia has brought new laurels to the Empire. They say that even now their king is in Rome paying homage to the Emperor.'

Domitia nodded gravely. 'You may find serving with my father more of an honour than you are comfortable with, tribune. His reputation as a disciplinarian is well deserved and I have no doubt that you are replacing some young officer who has failed to meet his standards.'

'Discipline comes easily to me, my lady,' Tiberius said offhandedly.

'But no soldier is so perfect that he cannot be improved by more training. I will use what time I have on board to prepare.'

She smiled. 'He would have been impressed by your display yesterday morning, though possibly not by the fact that I witnessed it.'

'My apologies, lady.' Valerius found his voice at last. 'We should have taken more care. From now on we will exercise in the stern. You will not be disturbed again, I hope.'

'Do not concern yourself, tribune.' Domitia gave a coarse little laugh. 'I found it most instructive. If ever I discover myself with a sword in my hand, at least I will know what to do with it. In any case, if blame there was, it was mine. I was curious and, as Tulia is always reminding me, sometimes curiosity takes you places you should not go.'

VI

Summer, AD 66

The Sun King looked out upon his people from the balcony of the great Golden House he had built over the ashes of Rome's third district and felt an unexpected surge of affection. Less than two years ago thousands of Romans lived their shabby little lives on this very land, but the gift of fire had allowed him to substitute splendour for squalor and magnificence for mediocrity. The houses and apartments had been replaced by a vast country villa in the centre of the urban landscape; three hundred and sixty paces from wing to wing, with three hundred rooms each filled with rare bronzes, gilt statues and the finest artworks in the Empire, all surrounded by trees and pasture and lakes, and a great park in which roamed wild animals from all over the world. A Golden House for a Golden Age, and this would be the greatest day of that age.

With perfect timing the morning sun rose above the hills and everything around him gleamed as its rays reached out to caress the gold leaf and gold paint and golden statuary which covered the front of the vast building. The effect was such that it blinded those unfortunate enough not to be shielded by the huge cloth awning which portrayed him in his chariot driving the four horses of the sun god. His heart swelled with pride. He wanted them to be blinded. Blinded by his magnificence. Awed by his power.

He was not a fool. He understood he had lost the Senate and the aristocracy. But he still had the people and he still had the legions and he still had his Praetorian Guard. These were the triumvirate which cemented his power, not the whining politicians who complained at every expense and every little excess. The Golden House, which stretched between the Palatine and Esquiline hills, had come close to bankrupting the imperial treasury. Tigellinus, his commander of the Guard, could only ensure its completion by ordering the officials to cut the silver content of the denarius, but it was all worth it, because this – and his heart beat faster as he considered what he had achieved – this was his legacy to his people. No longer could he be compared to Divine Augustus and found wanting. In the Golden House he had created a monument to Rome's glory that outshone anything his illustrious ancestor had been able to devise. A monument that would last a hundred lifetimes of ordinary men.

'Caesar?'

With a smile, the Emperor Nero Claudius Caesar Germanicus turned to his imperial secretary. He had been quite lost in his own thoughts.

'King Tiridates is here.'

'Thank you, Epaphradotus.' This was the second ceremony to welcome Armenia into Rome's keeping. The first, in the forum, had been a mere appetizer compared to what was to come. Nero looked to the rear of the balcony where the king of Armenia waited in his long robes. A swarthy predator's face, the clubbed beard reaching his chest, nose like an axe blade and heavy brows, topped by a shining thatch the colour of pitch and styled in tight ringlets. A savage face. But a noble head. A head awaiting a crown. Had another Emperor been in Nero's place, King Tiridates would now be in the *carcer*, Rome's prison, awaiting the bite of the strangling rope, for Tiridates had been an enemy of Rome. He and his brother, Vologases of Parthia, had fought two long, expensive wars against the Empire. If Nero had followed his generals' advice there would have been a third and Tiridates would have been crushed on the battlefield and slaughtered with his army. But wiser counsels had prevailed and now the king was here to pay homage to his Emperor and to Rome.

He called Tiridates forward, and as the king stepped out into the light the massed ranks below and on the surrounding hills, and on the far-off houses, erupted into frenzied cheering, so that the balcony was hit by an almost volcanic wave of sound. Nero felt himself grow along with the volume of applause. This was what he lived for, this adulation and proof of his dominion. This was what had spurred him to invest so much effort and expense in his voice and his bearing. For a moment, he was possessed by an overwhelming urge to sing; to give them the joy that came entwined as one with his talent. But the moment passed and now Tiridates was on his knees laying the triple crown at his feet and he was looking down at the mass of dark greasy curls and the cheering was ever louder. Together, the two serving consuls, Telesinus and Paulinus, handed him the jewelled diadem of laurel leaves. With great ceremony he placed it over the other man's head. Tiridates murmured something in his native Parthian. It could have been thanks or mortal insult, but Nero cheerfully offered his hand to his new brother king and drew him to his feet, bestowing a kiss to show his affection.

Turning to the crowd, he raised his hands and in that single movement commanded a hundred thousand people to silence. 'Let the celebrations begin,' he called in his high-pitched man-boy's voice, and the cheering re-erupted.

The two rulers took the broad stairway to the ground floor, where Nero deliberately conducted his guest through the shadow of one of the wonders of the Empire, the astonishing statue he had commissioned of himself as the sun god, Sol. Close to one hundred cubits in height and covered entirely in gold leaf, it was the largest marble sculpture in the world, dwarfing even the legendary colossus which had stood astride the entrance to the harbour of Rhodes. It portrayed a pensive, benevolent Nero, with the sun's rays radiating from his head like a crown, his left hand, holding a globe, stretched towards his people and in his right the whip with which he would drive the horses drawing his chariot. It was a glorious piece of uninhibited self-indulgence, a thousand lifetimes of wealth incorporated in a single piece of art. As he passed it, King Tiridates wondered at the colossal vanity of the unprepossessing, almost effeminate young man beside him.

There was more to wonder at in the great banqueting hall, where the Armenian king dined on the most sumptuous food the Empire could provide, in a bewildering room which revolved around its guests while the ceiling periodically showered them with flower petals and perfumed water. Such technological marvels impressed Tiridates profoundly, even more than the displays of military might Nero had been careful to provide. An Empire capable of sustaining such extravagance could send a dozen legions against him at any time. He had been right to make the treaty and his brother Vologases wrong to want to continue the war.

Nero contemplated Tiridates' bemused expression with satisfaction, and left the room to summon his Praetorian prefect, Offonius Tigellinus. Tall and thin with a long nose and a fringe of russet hair that clung to the back of his head like a stray squirrel, Tigellinus didn't look like the most dangerous man in Rome. He had the face of someone who had just drunk sour milk and the hangdog demeanour of an undertaker. Nero felt the familiar flutter of nerves when the man he depended on so completely approached. So many had abandoned him, or wronged him in some way that forced him to remove them. Of all the long list, Tigellinus was the only man left he could trust. What if something happened to him?

For years, the former horse trader had supplied all his needs. Nothing was beyond his reach: boys, girls, men and women, rich and poor and in any combination or number. Senator's wife or slave, concubine or virgin, Tigellinus knew where to lay hands on them and if he could not persuade, buy or terrify them into the Emperor's bed, his Praetorians would force them. If the Emperor needed money – and emperors always needed money – Tigellinus would find a benefactor who could be induced to contribute to the imperial purse. Licences could be granted, subsidies controlled and monopolies awarded, and the Praetorian prefect would maximize the profit. What was more, that long nose had an infinite capacity for smelling out traitors and the mournful expression hid a pitiless cruelty and fertile imagination. It had been Tigellinus who had torn the heart from the Piso conspiracy with his blades and his hooks and his hot irons, Tigellinus who had invented the exquisite refinement of torturing a man – or a woman – to the very brink of death and having them restored by a physician to face the same fate again, and again, and again. It had never failed. Nero had been so delighted by his aide's successes that he had awarded him the triumphal regalia normally reserved for senators and consuls and erected a statue of him in the Palatine gardens.

It had been Tigellinus who suggested removing Nero's former teacher, Seneca, once and for all when Piso and his nest of vipers were being stamped out. That was what he liked about Tigellinus: his clarity of purpose. No attempt to fabricate evidence or bribe witnesses, just a simple tying up of loose ends. Nero's agents in Seneca's household had reported that the old man had met his fate with dignity, protesting his loyalty to the last. A pity, but he had long since outlived his usefulness and he knew too many secrets to be left alive.

'A most satisfactory day,' he welcomed Tigellinus cheerfully. 'I have never seen the people so proud of their Emperor. King Tiridates was suitably awestruck by my splendour and overwhelmed by the power of their love for me. A triumph. A triumph for Rome.'

'A triumph for Rome's Emperor,' Tigellinus corrected. 'And a triumph for her legions.'

All the long years in the imperial court and his training at Seneca's knee had given Nero an ear for nuance. He caught a certain inflection in the Praetorian's voice. 'Yes, a triumph for her legions. And it is right that men should fear Rome's legions. You have news from Judaea?' A few months earlier the Syrian sub-province had risen in revolt after a punitive expedition against an assortment of religious fanatics had resulted in hundreds of deaths. In the violence that followed the best part of two legions had been wiped out and the eagle of the Twelfth Fulminata lost. It was the greatest military disaster of Nero's reign and it was imperative that it should be avenged swiftly and mercilessly.

'Gallus has been removed from his command. Vespasian will form a task force from the Syrian and Egyptian legions and lead them against the rebels. Meanwhile, General Corbulo has returned to Antioch and will offer what support he can to Vespasian.' There it was again, that slight change in tone he had come to recognize.

'Two of our finest generals,' Nero ventured. 'And our most loyal.'

'Just so, Caesar.'

A moment of clarity. 'But you have concerns?'

'General Vespasian is your own appointment, a *new man* who is intelligent enough to understand that he would never win enough support to aspire to the throne, and his hands will be kept busy for at least two campaigning seasons. General Corbulo . . .'

'Rome's most successful commander in the past ten years . . .' Nero's voice rose an octave as he was forced to come to Corbulo's defence.

'Has been heard to cast doubts upon your policy of reconciliation in Armenia and Parthia. There is talk of giving Armenia away.'

Nero waved a dismissive hand. 'A soldier's grumbles. Even Tiridates told me that I have no more loyal commander than Corbulo.'

'Of course,' the prefect said smoothly. 'I venture no accusation, I only caution.'

The Emperor stared at him, the piggy eyes narrowing. 'Proceed.'

'General Corbulo was appointed on the advice of Seneca,' Tigellinus pointed out. 'He has been in the east, in Asia and Syria, for twelve years, with the same legions. Some would say enough time to create his own personal empire.' Nero didn't have to ask which 'some'; he knew the Praetorian had agents in every military command. But Tigellinus surprised him with his next admission. 'He is a difficult man to get close to. His senior officers have been with him for years and are unfailingly loyal; the juniors take their lead from the legates. Only now have I been able to place someone in a position of trust, although, as I have said, it is generally known in his headquarters that he has been critical of your policy and your orders to act upon the defensive. His legionaries regard him as something close to a god.' Tigellinus saw the Emperor stiffen, as he'd intended. Only emperors could become gods. 'Normally this could be dealt with simply enough. A new posting to some less arduous front. A summons home for some new honour, a long and happy retirement on his estates in the north . . .'

'But?'

'But the situation in Judaea means that Syria is also vulnerable. It would only take one small spark for the rebellion to spread. Therefore it is important that Syria is in safe military hands, and there are no safer military hands than General Corbulo's.'

Nero nodded. 'And what does my faithful Tigellinus advise?'

'We wait and we watch. If General Corbulo does his duty and defends Rome's and the Emperor's interests, all well and good. If he were to overstep the mark, however . . .'

The Emperor stared from the window overlooking the luscious parkland, its vivid greenery nourished by the blackened bones of a thousand plebeians still lying in the burned-out ashes of their homes. Not Corbulo. Never Corbulo. But then Tigellinus had never been wrong before. So they would wait, and watch.

'Very well, see to it and keep me informed.'

Tigellinus saluted and walked from the room. The first piece was in place.

VII

'Sail to the north!'

At the sharp cry, Aurelius followed the lookout's pointing finger to where a faint strip of cream could be seen between swells on the far horizon. 'Julius,' the captain shouted. 'You've got the sharpest eyes. Get up the mast and tell me what you see.'

While they waited for the man's report, Valerius strapped on his sword and joined Aurelius at the ship's side. He noted with approval that Tiberius already had his men in full armour. Serpentius emerged from the hold where he'd been checking the horses to join the young tribune and the four cavalry troopers. It was early morning on the second day since they'd left Creta. The ship had called at the port of Hersonnisos to take on a cargo of timber and the island's olive oil, which was said to be the best in the Mare Nostrum and would sell for a good price in Antioch or Alexandria. They'd said farewell to their escort there and when the galleys left it felt as if they were losing an old friend.

Aurelius nodded when he saw the swords. 'Good. No need for concern yet, but best to be ready. Julius?'

'A small ship under full sail, could be a galley or a fishing boat,' the sailor guessed. 'Wait! I see regular flashes of white at her sides. A galley, under oars and making good speed on a course to intercept.'

'Anything else?' Valerius noted that the captain's voice had lost some of its customary assurance.

The lookout strained his eyes towards the tiny speck almost lost in a vast undulating carpet of azure. Julius thought he'd done well enough to mark the splash of the oars. But when he looked again there *was* something he'd missed: a flash of colour at the head of the other ship's mast. 'Looks like she's running some sort of signal?'

Aurelius jumped for the mast and, with surprising agility for such a big man, scrambled up to the main spar.

'Could it be one of the escort galleys with a message for us?' Valerius shouted.

'They should be halfway back to Misenum by now.' The captain didn't hesitate. 'Turn due south and run before the wind,' he shouted to the steersman.

When he returned to the deck he called Valerius to the stern. 'Pirates.' He spat over the side.

Valerius's hand automatically went to his sword, but Aurelius smiled and patted him on the shoulder.

'There'll be time yet for that, tribune.' He studied the sky to the north, where a few puffy white clouds had gathered. 'She's a scout, not one of their big fighting galleys, which gives us a good chance of outrunning her; outfighting her too, if her plundering bastard of a captain wants to push his luck. We'll give it an hour before we turn northeast again. That should still allow us a chance of making landfall on Cyprus before dark. It looks like we might be in for a bit of a blow, which will suit us better than her, because she carries less sail and she's lower in the water.'

'I thought we had got rid of the pirates along the Cilician coast long ago?'

Aurelius laughed bitterly. 'Just because they've disappeared doesn't mean they've been defeated. They can't take on the big grain convoys and most single merchants aren't worth their while, so when the navy raided their ports, crucified the most prominent captains and burned a few of their ships they simply vanished, like smoke. It doesn't take a great deal of effort to turn a pirate galley into a coastal trader and most of the pirates were as much merchants as they were thieves and murderers. But if a juicy target lands in their lap . . .' The seaman glanced towards Domitia's pavilion.

'The girl?'

'I doubt they are after the timber and olive oil in our holds, tribune. Someone will have seen us dock in Creta. In a harbourside bar one of the crew boasts that his passenger is the daughter of the famed General Corbulo. They wait. They watch. They see us leave unescorted. If they catch us, they might take us all, but probably not. No, it is the girl they are after. They will move her along the coast to a sheltered cove – past Tarsus, maybe – and smuggle her into the hills where they will sell her to one of the bandit kings who still rule in the disputed lands on the borders of Cappadocia and Armenia. Those men have little love for her father. They will ask for a ransom that will make his eyes water and he will either pay it or get her back one pretty piece at a time.'

'Then let us hope they don't catch us.'

Aurelius sniffed the air as if testing the wind for scent. 'Sharpen your swords and pray.' Valerius nodded. 'And tribune? Don't mention this to the general's daughter. The last thing I need is a hysterical woman panicking all over my deck.'

Three hours later there was still no sign of the poor weather Aurelius had predicted, but they were back on course and there'd been no hint of the other ship for more than an hour. Aurelius had a man permanently at the masthead, but the captain still stood on the steering platform scanning the northern horizon with a worried frown on his tanned face. Valerius wasn't certain whether he was concerned about pirates, the clouds, which had turned into a brooding, dark-fringed pyramid, or the atmosphere, which had become sticky and breathless, though there was still enough breeze to stir the sails. The frown deepened when Domitia left the curtained tent with one of her serving girls and approached the stern.

'Good morning, captain.' She gave Aurelius a smile that would have melted another man's heart. 'I wonder if I might trouble you for some fresh water to use for washing. Sea water is all very well, but . . .'

'I'm sure that can be arranged, lady,' Aurelius said briskly. The dwindling water reserves had been on his mind, but if they made port as planned at Cyprus it wasn't a major concern. If for any reason they missed their landfall he would have to turn north to seek water at some settlement or river outlet on the Asian coast. He had no doubt he would find somewhere suitable – he'd sailed these waters since he was ten years old – but it would take time and he would prefer to preserve stocks if he could. Still, it would be worth a pint or two to get the general's daughter off his deck.

'Julius, a bucket of clean water for the lady and her serv—'

'Sail, due north!' The whole ship froze at the sound of the lookout's voice. 'And another just to her east.' His voice faded and he muttered what sounded like a prayer.

'What else?' Aurelius snarled.

'Captain, a third, a mile further east still.'

Aurelius darted another look at the clouds gathering in the north, but there was no help there. He turned to Domitia. 'I'm sorry, lady,' he said quickly. 'I'm afraid your request is denied and I must respectfully ask that you and your slaves take up your quarters below decks. It will be safer there.'

Domitia Longina lifted her dainty chin and glared at the captain. 'I will go below decks when I see fit, and not before,' she snapped. 'Safer from what, captain?'

'Lady, I command this ship and I do not have time to argue. You will go below. Tribune, will you escort the lady Domitia and explain our situation?' He nodded to Valerius and ran off, roaring to the helmsman, 'Cronos! Set course due south. I want her running before the wind with every ounce of speed she has. Sailmaster. Check every rope. We need every stitch straining.'

Domitia was left staring at the captain's disappearing back, caught between a patrician's natural inclination never to accept defeat and the knowledge that if Aurelius was concerned perhaps she should be also. Finally, she turned her anger on Valerius. 'Well?' For a moment he thought she might stamp her foot.

'If you would accompany me, I could explain our difficulties as we go.'

45

'Do not patronize me, tribune.' Her eyes – he noticed for the first time that they were a deep walnut brown – threatened to catch fire. 'I am my father's daughter and I will not be made light of. I . . .'

Valerius heard a shout from the deck and looked up to see the pale ghost of a sail on the far horizon. This was no time for talking. 'If you are your father's daughter you should be able to obey orders.' He took her arm and bustled her to the hatch which led below decks. He saw Serpentius grinning and Tiberius looking on with a puzzled frown and it only made him more angry at her foolishness. 'That sail belongs to a pirate galley. You understand about pirate galleys? Well, these pirates want you. And when they get you they will use you to destroy your father. If he pays the ransom and leaves them alive, he will no longer have his honour. If he does not, he will no longer have you, and that will be infinitely worse.'

In an instant the wildcat inside her retreated. His final sentence, and the way he said it, first confused then intrigued her. She frowned and shrugged herself free as they reached the ramp. 'If you had explained yourself so eloquently a little earlier,' she said sweetly, 'perhaps we would not have had this misunderstanding. Come, Suki.'

Valerius couldn't help noticing the way her body moved under the thin skirt as she walked down the steps into the hold. He shook his head. Idiot to think of something like that when they could all be dead in the next few hours. He ran to the stern and prepared to face the enemy.

VIII

'They're gaining.' Aurelius's voice remained steady, but the concern was written stark in the lines of his weathered features. 'I thought we were holding them, but they are making ground on us with every minute.' His eyes darted constantly between the heavens and the waves and the three sails that were now clearly visible on the horizon. 'They will not use their oars until they are close, because their rowers can only maintain their hunting speed for a short time. There is no point in using up their strength until they need it. But all is not lost. We may be fortunate yet.' His hand reached up automatically to touch the carved figure of Poseidon where years of habit and countless maritime dramas had worn a shining circle on the knee.

Valerius tried to judge the distance between the three pirate craft and the *Golden Cygnet*. How much time did they have?

Aurelius read his mind. 'We have a following swell and that tells me there is more likelihood of the wind's freshening than backing. There are still four hours till dark, but if we don't lose a steering oar or snap a rope we should be able to stay ahead and they will not relish continuing the chase after dusk. They are cowards at heart. They will always seek a profit, but not if it is likely to cost them blood. We may be only a single ship, but we can still put up a fight. The only reason they have not turned tail already is because of the prize.' He frowned and spat.

'Very well, Aurelius.' Valerius's voice took on the authority of a man who had commanded a legion – an African legion, but still a legion. 'You are in command of the ship, but who is in command of the defence of the ship?'

Aurelius nodded solemnly. 'My men are not fighters, though if it is fight or die they will fight. But understand this. If it is a choice between fight and run, we will run. What do you need to know?'

Valerius signalled to the watching Tiberius, who ran to them and saluted. 'Sir.' The young tribune's eyes were bright with expectation and Valerius thought: here is one man who will defend the ship to his last breath. A man to fight alongside. Another man to fight alongside was standing a few feet away, trying to look uninterested, but Valerius knew Serpentius would be listening to every word.

'First we need to know how many weapons are on board and how many of your sailors you can spare to fight.'

'I have a crew of twenty and in a stern chase I can give you a dozen of them, armed with either a sword or a spear, though I doubt they'll be much use with either.'

Tiberius snorted dismissively, attracting a glare from the captain, but Valerius only looked thoughtful. 'What about axes?'

Aurelius brightened. 'Oh, yes, they can all handle an axe. Give a sailor an axe and watch the blood and teeth fly.'

'So, we have seventeen, including the tribune's cavalrymen and my servant. Tiberius, we will leave one of your troopers to provide protection for the lady Domitia and her staff. The question is how many will oppose them?'

The captain chewed his lip. 'The Cilicians pack them in tight. A big pirate galley can ship fifty men over and above those on the rowing benches.' Tiberius gave a short whistle. 'But at least one of the galleys is the scout ship we saw; he will carry no more than twenty.'

The figures were double what he had expected, but Valerius hid his concern. 'Very well. Tribune Crescens. I have my own thoughts on the defence of the *Golden Cygnet*, but I would value yours.'

Tiberius struggled to hide a grin. When he spoke his tone was professional and his words considered. 'As I see it, from a military point of view the *Golden Cygnet* is simply a walled fighting platform and it can be defended in the same way I would defend any fortification. If we can get enough men to the point of attack we can fight off a force of greater numbers, especially a force of pirate scum.'

Valerius smiled. 'I wouldn't underestimate the pirate scum, Tiberius, but I agree with your conclusions. My only concern would be if we were attacked in more than one place, which I'd suggest we have to assume is a possibility.'

Aurelius nodded gloomily. 'These pirates, they climb like the monkeys they are. Given even the slightest opening they will swarm all over the ship.'

Valerius exchanged glances with Tiberius. 'Then we must consider another option. We can't let them get on to the *Cygnet*.'

The younger man glanced uncertainly towards the pirates. 'We fight them on their own ground?'

'Fight them on their own ground and kill them on their own ground.' Valerius turned to the captain. 'Do you have anyone on board who has served on one of those galleys?'

Aurelius didn't need more than a second. 'Capito!'

The wizened sailor who had met Valerius and Serpentius on the wharf in Ostia ran up to them. He looked abashed to be singled out, but brightened when he realized what he was being asked.

'Aye, they had me chained to an oar for nine months and would have thrown me and those chains overboard if yon navy lads hadn't been so quick.'

'Can you draw a picture of a galley and point out its strengths and weaknesses for me?'

The sailor told them, 'I can do better than that. I can show you.' He ran below and returned with a lovingly carved wooden model, every spar and every oar in its place. 'Now this here is the biggest of the type. Twenty oars a side, fifty feet stem to stern, and a dozen across the beam.' He pointed to the centre of the ship. 'Your scouts, they have but ten a side and are maybe eight feet across.'

'And besides the oarsmen the bigger ships carry say fifty fighting men and the smaller twenty?'

Capito frowned. 'That would be as a rule. Sometimes less, some-times more. A pirate chief, he would be hard put to it to fill his bigger ships these days, with the pickings so slim.'

'They must have a weakness,' Tiberius said, studying the little model critically.

Capito looked blank as if the thought had never occurred to him, but after a few moments his face broke into a gap-toothed grin. He patted the solid oak of the side of the *Golden Cygnet*. 'Their weakness is that they won't ram this. Their captains are savages: thieves and murderers who revel in torture and cruelty. They abused us slaves horribly. But they are also businessmen. The galleys are built for speed, light fast craft that can fairly skim across the water if the oarsmen are driven. But that strength is also their weakness. I've seen a Roman galley shear clean through a pirate hull.'

Capito returned to his station and the three commanders discussed the situation for a few minutes more before Valerius made his decision. Aurelius, in that curious ebb and flow of confidence that affects men before a battle, had pondered whether they should turn and use the ship as a sea-borne battering ram. It was an idea that appeared to have merits, but Valerius pointed out that while they were tangling with one ship the other two would undoubtedly converge on them and they would eventually be overwhelmed by sheer numbers.

'No,' he said firmly. 'The answer is to try to outrun them if we can, but to engage them one at a time if there is no other alternative.' He looked out over the waves. The little group of sails was closer still. 'We need to lighten the ship.'

In the depths of the hold Valerius's eyes took time to adjust to the gloom and bring into focus the individual objects around him. Aurelius's face had crumpled when Valerius had announced his decision. He had argued and growled and 'I'll be damned' until it had been pointed out that his most precious cargo was the general's daughter, and that if they lost Domitia they were unlikely to survive her father's wrath, or Nero's.

Valerius's gaze fixed on rank after rank of earthenware *amphorae*. He nodded to Aurelius. 'Form a chain and over the side with them.'

Aurelius winced. He could have wept, seeing his profit for the entire trip jettisoned, but he waved forward the men who had been waiting by the ramp.

'What's in here?' Valerius pointed to an enormous stack of odd-shaped parcels and packages set to one side of the hold.

'The lady Domitia's personal baggage.' Aurelius's eyes widened. 'You wouldn't . . .'

Back on deck, Valerius studied Capito's model of the galley and tried to ignore the closing presence to the north. Above the familiar creak and groan of the constantly shifting puzzle of ropes and jointed wood that was the *Golden Cygnet*'s rigging, he heard the rhythmic splash as the ship's cargo of finest Cretan olive oil was consigned to the depths.

A sharp feminine shriek broke his concentration and he looked up to see Tulia, Domitia's companion, wrestling with a sailor who was attempting to push a crate over the side. The crewman was twice Tulia's size, but from what Valerius could see he was getting the worst of the encounter and would bear the scars for some time to come. He was about to intervene when the general's daughter emerged from below decks. She took in the scene and he saw her fists clench and her eyes narrow. Her face took on the combative look he'd last seen on an Iceni warrior charging a Roman shield line. She advanced on the struggling pair.

'What is going on, Tulia?' she demanded.

The freedwoman disentangled herself from her opponent. 'They are throwing your things overboard, my lady,' she said tearfully. 'The tribune says anything heavy must be sacrificed.'

Valerius felt the moment she turned on him, and when he raised his head it was like looking into the mouth of a volcano. Before she could speak, he nodded towards the stern. Her eyes followed his and widened as she realized how quickly the pirate had closed since the last time she had been on deck. In that instant her whole demeanour changed and he was reminded of the difference between other women and a Roman lady bred to rule. The aggression drained from her to be replaced by a languid grace, and the headlong charge was transformed into a neat turn.

'Then if the tribune says they must go, they must go, Tulia. Kindly show them where to find the tableware and the boxes containing the statuary.'

Valerius rose and went to her side. 'Thank you, my lady, I appreciate your cooperation. If it had not been necessary . . .'

She shook her head and looked again at the pirate galleys, which were now less than half a mile away. 'In times of war we are all soldiers, tribune, and we must all make sacrifices.' She turned, and forced him to look deep into her eyes. 'Is that not so? We place ourselves in your trust.'

When she was gone and his heart had stopped thundering he forced his attention back to their pursuers, wondering at the turmoil she awoke in him. Another complication he didn't need. He imagined the big galleys gaining stroke by stroke, coming closer and closer until they touched hulls with the *Cygnet*. What would he do then? How could he confound his enemy? He thought back to the defence of Colonia, when he had tempted Boudicca's warrior chiefs with the only remaining bridge to the city and they had taken the bait. This was different. He was being hunted by three wolves, and when the first wolf's jaws closed the others would move in and together they would tear him to pieces.

'Look!'

He joined Tiberius at the side.

'Something strange is happening,' the younger man pointed out. 'Perhaps they are abandoning the chase.'

Valerius looked back to where two of the galleys had closed and their movement seemed to stutter. For a moment his hopes rose, before the ships parted and the smaller of the two suddenly surged ahead of its brethren.

'What's happening, Aurelius? I need to know what they're planning.'

The *Golden Cygnet*'s master scratched his head. 'I do not know, unless . . .' He looked again to where the single galley was powering towards them, each stroke bringing it closer and allowing him to see it with more clarity. 'Capito, come here. Tell me what you see.'

The old sailor hurried to his captain's side. He understood in an instant.

'Poseidon save us. I've seen it done before, but only once. They'll have run a plank between the sterns of the two ships and reinforced the crew of the smaller one. When a slave tires they throw the poor bastard overboard and he's replaced by a fighter. It means that they can maintain their highest speed but you'll face up to forty pirates instead of only twenty.' He took in the distance between the scout galley and the *Cygnet* and his voice faltered. 'They'll be upon us in minutes.' Valerius saw the moment Capito's nerve snapped. The sailor's eyes spun in his head and he let out a terrible cry. 'They won't take me again!'

Before anyone could stop him he ran to where a stack of *amphorae* lay against the side of the ship, picked up one of the great stone jars and leapt over the rail. Valerius searched the spot where the wizened seaman had jumped, but it was as if he had never existed. The weight of the *amphora* had taken him straight to the bottom. In the appalled silence that followed Aurelius barked an order and another sailor picked up one of the *amphorae*, preparing to heave it over the side. Valerius put a hand on the man's shoulder.

'How many left?'

'These are the last twenty I think, sir.'

'Keep them. I want the oil poured into as many buckets as you can find. And get me a couple of iron files. Big ones.'

Tiberius looked at him as if he'd gone mad, but when Valerius had explained his plan the young tribune shook his head in admiration.

'Madness. But it might even work.' He drew himself up to his full height. 'It is a soldier's privilege to volunteer to commit suicide, tribune, and I ask to be first over the side.'

Valerius shook his head 'There is someone better qualified, Tiberius. You are young; you will have other opportunities for glory.'

'You're right.' Tiberius grinned. 'Where you lead, I will follow. In any case, I doubt any of us will get back alive, even if we succeed.' His grey eyes turned serious. 'I underestimated you, tribune. For all your laurels, I thought you had gone soft, but I was wrong. You're as hard as the iron in that *gladius* you wear. Are you sure they all have to die?'

'All we can reach. We will have one chance. If we can't sink the galley we have to disable it.'

The sailor returned with a pair of heavy metal rasps. Valerius handed one to Tiberius. 'Here. You know what to do.' He took the other rasp to where Serpentius sat near the stern, calmly running a whetstone up and down the edge of a sword. The Spaniard nodded as Valerius took his place beside him.

'So we fight?'

'Fight or die. Maybe both.'

'Isn't it always so?'

'I have a job for you. A special job.'

Serpentius gave a bitter laugh. 'Isn't it always so.' He handed Valerius the sword, which was the one with the silver pommel. Valerius took it and nodded gravely before he bent and removed his sandals. The Spaniard's eyes widened as he started working on the leather sole with his knife to further expose the metal studs in the base.

'Why would you be ruining a perfectly good pair of marching boots?'

So Valerius told him.

IX

'I need five of your strongest and steadiest men. Have them issued with axes and tell them to report to me for their instructions. You know what to do when they reach us?'

Aurelius nodded. He didn't trust himself to speak. His eyes never left the pirate galley three hundred paces away, powering its way towards them through rising, white-capped waves whipped up by a wind that strengthened with every passing minute. The two larger pirates, hampered by their low freeboard in the heavy seas, had fallen back, but were still less than a mile away. Valerius studied their motion and reckoned that he had five minutes at most to do what he needed to do.

He replayed the plan in his mind and thought about the decision he'd taken. Was there any other way? The answer, as it had been every time he'd considered it, was no. But it didn't make him feel any better. It was murder, pure and simple. Not war. Not self-defence. Murder.

Tiberius waited by the side with his cavalrymen. They had expected nothing more than an uneventful cruise nursemaiding the general's daughter and it showed on the drawn, tense faces. Would they follow him? Only the gods knew, and Valerius had never placed much faith in the gods. He gripped his sword tight and it seemed to shrink in his hand as he lived the next few minutes in his mind. It was a sword that had been forged in the fires of victory. A sword of honour. The gold crown Nero had placed upon his brow might have given him fame, but the sword Suetonius Paulinus had placed in his hand had given him freedom. Freedom from the guilt of survival. Freedom to live again. Was he about to sully it?

He looked round and found Serpentius's shrewd eyes on him. The Spaniard knew. Without a word he took the blade and returned a few minutes later with another from the *Cygnet's* armoury. Valerius nodded his thanks, but Serpentius had already turned away to focus his attention on the pirate, judging the effect of every wave and every stroke of the oar with the fierce intensity of a man who knew his life depended on it. The sword he held was a long cavalry *spatha*, a double-edged bludgeon of a weapon that only someone exceptionally strong could wield with any finesse. Serpentius could use it, though. Valerius had exercised with him most mornings since they had met and outmatched him only once, and that by trickery. The Spaniard could weave mesmerizing patterns with the heavy sword that left a man dazzled by a whirlwind of bright iron. Old Marcus had boasted affectionately that he could remove your liver and serve you it for dinner before you even realized it had gone, and he had only been exaggerating a little. Each of them had a dangerous job this day, but Serpentius had the most dangerous one of all.

When he heard that the Spaniard was to lead the attack, Tiberius had argued against it until Valerius explained why he had made the choice. Serpentius, the gladiator, had faced five and even six fighters in the arena and lived to tell the tale. He knew how to kill and he knew how to survive and the second of those skills was as important as the first if the men Valerius led were to get back to the ship alive.

Fight the enemy on his own ground, the naval prefect had said. Well, that was what he planned to do, but first he had to get there and then he had to stay long enough to make it count.

A cough from behind made him tear his eyes from the galley and he turned to find the sailors Aurelius had promised in a small jostling group behind him. A couple wore nervous grins, most were grave-faced, but one or two were clearly terrified. The five burliest men held axes, although only two were of the brutally effective long-handled type Valerius had hoped for. Tiberius took them aside and explained what was expected of them, and Valerius was pleased to see that none flinched when they heard their orders. He told the rest to be ready to resist any boarders from the galley and lined them up behind the buckets full of olive oil.

Four ship-lengths. He looked back to the stern where Aurelius stood by the steering platform talking urgently to the broad-shouldered steersmen – four now, for the manoeuvre he planned would place a huge strain on the big steering oars. Beside the mast waited the big Nubian sailmaster, Susco, his face tense and his eyes on the men who stood by the lines that secured the sail. It was up to them now. Aurelius assured him it could be done. If he was wrong they were as good as dead.

The outcome depended on how well the *Cygnet*'s captain could judge the speed of his ship, and the speed of the galley. How well he knew the capabilities of them both. The timing had to be perfect.

The sea and the wind were rising all the time. Salt spray whipped across the deck and every few seconds the ship would lurch as another wave pounded the sternpost. Was he imagining it or had the course changed fractionally to the west? Would the captain of the galley notice?

Three ship-lengths. He could see the pirate crew as an amorphous mass with the occasional movement as they hurriedly switched places when a rower slumped forward exhausted from the mighty effort of powering the galley forward minute after muscle-tearing minute. He thought he heard a scream as another scarecrow figure went over the side, but he couldn't be sure.

Fight them on their own ground.

It had sounded so simple when the naval officer had said it, but now, looking at the galley, so slim and so deadly as it slipped through the waves, he felt his mouth go dry. Somehow he kept his face impassive. The others deserved that much. Inside, his guts were churning and something liquid had formed at the base of his stomach. He was Gaius Valerius Verrens, Hero of Rome. He had been through the fire and the iron of the Temple of Claudius and he had lived. He had faced

Boudicca's horde on the field before Colonia and he had never taken a step back. But he had never fought on a ship. Fear was a warrior's enemy and he had never felt a fear like this. He looked at the churning waters between the galley and the *Golden Cygnet* and he imagined what it had been like for old Capito. What had he felt as he plunged into the depths still clutching the *amphora* he had chosen as his doom? Valerius adjusted his iron helmet with the reinforced crown and heavy cheekpieces, and checked the straps of his *lorica segmentata*, the jointed plate armour that covered his shoulders, chest and back which he had chosen rather than the pretty, but less protective, leather breastplate. The armour would be his doom if he made a single slip in the next few moments. Tiberius had set aside a shield for him. The grip had been subtly altered so that he could release it with a twist of his wrist. It was potentially dangerous, because it was less secure, but he might have to move fast and the ability to jettison it could be the difference between life and death. He slipped the walnut fist into place and took up his position at the ship's rail a pace from Serpentius. 'Ready?'

A dismissive snort was the only reply. Behind him, where Tiberius and his cavalrymen stood, he heard someone mutter a prayer.

Two ship-lengths. The pirates were visible as individuals now, no jeers or threats, just fierce bearded faces waiting implacably for the moment of contact.

'Now!' The roar came from Aurelius at the stern.

In a single smooth movement the spar holding the huge mainsail dropped towards the deck, instantly slowing the ship's forward momentum. At the same time, the four steersmen leaned on the steering oars and the big merchantman leapt like a bucking horse, straining against the enormous pressure as the sea forced itself against the broad wooden paddles. The ship seemed to stop and turn simultaneously, its remaining impetus taking it across the path of the galley. Valerius clutched the side to steady himself. He heard a roar of surprise which immediately turned to triumph as the Cilicians concluded, as Aurelius had planned, that the *Cygnet* had lost a spar and was now disabled. The manoeuvre had been timed so that even the pirate's master, a man who had spent a lifetime at sea, would have no chance to alter course.

The galley would meet the bigger ship bow first, amidships, exactly as Valerius had hoped.

The pirate chief's frantic orders rang in his ears and he saw the flash of backing oars before the galley struck the *Golden Cygnet's* hull with a heavy crash. In the same instant the first of the grappling hooks fell on the deck and were hauled back to catch the ship's side. This was the moment. Even as the hooks landed, five of Aurelius's crewmen hurled the contents of their buckets on to the men in the prow of the pirate galley. Of all the elements, fire is the seaman's greatest enemy and when they felt the viscous liquid covering their bodies the pirates took an involuntary step back, then another, as they looked up in fear for the lighted torch that was certain to follow.

But there was no torch.

Only Serpentius.

The Spaniard landed like a cat on the raised platform in the bow, his sword ready and his eyes promising death. Confused by the oil, the vanguard of the boarding party took vital seconds to recover. They had crammed into the first dozen feet of the galley and were hemmed in by the rowing benches and their surviving occupants. The deck beneath them was slick with oil and their feet slithered and slipped on the planking as they fought to stay upright. The long *spatha* flicked out and the first pirate fell before they even realized Serpentius was among them. A growl went up and the leaders prepared to surge forward, but the gladiator's blade was a blur of bright metal and the surge died stillborn. Instead of attacking they were forced to retreat a step, and then another.

Two steps were enough. Valerius launched himself from the deck of the *Golden Cygnet* and crashed on to the bucketing galley in the space the Spaniard had cleared with his sword. The wooden planking was made treacherous by the olive oil, but the sharpened hobnails of the Roman's *caligae* gave him a purchase that was denied the barefooted pirates. A heartbeat later he was at Serpentius's left shoulder smashing his shield into the bearded, wild-eyed faces in front of him. Another thud told him that Tiberius and his men were following, and a second later the young tribune's shield locked into place beside his. Within moments they had been joined by the three cavalrymen and Serpentius was able to step back, his job done.

Valerius's wall of shields created an impassable barrier across the narrow breadth of the scout galley, anchored at the flank by the curve of the ship's wooden sides. The pirates could only attack two at a time up the narrow passage in the centre of the ship, or over the crowded rowing benches, and that meant they would never be able to focus enough power, momentum or numbers to break through. But it wasn't enough. Already Valerius could hear the sound of Aurelius's men reaching the deck behind him. And those men needed room to work.

'On me,' he roared. 'Now.' As one, the five shields battered forward with the automatic twist of the wrist that opened a gap for the lunge of the *gladius*. At the same time, the five men stepped into the space before the first of the wooden benches that would hamper their further progress as much as it hampered the pirate attack. Valerius was on the left of the line where his left-handed sword would do most good, with Tiberius to his right. He could feel Serpentius's comforting presence behind him, ready to aid the hardest pressed or fill any gap in the line. Now was the moment for the pirates to feel the scorpion's sting of the *gladius*. In an instant three or four of them were writhing on the deck and only the cavalrymen in the centre remained face to face with their attackers.

Chained to the bench in front of Valerius, a blackened husk of a man with shoulders whipped to raw meat by the overseer's lash raised his hands and pleaded for release. But the chains were an inch across and the only way they could be removed was if the galley were to be captured. Valerius had always known that six men could never take the ship.

'Two inches in the right place is better than six in the wrong one.' He heard the words of his first instructor as the triangular point of his short sword punched through the breastbone of the captive oarsman and into his heart. The man's eyes widened and his body slumped to the side, leaving just enough room for Valerius to take another step into the centre of the ship. If he could not kill all the pirates, the only way to save the *Golden Cygnet* and Domitia was to disable their vessel. The galley slaves had to die so that the general's daughter might live.

The slaughter had begun.

Valerius had killed before, more times than he could count, but the men he had killed had either been trying to kill him or deserved to die. He had never done murder. He took another step forward, screaming at the pirates to come to him, and his sword flicked out again. More than anything else he wanted to take a life that deserved to be taken, as if that would cleanse him of the slaughter of innocent men. When he had landed on the pirate galley's bow he had felt a terror that had never affected him on land. The lurching deck and the cramped confines of the fragile wooden hull tested his courage and his confidence. But now that the killing had begun, the battle calm settled over him.

A hulking unshaven brute in a loincloth clambered between the slaves at the rowing benches and stabbed at his eyes above the shield with a short spear. Valerius used the curved rim of the *scutum* to force the point up and was rewarded by a howl as his *gladius* pierced the man's unprotected belly, spilling blood and entrails on to the boards. To his right, Tiberius and the man beside him carved a path through the pirates in the central aisle. The water in the ship's bilge swirled and slopped an awful slaughterhouse pink and Valerius's nostrils filled with the stink of gore and oil, raw fear, ingrained sweat and the dried shit that painted the galley sides.

An enormous figure, naked to the waist and with a shaggy pelt like a bear, burst from the pirate ranks and vaulted the rowing benches on the right of the Roman line. Before the cavalryman facing him could react, the giant tore the man's shield from him and tossed it away, then picked the soldier up and threw him shrieking over the galley's side. The big pirate howled in triumph and turned towards the next man in the shield line, but before his comrades could profit from his victory Serpentius had stepped forward and sunk his long sword into the man's belly, ripping the blade free with a twist of his wrist. The Cilician collapsed disbelievingly into the ship's bottom and the Spaniard snarled defiance at his enemy and called more of them forward to die.

They had won three benches before Valerius heard the sound he had been waiting for. The sharp *thunk* of axes chopping into the galley's wooden hull brought a howl of dismay from the pirates and a screamed order from their captain that launched a ferocious attack on the Roman line. Another spear flicked off the rim of Valerius's shield and caught him a glancing blow on the cheekplate as he fought off two pirates, one of them, he noticed dispassionately, in a rusting Roman helmet of a pattern that hadn't been in use since the days of Pompey the Great. With a cry, the first of the men fell into the gap between two rowing benches where a galley slave already cowered. For a moment Valerius puzzled over whose sword had accounted for the pirate: it was a mistake that almost killed him. Just in time he sensed movement and darted a look towards his feet. The pirate had wriggled below the benches and was now readying his sword to stab upwards into the Roman's unprotected groin. It was too late to bring his own sword round to meet the blow, and evasive action was impeded by the body of an oarsman he had killed earlier. He saw the fierce light in his killer's eyes even as an axe blade from behind split the grinning head in two, spattering blood and brains on his legs. He shouted his thanks to his saviour, who turned out to be Julius, the lookout, but the sailor was already gone, throwing an oar overboard and bringing his big axe down to bite into the ship's bottom with all his weight behind it. How long had they been fighting? Valerius had no idea, but the bloody water at his feet reached past his ankles now. The ship was holed and that meant they couldn't fight for much longer. The other pirate galleys would be closing fast. They had done what they could. Now they had to do the impossible. Without taking his eyes from his enemy he shouted the command. 'Prepare to disengage!'

Tiberius grunted to acknowledge the order as he flicked a spearpoint aside with the edge of his shield.

'One step at a time, on my shout . . . Now!'

Somehow keeping his shield steady and fending off his attackers, Valerius made the awkward step back over the rowing bench and the body that was still chained to it. He could only hope that the other men were doing the same. In front of him the pirate crew howled as they realized what was happening and renewed their attack with redoubled fury.

He risked a glance at the boards and saw water gushing through a jagged hole low down on the side of the boat. A sword stabbed at his throat, forcing him to duck behind his shield, and another hacked at the leather covering, drawing splinters from the wood.

'Now.'

At last, the galley walls began to curve inwards and he could hear cries from the *Golden Cygnet* as the axemen clambered back on board. 'Tiberius,' he cried. 'Get your men out of here. I'll close on you and we'll hold them from the centre. Serpentius? You follow them.'

By now the pirates were fighting with the frenzy of the damned as they realized they had to regain control of the galley before it sank under them. He could hear the captain's roars above the howls of the gutted and maimed and the groans of the dying. Someone must have found a bow, because for the first time arrows began to zip past Valerius's head. One hit his shield with a sharp crack and a cry from behind told him another of the shafts had struck home. He felt hands working at his waist below his armour, but he didn't have time to wonder what was happening.

'Tiberius?'

'Sir,' the tribune gasped. His own breath rasping in his throat, Valerius found he was uncommonly pleased that the younger man was showing signs of tiring. At least it showed he was human.

'When I move forward, you go.'

'I can hold them.'

'That's not a suggestion, tribune. Get back to the ship. Now!' As he shouted the word Valerius smashed his shield at the pirates contesting the narrow passageway. He hadn't worked out what came after. All that mattered was to give Tiberius and his men time to escape. The other galleys would be almost on them now and Aurelius had orders to get the *Golden Cygnet* under way before they were in a position to threaten him, no matter who was left on board. Sword blades clattered against the big wooden shield and he knew it was only a matter of time before someone worked their way over the oar benches to flank him, or stabbed his legs beneath the shield. The pressure was almost unbearable. He remembered the last moments in the Temple of Claudius and realized he was grinning.

'Lord? Valerius?' His heart quickened further at Serpentius's shout. 'Now.'

A hail of spears arced over his head into the crowded passage in front of him and the pirate crew hesitated for a precious moment.

With a twist of his wrist the shield dropped free and he ran.

X

With the pirates so close behind that he could feel their breath on his neck, Valerius sprinted towards the galley's bow. The crew of the *Golden Cygnet* had cast off the grapnels and the big merchant ship was already five feet away, with the gap widening every second. He glanced up to see a row of anxious, wide-eyed faces and registered the ropes hanging from the bigger vessel's side.

Still travelling full pelt, he mounted the low platform in the bow and dived for the ropes, reaching out with his left hand. Even carrying the weight of his armour he would have done it. He was certain he would have done it. But, as he launched himself, a callused pirate hand clipped his heel and turned the leap into a sprawling tumble that smashed him against the ship's side. His helmet struck the seasoned oak with a clang and the impact knocked the breath from his body, before he plummeted into the blue-black void under the *Cygnet*'s rail.

The shock of the freezing waters seemed to stop his heart and for a fleeting moment he had no idea what was happening. His bewildered mind registered the ship's weed-streaming timbers through the opaque curtain of blue water and silver bubbles as the light above him faded to a tiny window. As he sank, the fingers of his left hand scrabbled for the straps of the armour that was carrying him to his death, but he knew it was useless. He had drowned before, trapped in the narrow aqueduct tunnel below the Viminal Hill, but that had been a terrible, violent drowning, while this was almost dreamlike by comparison. He made no conscious decision to hold his breath. His body's natural inclination to survive was automatic. But he could only hold it for so long. Gradually, the pressure grew in his chest and his nose and throat began to fill. He looked up at the wooden hull for the last time before a convulsive jerk made him choke and the darkness closed in.

'I've seen it done before.'

The words seemed to come from very far away.

'Put him on his stomach and pump his back.'

He felt himself being turned over and the pressure of strong hands on his ribs. At first nothing happened; then he felt a burning sensation in his chest and throat.

'One of the steersmen fell overboard in the harbour at Alexandria. We thought he was gone, but his bunkmate who was sweet on him lay on top of the body and gave him a good squeeze. Suddenly all the water came out and he was good as new.'

Valerius noisily vomited what seemed like gallons of salty water. His eyes opened and he watched the contents of his lungs and stomach slowly spreading across the smooth planks of the deck. Good as new? He tried to raise his head, but it seemed terribly difficult. Someone turned him over so that he was looking up into a patch of darkening sky circled by a ring of inquisitive, concerned faces. Rough hands pulled him into a sitting position and his head spun as if he was on his third jug of wine.

'Tribune?' Tiberius stared at him as if he were a ghost, which he supposed, in a way, he was. How many deaths must one man endure? He tried to speak, but the drowning and the vomiting had torn his throat.

'How . . . ?' It was a sound really, not a word, but Tiberius seemed to understand.

'Your slave is a man of some resource,' he said cheerfully. 'When you ordered him away he tied a rope to your waist. The sailors were able to haul you in like a fish after you fell, but it took so long we thought you must be dead.'

Someone – Serpentius? – placed a cup in his hand. He looked at the clear liquid suspiciously, but other hands raised it to his lips and the water was cool and soothing as it ran down his ravaged throat.

He nodded his thanks. 'The pirates?' The water seemed to have helped his voice.

'They are gone. Our axe men must have done their work well – the galley foundered. The others ran, not even attempting to rescue their friends.'

For the first time Valerius realized that the deck was pitching much more wildly than when he had left it. He looked up at the big mainsail, taut and straining at its stays, the wind whistling through the ropes. Tiberius pulled him to his feet and Serpentius wrapped a cloak around him. Not for the first time, he owed the Spaniard his life. It was only then that he noticed the other little group huddled over a bundle by the ship's side.

Tiberius saw the question in his eyes and shook his head. 'Aurelius. He wanted to help and picked up a spear. It was just bad luck really.'

Valerius pushed his way through the crowd and knelt by Aurelius's side. The captain's face had taken on the colour of old parchment and already bore the unmistakable stamp of death. He saw immediately what had happened. Aurelius must have been lifting the spear to throw when the arrow pierced his lower right chest, angling its way up towards the heart. They had torn away his tunic and there was very little blood, but the point was buried deep, with only a short span of shaft and the feathered fletching showing above the bruised flesh. Each laboured breath was accompanied by a hoarse groan and small frothy bubbles of red that clicked as they burst on his lips.

The captain opened his eyes and beckoned Valerius nearer. His voice was the merest whisper and the Roman had to lean close to hear what was said.

'East,' Aurelius gasped. 'You must go east. Judaea. Settlements by shore. Plenty of them. Cronos is a good seaman, but a poor sailor. He will want to go south for Egypt, because it is easier to run before the wind and a storm is coming. But by the time you get there water will be short, and unless Fortuna favours you, all you will find is desert.'

He closed his eyes and drew in a long, agonized breath. For a moment Valerius thought he was dead, but even though the captain was drowning in his own blood he had one last message to impart.

'Good crew, but keep the women out of the way. Shouldn't allow women on ships. Bad luck. Pour a libation for Poseidon and give his knee a rub for me. He has never let me down.' A smile flickered on his lips, he sighed once, and was gone.

No funeral oration dispatched Claudius Aelius Aurelius to join his beloved sea god. Four sailors carried him to the side and weighted the body before consigning it to the depths as was their custom. In the nervous silence that followed, Valerius called Tiberius and Cronos to the steering platform. By now the wind had risen to a low howl and the sky was dark, though it could only be mid-afternoon. He addressed the helmsman. 'With Aurelius gone, you are the man we depend on for our knowledge of the sea, Cronos. What is your understanding of our situation?'

Cronos frowned. He was a heavily built man with well-muscled shoulders from working the big steering oars, but he had a petulant mouth and a truculent, almost dismissive demeanour. Valerius had had little contact with him during the voyage, but he seemed capable enough. Perhaps the sullen attitude could be explained by the sudden change in his responsibilities. A fine seaman, but no sailor, Aurelius had said.

The man looked up at the brooding sky as if measuring their chances. 'We were a day's sailing from Cyprus when we first sighted the pirates, but we have been driven far south off our course. By now we are at least two days from land and must keep the wind at our back. This,' he gestured at the sky, 'is Poseidon's punishment for taking women on board without sacrificing to him first. If we do not placate him, the god will whip up a storm above and below and when the time is right he will rise from the depths and drag us all to his lair.'

Valerius felt Tiberius's eyes on him. 'Then we will make a libation to him at the appropriate hour and ask his forgiveness.'

'A few drops of olive oil or wine will not be enough to placate the god for this insult.' Cronos glowered. 'If we are to survive we must make a suitable gesture. I have spoken to the crew. We should make a gift of one of the women.'

Tiberius stiffened and his hand strayed towards his sword, but Valerius only nodded, as if he understood the crew's concerns. He lowered his voice and laid his hand on the seaman's shoulder. The physical gesture was reassuring, almost friendly, but the fingers closed like a claw, digging into the flesh, and the words that accompanied it held all the threat of a drawn blade. 'I want you to understand, Cronos, that whatever you and your friends believe, I command here and I would sacrifice every one of the crew before I would allow harm to come to the general's daughter or her women. Let it be known that if there is to be a sacrifice I plan to be generous, and storm or not the ship's master will be first over the side.'

It took time for the words to sink in, but Valerius was satisfied to see the man go pale beneath his sun-scorched skin.

'We will not sail with the wind at our backs,' he went on. 'We will turn east, for Judaea, where there is more likelihood of making landfall close to some community who can supply us. In the meantime, I want all food and water to be placed under guard – Tiberius will organize it – and we will ration its use.'

Cronos bristled at the order, but he had no choice but to accept. Valerius saw the hatred in his eyes and knew that before long it would be reflected by the whole crew. Sailors were superstitious by nature, and if Cronos told them the storm had been caused by Poseidon's anger and the presence of the women he would be believed. Pouring a libation wouldn't be enough, unless the winds died down.

Instead, they worsened.

Two hours later Valerius stood beside the steering platform whipped by spray and soaked to the skin. The steersmen battled to keep the *Golden Cygnet* on an easterly heading, but time and again her hull rang as it was battered by a big wave from the flank and she took a lurch southward. The winds had redoubled in force to a full gale and Cronos ordered the curtained awning on deck to be dismantled before it was torn away. Now he studied the cloth sail with anxious eyes as it rippled and cracked because of the angle of the wind across its surface.

'If we don't run before the storm we will lose it, tribune.'

Valerius reluctantly nodded his agreement. Clearly, Aurelius had never envisaged a tempest of this magnitude. The largest of the waves carried a terrifying power. Each time one struck, the whole ship lay over so that anything not secured cascaded across the deck. If they carried on with their eastern course there was a danger they might capsize. An unceasing bellow like an orphaned bull calf's filled the air, so that even a shouted conversation became difficult, and every so often a rainstorm swept out of the darkness with the sound of arrows striking a cohort's shields. Time meant nothing in this whirling vortex of wind and water. At one point Valerius's senses told him he should sleep and he huddled in his sodden cloak jammed between the steering platform and the ship's side, but fear, discomfort and the constant motion denied him the oblivion he sought.

Daylight brought little respite. If anything, the winds strengthened, shifting at the same time so that Cronos believed they were now being driven east. All through the long day Valerius watched the seaman and his exhausted crew fight to keep the *Golden Cygnet* afloat, cursing at his own impotence. Around nightfall the motion of the ship subtly changed, and he could feel her wallowing beneath him as if she was trailing an anchor. A shadowy figure crawled out of the darkness and Tiberius shouted something into his ear. He had to repeat himself three times before Valerius worked out that he was wanted below. Together they staggered across the pitching deck just as the next rain shower arrived, driven horizontally so that every giant drop stung like a slingshot against exposed flesh. Tiberius hauled open the hatch and Valerius felt a surge of relief as they slipped below and away from the incessant howl of the wind.

His respite was short lived.

When he reached the base of the ladder he was up to his knees in water that surged and foamed with the motion of the ship, the disturbance intensifying the bitter stench of decay, bodily ordure and fresh vomit. The torment of the wind was replaced by the incessant creaking of the ship's planks and a tortured rending as some piece of cargo worked itself to pieces. As their eyes adjusted to the gloom an almighty crash shook the whole ship, instantly followed by the terrified scream of a panicking horse and a series of smaller thunderclaps.

'Your slave Serpentius is with the horses. They are kicking their stalls to pieces, but that's not the worst of it.' The ship reeled beneath their feet and something huge and pale sailed past Valerius and crashed into the side with enough force to make him wonder that the hull hadn't been stove in. 'Some of the timber cargo has worked its way free,' Tiberius explained in a voice that was an eye of calm amidst the echoing clamour of the hold. 'The crew are securing what they can, but there's still enough loose to shake the ship to pieces unless the storm dies down.'

He led the way to where the sailors had erected a temporary cabin for Domitia and her women. Valerius realized he'd been so busy and so exhausted during the past few hours that he'd forgotten the other passengers. Only now did he understand the agonies they had suffered as they lay here in the pitching bowels of the ship, battered physically and mentally in a groaning, waterlogged chamber that must have felt more tomb than sanctuary.

'I'm not sure how much more of this they can take,' the young tribune said. 'They're being very brave, but . . .'

Somehow they'd managed to light a small oil lamp and Domitia held it aloft to identify the intruders. All the patrician arrogance had vanished. She was just a pale, frightened face – more child than woman – in the flickering yellow glow of the flame, her expensive cloak stained by the vomit that dribbled from the corner of her lip. Yet the dark eyes still contained a reservoir of pride and defiance, as if Domitia Longina Corbulo had vowed to go to her death undefeated by the elements. She sat on a couch, just clear of the stinking bilge waters, the cloak encircling the slave girls who huddled at her side. Tulia lay with her head in her mistress's lap, eyes closed and her face a deathly shade of green.

'My lady, I apologize for your discomfort, but I . . .'

Domitia raised her head and his heart lurched as he saw how close

71

to collapse she was. It took her a second to recognize him and her voice was barely audible above the noise of the storm. She managed a bloodless smile. 'I'm sure you are doing everything you can, tribune. We understand that our fate lies with the gods now.'

He shook his head. 'The ship was built to withstand these conditions. It will be unpleasant for a time, but we will survive.' Even as he said the words the gods were laughing at him.

She frowned. 'I believe the water is rising faster than before.'

'The lady is right,' Tiberius cried. For a moment Valerius was almost overwhelmed by the troubles which threatened to overwhelm him. The women's situation among the darkness and the filth was unspeakable, but on deck they would be exposed to the driving rain and the knife-edge of the gale. He considered trying to create some sort of shelter, but knew it would be torn to pieces within moments. But what choice did he have now? In the seconds he had taken to consider it, the water had risen another inch. Serpentius appeared in the doorway with a question in his eyes. The horses? It would be a release, but something stopped him from agreeing.

He shook his head. 'We've no time. Tiberius, get your men to carry Tulia and the girls on deck. Serpentius, help me with the lady Domitia.'

He reached out a hand, but an almighty crack from the deck above froze everyone in position.

XI

Valerius was first to react. 'Get them out.' He raced for the hatch and looked up to see that the big linen sail had split and was now hanging in long, streaming tatters that flapped and cracked like a slaver's whip in the fierce wind. The *Golden Cygnet* was now at the mercy of the waves, which were already turning her side on to the storm. If that happened it could only be a matter of time before the ship was battered into splinters.

A shout alerted him and he ran up the steps and across the lurching deck to where Cronos and three other sailors wrestled with the great steering oars.

'Take my place,' the captain ordered. 'Our only chance is to get her stern on to the wind again.'

Valerius took the thick wooden shaft under his left arm and heaved with all his might as it kicked against his body. A flash of lightning split the night sky and he saw a huge wave approaching the side and braced himself. It broke over the deck in a foaming white surge just as Tiberius emerged from the hatch with Domitia's freedwoman. Valerius shouted a warning that was lost on the wind and when he looked again the young tribune was clinging to a wooden stanchion as the wave receded around him. Tulia had vanished as if she had been plucked from the deck by the gods.

Cronos reappeared with two lengths of thick rope and with shaking hands quickly fixed the steering oars in position. Gradually, Valerius felt the motion of the ship steady as the action of wind and water on the paddles brought her bow round so that her stern was to the waves once more. He ran to where Tiberius still floundered.

'Serpentius?'

Tiberius shook his head with a look of stunned bewilderment. The hatch was a few paces away and Valerius waited until the next wave that battered the stern broke across the deck before he dashed to open it. Serpentius stood unsteadily at the bottom of the ladder with blood masking his face and the women holding him upright.

'He fell when the wave hit us.' Domitia's dress clung to her body beneath the cloak and she was shivering, but her voice was calm. 'I think he is only stunned.'

The general's daughter ushered her girls up the ladder and Serpentius groaned as Valerius helped him follow. When they emerged into the wind and rain they saw Domitia and her slaves huddled in the lee of the ship's stern where most of the crew had taken cover, and joined them there.

Cronos stood by the steering platform peering into the murk ahead.

'What can we do?' Valerius shouted.

'Pray,' the steersman mouthed.

'Food and water?'

Cronos laughed. 'You really believe we'll survive long enough to be hungry?'

'Better to be prepared.'

The seaman nodded and put his mouth to Valerius's ear. 'Take Julius. He'll show you where the spare water skins are stored. Fill them all. Don't worry about the food. If we need it we'll find it.'

Valerius beckoned to the tall sailor, who reluctantly struggled to his feet. Together they fought their way back to the hatch and into the hold, where the water was now waist deep. Julius muttered to himself as they inched their way through the darkness, but he never missed a step and steered Valerius past trouble until they reached the butts. The first they tried had been contaminated by seawater, but the second was sweet, if musty with age. They filled twenty skins and took them to the deck, where Valerius stored them at Cronos's feet and placed one of Tiberius's men to stand guard over them.

Despite the loss of the sail, the wind and the waves continued to drive the ship forward at astonishing speed. More than once he feared the ship would pitch sideways and broach, but the twin steering arms stabilized her course. 'Now we must endure and survive,' Cronos said solemnly, and reached up to touch the figure of Poseidon.

The lookout in the bows must have been asleep or blinded by the spray, because the first warning of disaster was the sound of the foot-thick oak mast snapping just as the ship crashed to an abrupt halt and twisted side on to the waves. Valerius was thrown helpless across the deck and smashed into the ship's rail, where he lay for a moment feeling strangely detached as Cronos, who must have been on the steering platform testing the oars, was catapulted screaming over his head into the darkness. In seconds, the deck became a chaos of panic-stricken, wailing shapes who screamed all the louder when the next wave smashed into the ship's exposed side. The snapped mast saved them, or perhaps Poseidon approved of Cronos's sacrifice. It had fallen forward across the bow and was still attached to the ship by a tangle of ropes. Crossed by the spar that had held the sail, the twenty-five feet of oak acted as a sea anchor and when the next wave struck, instead of capsizing the *Golden Cygnet*, it threw the stricken ship on its axis with the stern closest to a shore which was just visible as a faint fluorescent line of breaking surf four or five ship-lengths away.

'Valerius?'

Serpentius's shout was just audible above the screams and the smash of the waves. He picked out the Spaniard in the crush of people in the centre of the deck. 'Here,' he called. A shadowy figure detached itself from the dark mass, dragging a second, smaller figure with him.

'Take your hands off me. I will not go without my girls.' Domitia struggled against Serpentius's wiry strength, but he pulled her effort-lessly to Valerius's side.

'The slaves are with Tiberius,' the Spaniard said, bracing himself against the rail as another big wave crashed sickeningly into the bow. 'We need to get off the ship before the sea smashes it to pieces. If that mast goes, we could only have seconds.'

Valerius ran to the side and as a flash of lightning lit the far horizon his heart quailed at the rush of brown water churning past the hull. The ship's bottom appeared to be sitting on sand, which gave him hope, but the power of the waves would knock anyone who tried to escape that way off their feet and suck them under. The stern showed more potential. Here the wave line was broken by the ship's mass and there was a chance that at least some might escape.

With his knife, Valerius cut the ropes holding the steering oars and Serpentius retied them so that they dropped over the rail into the area of relative shelter in the lee of the stern.

'Can you swim, lady?' Valerius demanded.

Domitia shot him a startled look. 'I was taught as a child.'

'Then get ready.' She hesitated only for a moment. It was clear that if she took to the water in her long *stola* of fine wool she would drown in seconds. She dropped her cloak and began working at the ties of the dress. The outer garment fell to the deck to reveal a short tunic of filmy material which, in the rain, clung to her body like a second skin. Her slight frame shook with the cold and Valerius picked up the cloak to cover her, taking her in his arms at the same time to provide her with the warmth of his own body. He felt her start and thought she would break away, but she only moved a little closer. For a moment he was torn between a burning need to keep her safe and the greater responsibility he had to the surviving crew of the *Golden Cygnet*.

'We don't have much time.' Serpentius's voice cut through his thoughts.

'You go first. I'll lower the lady Domitia down to you. See, there, that line of white? The beach will be just beyond. Make your way there and I'll join you when I can.'

Serpentius disappeared over the stern. When the Spaniard shouted, Valerius led Domitia to the rope. 'You'll be safe with Serpentius. There is no better man in a crisis.'

'My girls?'

'We will get them off next.'

She gave a little nod of thanks and picked up the fallen dress before scrambling over the side. It was such a female thing to do that it made him smile, but his heart sank as her head disappeared below the waves. He only breathed again when she surfaced and Serpentius appeared at her side to support her through the heavy surf.

Tiberius arrived at the stern with the two slave girls already stripped like their mistress. A collective growl went up from the seamen crowding behind.

'No slave is leaving this ship before me.' Julius, the tall lookout who had saved Valerius on the galley with his timely axe stroke, forced his way to the front of the crowd. 'You can go, tribune, and your little fighting cock here, but I'll be next down that rope.'

'You'll stay until these women are off the ship.' Valerius stood between the sailor and the slave girls. He knew any sign of weakness would trigger a mutiny. 'If we maintain discipline and do our duty we'll all come out of this alive.'

'Like fuck I will.' Julius produced a long knife from his tunic and dashed forward. Valerius reached for his sword, only to discover it had slipped from its scabbard when the ship struck. He looked for something he could use as a weapon, but Julius was almost upon him. A glittering dart flashed across the deck and Julius stopped as if he had walked into a marble pillar. With a terrible choking noise he collapsed to his knees and keeled over on his side. Without a word, Tiberius stepped forward and lifted the dying man's head to retrieve the knife that was buried to the hilt in his throat.

Valerius went to stand at the young soldier's side. 'Your shipmate received the justice he deserved,' he shouted. 'And anyone who thinks otherwise should say so now. There will be no more mutinies. Prove that you are Romans, not pirates, and nothing more will be said. If we survive this, we may be here for days, so we'll need all the food and water we can gather.' The grumbling had been replaced by a sullen silence and Valerius hesitated as another big wave pushed the ship further aground. 'Tiberius, get the girls off now.' He placed himself between the crew and the stern, but no one moved to stop the young officer. 'I will be the last man off the ship, but now I want you to collect up the water skins and anything else you can carry.'

There was a moment's hesitation before they moved off to gather water skins from where they'd scattered when the ship ran aground. Valerius heard a frightened whinny from the hold below and realized he'd forgotten the horses. He lifted the hatch and dropped into the surging waist-deep waters of the hold. Two of the beasts were down, their eyes opaque in the gloom and their already bloated bodies floating among the swirling filth of the stall, but a pair of frightened white discs told him the gelding still survived. He drew his dagger and stepped closer to the big chestnut to place the point just behind his ear. There was an odd moment of calm when he could feel the horse's warmth and trust. He steeled himself for the killing stroke, but something made him hesitate. Quickly, he ran to the hatch and somehow manoeuvred the hinged ramp into place. The gelding shook violently as he was cut free and Valerius spoke gently into his ear before covering his head with a blanket that hung by the side of the stall. The big horse seemed to understand what was required of him and allowed himself to be led up to the deck.

A drop-down panel gave access to the gangplank when the ship was in harbour and Valerius unhooked the bolts that held it in place. There was still an eight foot plunge to the sea, but the gelding would have to take his chances. He slapped the horse on the rump and whipped the blanket from his head as the animal leapt over the side and vanished into the darkness.

By now, the last of the crew were disappearing over the stern and his legs said he should join them. Instead, he forced himself to fight the fear that threatened to overwhelm him as the ship rose and fell in the surf, her keel crashing against the bottom with each hammer blow of a wave. He searched from bow to stern, shouting into the hatches as he ensured that no one was trapped or injured. As he struggled towards the stern the last frayed rope securing the shattered mast to the *Golden Cygnet* finally parted. No longer anchored, the whole ship spun side on to the waves and canted over until the deck was almost vertical. Valerius made a frantic grab for a stanchion as he flew over the side rail into the angry sea, where the surf picked him up and spun him like a falling leaf in an autumn storm. There was no up or down, just a rolling vortex of brown water that forced its way into his nose and mouth. His face broke the surface and he sucked in a breath that was as much sea as it was air, but in the same instant he was under again, dragged along the bottom where shells and gravel tore at the bare skin of his arms and legs. He tried to control his momentum, but the power of the surf had him in its grip and gradually he began to weaken. Just when he thought he was finished a hand grabbed the neck of his tunic and hauled him clear of the water. He found himself blinking into Serpentius's glaring face.

'Only a fool would sacrifice himself to save a horse,' the Spaniard snarled. 'Since when did you become a fool?'

'Domitia?' Valerius choked out the name with a mouthful of sea water.

'Safe, but she twisted her ankle when she dropped from the rope. She won't be walking anywhere in a hurry.'

They struggled along the beach to where the former occupants of the *Golden Cygnet* gathered in two distinct huddles whipped by the wind-driven sand. Closest to the shore the dejected crew shivered where they'd crawled from the pounding surf. Further back Tiberius and two of his surviving cavalrymen provided what shelter they could for the lady Domitia and her two slaves. The third German trooper lay nearby, still alive, but halfway to another world, empty eyes staring into the rain and a purple dent four inches across in his forehead. Somehow, Tiberius had retained his cloak and the general's daughter had wrapped it around herself and the girls.

Valerius spoke reassuringly to the crewmen and ordered them to gather the food and water and place it conspicuously between the two groups. He knew better than to risk angering the sailors by seeming to monopolize the supplies so soon after the wreck. Better to wait to reimpose military discipline until their situation became clearer in the morning.

Serpentius offered him a drink from one of the skins, but he refused. 'It can't be long until first light. We'll issue a ration then. But I want

79

you to stay close and make sure no one else touches it.' He left the Spaniard and walked across the soft sand to where Domitia sat. One of the slave girls was tying a bandage round her ankle.

'I hope it's not too painful, my lady?'

She looked up. By some miracle the girls had managed to make her hair and clothing presentable. 'It barely hurts at all, tribune, although it is a little swollen.' He smiled at the lie. 'I must thank you for what you did,' she continued. 'If we had stayed on the ship we would all have drowned. I was wrong to delay you.'

'Sometimes it is more prudent to retreat than to stand your ground, but the decision is never easy, especially for a soldier – or a soldier's daughter.'

She nodded at the compliment, and in the pause that followed they could hear the sound of timbers shattering as the breakers continued to hammer the ship. 'How long are we likely to be here?' It was a foolish question, a little girl's question, and he experienced a moment of irritation. Already, he felt crushed by the weight of expectation. Unless they were very fortunate he would soon have to take decisions that would mean the difference between life and death for every stranded survivor; decisions founded on the most basic of knowledge. He didn't know how well equipped he was to do that, but whatever happened in the coming hours or days it was vital to keep their spirits up.

'Perhaps a few days.' He kept his voice confident. 'We will know better in the morning. We may have landed on the Judaean coast, but we have no real idea. We were driven far south and I think even poor Aurelius would have struggled to place us. If we *are* there, it is a fertile area and we should be within walking distance of some sort of settlement. In the meantime, please rest. It could be a long day tomorrow.'

'And if we are not?'

'Then we must endure and survive until help comes, my lady. Sailors have many useful skills and we are fortunate to have resourceful men with us. I do not fear for our future.'

It was surprising how easily the lie came. He knew there were things he had to do, but first he called Tiberius across. 'You were right to kill the lookout. Thank you.'

'I was only doing my duty, tribune.'

'No, Tiberius, it was more than your duty and I want you to know I appreciate it. If I can ever return the service . . .'

'Of course, sir. Perhaps you might commend me to General Corbulo,' Tiberius said seriously. 'This posting is a great opportunity for me and I would not want to waste it by being sent to some obscure outpost in the mountains.'

Valerius fought the urge to laugh. Here they were stranded only the gods knew where with barely enough food and water to last a week and Tiberius was concerned about his career. 'I think the general will find a better use for a man with your qualities. Julius, fool that he was, called you a fighting cock and he was right. You could be a great soldier some day. I have served with great soldiers and I recognize their qualities in you.'

The young man was clearly embarrassed and Valerius regretted being so forthright. He sounded like a foolish old veteran polishing his armour by the fire for his retirement parade. He opened his mouth to apologize, but Tiberius suddenly grinned shyly and reached for his belt.

'I found this lying on the deck.' He handed Valerius a legionary *gladius*, the one Suetonius Paulinus had presented to him in the aftermath of the British rebellion. 'I did not think you would want to lose it.'

Valerius had thought he would never see the sword again and he'd resigned himself to its loss, but now he had it in his hand he felt its power running through him. Still. He held the blade out hilt first to the younger man. 'It was given to me for what the general believed was an act of great bravery. Perhaps you deserve it more.'

Tiberius looked down at the sword, but his hand didn't move towards the blade. 'Even if I were to win the Gold Crown of Valour it would not equal the honour you have already done me. You ask me if you can do me a service?' He hesitated and shook his head. 'You will think me less of a soldier.'

'No, Tiberius. Ask what you will.'

Tiberius took a deep breath. 'I have never known a man I respect more than Gaius Valerius Verrens, Hero of Rome, and I can think of nothing finer than to call him my friend.'

Valerius laughed out loud, and felt the stares from the sailors down by the shoreline. Who could laugh at a time like this? But if anything could raise his morale in these dire circumstances it was this competent, agreeable young man, a tribute to his class, believing that his friendship meant something. He held out his right hand and Tiberius took the walnut fist in his.

'Of course, it will make no difference to our military relationship . . .' Tiberius stuttered. He was interrupted by a familiar snicker and a substantial form plodded out of the wind and the darkness to nuzzle Valerius's hand.

Valerius grinned at the younger man. 'We needed a gift from the gods and they have delivered one.' He patted the gelding's shoulder. 'Come, Tiberius, we have plans to make.'

XII

Theatre of Pompey, Rome

A storm was coming. He could feel it in the tension in the air and the oppressive heat that lay like a dirty blanket over the city, and he prayed that rain would not spoil the entertainment. All around him was a cacophony of noise: how they roared, the common people, and how quickly they forgot. Afranius had written *The Fire* as a tragedy, but an Emperor could not be confined by mere convention and he, Nero, in his wisdom, had reconfigured the play as a comedy. Of all the theatres in Rome only that of Pompey the Great had a stage large enough to contain it. Capable of seating twenty thousand people, the vast semicircular auditorium was filled to capacity, with the front six rows packed with evil-smelling plebeians of the lowest rank, lured by free entry and the promise of rich pickings. For this was a play like no other.

He loved the theatre, because it allowed him to escape for a few hours from the increasing cares of state. Sometimes, alone in his great palaces, he had the feeling that the walls were closing in on him. He had lived with the scent of fear his entire life; first his own, the unloved child in a house full of enemies. Then the infinitely more preferable scent of other people's fear as his power and – yes, he would not deny it – his malevolence grew. Other men's fear gave him an almost godlike sense of omnipotence that he normally only felt on the stage or on the podium. So why was it so different when he smelled the fear on Tigellinus? Because Tigellinus, of all people, had no reason to be frightened of him. If Tigellinus was frightened it meant that Tigellinus felt vulnerable, even threatened. If Tigellinus felt threatened, it was because he believed his position was weak. And if Tigellinus was weak, where did that leave the Emperor who depended on him? It was a question he would never ask the man standing next to him, for fear of the answer he would receive.

He took a deep breath to still his growing panic and thrust the melancholy thought aside. From his favoured place by the *proscaenium* wall he was able to look up to where the statues of the mere mortals who had dominated this very stage – Aesopus, the tragedian, and Roscius, who had made laughter into an art form – stared blankly from their niches out towards the great pillared temple where Venus Victrix ruled. Surely they would have appreciated the genius of his production?

The full-sized, five-storey house, a replica of the ubiquitous *insula* apartment blocks that lined Rome's streets, was blazing cheerfully now, each room visible to the audience because it had been built without a façade to ensure an uninterrupted view. Inside, the professional actors were doing their bumbling best to ensure that the conflagration would be terminal. It was almost time.

'Help, help,' cried the actor playing the brothel owner. 'Help us save what we can.'

The signal triggered a crazed rush from the front ranks of the audience as hundreds of excited plebs heeded the call. When they reached the wooden structure, the most fearful hesitated, quelled by the searing heat of the inferno. The fire had been skilfully set so that there was only one way into the building, a narrow passage which was alternately filled with flame and clear. Each floor of the block was strewn with treasures which rose in value with succeeding storeys. The lower floors contained furniture, ornate tables, chests full of who knew what valuables, and sacks of grain, the sale of which would keep a family in plenty for a month and more. On the fourth floor a table had been set for a banquet with fine silverware that would provide a man with the wherewithal to buy a small farm. Tethered beside the table, the comely, talented and equally valuable slave girl who had played the prostitute was now screaming frantically in a manner that might convince you she actually feared for her life.

But it was the top floor, the fifth, which had drawn these people, the dregs of Rome, the debtors and the dispossessed, to the theatre of Pompey. The man who found his way through the flames to the top floor, if he returned at all, would return rich, thanks to the chest that had been hidden there by the girl, and contained vessels of gold, glittering jewels and enough golden *aurei* to set someone up in style for the rest of their life.

'See how they cower, Tigellinus, burdened by the lack of courage ingrained in their breeding.'

The Praetorian nodded gravely and tried to look interested. This was the fifth time he had seen *The Fire* and he knew that only by taking immediate advantage would any of the men have the chance to reach the top floor before it was consumed. 'He who hesitates loses all, Caesar,' he agreed in a bored voice.

One man, a tall dark-haired fellow braver than the rest, broke the spell, timing his run to coincide with a gap in the flames. His courage inspired or shamed another, and then four or five. As one, they rushed for the stairs, ignoring the inferior treasures on the ground floor which would be secured by those less brave. But the stairway was only wide enough for one man. The dark-haired pleb made it first, with a stocky peasant, a thief by trade, with ugly misshapen features and a missing eye, hard on his heels. The others jammed the narrow space and fought for progress, kicking and punching, until one pulled a dagger and kept his snarling fellows at bay long enough to dart upwards. The house was of particularly cunning manufacture. The builders had used hard and soft woods, and designed damp and dry areas, so it burned in a particular way. This left the upper floors clear of fire, but difficult to access, while those below burned quickly, but still left enough of a way out for a man making his way to the top to believe he had a chance of escape. Already flames were consuming the third floor and those who risked their lives to reach that level had to dash through the narrowest of gaps to reach the next stair. The tall man and the one-eyed thief both made it through, but the man with the knife took one look and retreated. One of his companions darted past and made a grab for a pot overflowing with bronze coin, only to drop shrieking through a gap in the floor and into the maw of the flames on the level below. A roar of applause and guffaws of raucous laughter from twenty thousand throats accompanied his demise.

By now the first man had reached the silver level. He was clearly the crowd's favourite and they cheered him on, screaming at him to go for the gold. The slave girl, her *stola* already smoking in the intense heat, howled at him for help, but her voice was almost drowned out by the jeers of the audience. Remarkably, he hesitated. It was only for the merest fraction of a second, but long enough for the thief to smash him aside and send him sprawling. Still, he recovered quickly; without another glance at the girl he bounded for the stairs, taking them two at a time, only to be met at the top by a flying boot that took him clean in the face. He tumbled down the stairs and lay motionless at the foot. The crowd howled in outrage, but the thief put the chest to his shoulder and charged downstairs, leaping over the prone figure who clawed weakly at his legs. Time was running out. Every floor but the uppermost pair was a mass of flame, and it was clear these would soon be enveloped. Only the stairs provided a tantalizing, narrow and fast closing avenue of escape.

The tall man rose groggily to his feet and the crowd could sense the calculations running through his mind. He hadn't risked everything to leave empty-handed and his eyes flickered between the silver and the girl. They screamed at him to take the silver, but he could see it was impossible to carry it all. The girl was as valuable, perhaps more so, as anything he could take in his hands. He ran across floorboards glowing with heat, untied her hands and feet and pulled her upright. At first, she didn't understand what was happening, but gradually a smile crossed her face. She said something to the tall man no one would ever hear and gave him a hefty push that sent him staggering backwards until his feet met air and he plummeted through the flames of the lower floors to land with a sickening crack on the flagstones four storeys below. As the crowd roared, the girl grabbed what she could from the table and ran for the stairs.

Two floors below, the one-eyed thief exulted in the knowledge that he was a rich man. Clutching the casket to his chest he groped his way through the smoke to where the stairs to the ground floor smouldered. As he reached them, a faceless figure with the blackened remains of singed tunic protecting his face rose up and stabbed him deep in the guts. The thief screamed at the white-hot agony in his vitals and watched helplessly as the knife man prised the chest from his unprotesting fingers and disappeared from view. He tried to move, but his legs wouldn't work. The pain in his insides was like nothing he had ever experienced, but when the flames reached out for him it paled into insignificance and his dying shrieks goaded the crowd to ever greater rapture.

As the peasant burned, the knife man was making for safety through the flames of the ground floor and was already mentally spending his money when his foot hit some hidden pressure point. Before he could even scream a jet of burning liquid erupted between his feet and made him one with the inferno that surrounded him.

Now the only living thing in the burning building was the slave girl. When she reached the first floor she could tell the location of the stairs by the blue flame that consumed the thief's fat. She knew there was no escape by that route but she had lived by her wits for half her life and now it stood her in good stead. Still holding her loot, she ran directly into the flames and leapt through what had been the open front of the room. It was only a single storey, but when she landed she felt her ankle snap and she realized her hair was on fire. Her only consolation was the cheers of the crowd and the silver scattered around her.

As she lay exhausted, the applause grew louder and she looked up into the face of the Emperor Nero Claudius Caesar Germanicus, who regarded her with a benevolent smile. 'Get rid of her, Tigellinus. She's no good to anyone now.' He turned away to accept the justified acclaim of the mob. Had there ever been a better entertainment?

Just then, the storm broke and great droplets of rain hammered down on the dry stones and hissed among the burning timbers. He looked up to the heavens and allowed the cool water to pour over his face. It was a sign. He was still the favourite of the gods.

XIII

When Valerius opened his eyes the storm might never have happened. After a night shivering in the open he luxuriated in the warmth of the first gentle rays of the dawn, but instinct told him he would be cursing the sun by the day's end. It rose in the east, as always, creating a golden corridor across the darkened sands, but east was not where he expected it to be. It should have been behind him, as he faced the sea; instead, it was directly to his right. As he watched, the sands glowed first a fiery, orange red before mellowing to a deep pink, and he gradually became aware of his surroundings. The dangerous beauty of it assaulted his senses and the terrible reality turned his viscera to liquid ice.

The two small groups of survivors were the only living things on a flat sandy beach that ran as far as the eye could see to east and west. Worse, when he looked inland the landscape consisted of fold after fold of rolling dunes stretching far into the distance. Not a tree or a blade of grass. No hint of water or habitation. Not even a scrap of cover. He tried to recall the details of the maps he had studied of the eastern Mare Nostrum. Unless the contours of the coastline were deceiving him, it seemed clear they had been driven much further south than any of them had anticipated. Not to the shores of Judaea, but to Egypt, and not to the fertile area of Egypt which flanked the Nile delta, but a much more forbidding shore: a sixty- or seventy-mile strip of deserted, barren coastline where even the nomads of the interior were reluctant to venture.

Only when he turned back to the sea did he find any reason to hope. The *Golden Cygnet*, or at least part of her gilded hull, had somehow survived thanks to her solid construction. It rocked placidly in the waves of a wide, shallow bay, battered, but more or less intact, a hundred paces from the shore. Exhaustion weighed him down, but he knew he had to stir himself. Already he could feel the strength of the sun growing. They needed to act or die.

He called to Serpentius to issue a ration of water – two precious mouthfuls for every man and woman – and while it was handed out he gave his orders. Twelve crewmen survived from a complement of twenty, two of them with broken bones and another who was coughing blood and probably wouldn't last the day. He tried not to give thanks for the five extra mouths who had perished in the surf as they escaped the shipwreck, but he knew their deaths and those of Aurelius, Capito, Cronos and Julius might mean the difference between death and survival for the rest.

He called the sailors together, but kept Tiberius's guards aside in a separate group. 'We need to strip the ship of everything worthwhile.' His voice sounded hoarse from two days of shouting against the wind. 'The first priority is water, of which there may be more, even if it is slightly tainted. But we must also have shelter or the sun will roast us alive.' He pointed to four of the men. 'You will concentrate on shelter. If it has survived, bring the covered awning that was on the deck for the women. There must be a spare sail; bring that also, and rope.' The others he tasked to scour the ship for water, food and any timber or tools that might be useful.

'Why tools? If we're here long enough to build something we'll already be dead.'

Valerius tried to keep the irritation out of his voice. Why must they waste precious time? 'Because with tools we can make fish hooks and spears. You've all speared flatfish? The sandy bottom is perfect for them. We can eat the flesh and drink the blood. If we move from here we can use the tools to fashion litters for the injured and to carry the food and water.'

'Aye, blood,' moaned another. 'Flatfish isn't the only thing in these waters. There's sharks as well, I've seen them, long as a steering oar and with a mouthful of teeth that can tear a man's arm off, begging your pardon, sir.'

Valerius laughed with the rest and tossed the man his knife. 'When it comes for you, kill it and we'll have it for dinner. Now get on with it, before the sun broils our brains.'

When they set off fearfully through the shallow seas – he had never met a sailor who was happy in water – he summoned the two fit cavalrymen. 'Do it carefully,' he told the senior of the two men, a Batavian named Civilis, 'and without making it noticeable, but I want every weapon on that ship brought to me. Every spear and sword.'

Tiberius had stood silent as Valerius gave the orders and now he nodded his approval. 'We keep the weapons, the food and the water under our control, and build two separate shelters far enough apart to give the lady Domitia privacy.' He studied Valerius seriously. 'You realize that some of them saw her in her shift and liked what they saw? I have seen them looking at her. They are hungry, and not just for food.'

'Why do you think I made certain the weapons will be in our hands, not theirs? They are decent enough by their own lights, but when a man thinks he's going to die he will resort to desperate measures to get what another man is keeping from him. The second shelter will be split by a curtain to give the general's daughter a space of her own, but allow one of us to always be with her.'

Tiberius bowed. 'I will guard her with my life.'

Valerius shook his head. 'I have another task for you, Tiberius.' They walked to where Serpentius sat casually by the spot where they'd buried the pile of water skins to keep them out of the sun. The Spaniard was feeding the gelding with a mouthful of oats he had found among the foodstuffs they'd managed to rescue. The horse Tiberius had lost in the wreck had been one of the finest animals Valerius had ever seen and he guessed that the young tribune was more at home in the saddle than any of them. 'I want you to ride for help.'

Tiberius gave a little whistle. He looked up at the sun and then took in the scorched, barren landscape all around them. He knew he was being asked to commit suicide. 'Of course, tribune.' He produced a grave smile as he agreed to ride to almost certain death.

'Serpentius? How many water skins?'

The Spaniard shrugged. 'Twenty at the last count, but maybe they'll find more in the ship.'

Valerius drew a curve in the sand. 'If I'm right, here is Judaea to the northeast. To the west, Egypt proper where most of the settlements will be clustered along the valley of the Nile. Sixty miles between them. Which puts the wreck somewhere around here.' He pointed to a patch of sand in the centre of the curve between the two areas he'd circled. 'So, east or west?'

Tiberius studied the impromptu map, frowning as he concentrated on the scrawls in the sand. 'East or west?' he repeated. 'Thirty miles. Two days in the saddle if I rest at night. Thirty miles at most if we choose correctly, but there is no guarantee that we are in the geographical centre, so anything up to forty or fifty if we don't.'

Valerius nodded. They both knew that if they chose wrongly they were probably all dead. 'We'll split the water and pour as much into the horse as he'll take. You can carry what's left of your half with you.'

Tiberius shook his head. 'That only leaves ten water skins among twenty,' he pointed out. 'Two pints to a person. Even if I reach help on the third day it will take us another two to get back here. You'll never survive on two pints of water a man in this heat.'

Serpentius snorted and the two men looked at him. 'I know, it's a terrible plan,' Valerius said. 'But if you can think of anything better I'll be happy to hear it.' He waited, but it seemed no one could. 'In this heat, ride through the night when it's coolest. You'll save the horse and save on water. I say go west. There's a rebellion in Judaea and when there's blood in the gutter people don't take kindly to strangers. Even if you do reach a settlement there's a good chance they'll cut your throat just for being Roman.'

Yes,' Tiberius said slowly. 'I agree. West. If I keep the sea always to my right and follow the beach I could make good time.'

Valerius nodded his approval, relieved that the decision had been taken. It was only later that the awful twisting in the guts of not knowing whether it had been the right one would come. But this was no time for doubt. He clapped the young man on the shoulder.

'Then let's get it done,' he said decisively. 'You can make ten or fifteen miles then hole up in the nearest shade, if you can find any, until nightfall. I want you out of here before the crew returns from stripping the ship. If they find out we only have half the water they think we have I'll have another mutiny on my hands.'

Serpentius was already digging for the water skins and Tiberius took the horse aside to check his gait and hooves. Valerius knew by the way he vaulted on to the animal's back that he had made the right choice.

'Does he have a name?' Tiberius asked.

'He's a soldier's horse. He doesn't need one.'

'Then I'll call him Hercules.' Tiberius grinned. 'We need a hero.'

While they were waiting for the water, Domitia hobbled up with her arm round Suki, the African slave girl. Valerius explained Tiberius's mission.

'I pray for Fortuna's good wishes, and may you travel with the speed of Mercury,' Domitia said, and Valerius could have sworn Tiberius glowed in the light of her favour.

'I will not let you down, lady,' he assured her with a shy smile.

While Serpentius watered Hercules. Valerius gave the younger man some last advice. 'Take it gently at first. Get used to each other. When night comes make the best speed you can, but don't push too hard. Don't kill yourself but, more important, don't kill the horse. I want him back.'

Tiberius smiled at the poor jest and mounted Hercules, with the water skins draped around him. Before he rode off he leaned from the saddle and took Valerius's wooden fist in his hand. 'I promise I will not fail you, my friend.'

Valerius turned to find Domitia staring at him. For a moment he was lost in the dark eyes, before he remembered that she was the general's daughter. It was the first time in days he'd thought about his original mission. Paulinus's appearance at the villa seemed a long time ago; Domitia's father's guilt or innocence insignificant. Even the thought of the threat to Olivia produced nothing more than a dull ache. These things were beyond his control now. They could be left to the Fates.

His immediate priority was to keep Domitia Longina Corbulo alive, at least until everyone else was dead. He hoped it wouldn't come to that, but you couldn't drink hope. He picked up one of the water skins. It would deprive someone of their share in thirty-six hours or forty-eight, but it might mean she lived for the last hour it took for help to arrive, and that made it right.

He held out the skin. She licked her lips, but shook her head. 'I will drink when everyone else does.'

Valerius resisted the temptation to insist. Clearly, keeping her alive was going to be more difficult than he had anticipated.

The first sailors returned carrying pieces of the curtained awning and it was the work of a few minutes to erect a tent on the sand. Domitia and her girls retired gratefully away from the worst glare of the sun. He noticed that the sailors were very keen to return to the ship, and also that those he had sent to fetch water still hadn't returned. That made him wonder, and the suspicion prompted him to order Serpentius to disinter two of the water skins from the pit and conceal them somewhere else. Perhaps he was wrong to put so little faith in the men's honesty, but he doubted it. The Spaniard laughed and Valerius realized he'd already taken the precaution of laying one or two aside.

The bulk of the men returned thirty minutes later, suspiciously cheerful and a few of them carrying water skins that they dumped in the sand at Valerius's feet. Still not enough for five days, but an improvement. The haul of other goods was better than he had expected, including a flint and iron from Aurelius's belongings that would allow them to start a fire if they could find something to fuel it. There were sacks of damp wheatmeal that would only be a little saltier than normal when they turned it into porridge, and sufficient board and sailcloth to make a second shelter and provide a substantial enough partition for Domitia's pavilion to make it respectable for her guards to sleep there. He waited until they had all returned and Tiberius's German cavalrymen had deposited their clanking sacks with Serpentius before he gathered the sailors in an untidy mismatched rank to thank them for their efforts. A few just stared at him, but enough of them were hiding grins and shuffling their feet to make him sure he was right.

He smiled at them. 'I'm only going to ask you once, so let's be certain. You've returned with a fine haul, I can see that. But I'm wondering to myself if you had enough time to make a *proper* job of searching the *Golden Cygnet*.' He looked along the line, meeting the eyes of each man in turn. 'In the legions, if a man failed in his duty, let's say by not quite finding all the water on the ship, then it would be up to his tent mates, his *contubernium*, to punish him.' He saw them looking at him uncertainly, as if they weren't sure he was serious. 'So if I were to send Serpentius here out to the ship, and he were to find more water, it would mean you'd have to choose one of your own,' he paused, and now they were looking at one another, 'and I'd have to watch eight of you beating him to death with those wooden staves you've so kindly brought back.'

Someone muttered defiantly, but by now Valerius knew the German guard was at his back and most were staring at him with fear in their eyes. They weren't soldiers but sailors, rough men who liked to fight, and if someone died, too bad, but they weren't professional killers. Valerius was. 'So,' he said, 'I'm going to give you another chance to get back out to that ship and bring back every drop of fresh water.'

They waited until he nodded, and almost knocked each other over in the rush to reach what remained of the *Golden Cygnet*. 'Do you think I can trust them now?' he asked Serpentius.

The Spaniard shrugged. 'I'd always trust a terrified man before one who tells me he's honest.'

Valerius went back to the makeshift pavilion and met Domitia in the doorway. He bowed and waited for her to move either forward or back, but she stood there studying him seriously.

'Would you have done it?' There was curiosity in her voice, but no hint of reproach.

'Without discipline there is only chaos and death.'

'I'm aware of that, tribune, but I ask you again, would you have ordered those men to kill one of their own?'

He hesitated. Truth or lie? 'An officer should only ever give an order when he knows it will be obeyed,' he said. 'You will not find that in any military manual, but it is the unwritten code. Even with Serpentius at my back I doubt I could have forced them to kill their comrade.'

'Then they would have won. *Without discipline there is only chaos and death.*' She quoted the words back at him without irony.

'You're right,' Valerius conceded. 'I could not let them win, because then we would all die.'

'So what would you have done?'

'I would have chosen one of them myself and I would have cut his throat.'

She tilted her head to look up at him and he became conscious of the intriguing shadows deep in her eyes.

'You remind me of my father.'

XIV

Valerius could feel their discontent. It simmered in the broiling sun like a gently boiling pot, but it was still only mid-morning on the third day and by the time the sun reached its high point the pot would be ready to boil over. The sailors lay beneath their inadequate shelter like haphazard lumps of black rock. Valerius sat in the paltry shade of Domitia's pavilion twenty paces away listening to the stricken cavalryman's harsh, uneven breathing and waiting for him to die. The other mortally injured man had died during the night and lay wrapped in a sailcloth shroud at the top of the beach, but no one was going to dig two graves when one would do. It was incredible how a man's strength could ebb away in such a short time. He heard a hacking cough. He knew what they were thinking, because it was driving him mad too. About water. Clean, pure, cool water, not stinking blood-hot dregs thick with the saliva of ten other men who had already drunk from the same skin. He had rationed them to a tiny amount each, four times a day, knowing even that would deplete their dwindling supply too quickly. Two swallows. But he had discovered that two swallows was only enough to keep a man on the brink of death, not alive, in this sweltering furnace of a place that leached the fluid from the body like wine from a fractured *amphora*.

Thirst was the enemy. Thirst was tight-skinned, pinched faces

97

and narrow, red-rimmed eyes filled with hate. Thirst was when your tongue cleaved to the roof of your mouth and your throat felt as if it was scoured with pebbles. Thirst was cracked and bleeding lips so painful you wanted to cut them away with a knife and a head that felt as if your skull was being ripped off. Thirst was always wanting to piss, but never being able to. Thirst was the agony of knowing the next two swallows were four hours away, but they would only increase the torment until the next pointless sip of taunting nectar. Two swallows teased, but didn't satisfy. It lubricated cracked lips, but barely reached the throat. A momentary glimpse of paradise snatched away before it could be savoured. Like the glorious turquoise sea that lapped at the shore and formed small pools in the sand, so cool and clear and wet, but so deadly. Liquid that tempted and tormented, but could never be drunk because it would multiply a man's thirst ten times and push him beyond the edge of sanity. He suspected that more than one of the crew had already succumbed to the lure, and, as if the gods wished to confirm his suspicion, a man staggered to his feet among the sailors and stepped into the fierce light of the sun.

Valerius recognized him as one of the steersmen, a man whose skill had saved all their lives in the encounter with the pirates. The seaman croaked something unintelligible from a thirst-scarified throat and wandered aimlessly between the two groups, repeating the word over and over, his face and hands raised to the merciless sun, before falling to his knees and digging frantically in the sand. The sailors knew Valerius had ordered the goatskins to be buried, but not where. Now the sun-crazed steersman scraped and dug ever more desperately until he gave what might have been a howl of triumph and heads rose sharply among his shipmates. Valerius wondered what he'd found. It certainly wasn't water, which was safe on the far side of the pavilion from the seamen. A second later the sailor dipped his hands into the hole and raised them to his lips. Valerius gagged as he realized what was happening. The demented sailor's cupped hands were filled not with water, but with sand, and he poured it into his mouth, repeating the gesture again and again until, with a choked groan, he collapsed on his face and lay still.

Someone appeared in the doorway beside him. He knew it was Domitia before he stood up because she smelled different from everyone else. After dark, she bathed in the cool waters of the bay, resisting the temptation to drink that would have destroyed Valerius, and it gave her a salty, wholesome scent. Still, she suffered as much as anyone in the heat, and her face and eyes were puffy and distended as she swayed on her feet.

'Is he dead?' The words were slurred by her swollen tongue and saliva as thick as mud.

'Yes.'

'Good.'

He nodded. One less mouth to drain their precious supply.

'The trooper, too.' Valerius noticed for the first time that Ferox, the injured cavalryman, was silent at last. 'We'll bury them after dark.'

She nodded, and the movement seemed to use up the last of her strength because she would have fallen if Valerius hadn't caught her. She slumped in his arms, slim and soft, the curves of her body nestling against him. Something exploded in his head and he was filled with a terrible need. He crushed his face into her dark hair, inhaling a honeysuckle scent that acted like an elixir. She felt it too, because she squirmed against him and her head came up and he felt cracked lips against his. Her cloak dropped away and he could feel her skin through the soft material of her shift. They held each other like that for a few moments before he realized what he was doing. This was madness. He was as crazed as the poor fool lying in the sand not five paces away had been.

'No.' He tried to draw away, but her arms held him close and his body wouldn't obey him anyway.

'Please.' Her eyes opened and he saw tiny damp buds in the corners that might have been tears.

He shook his head, and pulled away.

The emotions surged across her ravaged face like storm clouds over a field of wheat: desolation and heartache, pain and rejection, and finally fury. She stepped back and he wondered if she was going to hit him, and what he would do if she did. 'Coward,' she hissed, and turned and staggered away through the curtain that separated the two sides of the tent.

He closed his eyes and shook his head. He had been awarded the Gold Crown of Valour for defying fifty thousand of Boudicca's blood-crazed warriors, yet he had failed every woman he had ever loved. When he opened them again, Serpentius was standing watching him.

'If Tiberius doesn't get back soon we're finished.'

'Maybe we already are.'

'It's time.'

Valerius nodded. 'Get the water.'

Two and a half water skins a day. They'd started with fifteen. By tonight they would have five left, plus anything Serpentius had kept in reserve. Three days, at most, if he cut the ration, but it was barely enough to keep them alive now.

Where was Tiberius?

It had all seemed so simple. Keep the sea to your right, ride during the night and try to find some precious shade during the heat of the day. Keep going until you win or you die. For Tiberius Claudius Crescens it was the ideal mission. The kind of mission with no complications and no regrets. Win or die.

But he hadn't reckoned on being killed by his own stupidity.

The landscape he had ridden through was as forbidding as it was intimidatingly beautiful. A landscape that could destroy you just by its very existence. Ahead, the never-ending surf-washed line of the beach, flat as the freshly brushed surface of the Circus Maximus on a race day. To his right, the broad expanse of the ocean, a marker, no more than that. To his left, inland, a treacherous dustbowl and salt flats which turned quickly into an anonymous sea of rolling sand dunes. Tiberius recognized, without any sense of inadequacy, that he was a man of little imagination. It was, after all, a desirable quality in the type of soldier he had chosen to be. But the thought of becoming lost in that great sandy waste made him feel like an ant on a roasting plate: a tiny insignificant creature whose fate was beyond its power to change.

Yet none of it was as great a threat as the challenge which faced him now.

Someone more romantic might have said he appeared to be standing in the centre of a gigantic silver plate, of the kind that graced a senator's banqueting table. On three sides moonlight glittered across waters as unruffled as the flat sand he had ridden over, always keeping the sea to his right, since he had left Valerius three days earlier. He was so close. He knew he was close because he could see the flickering pinprick of light that identified a home in some Egyptian settlement and smell the smoke of a dung fire in the still air. He looked over his shoulder. The first pale ochre hint of dawn was a ghostly betrayal on the eastern horizon. An hour at most?

Hercules whinnied behind him and nuzzled his back. He had two more leather water skins left of the original – was it six? – and of the four that had been drunk the horse had consumed three. He put a skin to the gelding's mouth and held it there until it was empty.

His mistake had been not to take a path a little further inland. He realized that now; too late. By staying close to the shore he hadn't noticed when he strayed from the beach on to the mile-wide spit of sand that had finally narrowed to this thin streak which ended at a channel a few hundred paces wide but the gods only knew how deep. How far had he come? Ten miles? Twenty? He had been riding all night. It was impossible to tell.

He had no choice. Turning the horse the way they'd come he kicked him into a trot, then a canter and finally a full gallop. Speed was his only hope. In the moonlight, the evidence of his pride and his arrogance was clear in the single line of hoofprints that vanished into the distance. He had no choice. He had to make as much ground as he could before daylight. His mind cleared. He felt no fear. It was all simple again. He would die, today or tomorrow; but he would die trying.

The big horse carried him uncomplainingly, mile after mile, hour after hour, through the dark and into the dawn, but daylight mocked him with a flat expanse of blue lagoon to his right, and no end in sight. He had no choice. The gelding's sweat soaked his legs and he could already feel the sun roasting his neck. Soon it would be so hot it would be like breathing the flames of a furnace. He dug his heels into the horse's ribs and urged him on harder. Hercules had a huge heart, but even huge hearts have a breaking point. Tiberius felt a surge of hope when he realized the lagoon was finally petering out, but only for a moment. Seconds later the gelding collapsed under him as if he'd been shot in the chest by a ballista bolt. Tiberius hit the ground shoulder first and rolled to a halt in a cloud of sand. By the time he'd rubbed the grit from his eyes Hercules was bravely trying to get back to his feet, but the power had gone from his legs. Pink foam frothed from the horse's nostrils and mouth and sprayed across the sand as he shook his great head in frustration. As Tiberius watched, the animal's struggles grew weaker and he rolled on to his side, his gleaming flanks heaving and slick with sweat. To the young tribune, the gelding was nothing more than a mode of transport, to be used and discarded, and, his father would have said, eaten if necessary. He knew horses, admired their strength and stamina, but he felt no affection for them. Still, he respected courage and he placed a hand on the gelding's forehead and smiled into the trusting eye as he killed Hercules with a single thrust of his sword behind the right ear.

There was no time to rest. He stood up and felt the sun's heat boring through his dark hair. A few minutes and it would boil his brains and render him senseless. He removed his tunic and fashioned a covering for his head and shoulders. With a last reproachful glance at the sand spit that had killed him he allowed himself a single sip from the final water skin and set off westwards.

At first it was merely a trial. The furnace temperatures made it difficult to breathe and he could feel the skin on his arms melting, but he made reasonable progress. Very soon it became a torment. The relentless heat seemed to suck the strength from his legs. The sand shifted beneath his feet and he found himself fighting for every step. His mouth and nose might as well have been filled with sand. Grit scraped his eyeballs and his vision blurred, making it difficult to keep his course. Water. He must have water. But Tiberius knew that when the water skin was empty he was finished, so he denied himself until he could endure no longer, then denied himself again. What seemed like a mile later, he scrabbled for the water skin and gulped down a single mouthful, though it took all his resolve not to drink more. He risked a look back the way he'd come and let out a tormented groan. A few hundred paces away the dark bulk of Hercules lay in the sand. He had been walking for what seemed like hours and he had travelled only a quarter of a mile. A lesser man might have fallen on his sword in despair, but Tiberius Claudius Crescens was no lesser man. His brutal upbringing had had but a single purpose. To make him hard. Hard as the iron that forged his sword. Hard as the stones he had carried to build his strength. His father had taught him to hate, and to endure. He slung the water skin over his shoulder by its leather strap and began walking again.

The makeshift hood suffocated him, but when he removed it the super-heated air burned his face and throat and the sun seared his scalp like a fish on a griddle. The heat played tricks with his mind. At one point he marched at the centre of a full cohort of legionaries, fully equipped with sword, shield and spear, their helmets glistening and their centurions calling out the marching beat. Every one carried a full water skin that sloshed and gurgled with each step he took, but the moment Tiberius turned to ask for a drink the whole unit vanished. A mile later his father rode past on a pale horse, even though he was long dead, but when Tiberius picked up his pace to ask the questions he'd always wanted to ask, the horse turned into a dog and ran into the desert.

He would have kept the sea to his right, but the sea was long gone. That told him he was lost, but it didn't matter because when he saw his tracks he realized he had been walking in circles. When he saw the city moving towards him he started laughing. Through his delirium he knew that it was just another joke the gods were playing on him. He only felt threatened when he saw the armoured giants. They shimmered across the flat plain, growing larger with every step and walking three feet above the ground. Well, he would fight them. He drew his sword and it felt good in his hand. But the reality was that he'd thrown the sword away with his empty water skin twenty minutes earlier. When a hand touched his shoulder, he believed he was fighting for his life. He would have killed anyone who said he was pleading for it.

XV

'He is not coming back. We all die if we stay here.' The sailors' spokesman, Susco, the Nubian sailmaster, was a big man but heat and thirst had shrivelled him like a piece of animal hide in a fire. His words emerged as a choked, belligerent challenge from a throat dry as dust. Behind him his shipmates stood in a tattered, swaying line, red-rimmed eyes squinting from faces blackened by the sun. Valerius noted that they had waited until the water had been distributed to make their challenge. It had given them renewed strength and fuelled their determination.

'We should go, tonight when the sun sets,' Susco continued. 'East. If the tribune could not reach help in the west on a horse, we must go east.' Valerius nodded, not in agreement, but because he understood the logic of desperation. Susco mistook it for approval. 'We will take all the water and travel light. We can make sixteen miles before dawn.'

'Aye,' a ragged growl of approval from the sailors.

'No.'

The Nubian shook his head. 'You are outvoted, tribune, and outnumbered.'

Valerius laughed at his naivety. 'Do you think you are in the Senate, Susco? Do you believe that what you say carries some sort of authority?

Then you are mistaken. There is no vote. I command here and as long as I command we stay.'

'It is you who are mistaken,' Susco growled. 'There are no patricians and no plebs here. Just desperate men looking for a chance of life and their fair share of what they are entitled to. If you want to stay, we'll take what's ours and go.' Susco took a step forward, his fists bunched, and there was a growl as the men moved with him towards the tent. Valerius felt Serpentius moving in behind him, but he made a calming motion with his left hand. This could still be settled without violence.

'And what about them?' Valerius pointed to the two injured sailors lying in the shade of the makeshift awning. 'Will they get their fair share too?'

Susco shrugged. They would die soon enough and had not been part of his plan, but he knew his supporters would never abandon their shipmates. 'We'll carry them.'

'Then you won't make sixteen miles. More like six. And what will you find? Exactly the same as you have here. More sand, more rocks and more sea. Only you won't have shelter and your water will run out by noon and you'll be dead by nightfall.' Valerius sensed confusion in the men behind Susco. The sailmaster had convinced them that anything was better than the hell they were suffering here, but if Valerius could persuade them they would be better off together they still had a chance. 'And what if you do leave at nightfall and Tiberius is just five miles down the beach, with help? Those who stay will be drinking sweet water and on their way back to civilization while you are dying by inches in the sand.'

Susco glanced to his shipmates for support, but one glance told him he'd lost them. His shoulders slumped and Valerius sighed with relief.

'We—'

'A Roman officer does not negotiate with scum, tribune.' Domitia's imperious voice rasped through the silence like a saw blade and Valerius saw the men stiffen. He turned. She was standing just outside her tent, tall and straight as a legionary centurion, her small breasts rising and falling beneath the thin shift. She glared at the sailors, eyes filled with contempt and the utter conviction of a lineage that gave her dominion over men like these. 'Mutineers and deserters deserve no water and they will have none. Get back to your places or I will have you cut down by my guards. My father will hear of this when we reach Antioch. The punishment for mutiny is death and you can be sure I will urge him to show no mercy.'

The big sailor stared at Domitia. 'We won't take orders from a girl and we won't be treated like dogs,' he said. 'We'll have the water now and we'll butcher you to get it if we have to.' When Susco spoke there was a catch in his voice that betrayed his intentions and Valerius knew in that moment that he would have to kill him. With a growl the crew moved towards the tent and he felt the familiar glow of coming battle flare inside him. He drew his sword and heard the distinctive hiss of another blade being unsheathed as Serpentius stepped to his side.

'Are you willing to die for it, Susco? Or you? Or you?' Valerius was smiling now. The savage smile of a born killer. A victor's snarling mask. To the men facing him, he seemed to grow, a warrior god come to earth, the scarred face offering only one thing: death. 'A water skin is no good to a man with a cut throat or a hole in his guts. Get back to where you belong. We'll issue the next ration at first light and Tiberius will be back before noon. Obey my order and there will be no executions. Obey and we will all get out of this alive. You have my word on it.'

They backed away, unwillingly, but they went. He knew they would return.

When they were a safe distance away he turned to Domitia. Her eyes had lost none of their certainty.

'I expected more of you, tribune,' she snapped. 'Your duty is to protect me.'

He took her by the arm and pulled her back to the tent. She made no attempt to break away. 'My duty is to get as many people out of this alive as I can, lady, and you have just made that more difficult. In fact, I think you may have killed us all.'

She looked at him and he wondered if it was contempt in her eyes. Only later did he realize it was pity. 'Perhaps you are not like my father after all.'

He left her and went to where Serpentius was sharpening his long sword.

'They'll be back,' the Spaniard said. 'And we should be ready for them.'

Valerius nodded absently. 'I made a mistake. I should have killed Susco.'

'Better that way.' Serpentius spat dryly. 'They only had a few sailors' knives; it would have been like killing rabbits. Might be different later.'

'Four trained soldiers against a rabble of sailors armed with a few sticks?'

'Maybe not just a few sticks, and more likely two than four.'

'What do you mean?'

Serpentius's eyes flickered towards the tent. 'You were too busy to notice. When the general's daughter was trying to get us killed, you were watching the sailors. I had my eye on our German mates. They'd already pulled their swords when you went for yours, and the only reason they didn't kill you was because I was watching them.'

As darkness fell, Domitia trooped down to the beach with her servant girls to wash in the waves as had become her custom. The two slaves held up a length of curtain to allow her privacy, but Valerius noticed something he should have seen before: the way they were followed by the hungry eyes of the stranded sailors, and more hungrily still by the two German cavalrymen who sat together on the far side of the tent. He cursed himself for a fool. He had been concentrating on keeping them alive when he should have been aware of the currents flowing between the two groups, and between Domitia and her guards. Of course men forced into close proximity with three young women for weeks on end would be affected. He had discovered in Colonia that imminent death was more likely to heighten lust than to suppress it.

But was Serpentius overreacting? He approached Civilis, the senior of the two guards, and arranged that he should take the first watch.

The German nodded grimly and saluted. 'If they come, we will be ready for them,' he assured Valerius. But when Domitia returned from her bathing, his eyes never left the general's daughter.

✻

Valerius slept fitfully, tormented by dreams of lakes and rivers and bubbling streams. It could only have been an hour before he felt a looming human presence and realized Serpentius had come to wake him for his watch. But when he opened his eyes the first thing that drew his attention was the faint, unmistakable gleam of edged metal. The second was that the figure leaning over him was much bulkier than the whip-thin Spaniard. His left hand groped for his sword, but his mind told him he was already dead.

Without warning his assassin stiffened and gave an agonized groan as six inches of pointed iron emerged from the centre of his body. A point that violently twisted, making the man jerk and shudder as his vitals were torn by the long double-edged blade, the groan becoming a scream that was instantly muffled by a leathery hand. The iron point disappeared and the body slumped forward. When the hand was removed Valerius's face and chest were drenched in a rush of warm liquid that fountained from the gaping mouth. 'Bastard,' he spat, and wiped Civilis's blood from his mouth and eyes. 'Did you have to make such a mess?'

'They're coming.' Serpentius ignored his master's complaint. 'The other guard has gone to join them. I think he's taken the weapons, but I thought I'd keep an eye on this one.'

As Valerius strapped on his sword, the curtain that split his sleeping area from that of Domitia and her women twitched and a wide-eyed brown face appeared. When Suki saw the gore-drenched figure with the sword she opened her mouth to scream, but Serpentius clamped his hand over her mouth and shushed her. A moment later Domitia pulled back the curtain and gaped as she recognized Valerius behind the bloody mask.

'If it comes to it, you might be advised to use this.' He tossed her the dagger at his belt and she caught it deftly, studying it in her hand. Her chin came up and her eyes were steady.

'Only to kill those who come to take what is only mine to give,' she said. And he believed her.

Serpentius disappeared from the tent and, with a last glance at Domitia, Valerius followed him.

Was it a rustle of feet through sand, or the gentle swish of surf on shore? They were only just in time. Movement, a lighter darkness against the true night and less than ten paces away. Shadowy silhouettes moved across the beach, but their stealth was illusory when faced with a hunter of the night. A sharp scream rent the air as Serpentius, the veteran gladiator, found his first victim. Valerius remained where he was between the attackers and the tent. In another fight the two men would have stayed together, each covering the other's back, but this was no time for elaborate tactics. Serpentius was like a fox among chickens, moving silently through them, his long sword seeking out his next prey. A clash of iron on iron confirmed that the mutineers had been given weapons, but that would not save them. The darkness was Serpentius's element, his speed their doom. A second man shrieked, then a third, and now the rest nervously shouted encouragement to each other, making them all the easier to identify and to kill. Valerius knew that those who stayed silent would be the most dangerous. By now his senses were in that high state of readiness that comes only to a warrior in battle. The first hint the man who came out of the darkness had of his presence was the sting of the *gladius* that sliced the tendons of his throat and severed his jugular, so that he died silent and bewildered, blood fountaining and feet scrabbling in the sand. Valerius registered without regret that he had just killed the surviving German guard, and waited for his next victim.

Out of the pitch dark a torch flared followed swiftly by another, and a circle of light encompassed the sandy battleground like a golden arena. Before Valerius could identify the foremost torch bearer as Susco, Serpentius appeared by his side with the same bewildering fluidity with which he had gone. Four men down, including the guard, only five left, but five men armed with swords, whose eyes glinted like ravening wolves' in the torchlight. Five men driven beyond fear by the scent of buried water and the delights Susco had promised them with the women in the tent. But to sample those delights they first had to kill the two men who stood in their way.

Valerius waited, as he had waited in the Temple of Claudius for

Boudicca's warriors to break through the door and slaughter the last surviving Romans of Colonia. He had not felt fear then, and he did not feel it now.

'Kill them. Kill them all,' he said softly to Serpentius, the gladiator who had never lost a fight.

But Susco had other ideas.

The torches were wooden staves salvaged from the ship, capped with torn cloth from the tunics of those already dead and soaked with pitch secreted away during the forays to the wreck of the *Golden Cygnet*. Susco held one, a second crewman the other, and it was he who tossed his flaming brand over Valerius's head and on to the roof of the pavilion where Domitia and her women waited for the outcome of the fighting they could hear so clearly in the still desert night. The cloth of the tent had spent four days in the burning sun. At the first lick of flame the tinder-dry fabric erupted with a soft *whump*, the fire instantly running the length of the roof.

A terrified scream jolted Valerius into action.

'Go,' he ordered Serpentius. 'I will hold them here.'

Another man might have hesitated for a vital heartbeat, but the Spaniard slipped away without a word and left Valerius to face his enemy alone.

The odds of five to one seemed impossible. Susco thought so. He wore a mocking smile that said his victory was already certain and the fruits of it his to take at his leisure. 'They'll taste all the sweeter for a little roasting,' he sneered. But delirium and thirst had impaired his judgement. He had forgotten the kind of man he was facing.

Valerius sprang forward over the sand, angling his run so that Susco's bulk shielded him from the remainder of his attackers. He knew it had to be fast and it had to be certain. Susco drove his torch towards Valerius's face, expecting him to meet it with his sword, which would leave Susco with a simple thrust into the Roman tribune's exposed body. But Valerius didn't hold his sword in his right hand. His right hand was buried in the burned-out ruins of Colonia. Now the carved walnut fist which had replaced it came up and knocked the torch aside. He ignored the heat and the stink of singed hair as it brushed his shoulder, at the same time stepping inside Susco's clumsy lunge. It gave him the heartbeat he needed to rake the inside of the other man's arm, flaying skin and muscle from the bone with the edge of the *gladius*. While Susco was still reeling in shock the sword came up in a scything backhand sweep that took him below the chin and severed his head from his shoulders. The sailmaster's trunk swayed for a moment as a thick dark spray spumed from the neck, before it toppled slowly backwards into the sand. The surviving attackers were sailors, not fighters. When he hacked the next down without even meeting a challenge the rest dropped their swords and fled into the darkness.

Valerius turned to find Domitia's pavilion a raging inferno.

XVI

He reached the burning tent as Serpentius staggered from the doorway with a cloak over his head and a slave girl under each arm. The Spaniard collapsed in the sand, his chest heaving and utterly spent. Valerius ran to him and dragged the group clear of the flames. Where was Domitia?

'She wouldn't come,' Serpentius choked. 'Ordered me to take the girls first. I . . .' He tried to get to his feet, but his legs buckled beneath him.

'I'll go.' Valerius picked up the cloak and rushed for the tent.

A wall of fire met him where the curtain had hung. Nothing could survive in that holocaust of flame. Then she screamed, long and shrill, the scream of a woman in mortal agony or mortal fear. 'Sweet Minerva aid me,' Valerius whispered. He swung the cloak over his head and charged the flaming barrier.

Domitia's scream had used up the last of her strength. Her lungs seemed to be filled with something solid and she struggled for each breath. Dense smoke wreathed the upper part of the pavilion and above it the ceiling glowed red. In front of her was nothing but flame. She had thought the heat of the Egyptian sun unbearable, but the radiation from the fire felt as if it was melting her flesh. She had used the little knife Valerius had given her to try to cut through the fabric of the pavilion, but it was thick cloth, almost a rug, woven tight to provide shelter even from winter gales, and she barely scarred it. All hope fading, she slumped closer to the floor where the air was cleanest and waited for death. When the wall in front of her exploded in a shower of sparks and flaming fabric she believed it was Vesta, goddess of fire, come to carry her off.

Valerius tore off the burning cloak and rushed to the general's daughter. Domitia lay face down on the sand with one arm thrown towards the doorway and the flesh of that hand bubbled like a boiling pot. He picked her up and turned to make his escape the way he'd come, but one look told him it was impossible. The cloak that had protected his flesh from the blistering heat was a smouldering mass on the floor. They were trapped.

In seconds the smoke wrapped itself around him, and before he knew it, it was choking him to death. He felt the moment his mind began to shut down.

Act or die. He had not come here to die.

He shook his head to clear it and again studied his surroundings. The awning at the door collapsed in a cloud of flame and sparks, and he knew it was only seconds before the ceiling followed it. No chance of digging their way out in time; they'd anchored the base of the tent with two-foot mounds of sand. His eyes took in the heavy cloth walls and he saw where Domitia had made her pathetic attempt to escape with the knife. Was there any hope? He laid her at the base of the wall and drew his sword. With the strength of the damned he hacked at the cloth, but barely made an impression. In desperation, he stabbed with the point and, little by little, the iron blade disappeared into the close-woven material until it finally broke through. Using his left hand and his right arm he brought all his weight to bear on the hilt. Slowly the fabric began to tear and he increased the pressure, sawing with the blade. Eventually he created a rip a sword's length in height, but it was still not enough. He worked his way left and right, hacking at the threads until it was wide enough to wriggle through. Sweet fresh air poured into his lungs and the temptation was to lie and glory in it, but he stirred himself and reached back to pull Domitia away to safety.

Not a moment too soon. The roof collapsed and the burning fabric engulfed the ground where she had lain a second before. He dragged her unconscious body a safe distance and watched the entire structure burn like a funeral pyre.

Sleep or exhaustion must have overcome him, because when he woke it was to the sound of a diabolical ululating wail. Domitia lay by his side just outside the circle of light thrown by the glowing heap where the tent had been. He feared he had lost her because the rise and fall of her breast was so shallow, but gradually her eyes opened and looked into his. They were puffy and red-rimmed, but something glowed in their depths that told him she was unscarred by her ordeal. She gave a little ladylike sneeze and laughed.

'You have no eyebrows and your hair is all patchy.'

The statement made him smile. If that was the only price of last night's mayhem he could count himself fortunate. 'So is yours,' he pointed out.

She frowned and her lips formed a pout. 'But I am still beautiful?'

'You will always be beautiful, lady,' he said, and she accepted it as her due.

'What is that noise?'

'It sounds as if someone has died.'

'Then perhaps we should resurrect them.'

He hesitated, caught between what he knew was right and what he knew she wanted. Knowing that he wanted it too. Just to stay here a little longer in each other's company. Not Gaius Valerius Verrens, Hero of Rome, and Domitia Longina, daughter of General Corbulo. Just a man and a woman. But duty was duty. He held out his hand to help her to her feet and she took it reluctantly, wincing as they touched. For the first time he saw the sacs of pus-filled flesh hanging like over-ripe grapes from her fingers and realized the agony she must be suffering.

He led her back into the light and round the fire to where her servant girls knelt with their heads covered, producing the plaintive wailing they had heard.

Serpentius stood behind them staring distractedly towards the

114

glowing remains of the tent. As the two figures emerged from the darkness his hand automatically went for his sword. When he recognized Valerius, his eyes widened and he made the sign against evil.

'Mars save us.' He strode towards the Roman and Valerius thought the gruff Spaniard was about to take him in his arms. At the last moment Serpentius stopped short, grinning wryly. 'You'll have to show me that trick. Did Hades spit you out?' He bowed to Domitia. 'My lady, I am glad to see you safe.'

Domitia smiled and walked to the two slaves, who stared at her with their mouths gaping before they ran shrieking into the darkness.

Serpentius laughed. 'By the gods, I've never been so glad to see you.'

Valerius raised what had once been an eyebrow. 'Because you miss my company?'

'No, because I thought that screeching would never stop. I would have jumped into the fire myself to get away from it.'

When the girls had been rounded up and convinced that Domitia was no ghost they gathered by the fire. Valerius dug up one of the precious water skins and allowed everyone to drink their fill. Serpentius vanished for a time and when he returned he reported no sign of the surviving crewmen, including the injured.

'They will still want our water, but I doubt they'll be back,' Valerius said. 'The men who escaped were those whose hearts weren't with Susco. Whether that makes them the best of them or the worst doesn't matter. They know what awaits them here. Either we'll kill them or they'll be tried for mutiny and suffer a worse death. Better to keep walking until you drop.'

'At least they've left their shelter. We can salvage what's left and move across when the sun comes up, once I've cleared away their filth.'

Valerius nodded and walked over to where Domitia sat huddled between the two slave girls. 'Let me see your hand,' he said gently.

She held it out and he studied it. He knew a lot about cuts and wounds, but very little about burns apart from the remedies which had been used on the estate. Perhaps it was better to leave it alone if he wasn't certain what to do.

Domitia saw his confusion. 'I can suffer it, tribune. I am a soldier's daughter.'

'Grease,' Serpentius said decisively. 'Cover it with grease and leave it for a week.'

'And where will we get grease?' Valerius demanded. 'I'm not a magician.'

'Always grease on a ship,' the Spaniard pointed out. 'I'll swim out to the wreck tomorrow and see what I can find. If you can wait that long, lady?'

'Of course,' Domitia said gracefully. 'I am glad that someone is looking after my welfare, Serpentius.'

It was the first time Valerius had seen the Spaniard blush.

Late in the night as he lay in the sand beneath his cloak, Valerius felt someone move in beside him. Warmth and softness and the scent of salt water and smoke.

'You may put your arms around me, tribune. I am cold.'

So he did.

XVII

Valerius dreamed of a river nymph with Domitia's face dancing naked beneath a cascade of cool, clear water. Strangely, for the first time in days thirst was not uppermost in his mind. Instead, the vision stirred a feeling that had lain dormant for a long time, accompanied by a reaction that would have made Priapus proud. He woke with something soft, warm and round in his left hand and a thunderstorm building inside his skull as he realized that the thing squirming against his groin was a pair of firm female buttocks that were only just covered by the short tunic their owner wore. He tried to release Domitia's left breast, but her hand clamped over his, and when he attempted to move away the buttocks squirmed all the harder, making the sensations he was experiencing close to unbearable.

'Do not move, Valerius, I beg you,' she whispered.

She wriggled round beneath the cloak to face him and her mouth came to his, her breath still sweet despite the days without water. He knew that the two slave girls were sleeping less than twenty paces away, but it was the most natural thing in the world to kiss her and to feel her body moulded against his. More natural still that when the tunic rode up above her hips his hardness should find her softness and with a wriggle of her hips it was as if he had been engulfed in oiled silk and the heat of it made him groan. Domitia crushed her lips against

117

his so fiercely that he could feel the individual small white teeth behind them as she fought to suppress a moan of pure pleasure. Valerius wrapped both arms around the slight figure and held her to him, the passion flowing between them, the frustration of being unable to give it full rein making it all the more intense. Suddenly she stiffened, her eyes opened wide and she shuddered against him and he could not prevent himself from following her. Slowly she relaxed and he felt her lips nuzzling his cheek.

'I have prayed for this day, ever since the morning I watched you exercising with your soldiers.'

Valerius smiled. 'I thought you were looking at Tiberius.'

'Tiberius is nothing but a boy,' she said dismissively. 'And I think that Tiberius is only capable of loving himself. You were different. I looked at you and saw a man.'

'But not a whole man.' It was part of the burden he carried that if the hand was not mentioned he must point it out.

She wriggled closer. 'Your wooden hand is as much a trophy of war as the *phalerae* you wear or the Gold Crown of Valour you hold. Even with a missing hand you are twice the man of any other I have met.'

He shook his head. 'It should never have happened. I should not have let it happen.'

A soft finger touched his lips. 'Do not say that, my love. It was meant to be. It is possible that by tomorrow or the next day we will be dead. Why should I allow the gods to deny me any longer?'

He had no answer, but he still knew it was wrong and he had a feeling that her gods would demand a reckoning in their own time.

'It must not happen again, Domitia. Your father . . .'

'Is hundreds of miles away. You are such a fool, Valerius. For us, there is no future. Only now.'

She slipped away and woke the two girls and together they went to wash away the smoke and the ashes of the previous night in the surf. Serpentius was already up and checking the bodies from the battle for signs of life. The skin on his shaved head was blistered and his face still black from his rescue of the slaves during the night. Valerius wondered just how much he had heard of what had happened earlier, and received a cool look that confirmed his fears.

'So we fight our way out of one trap to fall straight into another?' the Spaniard grumbled as he hauled Susco's headless corpse towards the sea where he'd already sunk three of the dead mutineers. 'By Mars' sacred arse, he's beginning to stink already.'

'A slave should mind his own business,' Valerius pointed out. 'I believe it was you who told me that.'

'How could I mind my own business when you made enough noise to wake Susco here?' the Spaniard complained, letting the body drop to the ground as he straightened to face the Roman. 'And even a slave knows that when an old tom cat plays with a leopard kitten he'd better watch out for the leopard.'

Valerius noticed that Serpentius didn't mention Corbulo by name, but the surge of guilt he felt was like a spear in his guts. How could he have let it happen? He was a man full grown, he knew the boundary between sex and love. And he had never allowed himself to cross it since his time with the British girl Maeve at Colonia. There had been slave girls aplenty in the proconsul's palace at Carthage where he had spent eighteen months as military aide to Aulus Vitellius. Yes, Domitia had come to him in the night, but a sane man would have sent her away again. Instead, he had allowed himself to be hypnotized by the heady brew of her youth and beauty and sensuality, and betrayed himself and her father.

He saw Domitia watching him from the shadow and he wondered what was going through her mind. Their coupling had been urgent and as unstoppable as the waves that had battered the *Golden Cygnet* to pieces. While it was happening she had whispered words like 'love' and 'for ever', but how much of it had been driven by the intensity of the events of a few hours earlier? He had experienced before how a combination of fear and the unlikelihood of survival could swamp the senses and warp the mind. Would she end up despising him for his weakness as much as she had praised him for his masculinity? He looked up and found the Spaniard still staring at him. 'The leopard is far away and I'm more likely to die of thirst than on another man's sword.'

Serpentius nodded thoughtfully and changed the subject. 'Maybe Susco had a point.'

'You think we should try to walk to Judaea?'

'Not Judaea. But I have been thinking there must be some kind of trade between Egypt and the Judaeans and the most likely route for that trade is surely along the coast. Perhaps if we strike inland we can find the road?'

'And if we can't?' Valerius said. 'What then?'

'Will we be any worse off?'

The Roman nodded to where the three women now lay beneath the sailors' awning. The sun had barely risen, but already they could feel the threat of its fierce glare. By midday it would be unbearable even beneath the shelter of the canopy, every drop of moisture leached from their bodies by a furnace heat reflected from the burning sand. Domitia's slave girls had been affected more than any of them by the dehydration and their condition had not been helped by the terror of the previous night. They moved with an almost pitiful lethargy and no longer responded readily to their mistress's commands.

'How long do you think they would last out there?' He pointed inland where the red dunes marched away in relentless tight-packed ranks beneath the blistering sun. 'At least here we have shade and we're conserving our energy. There may be a few things on the ship we've missed. No, we stay here and wait it out.'

'Then we're dead if Tiberius hasn't got through.'

'Tiberius is not the man to give up.'

'If he was coming back he should have been here by now.'

Valerius looked the other man in the eye. 'If you want to try it alone, I won't stop you.'

Serpentius shook his head. 'You were right. We have to stay together. These poor fools didn't understand that and look where it got them.' He picked up Susco by the arms and resumed dragging him away. 'When we're finished here, I'll go out and give the ship another search. I'm certain there's no more water, but I should be able to find some grease for the general's daughter in the galley or where they stored the horse harness.'

Valerius nodded absently and stared westwards across the desert as if he could conjure a rescue party by the force of his will.

'He's out there, I'm certain of it. If we can only last another two or three days we will survive.'

The dribble of water Valerius poured into his mouth did nothing to relieve his thirst; if anything it made the need sharper. Domitia saw that he was more generous to the others than he had been to himself and insisted he take more.

'We all drink or none drink. We all live or none,' she said.

They lay beneath the awning, but the sun's rays were so strong that the shelter of the thin canvas was largely illusory. Valerius did what he could to shade Domitia and her women from the worst as they lay panting in the sand, their flesh desiccated by the relentless heat, but soon he could only collapse beside them.

Suki, the elder of the girls, went mad as the noonday sun reached its highest point, her mind consumed by the knowledge that the next drink, or perhaps the one after, would be their last. She ran into the sea and no one had the strength to follow her. The last Valerius saw of her she was flailing her way towards the *Golden Cygnet*, but the next time he looked up all he could see was the glare of the ocean. Her fellow slave did not even raise her head.

Someone, it must have been Serpentius, found the fortitude to dole out the last of the water just as darkness fell, and none of them knew whether it would be sufficient to see them through to the next dawn. Valerius was beyond torment now, and beyond guilt. His last thought before he lapsed into unconsciousness was to cover Domitia's body with his own to fend off the chill of the night.

But he did not dream of Domitia. He dreamed of Maeve, the beautiful British girl who had captured his heart and then torn it in two when she had betrayed Colonia and the Temple of Claudius. He dreamed of lush pastures and soft rain; rain that fell on his cheeks and moistened his lips. The dream was so real that he could feel the water trickling down his throat, but he had lost the ability to swallow and choked on it.

'Not too much, or you will kill him.'

XVIII

'Titus Flavius Vespasian at your service, tribune.'

Through eyes swollen to narrow slits Valerius saw he was being addressed by a fellow *tribunus laticlavius*, but the name told him his saviour was a much more exotic member of the species. Titus was a fresh-faced, handsome man perhaps a year or two younger than Valerius, with strong, thoughtful features and the kind of natural authority that so often comes with good breeding. Valerius tried to speak, but the other man shook his head gently.

'There will be time for explanations later. I will send my physician to you once he has treated the lady Domitia. In the meantime I must make arrangements for her transport. You should rest now.'

Titus left and Valerius lay back and closed his eyes. Despite his physical condition he felt at peace. They were safe. Domitia was safe. After all that had happened – pirate attacks, shipwreck, mutiny and thirst – it was difficult to believe he was once more in a legionary's leather tent, with water and food to spare. He had a niggling feeling he had forgotten something important, but every time he tried to pin it down it slipped deeper into the recesses of his mind. Whatever it was, it could wait.

When he opened his eyes again he found himself staring into the face of something only half human. The features were puffy and distended, with alternating red blotches and patches of wrinkled skin covered in a revolting green salve, and the top of the shaven head seemed to glow bright red. Further inspection showed that the arms, legs and torso of the apparition were covered by loose bandages.

Tiberius read the look in his eyes and a grin creased the grotesque features. 'Before you say anything, tribune, you don't look a great deal better yourself.'

Valerius laughed and felt as if his throat had been cut.

'We have you to thank for our lives, Tiberius,' he whispered. 'I will be for ever in your debt.'

The young tribune said to him, 'Thank Fortuna. If it were not for her we would all be dead – and General Vespasian's son, of course.'

He slumped in a corner of the tent and Valerius insisted he tell the story of his long ride west. Tiberius recited the tale in a dispassionate voice that only changed when he reached the moment he realized he'd strayed off course and would have to retrace his steps for twenty miles.

'I came close to despair then, though it is not my nature. Only my pledge to you kept me in the saddle. When Hercules foundered I knew I would not last the day. The only thing that saved me was getting lost. I must have become delirious, because I had wandered into the desert and was walking in entirely the wrong direction. Numidian cavalry auxiliaries returning from a reconnaissance patrol saw me wandering in circles. They thought they had found one of their own, because I had been burned almost black and I could barely speak. It was a whole morning before I was able to explain to their Roman officers who I was. Of course, I wanted to return immediately, but the Numidians were also short of water and there was no point in coming without it. We took another day to reach the desert oasis where Titus had his headquarters, and he insisted on returning with me when I explained about the general's daughter. Apparently their fathers are friends. We had to wait until they had loaded the camels with water skins, but he drove the column until man and animal were on their knees to reach you in time. Still, I thought we would be too late. But they put me in a litter on the back of a camel and here we are.'

Valerius was curious. 'Just where is here?'

Tiberius pulled the knife from his belt. 'You were wrong.' He drew the broad curve of the coastline in the sand. 'This is where I met the Numidians, more or less.' He pointed to a spot at the western end of the curve. 'We are here.'

Valerius's heart sank as he realized his mistake. 'Twenty miles from the Judaean border, and I sent you to ride forty.'

'Closer to sixty if you take in my diversion,' Tiberius admitted without a hint of modesty. 'But you were right, the rebels are very active in the border villages. They would have been more likely to cut our throats than feed us.'

'Nevertheless, a ride worthy of a hero, and you can be sure I will report it to General Corbulo.'

'I could ask no greater reward, tribune,' the young man said earnestly.

'Of course, you could not have done it without my horse.'

'No, sir. I'm sorry about that. He was a fine horse.' A mischievous glint appeared in Tiberius's eye. 'But I thought the horse was probably less valuable than the general's daughter.'

It wasn't until the young soldier left that Valerius realized what had been lost in the euphoria of his survival. When he had believed death was certain he could ignore it, but now the shadow of Gnaeus Domitius Corbulo loomed like a hurricane cloud on the far horizon. And every step he took carried him closer to the moment of decision.

'You fought in Britain, I understand?'

Valerius noted the inevitable glance at his wooden hand and smiled. Titus Vespasian's splendid uniform, his spotless armour and the quality of his horse all proclaimed his status. He was the general's son and a young man with a glittering career ahead of him in the military and politics, but he could still be seduced by the physical proof of another man's sacrifice.

'I was with the Twentieth during the rebellion,' he acknowledged. 'But in the end I served as an aide to the governor, Suetonius Paulinus.'

'The Second Augusta,' Titus said. 'But I only arrived after the rebel queen had been killed.' Valerius was surprised. He had known the father had served on the island during Emperor Claudius's invasion two decades earlier, but not that the son had fought there.

'You must have been very young?'

'Seventeen,' Titus admitted cheerfully. 'The most junior of the junior tribunes and with less authority than a legionary of the second rank. It was not my most rewarding posting. You will have heard the story?'

Valerius nodded. Every Roman soldier who had been in Britain knew the tale of the notorious Second legion. How the camp prefect Poenius Postumus, who had been left in command, had refused to march to Paulinus's aid, brought disgrace to his unit and been forced to fall on his sword.

'While Paulinus hunted down the last of the rebels, the Second was kept in the west garrisoning Isca and far from any glory or plunder, and the men resented it. Of course, they took their frustration out on the tribespeople round about. I have never witnessed such cruelty before or since.'

Valerius remembered the gore-slick field after Boudicca's last battle and the swords rising and falling on enemy warriors even after they had surrendered. 'I saw enough cruelty and bloodshed in Britain to last me a lifetime.'

'And yet you are still a soldier?'

Valerius felt the shrewd eyes on him and wondered if he was being mocked, but he decided Titus was just being curious. 'My father wanted me to be a politician, but I don't think I'll ever be cut out for the Senate. I discovered in Britain that I actually enjoyed soldiering, even the worst parts of it: the discomfort and the cold and the waiting. The men are a bunch of devious, thieving rogues, but there is a real sense of achievement in sharing their lives and winning their respect. To lead them in battle is to walk with the gods for a day.'

Titus laughed. 'We are much alike then. A junior tribune's life is what he makes it, and my comrades preferred drinking and carousing to fighting or drilling, but my father's advice to me was to learn everything I could. So I let them laugh at me as I dug trenches and stood in frozen rivers building bridges, and when I rose in the dark to supervise drill while they were still in their beds. Perhaps soon I will be laughing at them.'

Valerius had seen the effortless way the younger tribune commanded his men and the respect the wild Numidian auxiliaries accorded him, and he had no doubt it was true. Titus explained that his father, the general, had just arrived in Alexandria to gather his forces for the response to the unrest in Judaea. Vespasian blamed the rebellion on the incompetence of the previous commanders, who had embarked on a campaign of brutality and military ineptness which first enraged and then encouraged the citizens of the province.

'They have a taste for Roman blood now,' Titus said. 'Between them Florus, the Judaean procurator, and Gallus, the propraetor, managed to lose the best part of the Third Gallica when they became trapped in the palace at Jerusalem. They should have chopped off the head of the snake then and there, but they waited too long. When they did counter-attack, Gallus was too timid and the Twelfth Fulminata lost their eagle in the retreat. Now my father is preparing to retake the province and I am to be his aide. You were fortunate that I was exercising my Numidians when they came across your young tribune. It is remarkable that he survived so long.'

Valerius smiled. 'He is a remarkable young man.'

'I have already dispatched a courier to Alexandria with news that the lady Domitia is safe, and my father will send word direct to Antioch. General Corbulo will be relieved to hear the news. Now I must escort you to my father. He will be very interested to hear your story.'

They rode on in silence and at a sedate pace suitable for Domitia's camel-borne litter, which was further down the column. Valerius had seen little of the general's daughter since the rescue, other than an uninterested exchange of glances as they ate with Titus on the evening before their departure from the beach. The night they had shared seemed unreal now, a true moment of madness that could never, should never, be repeated. Yet he still felt himself drawn to her in a way that went beyond the first shock of the physical.

A rider galloped up with a message for Titus. The general's son thanked the trooper and turned to Valerius. 'The lady Domitia Longina passes on her thanks for your efforts in keeping her alive and hopes to give them personally once she has recovered from her injuries. She too is remarkable. I have been impressed by her resilience. She seems more upset by the loss of a slave than by anything she has suffered herself. A rare combination of beauty, courage, virtue and devotion, don't you think?' Valerius started at the word 'virtue', but there didn't seem to be any hidden meaning in the young soldier's words. He almost missed what Titus said next. 'Lucius is a very fortunate man.'

Titus noticed his incomprehension. 'Her betrothed. Lucius Aelius Lamia. We served together in Germania. She tells me they are to be married when she returns from her visit to her father.'

Valerius felt as though someone had hit him with a hammer. Why hadn't she told him? He should have been jealous, or angry. But the truth was his only emotions were relief and a sense of release. Would it have made any difference if he had known? Probably not. But now he knew it would never happen again.

'Yes. He is a very fortunate man.'

XIX

The elder Titus Flavius Vespasian had set up his headquarters in an annexe of one of the royal palaces close to Alexandria's harbour. Staff officers and couriers came and went with the flurried regularity of ants from an anthill, beneath giant fans which shifted the overheated air in the great marble hall, but barely cooled it. At the centre of a sweating mass of clerks the red-faced general barked his orders and demanded up to date information.

'How many ships do we have to transport the two legions and their auxiliaries from Alexandria to Ptolemais?' The answer patently didn't please him. 'Not enough, but it will have to do. We had two thousand transports when Claudius invaded Britain, but we were landing on a hostile shore. Unless the rebels decide to invade Syria this will be different.'

Valerius stood with Titus while an aide interrupted the general to announce their presence.

Vespasian barely paused between sentences and waved Titus towards a nearby doorway. 'His private apartments,' the young soldier whispered. Valerius hesitated, but Titus ushered him forward. 'He will want to hear what you have to say.'

The general's offices were in a sumptuous corner room with a view of the harbour and they only had to wait a few minutes before Vespasian bustled in. He was in his late fifties, with the substantial belly that came with success and middle age, a fine nose and a grim-set mouth in a face that had long forgotten how to smile. Only in the eyes and the youthful energy was there a hint of the man he had once been, and Titus now was. The two young men saluted, Valerius rapping his wooden fist against the leather breastplate of his borrowed uniform, but the general ignored them as he took his seat behind a desk of pale marble.

'Wine,' he shouted. Seconds later the servant who had been hovering behind a nearby screen appeared with a jug and three embossed silver cups. Titus waved him away and poured the wine, which was white and surprisingly cool. Valerius's lips barely touched the rim of his cup, but the general took a deep draught and sighed with pleasure.

'Annius has been recalled to Rome, so I want you to take temporary command of the Fifth Macedonica until Corbulo can send us Marcus Bolanus,' Vespasian told his son.

Valerius saw Titus's face harden, an unusual reaction for a soldier who had just been given an appointment for which other men might wait a lifetime. 'That means . . .' The young man recognized his father's warning glance and kept the rest of his thoughts to himself, but Valerius could guess what they were. Annius Vinicianus was not only the legate of the Fifth Macedonica but Domitia's brother-in-law, the husband of General Gnaeus Domitius Corbulo's eldest daughter. His recall might have some innocent purpose, but at a time when the Empire's very foundations were still shaking from the effects of Piso's conspiracy it could just as easily result in arrest, torture and death.

'Whatever it means is between Annius and the Emperor,' Vespasian said firmly. 'We have a war to prepare for. I can't ignore politics, but I will not let them divert me from my main purpose. We must be ready to move as soon as possible.'

He paused and stared at his desk. When he looked up it was as if he was seeing Valerius for the first time. 'And you are the young man who saved Corbulo's daughter?'

Valerius straightened. 'Sir!'

'Then I must commend you, although I'm not certain what her

father will make of shipwreck and pirates.' He shook his head at the thought. 'His notions of discipline are somewhat different from mine.' The tone changed and Vespasian's eyes narrowed. 'Verrens? You are to be his second in command?' Valerius nodded.

Vespasian glanced at his son. 'Leave us.' Titus hesitated, with a look of puzzlement at Valerius, before he walked from the room. When they were alone, the general rubbed his hand across his forehead and let out a long breath.

'First, you should be aware that I know of your secondary commission from the Palatium.' Valerius's head came up with a snap, but Vespasian raised a hand before he could speak. 'Do not deny it. Let it be sufficient that I know, and that if I know, General Corbulo also knows. Second, let me say that I *need* Corbulo. No, let me go further. The *Empire* needs Corbulo in command of the Armies of the East.'

Vespasian walked to a large table over which was laid a map of the eastern Mare Nostrum from Cappadocia in the north to Egypt and Africa in the south.

'Here, Judaea.' He pointed to an area in the centre of the map. 'Lost to Rome for the moment thanks to those fools Florus and Gallus. Better that the pair of them had fallen on their swords, but they do not have the wit even to do that. A rat's nest of rebels from Galilee in the north to Jerusalem and Masada in the south. Fortress cities on the coast at Caesarea, Jotapata and Ashkelon, now in Jewish hands, and Roman bones bleaching in the streets of all of them. I will restore Judaea to Rome, with Corbulo's help, but what Rome will not currently recognize . . .' Valerius listened with ice water in his veins. If Vespasian knew of his mission why was he being told this? The general read his expression and the thin lips came as close as Valerius guessed they ever would to a smile. '. . . and what I cannot change is that General Corbulo has problems of his own in Parthia, where he believes King Vologases is ready to take advantage of his brother Tiridates' absence to return Armenia to Parthian rule. Corbulo knows how much a Parthian's word is worth. When he was given command in the east it was clear that if Parthia controlled Armenia she would quickly become a threat to both Cappadocia and Syria. Vologases' ambitions have remained unchanged for ten years. Corbulo recognized that when he crossed the Euphrates and took three legions into the very heart of Armenia, stormed three of Tiridates' fortresses in a single day and went on to burn his capital at Artaxata. Armenia remained under Roman rule for four years before Parthian treachery obliged him to intervene again. Corbulo forced the Parthians out of Armenia, not once, but twice. Vologases sued for peace and agreed that Tiridates should rule as Rome's subject, but now, with Tiridates in Rome and Judaea alight, he sees yet another opportunity.'

He paused and took another drink from his cup, and the grey eyes scoured Valerius's. 'You understand that I am taking you into my confidence, tribune? I do it for a purpose. It is my instinct that Gaius Valerius Verrens serves Rome and my certainty that Rome's best interests are served by stability in her eastern commands. Let me be frank. What I will say next I do not say in criticism of a fellow general, but as one officer giving another proper notice of what awaits him at his next posting. General Corbulo has been in the east for twelve years. Long enough to form friendships and alliances which may be of benefit to the region, but might be misconstrued elsewhere. Am I making myself plain?'

Valerius kept his face expressionless. The legate seemed to be confirming everything that Suetonius Paulinus had implied, but Vespasian's next words surprised him.

'Yet for all this Caesar has no more loyal general than Gnaeus Domitius Corbulo. You will form your own opinions when you reach Antioch, but I ask you to bear this simple fact in mind in all your dealings with the general.' He paused and stared out to the ships waiting beyond the breakwater, choosing his next words with particular care. 'Of course, if your own inquiries should conclude otherwise, you must act as you see fit. Nevertheless, you have a unique opportunity to influence the outcome of your own investigation, and for the good of the Empire. I see you doubt me. Let me explain. One of the most important functions of a good officer is to say what needs to be said, whatever the consequences and even if his commander does not want to hear it. It will not make him a popular officer, but it will make him a valued one. General Corbulo's staff have been with him for a long time, perhaps too long, and I fear they have forgotten this lesson. His inclination will be to attack Vologases, and his inclination may well be militarily correct, but *it will not be right*. It would be seen in certain quarters as impertinent. A sign of independence at a time when independence has deeper meaning. A good officer,' the grey eyes burrowed deep into Valerius's skull, 'would be doing his commander a service if he pointed out this simple fact.'

Valerius's first thought was that he was being drawn into a trap. If Nero had personally ordered the inquiry into the workings of Corbulo's headquarters, as Paulinus had insinuated, every word he had just heard and every suggestion implied was an act of treason and an invitation to bow his head before the executioner's sword. He had known the moment of decision must come. Well, this was it. A sensible man would stand up and point out that he had no choice in the matter, that he was the Emperor's agent and would do his duty. Yet he hesitated. A small voice in his head told him there were undercurrents here he could not see and did not understand. Titus Flavius Vespasian was the direct appointee of the Emperor. A trusted adviser with intimate knowledge of Nero's court. Where was the profit in entrapping a lowly tribune on his way to do the Emperor's bidding? A conspirator – and Valerius had ample experience of conspirators – would never have been so direct; there would have been subtle hints and cryptic asides, certainly an offer of advancement or reward and perhaps even the threat of extreme consequences if that offer was not accepted. Vespasian had spoken with the eloquence and passion of a man who believed everything he said, and with each unguarded word he heightened the odds of condemning himself. The message behind the words was that if Corbulo invaded Armenia without the Emperor's direct order he would be exceeding the authority granted by Nero, and in the present political climate that course of action was likely to have serious consequences which would, in turn, weaken the eastern armies. Yet, if that were the case, why had Vespasian himself not already taken steps to stop Corbulo?

The general read Valerius's look as if he could see into his mind.

'I have known Gnaeus Domitius Corbulo for many years, as a

colleague in the Senate, as a military commander, sometimes as a friend and sometimes as a rival. Our careers have had certain parallels. We shared our first legionary commands on the Rhenus frontier and he was of great help to me when I was preparing the Second Augusta for the invasion. Later I was able to help him in certain difficulties he had with Divine Claudius. Circumstances dictated that while his military career flourished, I was never able to repeat the successes of Britain. These are troubled times for the Empire.' Vespasian's voice took on a doleful tone and Valerius knew he wasn't talking only of the Judaean revolt, the unrest in Germania and the whispers from Gaul. Nero's revenge on the Pisonian conspirators had torn the heart out of the Senate and this man would have lost friends, and even though close to the Emperor would undoubtedly have come under suspicion himself. 'If I offered this . . . advice . . . as a friend, it might be dismissed as a provocation. If I offered it as a fellow officer it would be interpreted as an insult. His successes and the – let us not be coy about it – reverence in which he is held by those he leads make him a difficult man to persuade. No, he might listen to a member of his staff, if that man were courageous enough to speak out, but I doubt anyone else could divert him from his path.'

No signal had been given, but the light clink of armour told Valerius that Titus had returned. Vespasian took another draught from his cup and stared at the map. Titus went to stand by his side. Valerius knew he was being dismissed. He also knew when he was outmatched.

'In that case it would be better if I left as soon as possible,' he said.

Vespasian nodded absently. 'There is one more thing.' He approached so close that even his son couldn't hear what he whispered. 'Tell General Corbulo that, whatever he decides, I will support him.'

Valerius didn't know what to make of this cryptic message, but he nodded. Titus affected not to notice the exchange and accompanied him to the door. 'A courier will be leaving for Antioch by fast galley in two days, escorting the general's daughter, and you will be welcome to join him. In the meantime, I will see that all the equipment you lost in the shipwreck is replaced.'

Valerius thanked him. 'But perhaps the lady Domitia would like to

133

take a few days more to recover and travel in a little more comfort?' he suggested tentatively.

'No.' Titus smiled. 'She is eager to be reunited with her father. Her passage has already been agreed.' Valerius returned the smile, but his heart sank at the thought of sharing a cramped ship with Domitia for another three days. Titus's expression changed and his handsome face turned serious. 'You may be surprised by what you find in Antioch. Sometimes men who serve for long periods in the east can become set in their ways. Be very careful, my friend, and do not expect a warm welcome.'

Only later did he realize that there had been a moment of decision – a hesitation – during his interview with Vespasian, and that if the decision had gone against him he would never have left Alexandria alive.

XX

Rome

Everything was on fire. Everywhere he looked the flames crackled and roared and consumed: apartments of wood and wattle, warehouses filled with oil and wool and timber, even the great marble temples which had seemed so solid and safe and invulnerable had burned. And flesh. So much flesh. The smell of roasting meat filled his nostrils in the same way the screams of the doomed filled his ears. He tried to shut it out, but it was as if the screams were *inside* his head. He saw a gap and ran for it, but before he could reach safety a wall of fire blocked the street. He could feel himself burning.

'Mother! Make it stop.'

But Mother couldn't stop the flames even if she had wanted to. Because Mother was dead. At his hand. Or if not at his hand, by his will; like so many. They came to him now, all those he had called friend and lover and, yes, even brother. One by one they pierced him with their accusing eyes and he did not know which was greater, the pain of their contempt or the agony of the fire that was melting his flesh from his bones like wax dripping from a candle. He remembered a pillar of writhing flame, a blackened skull with burning eyes, and a name: Cornelius Sulla. So this is what it had been like.

He opened his mouth to scream and flames filled his mouth and his nose and he felt them flash down his throat, incinerating his lungs and exploding his heart. He raised his arms to the heavens in a last despairing gesture and before his eyes shrivelled in his head he looked out over the Rome he had created, the sea of fire that was his gift to his people, and saw a fiery orb arc across the sky, leaving a trail of sparks in its wake. A falling star? No. A fallen god.

'Tigellinus!'

He shot bolt upright with the sweat dripping from his face as if he'd just emerged from the baths. 'Tigellinus!' The waking scream echoed the unanswered one from the dream. The dream which had seemed so real that he could still feel the raw agony of the flame shooting down his throat. Running feet. Not Tigellinus, but the slaves who served his bedchamber. For a moment he wondered why Poppaea wasn't at his side, then he remembered that she was dead. Dead more than a year, along with the child.

'Send for my Praetorian prefect.'

By the time Tigellinus arrived Nero was curled in a ball on top of his bed, his whole body shaking as if he was suffering from a fever. The Emperor's personal physician stood by the doorway with a look of perplexed anxiety on his face.

'Is he sick?' Tigellinus asked the Greek. The physician shook his head and the Praetorian sighed. He had grown accustomed to late night summonses to heal crises of the body or the mind, to interpret dreams which promised triumph or disaster, to praise ideas of such genius no mortal man could turn them into reality, or simply to hear a song which had fixed itself in his master's head and must be heard before it disappeared for ever. Just lately it had been the dreams.

'Caesar?' He approached the bed.

'It is finished.'

The three whispered words sent a stream of ice water down Tigellinus's spine. In the past there had always been doubt. Here there was only certainty.

'No, Caesar.'

'I watched a burning god fall from the sky.'

'Falling to smite your enemies.'

'No, I was on fire. The whole city was on fire.'

'A memory. Remember how you fought the flames and saved your people.'

'I saved them?'

'You were everywhere,' Tigellinus assured him. 'Directing the rescue, organizing the water supply. Without Nero there would be no Rome.'

Nero opened his eyes. It had been almost three years earlier. He remembered a burning glow on the horizon. The smell of smoke. Ashes. Perhaps it was true. But the certainty was clouded by the fact that he had wanted it, and when he wanted things they tended to happen.

'The followers of Christus, Caesar,' Tigellinus pre-empted the next question. 'Vile creatures who sought to destroy Rome, and through Rome, you. Fanatics and purveyors of lies.'

'Yes, the Christus followers. They admitted their guilt under question.'

'Each one bore the mark of the fire.' The Praetorian commander remembered the careful selection. The refinements necessary to ensure that each confession should be exact in every detail. Yet still one had duped him.

'But the man Paulus claimed it was a portent of the end. He said Rome was the great whore.' The young Emperor reached out and gripped Tigellinus's hand with surprising strength. 'It must not happen. You will not allow it to happen.'

'No, Caesar.' Tigellinus's voice was soft and reassuring. 'Your agents are in place with the German frontier legions and in Hispania and Lusitania. The traitor Vinicianus will soon be in our hands. Thus far he has not implicated his father-in-law, Corbulo, and there has been a delay in my agent's reaching Antioch. But if he is guilty I will know it within the month.'

'Find them for me. Find my enemies. Hunt them down. Show them no mercy.'

'At your command, Caesar.'

'For Rome.'

'For Rome.'

XXI

Valerius stared out beyond the bow of the twin-banked bireme galley, hypnotized by the glint of sun on sea. He was so spellbound that he didn't notice Domitia emerging from the flimsy wooden cabin that had been built for her until she came to stand at his side. For more than a minute they stood a few decorous feet apart, as aware of each other's presence as if they were touching hands. He was searching for the word or the gesture that would breach the barrier that had separated them since the night on the beach when a pair of blue dolphins, lithe, swift and fearless, appeared from nowhere to carve their way effortlessly through the waters below the lovers' feet.

Domitia studied them for a while, her eyes never leaving the dark shapes as they rose and fell, triangular fins chopping the surface to leave a trail of silver bubbles, and even occasionally departing their natural element entirely. One was larger and seemed to take the lead, but the other mirrored its partner's every move, never more than a few inches from its side. Sometimes they were so close that their bodies touched.

When she spoke her voice was soft as the kiss of the sea on the galley's hull. 'Don't you ever wish you were free, Valerius? Free of duty and of obligation. Free to go where you want with whom you want. What if Poseidon were to grant you the ability to choose, this very moment, to turn into a dolphin and swim away with me, to spend our lives roaming the oceans together? Would you accept or would you stand here and watch me swim away alone?'

Just for a moment he was swayed, and the mesmeric rhythm of the sleek streamlined figures cutting through the water drew him to them. He remembered desire and softness and strength beneath the knowing stars of an Egyptian night. A night of magic. When he had been with her, anything had seemed possible, but . . . But he was Gaius Valerius Verrens, Hero of Rome. He had never known anything but duty and obligation. Duty to his father and the estate. Duty to the *cursus honorum* which had shaped his path through life. Duty to the men he had served with and served under. Duty to Rome and its Emperor. And his duty to the Emperor had made him a spy. What would she think of him if she ever discovered that he had been sent from Rome to spy on her father? He knew the answer well enough. She would despise a man so weak and disloyal. He did not tell her that he could have been free. That the marble deposits beneath his estate at Fidenae would have bought a hundred freedoms, or a thousand. He knew that when she said *free to go where you want with whom you want*, she actually meant *free to love whom you want*. But that was as much a dream as the dream of turning into a dolphin. The reality was that Domitia was betrothed to a man already spoken of as a future consul and Valerius would always be bound to the master within.

When he looked again, the dolphins were gone. He felt her eyes on him, but he dared not turn to see what was written in them. He feared her next words, but when she spoke it was lightly, though her voice was touched by a lost, wistful sadness.

'So we will not wander the oceans together, tribune? It is of no matter. It was a silly girl's whim. Better that we both forget that this ever happened. It was a momentary thing, and in any case, one which we will never be in a position to repeat. I am a respectable Roman lady, Valerius, and I rely on your discretion and your honour to ensure that *my* honour remains untarnished.' When she said the last few words he heard a smile in her voice. As she left him her hand brushed lightly against his.

Two days later they docked at the port of Seleucia Pieria, the magnificent harbour at the mouth of the River Orontes created by Antioch's founder Seleucus, one of Alexander the Great's generals. When they disembarked, a closed carriage awaited Domitia and she insisted on hurrying ahead up the paved road by the river to meet her father. Valerius, Tiberius and Serpentius waited until their equipment was unloaded and packed on a pair of mules before joining their escort for the ten-mile ride inland to Antioch.

And Corbulo.

They entered the city by an enormous twin-towered gate and along a broad avenue flanked by marble pillars. Alexandria with its towering palaces, secluded gardens and great trading port might be Rome's gateway to the east, but Antioch was the crossroads between east and west, a sprawling city of more than half a million people, its streets teeming with merchants and traders of every nationality. Valerius was struck by the scale of the walls, which challenged even those of Rome. This was where his hero, Germanicus Caesar, father of the Emperor Caligula, had finally succumbed either to some awful disease contracted in Egypt or to poison administered on the orders of his rival, another treacherous Piso. He wondered in which of these buildings the great man had died. On closer inspection many showed the filled cracks and wall repairs that were clear signs of earthquake damage, although not from a recent event. The river was always to their left, and when they turned off the main road towards it they were welcomed by a paradise on earth. Even the normally undemonstrative Tiberius gaped when he saw it. The governor's palace proved to be a place of cool waters and shaded cypress and laurel groves, where waterfalls tumbled from the surrounding hills to create sparkling pools filled with small darting fish and purple herons stood frozen among the reedbeds. Further upstream the enormously rich Syrian merchants of Antioch had built villas in the Roman style, but nothing could match the magnificence of governor Gnaeus Domitius Corbulo's official residence. Two storeys high with a roof of red tile, pale cream bricks and milk white marble, it dominated everything around it, stretching for close to a quarter of a mile along the bank of the Orontes.

Led by their escort, an exotic mix of Syrian mounted archers in pot-shaped helmets and green cloaks and bearded Scythian spearmen in fish-scale armour, they crossed the river by a stone bridge and turned upstream along an avenue of cypress trees. In the shade of the branches, still as statues, the soldiers of a full cohort stood at rest. The design on their curve-edged *scuta* was unfamiliar to Valerius. At the top of the shield, against a red background, a proud bull in silhouette dared any comer to challenge him, while below the metal boss a galley in full sail cut its way across the painted ash. On either side of the boss he was a little unnerved to see a pair of dolphins.

'The Tenth Fretensis,' Tiberius said in a low voice. 'General Corbulo's elite. They provide his personal bodyguard.'

There had been times in the last two weeks when Valerius believed he would never reach this point, and others when he had prayed he wouldn't. All he could think of was Vespasian's warning. *If I know, General Corbulo also knows.* He had revealed the true purpose of their mission to Serpentius during the voyage from Alexandria and the Spaniard had accepted the information with a bitter laugh. Now he surveyed their surroundings with the wariness of a stalking panther. They passed through a pillared gateway to be met by an honour guard and Serpentius draped Valerius's senior tribune's white cloak – a gift from Titus – over his shoulders. As they approached the palace, his heart stopped when he noticed the coach that had carried Domitia and her servant from Seleucia. That was the thing about guilt: it didn't matter where you went, it would always be waiting for you.

He checked in his sword at the door and an aide ushered him through a maze of corridors to a large receiving room with a colonnaded balcony overlooking the river. Vine stems writhed like snakes up the pillars and entwined to form a ceiling of emerald green through which the sun sparkled like so many polished jewels. It was early evening, but this was midsummer in the Orient and even in the depths of the Orontes gorge the force of the day's heat still lingered in the stones and the grass. Six men waited for him there, six men who surveyed him with looks that ranged from naked animosity to open contempt and in at least one case pure hatred. From their uniforms and insignia he guessed they were Corbulo's senior commanders, at least three of them legionary legates. There was no greeting, only the merest acknowledgement of his existence.

Valerius felt hot blood rise inside him, but he kept his expression blank. So that was the way it was to be. 'Gaius Valerius Verrens, reporting for duty to General Corbulo. I was told he would be here.'

'Since you have not lost your eyes as well as your arm, tribune, it should be clear to you that he has been detained elsewhere.' The insult was deliberate and accompanied by a humourless smile. It came from the oldest of the six, a handsome, narrow-faced patrician with cropped grey hair. 'You are interrupting an important conference. Surely your time would be better spent making yourself look like an officer for your interview and not some grubby recruit returning from his first patrol?'

Valerius bit back the retort that came to his tongue. The man's age and the scarlet band at his waist marked him as a legionary commander, even if it hadn't been already evident in the arrogant dismissal of a mere equestrian. He studied the grim faces and cursed Paulinus for his poor security. Then it came to him. Paulinus had made sure word of his mission preceded him. The consul knew that even with Olivia as a hostage, Valerius might be tempted to ignore his orders. Now he had little choice, because he was a pariah whether he carried them out or not. Yet something was not quite right with that theory. What . . . The legate's sneer cut across his thoughts. 'Perhaps you left your tongue where you left your hand? A gentleman would apologize and leave.'

'Enough.' The word snapped through the air like a cracking whip. Valerius's tormentor stiffened before acknowledging the order with the slightest nod of the head.

The figure who filled the doorway was tall, with a slim muscular build that belied his age and grey, challenging eyes that dared you to disagree with him. Deep lines scored his face and he had a long hooked nose that reminded Valerius of one of the desert eagles the nomad tribes of the east used to hunt foxes and jackals. He wore a long tunic of raw silk secured by a belt of gold links that gave him the appearance of an eastern potentate. Many generals Valerius had served under were more administrators than soldiers – Aulus Vitellius had been one – but Gnaeus Domitius Corbulo was a truly great commander because he could fight as well as he led. Valerius had heard the stories. If Corbulo negotiated, it was from a position of strength with a legion at his back. If he retreated, it was only to find a better way to attack. He was no longer young, but he knew how to wage war and he knew how to win. This was a hard man, body and mind forged in combat into a weapon as potent as the swords his legionaries carried. His enemies feared him, his officers respected him and his soldiers loved him as they would a strict father – or a stern unforgiving god.

'So, you are my new second in command?'

Valerius rapped the wooden fist against his leather breastplate. The unblinking eyes never left his face and the younger man swore he could sense the quiver of trapped energy and an air of deadly intent bordering on menace. Corbulo's scrutiny continued for more than a minute while the sweat ran down Valerius's back in a warm stream.

Eventually, the ordeal ended. Or perhaps it was only beginning. 'Come with me,' the governor said curtly.

He led the way through the palace to another, smaller room on the floor above and sat down behind a large desk with scrolls stacked neatly to one side and a stylus and a pile of wax tablets in front of him. A legionary of his personal guard stood on either side of the entrance and Valerius took his place in front of the desk. He caught the sweet scent of perfumed water and noticed a dark-haired figure reclining on a couch on the far side of the room playing with a small ball of fur.

'Your orders?'

Valerius reached inside the pouch at his waist and handed over the scroll.

'Ambiguous,' the general said after he'd studied the contents.

'Sir?'

'Your orders are ambiguous. You are to be my second in command, but I am to use you in any way I see fit in the service of the Empire. In

143

effect, I could make you part of the foundations of the new basilica I am having built and no one could question it. Do you agree?'

It was a dangerous question, to which there seemed no safe answer, but it demanded one. Valerius decided that attack was his best policy. 'I do not, but judging by the welcome I received a few moments ago some of your senior officers do.'

A sniff from the corner seemed to signify that Domitia held a different opinion. Valerius felt the dark eyes on him and wondered why she was here. Had her father arranged it to keep him off balance and increase his humiliation? Or was he simply indulging his daughter? The latter seemed unlikely, and perhaps it was neither, but Valerius still felt he was caught in a trap.

Corbulo glared in the direction of his daughter. 'They seek to protect me. Would you have them do otherwise? They look at Gaius Valerius Verrens and see a traitor in their midst.'

So it was out. Corbulo was aware of his mission and didn't care if he knew it. In some ways that made it simpler. 'I am no traitor. I was asked to prepare a report, nothing more.'

'A spy then?'

The hackles rose on Valerius's neck, but Corbulo raised a hand before he could reply.

'From my daughter, and from certain other sources, I have been given some notion of the manner of man I am dealing with. Unless I am mistaken, or misinformed, he is a man of honour. The fact that you have undoubtedly been proved in battle is of little significance. I have known brave men of little judgement and some of no judgement at all. On the other hand, when faced with pirates, shipwreck and mutiny, you conducted yourself with intelligence and imagination. I sense that you are not a man to be swayed by either blandishment or threat, and that is what has brought me to my decision.' The grey eyes brightened. Was there a mocking challenge in them? 'You will investigate where you will, with my sanction, and when you have done so you will make your report. Gnaeus Domitius Corbulo has nothing to hide and nothing to fear. Of course, while you are spying on my staff, my spies will be spying on you. You would expect nothing else, I'm sure?'

Valerius tried to hide his surprise. At best, he had expected to be banished to some remote outpost, and there had always been the possibility that he might conveniently disappear in a desert ambush. Again, there was that surprising sense of support from the silent presence behind him. Corbulo continued.

'The one stipulation I make is that, in the meantime, you serve under my command *in any way I see fit*. Do not thank me. I assure you it will be arduous, difficult duty and the manner of it may not suit you. I grant that you have fought and by all accounts fought well.' He glanced at Valerius's wooden fist. 'But you have no experience of campaigning in the east. You will find that having one hand is a greater handicap against the Parthians than against your Celtic queen. A man who has faced barbarian chariots and spearmen is of little use against mounted archers who sting like hornets and then fly off to fight another day. They have a habit of eating the young, inexperienced officers they capture for breakfast.'

Corbulo continued to regard him with an unblinking stare, but a soft *miaow* broke the silence and the governor failed to suppress a rueful smile. Clearly his notorious attitude to discipline didn't extend to his youngest daughter – or her cat. The general picked up his stylus and rubbed it thoughtfully between his fingers. 'Very well. Domitia, I believe the kitchen servants require your supervision.'

There was no hint of argument against the obvious dismissal, only a soft rustle of silk and the scent of perfumed oils before Valerius felt her presence beside him.

'I am glad to see you well, tribune.'

Her voice was lower and huskier than he remembered. Valerius turned and felt the familiar flutter as he looked into eyes the colour of polished walnuts.

'My lady,' he bowed. 'I thank you for your kind words and your good opinion.'

'Oh, I think I am in a better position to judge my saviour's character than a few wrinkled old generals,' she said, ignoring her father's growl of disapproval. 'Come, Puss Puss.' She walked out followed by the fluffy white kitten.

The general's expression softened. 'My daughter tells me that you saved her life . . . and her virtue?'

Once more, and from an entirely unexpected angle, Valerius felt the point of a dagger tickling his spine. 'The general's daughter is a lady of great character and fortitude and a credit to her father,' he said carefully. 'She withstood pirate attack, shipwreck, mutiny, thirst and fire without a single word of complaint. If anything she was strongest of us all.'

Corbulo nodded absently. 'And you were together for how long?'

How long? A lifetime. Valerius understood that the general felt the conversation had to take place and the questions had to be asked, but the room suddenly felt more dangerous than the slippery, blood-soaked boards of the pirate galley. 'I believe it was six days between the wreck and the morning General Vespasian's son came to our rescue. We had run out of water and I doubt we would have been alive an hour later.'

'She speaks very highly of you.'

'I did my duty and nothing more.' Valerius kept his voice steady and tried to think of anything but the night beneath the cloak. He had a moment of inspiration. 'I would commend the name of Tiberius Claudius Crescens to the general. Tribune Crescens is a remarkably resourceful young man. He rode close to sixty miles through the desert for help.'

The general nodded again. 'Very well, I will interview him later. In the meantime, I plan to convene a strategy conference with the officers you met below. You are aware of our situation?'

'General Vespasian was kind enough to brief me.'

'Good. That will save time. You will take up your position immediately. Your predecessor, Tiberius Alexander, was a good man; he will have left everything in order.'

'He must have been popular,' Valerius risked the rueful suggestion. 'His comrades do not appreciate the arrival of his replacement.'

Corbulo laughed. 'It's not your arrival they do not appreciate, tribune, or even the fact that they think you are a spy. It is because they think you are here to kill me.'

XXII

'General Gaius Licinius Mucianus, legate of Sixth Ferrata.' Corbulo introduced the handsome aristocrat who had insulted Valerius on the balcony. The sneer remained in place and the long nose twitched as if it had smelled something distasteful. 'Marcus Ulpius Traianus, Tenth Fretensis.' Traianus was younger than his fellow commander, fine-boned and heavy-lipped with piercing blue eyes. 'Aurelius Fulvus, commanding Third Gallica, and Gaius Pompeius Collega, Fifteenth Apollinaris.' The two men nodded and Collega, who had not been at the earlier conference, gave Valerius an uneasy smile of welcome. Only one other man remained in the room after Corbulo's aides had set out an enormous table with a series of overlapping maps, and the general presented him warmly as his camp prefect and quartermaster, Casperius Niger. Niger had dark hair shot with grey and the swarthy complexion and uncompromising features of a native easterner, but he was clearly one of Corbulo's most trusted members of staff.

Tension filled the room like a fog, mixed with that peculiar suppressed excitement and anticipation Valerius remembered from the conference where the Colonia militia had received their orders for the defence against Boudicca.

Corbulo stood hunched over the table, his eyes taking in every detail of the maps. This was ground he had covered many times, but he understood the traps and pitfalls that awaited him among the treacherous river valleys and the barren mountains, the dusty plains and featureless deserts. His commanders knew the situation well enough, but General Gnaeus Domitius Corbulo was Rome's greatest general because he considered every detail and his watchword was preparation. The first few minutes were a mirror of the summary Valerius had received from Vespasian. The situation in Judaea was worsening, the rebel strength and confidence increasing with every day the Romans failed to avenge the defeats suffered by Vespasian's predecessors.

'General Vespasian has almost completed his preparations in Egypt and he will begin shipping his main force to Ptolemais, here on the Judaean border, north of Galilee where the largest concentration of rebel forces is believed to be, while his cavalry carries out diversionary operations in the area between Ashkelon and the Dead Sea.' Valerius nodded. That explained Titus's mission into the desert. Corbulo's voice changed and Valerius caught a hint of irritation. 'I have orders to consolidate my position in Syria, while giving as much support as can be spared to Vespasian. To this end Sixth Ferrata, Third Gallica and their associated auxiliary units will march south from their positions at Zeugma and Cyrrhus to prepare defensive positions and stockpile supplies for sixty thousand men.'

Mucianus frowned. 'It will take all our reserves and I will have to strip every town and village between Antioch and Damascus.'

Corbulo fixed him with that steady gaze. 'Nevertheless it must be done. I have already sent to Sergiopolis and Palmyra to have their stores of grain, oil and wine moved to Damascus. I see no reason why it should not be waiting for you when you arrive there. Any shortfall will be made up by a special requisition from Cappadocia and Egypt.'

'If we withdraw entirely from Zeugma and Cyrrhus it will leave the main crossing of the Euphrates undefended and the road to Antioch open,' Collega pointed out. 'If you are wrong, the Parthians will be able to outflank our eastern defence line and Syria will be at their mercy.'

The other three legates looked at him and Valerius realized this was what they had been discussing during the afternoon.

Corbulo ushered his commanders closer around the map and motioned to Valerius to join them.

'I have recently received word from our spies in Parthia that King Vologases has sent out a call to raise a force of seventy thousand men – heavy cavalry, slingers, spearmen and mounted archers – and is preparing to march north from his capital on the Tigris,' he said solemnly. 'There can be only one reason for this. He means to take advantage of the rebellion in Judaea and the fact of his brother's absence from Armenia to retake control of that country. I cannot allow that.'

Again the four turned to their general, three of them nodding, but Collega's broad face showed consternation. 'Without two of your four legions and with explicit orders from the Palatium in Rome to consolidate your position I do not understand how you intend to stop him.'

Corbulo gave him a look teachers reserve for their slowest pupils, but Collega stood his ground and returned the stare.

'It is late in the season and he must move quickly if he is to force the mountain passes before the first snows,' the governor explained patiently. 'He cannot delay because he knows that Tiridates will return in the spring carrying Rome's blessing. The Armenian council will unite behind their king and the opportunity will be gone. The last report from our agents shows him still in Ctesiphon.' Corbulo used a centurion's vine rod to indicate a position in the centre of the map table close to a winding blue line Valerius calculated must be the Tigris river. 'Which means that even if he has already marched he cannot be any further than this position today.' The tip of the vine rod moved north. 'I think there is no doubt that he intends to reconquer the land his brother has negotiated away by first taking Tigranocerta, the fortress city which guards the only road north, and then turning northeast by the Sea of Van to reach the capital Artaxata. This is how I will stop him.' He used the vine rod as a measure to indicate the distance between Antioch and Tigranocerta, then between Vologases' army and the city. When it was done his face broke into a savage grin that revealed Corbulo the warrior. 'We will have at least six days' march on him. I intend to consolidate my position by garrisoning the fort at Zeugma and the Euphrates crossing with a vexillation of three cohorts from the Fifteenth Apollinaris and a mixed cavalry and infantry force of Cappadocian auxiliaries. Then I will march the Tenth Fretensis and the bulk of the Fifteenth to . . . here, north of Gazarta, where I will intercept my enemy and defeat him.' He looked around the room, the pale eyes daring any man to contradict him.

Valerius was stunned by the audacity of the plan, and more so by the fact that Corbulo was offering his head on a plate to his enemies. He remembered Vespasian's warning. Did he want to be liked or valued? He opened his mouth to speak.

'With the greatest of respect, general,' Collega's voice shook slightly as he interrupted. 'To take such a course of action would be at best risking your command, at worst . . .' He faded away as if his tongue was unwilling to speak the word they were all thinking. 'You intend to meet a force of seventy thousand Parthians with a Roman one of not much more than twenty thousand. This is a campaign which warrants months of preparation, yet you give us only days. Victory is far from certain; defeat would leave Syria open to King Vologases' army and risk the loss of the entire Roman east. Vespasian would be trapped between a victorious Parthian army and the Judaean rebels, who have already proved they can be a match for a Roman legion. I beg you to reconsider.'

Valerius came to attention, bringing a glare from Corbulo and a look of hatred from Mucianus that almost stopped his tongue.

'I must agree with General Collega. In my opinion you would be risking too much for too little. Even meeting such a formidable army on favourable terms would be dangerous. To meet them with such a weak force seems . . .'

'Madness?' Corbulo's arid voice completed the sentence for him.

Mucianus pushed his way round the table to face Valerius. 'So, the Palatine's spy shows his true colours and becomes an expert in eastern warfare in the same instant. What does a mere tribune know of grand strategy? We have been fighting these barbarians since you were issued your first *caligae*, soldier, and thanks to this man whose reputation you have the audacity to demean we have defeated them every time we have met them.'

'I am not . . .'

'Let us not fight among ourselves when the enemy may already be on the march.' Corbulo stepped in front of Mucianus, and turned to Valerius and Collega. 'Everything you say is true. No one knows better than I what we risk by this strategy. Yet I believe there is no other way. May I explain?' Collega bowed and stepped back from the table. 'My good friend General Mucianus is correct that we have been facing the Parthians and their Armenian allies for more years than I care to remember. No matter how many times we defeated them, no matter how strong the defences we put in place along the Euphrates, they were always a threat to Syria, and, by extension, to Asia and the east. Until now. I know Tiridates. He is not his brother. He would rather hold what he has than risk everything again. With Tiridates on the throne there is an opportunity for lasting peace. But he must be allowed to take that throne and rule with Rome's blessing. If we stand back and allow Vologases to invade Armenia we will be in danger of throwing away everything we have won, everything Roman soldiers have fought and died for in those gods-cursed mountains for twelve long years. Armenia will become a Parthian state, and our weakened condition ensures that Vologases will have the leisure to consolidate his rule. I will not let that happen.'

Corbulo straightened and his voice took on a power that mesmerized every man in the room. 'Once before, I stood on the banks of a river and obeyed a command not to cross. That river was the Rhenus and the command came from my Emperor, Divine Claudius. The German tribes were in disarray and at each other's throats. They were ripe for defeat. We had an opportunity to smash their power for a dozen generations, to emasculate them and enslave their warriors. To extend Rome's rule as far as Germanicus, who died in this very city, dreamed. But I turned back, and what has happened? We have had to fight each and every day since to keep what is ours. Thousands of brave men have died, and worse, our timidity has encouraged the tribes of the east to test themselves against us not just on the Rhenus, but also on the Danuvius. None of this would have happened if I had had the courage to do what was right.'

151

'But the Emperor . . .' Collega said.

'The Emperor and his advisers must do as they see fit, just as Gnaeus Domitius Corbulo will.' Corbulo slapped the table, indicating that the time for argument was over. 'Now, to the details. We will march in two days. General Mucianus will rule Syria while I am beyond the frontier. You, Gaius Collega, will hold the bridge at Zeugma.'

As the next hour unfolded, Valerius was astonished at Corbulo's grasp of every aspect of warfare. He outlined the timings, routes of march and even rations per man for each of the legions involved to Casperius Niger, who took notes as Corbulo rapped out a string of commands.

'And finally to the mounted element of the main force. As we know from long experience our cavalry is the key element in any combat with Parthian forces. Parthian mounted archers are among the best in the world. We have been relearning that lesson ever since Crassus was taught it so painfully at Carrhae.' The other generals murmured agreement and Valerius understood that the threat must be very real. 'Once we are in the hills, they will attempt to divide us using hit and run attacks from ambush and weakening us in a thousand pointless skirmishes. Anything but meet us in a full-scale battle. But time is my enemy's enemy. Parthia is a fractious state and the bulk of its army is drawn from those of a hundred different warlords. Vologases knows that he cannot stray from home for long or he will return 'to find another man on his throne. If we can convince his soldiers that they only have death to look forward to and not plunder, they will start thinking about home, hearth and wife. The legions which march to meet Vologases will be accompanied by three regiments of mixed cavalry, six *alae* of Numidian light cavalry and eight of mounted archers from Syria, Thracia, Cappadocia and Phrygia. A force of close to ten thousand men. Gaius Valerius Verrens will command that force.'

For a moment, the room went very still and Valerius would swear the birds stopped singing in the trees outside the window.

Mucianus, predictably, was the first to find his voice. 'You would place your fate in the hands of this untested puppy,' he spluttered.

'Hardly untested, and the puppy has teeth.' Corbulo smiled. 'Valerius

152

Verrens is a Hero of Rome, holder of the Gold Crown of Valour, last survivor of the Temple of Claudius in Colonia and scourge of the rebel Queen Boudicca. You have commanded mounted troops?'

'In Africa.' Valerius was as taken aback by his appointment as Mucianus. 'But only as part of legionary punitive expeditions.'

'What is this but a large scale punitive expedition?' Corbulo demanded of the room. 'In any case, it must be enough. The co-ordination between cavalry and the heavy infantry of the legions will be vital. I need a soldier with a proven record as a fighting officer and experience of combined operations.' He turned to Valerius. 'Your light cavalry will be issued with double the standard number of javelins and the archers will take as many arrows as they can carry. I know it will create weight issues, but we will conserve their energy as much as we can on the march. Do you have any questions?'

At least a hundred were running through Valerius's mind, but they were questions he had to ask himself, not the governor. They would have to wait.

The conference broke up with Mucianus still eyeing Valerius suspiciously, but as the other legates left Collega approached to shake the wooden hand and wish him luck.

'Until I saw the hand I had not realized you were the same Verrens. You served with my brother Marcus in the Twentieth and he spoke highly of you.'

Valerius thanked him. 'You were right to speak out.'

'And you, though I doubt you made yourself popular among the governor's inner circle. They are very protective of his reputation, which is a fine one. Perhaps . . .'

'Yes?'

'I may have done him an injustice. I have not served with him as long as some, but I have seen him on campaign and I respect his reputation. He is a man who knows his own mind and once it is made up he is unlikely to change it. But if Corbulo believes he can win, it would take a brave man to think otherwise.'

As Collega left, the general called Valerius back to the table.

'The first lesson a military commander learns is always to expect the unexpected. I must be seen to send Vespasian my most experienced cavalry leaders, therefore I must make do with what I have. You need not concern yourself with tactical considerations: the prefects of the cavalry units are veterans who know their business. Your job is to provide leadership and coordinate their actions with those of the infantry. Do not let me down.' He tapped the map. 'Rock and dust, chasm and cliff. It looks formidable, but we have been there before. We know the ground and we know the risks. Water for the men and fodder for the horses will be of vital importance, but I trust Niger to take care of that.' He chewed his lip and his eye fixed on a single portion of the map. 'The key is that we know the ground.'

Valerius waited for more than a minute in silence.

'Sir?'

Corbulo's grey eyes speared him. 'One thing you must learn, tribune, is that I do not care to be plagued with details.'

Valerius cleared his throat. 'I carry a personal message from General Vespasian . . . to be delivered in private.'

Corbulo went very still. 'Then deliver it.'

'He said: "Tell General Corbulo that whatever he decides I will support him".'

The governor frowned, the lines on his cheeks and brow creating dark fissures. Clearly the message troubled him. 'Those were his exact words?'

Valerius nodded.

Corbulo gave a sour smile. 'More politics.'

Valerius turned to go, but a word from the general stopped him.

'I have spoken to young Crescens. You were correct: an impressive soldier and of good family. You may tell him that he is to join the staff of the Tenth for the campaign ahead.'

Valerius left the room with his head spinning. He suddenly realized how far out of his depth he was. Taking a legion and its cavalry contingent on a four-day expedition into the Atlas Mountains was entirely different from leading ten thousand men into one of the most inhospitable places on earth. He had an incredible amount to do in the few short hours before they marched. Not only did he have to organize his own depleted equipment for a campaign that could take as long as two months, he had to find out what he could about the units which would be serving under him and the officers who commanded them. But where to start? He had a vision of a swarthy face. Niger would know. Niger seemed to know everything. Suddenly something occurred to him and he couldn't help smiling at the brilliance of it. At a stroke Corbulo had thwarted any plans he might have made to carry out Paulinus's investigation. The Army of the East's overworked cavalry commander would be fortunate to have a spare minute for weeks to come.

On his way to consult Niger, he called at the slave quarters for Serpentius. 'How are they treating you?'

'I've been in worse billets,' the Spaniard grunted. 'They wanted me to clean out the stables, but after I told the overseer I only answered to you and I'd cut off his balls if he thought otherwise, they seemed to see reason.'

Valerius laughed. 'You'll have the chance to shovel dung another time. For the moment, I need you to put together the essentials for a two-month campaign in the mountains. We'll be fried during the day, frozen during the night and the chances are some bearded Parthian will want *our* balls to take home as a present for his wife.' He handed over the small wooden tablet which bore his seal of office. 'From now on you are my freedman, not my slave. That means I can conscript you into the army and no one's going to kill you for it, except the enemy. Take this to the *beneficiarius* and get yourself a uniform, weapons and armour. Then check with the cavalry out by the gate. Those veterans have been fighting Parthians for years and they'll certainly have added a few modifications that will help stop an arrow. Oh, and remember to sign up to the funeral fund.'

Serpentius reached for the bronze plaque at his neck and untied it. It was the manumission Valerius had granted him after their near-fatal mission for Nero almost three years earlier. Not that the Emperor knew anything about it. His late wife Poppaea had been grateful enough to grease the wheels that would allow a gladiator his freedom. The Spaniard was as hard as the mountains that bred him and Valerius had

155

never seen him show emotion, but there was a catch in his throat when he spoke.

'I suppose no man is ever truly free, but I haven't felt like a slave since that day on the Danuvius when the Dacians were chasing us with their skinning knives. I always knew there would be a time, though, and I suppose this is as good as any. When I was waiting to fight in the arena, I used to dream of this day, but I never really thought it would happen. I suppose . . .'

'No.' Valerius stopped him with a smile. 'There's no point in thanking someone who's probably going to get you killed.'

Serpentius sniffed and brusquely changed the subject. 'What about horses? Those spavined, bow-legged nags they gave us at the port won't last a day where we're going.'

'I'm supposed to be in charge of a cavalry wing.' Valerius shrugged. 'We'll be in trouble if they can't provide their new commander with a decent horse.'

By now it was clear that the sense of suppressed excitement from the conference had infused the entire palace as word spread that the legions were on the move. He found Tiberius outside in the grounds. The young man was talking to a senior officer in the shadow of a grove of carob trees, but by the time Valerius reached him the other man had disappeared.

'My apologies, Tiberius. The general wanted me to tell you myself, but I see you already know.'

Tiberius looked up sharply, but relaxed when he recognized Valerius. 'I would not have this posting if it hadn't been for you, tribune. They tell me that the Tenth will soon be on the move. Judaea, I expect, with General Vespasian and Titus?'

Serpentius gave him a wry smile of congratulation and Valerius drew the young man aside. 'You are not going to Judaea, Tiberius,' he said quietly. 'The Tenth will be moving northeast, into Armenia. We have information that a Parthian army is on the march and General Corbulo intends to intercept it. There will be a battle.'

Tiberius looked puzzled and his eyes went cold. Was it possible that the young man was frightened? It seemed unlikely, but it was conceivable. No matter how proficient a soldier was with his weapons, the thought of his first real battle was enough to turn the veins to ice water. But the expression only lasted a heartbeat before the young tribune recovered and his face broke into a grin.

'So, I am to be blooded at last. I have waited for so long. It could only be better if you were able to fight by my side.'

Valerius heard a whisper in his head. He had a momentary vision of the younger tribune with blood on his face, but he kept his smile steady.

'I will ask the general, Tiberius.' He exchanged glances with Serpentius. 'Who knows what can be arranged.'

XXIII

Valerius awoke in darkness, his head buzzing with the information he'd had to absorb and the details he would have to deal with in the coming twenty-four hours. Of the seventeen auxiliary cavalry regiments which were now his responsibility, apart from escort detachments, only one, the Thracian Third Augusta, was camped nearby, and that at Cyrrhus, a good fifty miles to the east. The rest were scattered across northern Syria or on the Cappadocian frontier with Armenia and were already making their way to Zeugma, where the army would converge to make the crossing of the Euphrates. It meant he had to decide whether to ride out immediately after Corbulo's morning briefing, or wait until the Tenth had assembled and march with them. He washed and shaved in the baked clay basin the servant had brought before oiling the stump of his arm and fitting the carved walnut hand on its leather stock. He had decided not to wake Serpentius. The Spaniard's ingenuity and patience had been tested to the limit the previous day begging, stealing and borrowing, but mostly stealing, the equipment they would need for the campaign and the mules to carry it, when every unit and every officer was frantically seeking the same thing. No legion or auxiliary cohort would go on campaign under-equipped if it could find a way to avoid it.

Valerius had spent his time with Casperius Niger, attempting to solve the problem of the extra javelins and arrows his cavalrymen would have to carry. The Syrian armouries in Antioch, Palmyra, Damascus and Tyrus had been working night and day since the beginning of the Judaean insurrection a year earlier, but it wasn't just a question of sourcing the weapons. Valerius had to know how many extra spears a cavalryman and his mount were capable of carrying on the march, how many mules and camels would be needed to transport the numbers required to make up the shortfall in the general's order, how much fodder would be needed for the mules, and how many mules and camels would be needed for the extra fodder for the transport animals. Was it any wonder his head ached as if it was the morning after the last day of Saturnalia?

He was struggling into his sculpted leather breastplate when Serpentius appeared yawning in the doorway to help him.

'I told you to sleep until dawn,' Valerius admonished him. 'This could be the last time you have the opportunity.'

'I'll have plenty of time to sleep when I'm dead,' the Spaniard grunted. 'How could I lie there and listen to you cursing over those straps? You remind me of a turtle that's ended up on its back.'

Valerius didn't bother to reply. He was proud of his ability to get in and out of the armour despite his missing hand and he didn't care to be reminded that it sometimes took him longer than he liked.

'When you've eaten, get the horses and the mules ready. We may have to leave when I've finished with the general. And hunt up some bread and olives, and some wine for the journey. I doubt we'll be stopping before nightfall.'

He pretended not to hear Serpentius's mutter that it was only the mad and foolish who rode through the midday sun and killed themselves and their horses.

Gnaeus Domitius Corbulo looked fresh and relaxed when Valerius was ushered into his room. The young Roman was again surprised that the only other person present was Domitia, who sat a little to one side of the desk, and more surprised still by what he witnessed as he waited. In front of the general, instead of the usual tidy pile of scrolls, sat a wooden gaming board, and as Corbulo reeled off a string of military

roles, letters and numbers Domitia would take a carved wooden replica of the soldier he referred to and place it on a given square marked
on the board. When they had placed ten or twelve of the figures, she
smiled at her father and removed the pieces from the board again.
Corbulo then closed his eyes while she mixed up the pieces and placed
them on different squares.

'Now.'

He opened his eyes and Domitia counted to ten before sweeping the
pieces off the board and into a basket at her feet.

'Cavalryman: C4, C5, D6. Legionary: D1, D5, D8. Cataphract: F2,
F3, F6. Mounted archer: F . . .'

The game was repeated three times more as Valerius watched and as
far as he could see the general did not get a single figure out of place.
He found himself astonished by the mental dexterity Corbulo had
cultivated and wondered at its purpose; for if there was one thing he
now realized, Syria's governor never did anything without a purpose.

Domitia whispered something to her father and the general glanced
up. 'My apologies, tribune,' he said gruffly. 'One becomes engrossed. It
is a game, but a useful one since I believe it aids the memory, which in
my case is not what it once was. Would you care to try?'

The offer was made lightly, but the tone contained a hint of challenge that was mirrored in Domitia's dark eyes. Valerius had never
shirked a challenge. He took his place in front of the desk and studied
the board, which was split lengthwise into twelve sections, eight deep.

'A through to H,' Corbulo indicated the depth. 'And one to twelve.
Ninety-six squares on which my daughter will place twelve figures. All
you have to do is memorize which figure is on which square.'

It seemed almost childish. Valerius had studied under Seneca, com-
mitting vast tracts of dull Stoic philosophy to memory. His time in the
law courts and as chief of staff to the proconsul of Africa had given him
a mind as sharp as one of the jewelled ceremonial swords the governor
displayed on his wall.

'Close your eyes,' Domitia said softly, and her voice transported him
back to the shipwreck beach, smoke still heavy in the air, soft sand and
a lithe, sinuous body twisting against his.

160

'Now.'

He opened them again but his brain seemed to be frozen solid. He felt the first thrill of panic as Domitia began her relentless count.

'. . . ten.' A slim arm swept the pieces from the board. How . . . ?

'You don't have time to think on the battlefield,' Corbulo barked. 'Come on, man.'

Valerius licked his lips. 'Cavalryman: D7, D8, F . . .' He shook his head. 'Legionary: A4, A . . . 6.'

Corbulo drew an impatient breath and Valerius rapped out the rest of the names and numbers by pure guesswork. When he was finished the general's face was grim. Valerius had managed a pathetic five out of twelve correct. 'Perhaps we should move on.'

But Valerius had looked into Domitia's eyes and seen the flare of victory there. And in that instant it came to him: this wasn't a game, it was a battle. He remembered how it had been in the field before Colonia with the howls of fifty thousand Celtic champions in his ears and the scents of blood, death and fear that had filled the air like a fog. The flash of swords and constant threat of spear and arrow that had dulled the mind and cloaked the rest of the battlefield from him. He had found himself operating on two levels. The here, where blade sank into cringing flesh and shield beat off one screaming tattooed attacker after the other. And the above, in that place of calm where the mind took in every subtle change in the pulse of the battle and he could feel its rise and fall like the breast of a sleeping woman.

'One more time.'

Corbulo snorted and shook his head, but Domitia reached for the first figure.

The battle calm absorbed Valerius now. When the silken voice whispered that he should shut his eyes and he heard the pieces falling into place on the partitioned maplewood, it was as if he could see where each was placed. And when he opened them again it was as if they had never been closed. The figures and their locations seared themselves on the surface of his eyes and when it came time to place them he reeled off the locations without pausing for breath.

The general grunted approval. 'Fortuna favoured you this time.'

Valerius shrugged. 'Why don't we find out? But this time double the number of figures.'

Domitia's face lit up at this impertinence and she gave a delighted laugh.

'Impossible,' the general sniffed.

'I have only eighteen,' his daughter said innocently. 'Perhaps Father should try first?'

Corbulo glared at the girl, but the impish look on her face overcame his irritation and when he turned to Valerius he was smiling.

'I think we have had enough games for the moment. You have made your point, tribune. Now, to business. I have arranged for the prefect of the Thracian Third Augusta to join us here with as many of his senior officers as he can spare from the preparations. That will allow you to take the measure of your new command while we are on the march to Cyrrhus. I was a cavalry prefect myself and we are arrogant creatures, but if you can win his respect he will be able to teach you much that will be of use before you are called on to put it into practice. You will find that cavalrymen are as fickle as their horses, but guide them with a firm hand and they will never let you down. Report back to me when you have seen him.'

Valerius thanked him. 'On the subject of horses, sir, I've been having trouble finding suitable mounts for myself and my freedman. I have conscripted him to the ranks as an auxiliary, acting and unpaid, of course.'

Corbulo gave a thin smile. 'Naturally. I have already heard tales of his bargaining skills . . . and certain mysterious losses. Mucianus was most put out. He is old-fashioned in his way, and the thought of a slave wearing the Emperor's uniform had him calling for the lictors. But I have seen your man exercising and I can understand why you would want him close, and with a sword in his hand. He looks quite impressive. A Spaniard I would guess, from his looks and his tongue.'

Valerius nodded. 'A Spaniard and a gladiator.'

'A formidable combination. Would that more of my army had his bloodline and his temper. In any case, there will be no further obstructions. A cavalry-trained horse is at a premium in these troubled times, but I will issue orders that your needs be met.'

As he was leaving Valerius's eye was drawn to what looked like a model of a siege tower on a cabinet by the doorway. Corbulo noticed his interest.

'Another diversion of mine and one of my own invention. It is based on Caesar. I call it Caesar's Tower.' Valerius saw now that the tower consisted of four of the boards they had played the memory game on, set eight inches apart one on top of the other. Caesar was a game contested on a single level by legionaries in their short hours of leisure time. The two players each had twelve identical markers, white for one side and blue for the opponent. In addition, each had a thirteenth, smaller counter about the size of a rabbit dropping. The large markers could only move a single square at a time in any direction, but Caesar, the small token, ruled the board and could move anywhere as long as it was in a straight line. The aim of the game was to capture the opponent's stones by ambushing them between two of your own and it ended when one side captured the other's Caesar. It was a game of strategy that could be fiendishly complex when played by two skilled players, but this was different. 'I have developed it so that it is played in three dimensions,' Corbulo continued. 'I have never been defeated,' he smiled at his daughter, 'though Domitia has come close. Perhaps, when we are on campaign, you would care to try.'

Valerius could think of no worse field punishment than spending his nights being made to look a fool by his commanding officer, but he was a soldier and sometimes a soldier had to make sacrifices.

'Of course. I would be delighted.'

Domitia picked up the kitten which had been rubbing itself against her feet and stroked it. 'If the tribune could spare an hour this afternoon, perhaps I could teach him the basics of the game?'

Corbulo blinked and Valerius thought he saw a flare of suspicion in the grey eyes. He struck before it could develop into something worse.

'I fear I will be too busy with our preparations, lady,' he said quickly. 'Perhaps when we return.'

'Such a pity,' the dark-haired girl pouted. 'My father takes so much delight in beating his enemies into submission that it would have done him good to face someone who might show him the meaning of humility.'

While Corbulo glowered, Valerius bowed his farewell and made his escape. It occurred to him that Domitia was more dangerous than Boudicca.

XXIV

Valerius's Thracian cavalry escort set up camp outside Antioch close to the temporary mud-brick fort that was currently home to the Legio Tenth Fretensis. When they were settled, Valerius rode out to greet its commander, a solemn, bearded young man who introduced himself as Claudius Hanno, a Roman citizen, but born and brought up by his Syrian parents in the oasis city of Palmyra.

The main Thracian force remained at Cyrrhus, halfway to the crossing point of the Euphrates. Hanno reported their readiness was high, although he produced the usual list of complaints about the quality of the replacement horses and equipment they had been given.

'It will be good for once to have a friend at headquarters. Anything you can get for us in the way of harness and saddlery would help. Boots, too. The desert air is not kind to leather.' Professional eyes ran over Valerius's horse. 'Though I see from your mare that it is not worth begging for a new batch of remounts.'

Hanno's mood brightened when Valerius revealed Corbulo's order for the cavalry to carry extra javelins.

'He has something special in mind for us, then.' The Syrian grinned. 'The general always thinks two moves ahead of any other commander. He is a great man,' he said, almost reverentially. 'When he led us to Artaxata, he cut through the enemy like a sword piercing a beating

165

heart. The booty we collected there made me a rich man, may the gods give me time to spend it.'

On the Rhenus or in Britain, an auxiliary *ala milliara* would be a flexible mixed unit equally split between cavalry and infantry. In Syria, since the threat from the Parthians was mainly horse-borne and because of the vast distances they had to patrol, the Third Thracians were a thousand-strong wing of mounted archers and spearmen. Valerius watched as Hanno put the fifty men of his escort detachment through a series of exercises designed to show off their skills. The Roman had worked with cavalry often enough, but he was impressed by the horsemanship, speed and agility of the Thracians. The spearmen would ride full pelt at a man-shaped target, launch a pair of spears and turn almost in the same instant, and they never missed the mark. They rode in twos and swapped mounts in mid-stride; they leapt from the saddle and raced round behind their horses before remounting at the run. The archers could turn backwards in the saddle, fire three unerringly accurate arrows over their mount's tail and return to a normal riding position in less time than it takes to tell it. Afterwards, Hanno showed him the bow his men used, an exotic recurved weapon made of wood, bone and sinew that was half the length of the hunting bow Valerius had once owned, but shot arrows twice as far.

Valerius commented that the auxiliaries, whether carrying bow or spear, seldom touched the reins to control their mounts.

Hanno nodded gravely. 'All of our horses are trained to respond to heel and knee as well as to harness. It is a skill you will be familiar with?' the Syrian suggested, nodding in the direction of Valerius's wooden hand.

Valerius smiled, remembering the long hours of practice and the number of times he and Hercules had parted company as they decided to go in different directions. The horse he had been given at Seleucia was only trained to the rein. That didn't matter too much on the road, but it would be different in battle when he would need his left hand for a sword.

'I will require such a horse when we cross the Euphrates,' he said.

'Of course.' Hanno bowed. 'But if you are prepared to wait, I will choose him personally from our herd at Cyrrhus. You will have plenty of time to get to know him on the march. By the time we reach Tigranocerta you will have a proper cavalryman's swagger and a proper cavalryman's backside. Made of leather.'

Valerius joined in the laughter and decided he was fortunate to have this man under his command.

Dusk had fallen by the time he returned to the palace, but he decided it would be unwise to ignore Corbulo's instruction to report on his progress. He walked quickly through tiled corridors lit by oil lamps that created shadows on the painted walls and the statues of great men which lined them. Two guards checked him before he entered the general's private quarters, but there were none outside the study where he had met Corbulo that morning, which presumably meant he must be elsewhere in the palace. Valerius turned to go.

And froze.

It was the rhythm his mind detected first. Not his ears, because the sound was barely even a sound. His mind. As if he could feel someone's heartbeat in the air.

Slowly, he turned back to the doorway and moved the curtain a handspan aside. Now the sound was clearer, a gentle rhythmic hiss as if a hunted deer had stopped to listen with the breath blowing softly through its nostrils. Everything seemed peaceful, yet he could feel the danger as if someone had doused him with a bucket of ice water. His eyes ranged over the small area of the room he could see through the gap and his heart stopped as they fell on the kitten, Puss Puss. She lay on her side in the centre of the marble floor, with her front legs stretched out straight and two tiny spots of red halfway along the pale fur of her side. He froze as he noticed the animal's face: her eyes were wide and her lips drawn back in a rictus of agony, showing every tiny fang. Puss Puss was dead, but what had killed her? What was making the noise?

His hand crept to his belt and he cursed as he remembered he had handed his sword in at the palace entrance. Still, he couldn't ignore the threat. An inch at a time he squeezed through the doorway, careful not to move the curtain and alert whatever or whoever was waiting for him inside.

Gradually, more of the room came into view. On the far side, partially obscured by a high-backed couch, Domitia crouched in a corner. At first she seemed to be frozen in place, then he noticed that her head was rocking from side to side, the movement so slight that it was barely noticeable. He could see her face clearly, but Domitia's wide eyes were fixed on something in front of her hidden by the bulk of the couch. He edged his way carefully to the right, towards Corbulo's work desk. Still he could see nothing. He dropped lightly to the floor so he could look between the legs of the couch. At first whatever was there was lost in the gloom, but slowly a heap of sinuous, dark coils came into focus and his blood turned to ice.

He must have made a sound, because Domitia seemed to see him for the first time and her mouth opened. He raised a hand for her to be still, but too late, because from behind the couch came a sibilant, drawn-out hiss and Domitia drew her head back so it was touching the wall. Her body started to shake and he willed her to stop, because he knew that any sharp movement would provoke whatever kind of snake had her trapped. He looked again at the coils beneath the couch and a memory came to him of Africa. A hooded, swaying column of pure copper-scaled spite. Cobra!

Think!

She had backed into a recess beside a statue of the Emperor and she had no way of getting out without passing the snake, which must be close enough to strike. He had to draw it away from her. Draw it away and kill it. But with what?

The only furniture in the room was the general's desk and chair, a pair of couches for his guests and the cabinet on which the gaming tower sat, all of them too cumbersome to use as a weapon. The statue of Nero was one of a number in the room, including a painted bust of Corbulo himself. They might be used as missiles, but they were heavy and unwieldy and the chances of hitting such a difficult target slim. All he would do was provoke the snake into attack, which might be only seconds away in any case.

168

Domitia gave a convulsive sob and he knew time was running out. She was as courageous as any woman he had ever met, but courage had its limits and she was close to that limit now. He had to do something, quickly. Could he face it unarmed? The idea filled him with panic. But he must not panic. Find it. Find the calm that allowed him to win the memory game. With that thought his mind cleared and everything in the room came to him. The wax tablet and stylus. The rolled-up scrolls in their leather pouches. The ceremonial swords on the wall. Without taking his eyes from Domitia he reached behind him and groped across the painted plaster until his hand closed on a jewelled grip. Some decorative swords were just that, an empty scabbard with a decorative pommel. But this one wasn't empty and he breathed a silent prayer of thanks. The blade drew easily from the elaborate sheath with only the barest imitation of the snake's hiss. The gem-studded hilt made it a little awkward in his hand, but the weight and balance were perfect. The sword was a locally made replica of a cavalry *spatha*, forged from the blue-sheened iron that made for the strongest blades. It was longer and heavier than the *gladius* Valerius normally carried, but he was as proficient with the one as the other.

With three strides he crossed the room and pushed the couch aside. The sight of the huge snake almost paralysed him with fear. It was so big that its flared head, with its glinting bronzed scales and pale throat, was on a level with his chest. The raised body pulsed with energy and was the width of his arm at its thickest point. It turned to face him in a single smooth movement and its fanged head drew back ready to strike, the unblinking eyes like obsidian beads as they fixed him in their deadly glare.

Domitia made an involuntary movement and the monster's awful gaze was drawn back to the crouching figure. Valerius raised his right hand to still her. Instantly, the black beads fixed on him. He feinted with the sword, staying just out of range, and the giant head threatened once more. He found that each move he made was replicated by the flared hood, so it became almost a dance as the snake followed his sword hand. There was his solution. To save Domitia he must become the snake's only target. But how to do it without sacrificing himself and leaving her to its mercy? He could see the wicked hooked fangs in the creamy white mouth and he imagined the glistening drop of poison in each tip. One scratch from those needle points and the venom would condemn him to a terrible, agonizing death. The snake let out a long hiss and he sensed that its patience was at an end. As he edged closer it became visibly more agitated. He held the sword high and ready to swing. He must draw the strike and draw it so that in the same instant the blue blade swept down to bite into that scaled body.

He stepped towards the snake, reaching out with his right hand, and immediately the great serpent's head whipped forward with an astonishing speed and power. Valerius flailed with the sword, but the cobra was already inside his swing and he felt a shocking blow that numbed his right arm and made him cry out in horror. From somewhere close he heard a scream that echoed his own fear. He had gambled that the snake would be drawn to the walnut fist, but the gamble had failed. The whiplash strike had taken the flared head beyond the wooden lure to the thick muscled part of Valerius's forearm. Yet even in the instant his mind told him he was dead, he realized that Fortuna had favoured him. Instead of plunging into unguarded flesh the terrible fangs were hooked into the thick leather stock that held the walnut hand in place, jets of pale venom already darkening the tanned cowhide. Panicking, he swung the sword again, but the cobra's writhing coils made an almost impossible target as they whipped forward against his legs, horrible, clinging and sinuous. He only managed to inflict a cut which enraged the beast further. He felt the moment when it tried to withdraw and come erect for a second, lethal strike, the wide head shaking his arm with incredible force as it tried to free itself. But the fangs were sunk deep in the tough leather like a pair of barbed hooks. Valerius knew he had only moments. With a last convulsive heave the snake broke clear, but even as its head swayed back and the power flowed into its neck the young Roman's brain had calculated speed and distance and angle and the long blue sword flashed out to meet the snake's strike and this time the edge cut deep into the body just below the flared hood. The cobra thrashed back and forth in its agony and the fanged head whipped by a hair's breadth from his face. It was dying, but not dead, and Valerius placed himself for another cut as it fell back to writhe on the marble floor. The long sword rose and fell, the bright iron cleaving the sinuous body in two and clanging against the stone.

Breathing hard, Valerius took a step back and stood head bowed over the still twitching body of the giant serpent.

He heard a slight noise behind him and turned with the blade raised to strike.

'That is no way to treat a fine sword, tribune. See, the marble has nicked the edge.' Gnaeus Domitius Corbulo's voice was controlled, but his face had the sheen of polished ivory and his hand shook as he held it out to take the ceremonial *spatha*, which he wiped and replaced in its scabbard. He raised Domitia to her feet on trembling legs. 'Come my dear, you are safe now. You were not touched? Nevertheless, you should see my physician.'

Before they reached the door she dropped her father's hand and walked slowly back to where Valerius still stood, half-paralysed and as spent as he had ever been after a battle. He saw the dark eyes flinch as they looked again on the cobra, lying in two pieces, its blood staining the white marble. For a moment it was as if they were the only two people in the world and he wanted more than anything to take her into his arms and comfort her. He knew that a single movement from him would make it happen. But he also understood that to make the movement would bring disaster. He could feel Corbulo's stare and hear his hoarse breathing. Domitia saw it and took strength from the decision he made for them both. She drew herself up to her full height.

'It seems that once again I must thank you for saving me, tribune. You should know that I came to my father's quarters to continue the game of Caesar we had begun. I had pondered a move that would confound him and thought to astonish him with it on his return. It was only when the snake killed my kitten that I became aware of its presence. You must have heard my cry.'

There had been no cry, but it was a convenient explanation and avoided further questions. It wasn't only in politics that innocence was sometimes no defence.

Valerius bowed his head. 'It was fortunate that I came to deliver my

171

report at just the right moment. I am only glad I was able to help.' He turned to her father. 'What I don't understand is how such a large snake should be able to make its way so far into the palace unseen.'

Corbulo's eyes went cold. 'Stranger still that it is a species I have never heard of being found so close to the coast. This was no accident, tribune. You have many duties, but I must ask you to carry out an investigation. Question my guards. Find out who was in a position to deliver the snake and find out who gave the order. We have an assassin among us.'

XXV

They found him early the next morning.

Valerius had spent the rest of the evening questioning the legionaries of the headquarters guard. The centurion of the detachment, all men of the Tenth Fretensis who had proved themselves unfailingly loyal to the governor, explained what Valerius already knew. Guards patrolled the exterior of the palace day and night, with pairs alternating at each of the entrances, including the one leading to the palace from the slave quarters. Within the palace itself, only a few corridors connecting the working rooms and the governor's personal quarters were continuously under guard, and Corbulo's private offices were only secured when he was there, by the team of men tasked with his close protection.

From the answers he received, Valerius put together a list of people who had used the corridors in the hours before Domitia encountered the cobra. He placed Domitia at the top of the list and himself in second place. They were followed by the senior officers who had visited Corbulo during the day. Finally there were a dozen or so slaves who had access to the governor's rooms to bring him food, clean, and carry out all the normal domestic tasks of a slave in a Roman household.

When the list was complete he took it to Corbulo to update him on his progress.

'I'm sure there's nothing you'd enjoy more than interrogating legate

Mucianus,' the general said. 'But he and his camp prefect, tribune Niger and legate Traianus all came to see me while I was there, and left immediately. For the moment, concentrate on the slaves.'

Valerius sought out Serpentius, who, despite his new freedman's status, preferred to live in the slave quarters. 'If I question them alone,' he explained, 'they'll tell me what they think I want to hear. Your presence always ensures a little more objectivity. We'll make these four our priority. According to the guards, they were all carrying some kind of container.'

The Spaniard looked over the list.

'I think you can forget Perellia. From what I hear she does a lot more than give the governor his massage at bath time. Big girl, dark hair and well set up. If she wanted to murder him she wouldn't need a snake. She could kill him with kindness, if you get my meaning?'

'But she was carrying a basket, which still makes her a suspect. You're probably right, but the governor isn't going to thank us for taking his concubine off the list. We'll question her first.'

But when they ordered the overseer, a Syrian freedman, to fetch the four slaves they discovered they had more pressing problems than Perellia's basket.

'I'm sorry, sir.' The terrified man was visibly quaking as he confessed. 'Turpio is missing.'

'Turpio is the slave who was to replace the governor's linen?'

'Yes, sir.'

'Is there any reason why he should leave the slave quarters at night?'

The overseer shook his head. 'He should have been locked in with the rest. They said he went to the *latrina* and didn't return.'

'Who are his friends?' Valerius demanded. 'Come on, man. He must have had friends. How long has he been gone?'

'Three hours,' the man confirmed. 'They thought nothing of it. Sometimes . . . sometimes he sold himself to the guards.'

Serpentius gave a grunt that might have been a laugh. Now they understood why the Syrian was so frightened. If Turpio was regularly allowed to slink out of the slave quarters, it meant that the overseer or his deputy was getting a cut of whatever he was earning.

'Three hours,' Valerius calculated. 'He could be five or six miles away by now. Serpentius, get me the guard commander.'

The centurion arrived bleary-eyed and belligerent, but Valerius had no time for niceties. 'It seems you may have allowed the man who tried to kill the governor to escape.' The soldier's face went pale and it was clear Valerius now had his attention. 'I want patrols on the main road to Seleucia and Daphne, and on the roads north and west. Every other man will search the palace and the surrounding area.'

When the centurion had rushed out shouting orders to his men, Valerius turned to Serpentius. 'Let me know if they find him, though I doubt if they will. He'd have to be a fool to stay near the palace. He'll either be hiding in the city with his accomplices or somewhere on the road where he feels safe.'

'Where will you be?'

Valerius yawned. 'In bed. One way or the other it's going to be a busy day.'

It was easy to see why they hadn't found Turpio in the night. Who would have thought to look in the river?

The body lay face up and trapped between a fallen branch and a large rock. Turpio's young features were the bloodless, fish-belly white of unpainted marble and his mouth hung open showing yellow teeth and a stump of tongue. At first Valerius thought it had been cut out, which seemed overly cautious if you were going to kill the man anyway. On closer investigation, however, it seemed that it, like his eyes, had become a delicacy for the pair of ravens that had perched on his chest until he was discovered by a legionary making his discreet morning libation to the Orontes. The rock lay less than four paces from the bank and Valerius could clearly see the vivid scar of the second smile that had been opened below Turpio's chin.

'We'll never know who he was working with now,' Serpentius said cheerfully. 'He must have been meeting someone who had promised to pay him or help him escape, maybe both. Whoever it was decided they couldn't rely on him to keep his mouth shut.'

They waited while two legionaries dragged the body to the bank.

Turpio's threadbare tunic was ripped, probably where it had caught on the branch that had kept him from floating downriver towards Seleucia Pieria. The chest from the throat down had been sheeted with blood, but was now a washed-out pink. Valerius bent over the body and examined the wound. It ran horizontally from one side of the neck to the other, obscene and pink-lipped and deep enough to have cut almost to the spine.

The Spaniard crouched beside him. 'A nice piece of work.' Valerius was happy for Serpentius to take the lead. The gladiator knew more about creating wounds like these than was good for a man. 'Sword work, see? Too deep and clean for a knife if the killer was standing in front of him and too straight if he came from behind. One quick professional stroke that took out the big veins on either side and the windpipe too. Turpio the snake charmer would have bled out in about a minute and he wouldn't have made a sound. Your man probably used a *spatha* or something similar, because if it had been a *gladius* he would have been covered with blood. Gladiator work.' He rose to his feet and pirouetted, at the same time drawing his long sword and carving the air in a single whispering sweep that had the men standing closest stepping back. 'Maybe he would have got a few spots on his clothes or his boots, but it would only be noticeable if you really looked. Dump the body in the river and then go back to wherever he came from. He couldn't know that Turpio would hang around long enough to be found.'

'And tell us we're looking for not one assassin, but two.'

'What's that?' The Spaniard pointed at Turpio's clenched fist where a scrap of green was just visible.

Valerius forced back the dead fingers and pulled out a ragged fragment of bright green cloth. The same green cloth that the tunics and cloaks of the auxiliary escort were manufactured from.

'Cavalry?' Serpentius suggested.

Valerius looked across the river to where Antioch was beginning to shimmer in the heat of the morning. 'It would make sense, when you combine it with the heavy sword.'

'The Parthians, then. This King Vologases must have spies in Antioch, even amongst the governor's servants and the Syrian auxiliaries, who to my thinking would as well be Parthian as Roman. If he believes General Corbulo is planning to move against him it would make a kind of sense to kill him. A knife direct to the heart of the enemy. And a snake is a very eastern method of murder.'

'That's true, but there is another possibility.'

'Who supplied the escort?'

Valerius nodded. 'The Syrian auxiliaries are attached to the Sixth Ferrata, the Scythians to the Fifteenth Apollinaris. So Mucianus and Collega. Gaius Pompeius Collega is not one of the favoured inner circle and it's plain he disagrees with Corbulo's plan. What if he decided that the best way to gain the Emperor's favour was to remove a man who is not only exceeding his orders, but is also, for all his protestations of loyalty, a potential rival? But . . .'

'But?'

'I have only met him once, but Collega seems too . . . honourable.'

'Your friend Mucianus then?'

The Roman grinned. 'Much as I would like it to be, Mucianus has more to lose than to gain from Corbulo's death. He is the governor's man, linked to him through years of service and patronage.'

A commotion behind them heralded the arrival of the governor amidst a cloud of bodyguards. Corbulo was accompanied by his legionary commanders and Valerius found himself once more the target of Mucianus's unforgiving stare. The guards opened warily to allow Corbulo forward and Serpentius stepped back with a bow to give him room to join Valerius by the body.

'So my assassin is dead?'

'It appears so.' Valerius kept his voice neutral. 'He had the opportunity to place the snake in your quarters and he ran when the crime was discovered. Unfortunately, we had no opportunity to question him. His fellow slaves say they know nothing of his movements outside the palace, but he had . . . arrangements . . . which allowed him to come and go more or less as he pleased.' He mentioned the slave's sideline and Corbulo grunted in a way that said that someone would pay for the lapse. 'He undoubtedly had the opportunity to meet contacts in the city or among the men of the four Syrian legions who spend their furloughs here.' He explained Serpentius's theory about the way the man had died. 'It seems certain that he met his killer in the gardens last night, but we had more than two hundred men searching the palace grounds, including a century from the Tenth Fretensis.'

'Surely you don't believe one of them killed him?' Corbulo rapped. 'The men of my personal guard all have years of service under my command, and the Tenth is the most loyal of all my legions.'

Valerius could have pointed out that the more trusted a man became, the more dangerous he could be. In any case, loyalty could be bought and sold like any other commodity. All that mattered was the price. He stood his ground. 'There is no guarantee that he was murdered before the hunt began. The only way to be certain is to question the searchers individually and cross-check their movements against each other.'

'Which would take days.'

'And have little hope of success,' Valerius admitted. He showed the governor the scrap of green cloth. 'This was found in the dead man's hand.'

Corbulo frowned and rubbed the rough fabric between his fingers. 'Someone from an auxiliary cavalry unit?'

'It is possible,' Valerius told him. 'We can't be sure. There is one thing . . .'

'Yes?'

'Judging by the type of wound, the murderer's uniform may have been spotted with Turpio's blood.'

The governor shook his head. 'We do not have time to search every tent.'

'No, but if you order every second man to check his tent-mate's clothing and vice versa it's possible we will find our killer in less than an hour.'

Corbulo studied Valerius with increased respect. 'Then do it.'

Valerius issued the order and Corbulo went back to the palace, only to return twenty minutes later when the reports began to come in as the units concluded their searches.

'Nothing?'

'No, general. I . . .'

'Sir! You should see this.' The centurion of the guard addressed his words to Corbulo. He carried something in his right hand and refused to meet Valerius's eyes.

'What is it?'

The man held up a pair of the nailed sandals every legionary wore. Corbulo's eyes hardened as he recognized the familiar stains on the leather strapping.

'Blood?' he demanded. 'Where were they found?'

'In the slave quarters.'

'And who do they belong to?'

'Him.'

Every eye followed the pointing finger.

To Serpentius.

The guards took time to react. A long moment of dangerous silence that was broken by Serpentius's bitter laugh. Corbulo flinched as if he'd been struck and his bodyguard moved forward with a low growl, their swords ready to cut down the murderer at the general's command.

The Spaniard's hand hovered over his sword hilt and Valerius knew that the moment he touched it he was a dead man. 'Wait.'

Corbulo's head snapped round and the look in his eyes told Valerius that Serpentius's wasn't the only life on the line. 'You dare to interfere with justice? You who brought this assassin to my home?'

Valerius kept his voice calm. 'Justice is only justice if you have the killer, general.'

'You say he is innocent?'

'I say that a pair of bloody sandals isn't enough to condemn a man.'

'They were less than an hour ago, when the man in question was not your servant. Did you not tell me the wound was made by a *spatha* in expert hands? Who is more expert than a former gladiator? Take him.'

Serpentius was standing in the centre of the four armed legionaries of the guard and Valerius saw him tense. Another second and there would be blood on the ground and men would be screaming.

'Ask him if the sandals are his,' he said quietly.

Corbulo raised his hand and Serpentius relaxed as the guard backed away. 'Well?'

The Spaniard stared at him with eyes so full of menace that for a moment even Valerius wondered if he had misplaced his trust.

'No.'

'You can prove this?'

Serpentius shrugged. 'Even a fool can see that these are not a slave's.' Corbulo's nostrils flared at the implied insult, but the Spaniard appeared not to notice. 'My sandals are standard issue, the leather is hard as mahogany wood and I have to replace the studs every two weeks.' He bent and unwound the leather ties holding his left shoe. 'Here.' He handed it to the general. 'My spares are the same. Those belong to a rich man. An officer.'

Corbulo weighed the sandal in his hand. He motioned for one of the blood-spattered pair and compared the two. It was immediately clear that the second was of a much superior construction and the leather softer and more expensive. He studied Serpentius like an undertaker measuring a client for a shroud but the Spaniard met his gaze without flinching.

'You will vouch for your man,' he demanded, turning to Valerius. 'You are certain this is not his sandal?'

Valerius nodded. 'I would trust this man with my life.'

'That is not what I asked.'

'It is not his sandal. I would swear it on the altar of the Temple of Mars.'

The eagle's eyes darted from one to the other and Valerius could feel his heart thundering in his ears. Eventually, the general tossed the sandal back to the Spaniard and Valerius dared to breathe once more. Corbulo nodded, and Valerius knew that the incident would never be spoken of again. He had made his decision and it was as final as any court of law.

'I do not have time for these distractions. We have a war to fight and it seems I will be safer in my campaign tent than in my own palace.' He turned to Casperius Niger who stood at his shoulder. 'Are the preparations in place?' The camp prefect nodded. 'Then we will march at dawn. Verrens?' Valerius straightened and Corbulo handed back the scrap of green. 'Neither of the two auxiliary units which supplied the escort will cross the Euphrates. They will help screen the Sixth Ferrata and the Third Gallica on the march south to join Vespasian. I will leave it to you to organize their replacements with Casperius. You will suspend your investigations for the moment.'

Valerius saluted and Corbulo and his aides marched off, the governor spraying commands like slingshot pellets and the gods help the man who didn't catch his words the first time. Only Mucianus lingered, crouched over Turpio, studying the dead face and the awful red gash in the pale throat.

'I see no murderer,' he said carefully. 'All I see is a slave sacrificed for expediency.' He looked up and stared into Valerius's eyes. 'I know where your loyalties lie, tribune. I warned General Corbulo against keeping you too close. It would not be the first time a killer has played rescuer to reach his victim. You failed with the snake and used the general's daughter to redeem yourself. I have no doubt you will try again.' His unrelenting gaze moved to Serpentius. The wiry Spaniard tensed and Valerius willed him to keep his hand away from his sword. Mucianus's face twisted into a glacial smile. 'He has the look of a killer even without a blade in his hand. But the general has been warned. He will be watching you and the next time there will be no escape.'

He turned abruptly and walked off after the governor.

'What did he mean by knowing where your loyalties lie?' Serpentius asked, letting out a long slow breath.

'He thinks we have been sent here by the Emperor to kill Corbulo.'

The Spaniard spat in the direction of the retreating legate. 'I know who I'd rather kill.'

'We have enough problems without worrying about Mucianus.'

Serpentius nodded. 'Like who spattered blood on those sandals General Vespasian's son gave you?'

'When did you steal them?'

The Spaniard feigned shock. 'Not steal, my lord. Borrow. Only until my spares are mended. Thanks for that.'

Valerius turned to him. 'You didn't kill him, did you?'

'No, but whoever did it is very good.'

'As good as you?'

Serpentius grinned. 'I hope we'll find out.'

Valerius looked again at the green cloth that had been in Turpio's hand. 'There's one thing I don't understand. If this was planted on Turpio to point us in the direction of the auxiliaries, why bother implicating you? Bluff and double bluff? It just seems too complicated.'

'There's a simpler explanation.' Serpentius bent to tie the straps of his sandal. 'Someone in the palace hears that Turpio's been found with his throat cut and decides there'll never be a better opportunity to get rid of us.'

'Which means that we don't have just one enemy to find, but two, and the chances are that they're both about to accompany us five hundred miles into Armenia.'

XXVI

'My cavalry commander must have a horse worthy of him.'

If beauty is the perfection of form, she was the most beautiful thing Valerius had ever seen. A groom held the reins to steady her noble head and Gnaeus Domitius Corbulo, proconsul of the east and governor of Syria, stood by her shining flank. The sword that hung from the four-pommelled cavalry saddle was the ceremonial blade Valerius had pulled from Corbulo's wall, but it had been modified for war.

With a flourish the governor drew it free and the blue-sheened blade glinted menacingly in the morning sun. 'It has a great history and it is not right that it should spend its life as a decoration.' Corbulo's voice contained that unsettling mix of steel, certainty and charm that made him who he was. 'I have had the jewels removed and the hilt bound with leather strips to improve the grip. It is a soldier's weapon now. The balance is a little unusual. You will notice that it is weighted towards the point, but that can be an advantage when you are using a sword from horseback. Here, take it.'

Corbulo spun the weapon with a soldier's practised hands so that the hilt was towards Valerius. The young Roman took it remembering the weight and the feel from his encounter with the snake. The sword's energy ran through him like heat from a blazing fire. He tried two or three cuts and it was as if the blade had a life of its own. Still, he only had eyes for the horse, and when Corbulo spoke again it was with an old cavalryman's pride and a glint in his eye.

'I owe you my daughter's life, tribune Gaius Valerius Verrens, not once, but many times. I hope you will accept this gift in part payment. She is an Akhal-Teke, from my own stables: the horse of kings.'

Valerius stared at the astonishing animal whose forefathers had carried Alexander the Great from Athens to the shores of the Indus; freshly groomed she was a work of art in polished bronze, her coat of fine hairs gleaming in the sunlight. He approached the horse's head and allowed her to take in his scent through wide nostrils which flared and snorted as he stroked her silken ears with his good hand. Only when he was sure she knew him did he look into the glistening dark eyes behind curling lashes and knew she was his for ever, and he hers.

'They are by nature a desert breed,' Corbulo continued. 'But she has a touch of Karabakh in her; not enough to affect her speed or her stamina, but enough to accustom her to the mountains. They are hardy stock and need little water.'

She was long and lean with an elegantly curving neck and a proud head. Her breast was narrow, shaped like a ship's prow and made for cutting through the desert air when she was given her head to run free on the long, slim legs. 'I will call you Khamsin, after the hot desert wind Hanno warned me about,' Valerius thought, only he must have spoken aloud because Corbulo nodded. 'Yes, Khamsin. A great name for a great horse.'

'Why don't you try her?' The familiar soft voice was betrayed by an edge of suppressed emotion. How had he not noticed she was there? He turned and realized that Khamsin was not the most beautiful thing in the world. Today, that honour belonged to Domitia Longina Corbulo. She wore a long dress of virgin white, belted with gold, that left her shoulders bare beneath the walnut tresses that flowed left and right of her wide forehead and framed the oval of her face.

'With your permission, lady?' He handed over his helmet, bringing a gasp of surprise from one of the watchers.

Domitia accepted the burden and nodded imperiously. As she watched, Valerius whispered encouragingly in the horse's ear before using his left hand to help him vault into the saddle. The groom handed him the reins, and oblivious of all but Domitia's gaze he walked the mare slowly to the gate. Beyond the trees lining the road lay the sandy ring of the governor's personal circus and it took all Valerius's patience to keep Khamsin to a walk. He was not the only impatient one. He could sense the controlled power surging below his loins and imagined the great heart thundering in her chest. She had a fine, high-stepping walk as befitted a mare whose sire a hundred generations earlier may have been brother to Bucephalus. His left hand was free to control the rein, but he wrapped the leather around the walnut fist of his right and used his thighs, knees and heels to command her. When he reached the circus he kicked her gently into a trot, feeling the free-moving muscles working sweetly beneath him as she danced across the packed sands. The warm breeze kissed his face and he laughed for the joy of it. Khamsin felt it too, pricking up her ears and shaking her head from side to side.

'Very well,' Valerius grinned. He reached to pat her neck and nudged her into a canter. The change was immediate and effortless, a surge in pace, and now she wasn't just moving but flowing over the ground. Too soon, they reached the far end of the arena and he shifted in the saddle. Left knee forward, right knee back, and she pirouetted like a leaf falling from a tree. Not falling, dancing. A single fluid movement that left them facing the way they had come. Khamsin must have sensed his exhilaration because she whinnied with pleasure. There was no stopping it now. He dug his heels into her flanks, but truly she needed no encouragement. She moved straight to the gallop and suddenly they were speeding arrow-straight down the length of the arena. Valerius crouched low over her shoulders and saw the ground flying past in a blur below. He had never travelled at such a speed, but he felt no fear, only the astonishing sensation of the blood bubbling in his veins and thundering in his ears. She seemed to shift beneath him to ensure that he stayed fixed in the saddle and her movement was so smooth that he might have been in a carriage. He wanted it never to end, but here were Corbulo and his staff at the entrance, watching in astonished wonder. He saw Domitia's face flash past, her eyes wide with delight and her mouth gaping, decorum forgotten as she clutched the fair girl who had replaced Suki. A ragged cheer broke out and for the first time he used the reins to gently coax her to a halt. He slipped from the saddle and stood by the horse's head, whispering his thanks for her efforts. Her chest rose and fell as she breathed, but he could tell it was with excitement, not exertion, and she gave off the satisfied feeling of a job well done. He wished he had something to reward her for her efforts.

He turned at the sound of running feet to find Domitia approaching with his polished iron helmet in her hands. For the first time he truly saw her for what she was. A girl, not a woman. A girl on the verge of womanhood, perhaps, but one still with the ability to become lost in childish glee. After the exhilaration of the race he was overwhelmed by his own emotions and if she had come three paces further he would have swung her into his arms. But she stopped, took a deep breath, and with a mischievous smile handed him first the helmet and then a shining red apple, her fingers brushing the leathery palm of his left hand as she placed it there.

'I must congratulate you on your horsemanship, tribune, and my father on his choice of gift. Truly she is a wonderful horse.'

He returned her smile, feeling like a boy again for the first time since he had left Rome for Britain to join the Twentieth. 'The finest I have ever ridden, lady, and unless I am mistaken the choice of gift was not only your father's.' He accepted the fruit and Khamsin scented the apple and nuzzled his fingers until he handed it over. 'A horse like Khamsin never forgets generosity,' he added chivalrously, and more quietly, 'and like Khamsin I will never forget this gift.'

She heard the catch in his voice and a shadow fell over her eyes. 'Is it always like this when a woman sends her man away to war?'

His heart tripped at the phrase *her man*. 'Seneca called it "this magnificent melancholy". At the time I dismissed him as unduly sentimental because he was a fat old man who had never gone to war. But that wasn't true. He had served on the Rhine frontier as a tribune.'

'This magnificent melancholy.' She ran the words over her tongue and liked them. 'Yes, I can understand that. A mixture of feelings.

186

Pride and sadness. Loss and . . .' She couldn't finish, but her eyes filled and again he felt that surge of need.

'Tribune.' There could be no doubt that Corbulo had seen what had passed between Valerius and his daughter, but the tone was almost kindly. 'Your command awaits you. Work them hard and use them well. When you have fixed your defensive positions come to my headquarters tonight and we will see whether you can master Caesar's Tower as well as you can master a horse.'

He nodded and offered Domitia his hand.

As they walked away, Serpentius ran up grinning. 'Now that,' he said with enormous understatement, 'is a horse.'

XXVII

For a frontier town, Zeugma, a sprawling community of mud brick and marble built across a low hill which sloped gently down to the Euphrates, was a surprisingly sophisticated place. Or perhaps not so surprisingly. Hanno, who had proved a wellspring of knowledge and experience during the six-day march from Antioch, informed Valerius that the city was another creation of Alexander's general Seleucus. It had been built more than three centuries earlier, and until it had been conquered by Pompey the Great it had been known, like Antioch's port, by his name.

'Now it is Zeugma, the place of the bridge.' The Syrian gestured towards the crossing, which was of a construction the Roman had never seen before. A bridge of perhaps twenty stone-built arches stretched two thirds of the way across the river and ended a hundred paces from the near bank. The gap between was filled by ten or twelve sturdy boats which carried a jointed wooden platform to complete the link to the bank. Hanno noticed his interest. 'For two reasons,' he said, holding up scarred fingers. 'First, when the river floods the prefect in charge of the bridge will order the pontoons to be detached. If he is fortunate, they will swing back to the bank and he will recover them. If he is unfortunate, the river will wash them away. But he will only have lost part of the bridge and they are easily replaced, whereas if it was entirely of stone he would lose much more and it would be a major project to rebuild. Second, in time of war the pontoons can be removed and any invasion force from the east must find another place to cross.'

'But we are at war now,' Valerius pointed out.

'Yes,' Hanno grinned, his white teeth shining in the dark face. 'But *we* are the invading force. The pontoons will remain in place until we return, either in triumph or, may Mars preserve us, pursued, as the lion sees off the jackal, by King Vologases' cataphracts, his armoured cavalry.'

Valerius felt a shiver of unease as he looked down at the narrow structure and imagined a defeated army packed on to the narrow cross-ing with the Parthian army pressing it on every side. Arrows sheeting the sky. Carnage and chaos. Men fighting and dying. Bodies in the river and the sparkling grey-green waters running red with Roman blood. He shrugged off the unhappy thought.

'I'm sure that will not happen, prefect. Everyone has complete con-fidence in the general. You said so yourself.'

'Of course,' the Syrian said. 'But they will be many and we are so few. Thousands of cataphracts – armoured lords on great horses, swathed in iron so our arrows cannot kill them. Swarms of mounted archers who live, eat and sleep in the saddle. Horses are their currency and their passion. A Parthian would sacrifice his wife before he would sacrifice his horse.' His eyes ranged over the legionary camps on the near and far banks, their scale almost equalled by the tented towns which had grown up since Corbulo had closed the busy crossing to civilian traffic. 'Much will depend on the enemy's mood. Sometimes, he is like the jackal. He prefers to bark rather than fight. But then he can be like the leopards which once roamed here. He will come fast and silent, and he will come for the throat. Beware of Vologases the leopard, tribune.'

On Corbulo's instructions Valerius had divided his cavalry between the east and west banks of the great river. Hanno's Thracian Third Augusta was camped with two other thousand-strong *alae* and two of the smaller five-hundred-strong wings alongside the permanent fortress now occupied by the Fifteenth legion Apollinaris. The rest of the units had orders to range the eastern bank of the Euphrates and harry or destroy any enemy forces they found there. The Tenth Fretensis had already crossed, and the Fifteenth, minus the three cohorts who would have to hold the bridge in their absence, would cross tomorrow, along with the rest of the auxiliaries, cavalry and infantry. All around them the tent lines buzzed with activity as units and individual soldiers frantically made their last-minute preparations for the advance into enemy territory. The air was heavy with the scent of burning charcoal as the armourers of the Fifteenth sweated to repair swords and plate armour, the ceaseless clatter of hammer on anvil punctuating their efforts. Hundreds of carts had been requisitioned to carry the supplies essential to feed more than twenty thousand men and as many horses, mules and camels, in a land that would yield barely a tenth of what was needed to keep them alive. Now those carts must be checked to ensure their wheels were sound and the base and walls undamaged. A single axle break could mean a century going hungry. Valerius was surprised to see the legion's carpenters dismantling the unit's siege weapons ready for transportation. It seemed an extravagance for an expedition that was otherwise designed to travel light and had no plans to invade town or city.

When Hanno left to join his men for the evening meal, Valerius stood for a while at the edge of the camp and contemplated the distant mountains on the other side of the river; just a dusty line on the far horizon that shimmered in the dry heat of the late afternoon. He found that the very land oppressed him. Once they had left the fertile strip by the sea they had marched fifteen miles a day over a bleak patchwork of dirty brown and scorched ochre, the monotony only broken by the occasional barren height where eagles and vultures soared, or some blessed river valley where they were able to water themselves and their horses in the cool of the stream. The experience had left him longing for the lush green plains, swampy moors and damp valleys of Britain, where he had once cursed the mud and the rain, or even the shady, ordered olive groves of the estate at Fidenae. After six days, they had found relief at Zeugma, where the Euphrates ran like a broad ribbon of grey and emerald through the sun-blasted rocks, spreading its bounty a mile and more to each side of the fast-flowing waters. Beyond the river lay a true wilderness where the midday sun burned hot enough to crack rocks and a man could ride for days on end before finding water. Yet Corbulo had not only taken his army all the way to Tigranocerta and Artaxata, but fought there and won. Won against incredible odds. Now he was going back, and Valerius would journey every last step with him.

He flinched at the old familiar pain in the bones of a hand that lay among the burned-out ruins of a town two thousand miles away – a pain he knew would never leave him – and walked towards the walls of the city and his nightly lesson from the general.

Surprisingly, what had begun as a trial had quickly become a pleasure. Valerius amazed himself by becoming proficient at the governor's version of Caesar, though the game was mind-numbingly complex and he was certain he would never become as skilled as his tutor. His proximity to Corbulo inspired jealousy and he was forced to ignore the stares of his fellow officers of the general's staff who believed him a spy or worse. In time he understood that suspicion of an outsider was too entrenched to break. If they didn't quite hate him, they resented and feared his presence in equal measure.

Corbulo had set up his headquarters in a villa overlooking the river, owned by the leader of the *ordo*, Zeugma's council of a hundred leading citizens. The man had been only too happy to give up his home, one of the finest in the city, to his old friend the governor.

Valerius found him hunched over the mass of reports his officers and their agents brought him every day. From here he dictated the orders for tomorrow's movements: miles to be covered, rations to be replenished, waterholes' positions and the forces that would be needed to secure them. His voice rose in irritation at the news of a shortage of mules – this in a land where every second animal was a mule – when it was too late to requisition more from Damascus or Antioch. He ordered that every transport animal in Zeugma and for ten miles around be rounded up, but it still meant the legionaries would have to carry an extra two days' rations on their backs.

Valerius passed the time studying the mosaic floor, which depicted a marine scene featuring a heavily bearded man with lobster claws for horns looking soulfully at a woman with long dark hair and wings growing from her forehead.

'Enough. Leave us and order some food and drink.' He looked up as Corbulo dismissed his clerks and rubbed his hands across his eyes. Despite his concentration on military problems the general had observed Valerius's interest in his surroundings. 'It is a depiction of Oceanus, the Greek god of the rivers, and his wife Tethys. Nikolos, who owns this house, is very proud of it. A little rustic and not quite the quality you would find in a villa at home, but pleasing enough in its own way.'

Valerius nodded his agreement. It wasn't the standard of the mosaic or even the subject that caught his attention. It was the glowing pink figure of Eros, the god of love, who sat cheerfully in the top corner riding a dolphin across a sea of Aegean blue, and reminded him of the day on the galley when he had stood with Domitia with the dolphins playing beneath their feet.

A servant entered with a jug of wine and food on two individual platters. Valerius watched as the Syrian broke off a piece of bread on one of the plates and dipped it into the spiced goat stew, then stood back before swallowing it. Corbulo nodded. When the man left the room, the governor noticed Valerius's puzzlement.

'My aides insist that my food is tasted.' He smiled. 'After the incident with the snake, it seems they fear I might suffer the same fate as Germanicus, he who might have partaken of the wrong type of mushroom.'

Valerius picked up the wine jug and poured two cups. Very deliberately, he lifted one of the cups and put it to his lips. Corbulo laughed. 'Your sacrifice does you credit, but the wine was tested earlier.' He beckoned Valerius across the room to where Caesar's Tower had been set up with the pieces exactly as they'd left them on the previous evening.

'You see where you went wrong?'

Valerius nodded. 'I allowed you to dominate my flanks and I did not have the strength to hold you back. The vertical movements weakened me at the moment I needed to be strong. I think I should have reinforced from the centre, but even then I suspect you would have prevented me. I still do not think in the third dimension.'

'Good. You have made another step forward.' Corbulo began moving the pieces back to their starting positions. 'I think this game is beyond recovery, but we will begin another.' He settled down on a chair on one side of the board and waved Valerius to the other. The evenings always started this way, with the game taking up the commander's attention, but Valerius had noticed a subtle change as they had gradually become more relaxed in each other's company. The breakthrough had come on the third night, when they had played in the governor's pavilion beneath a stony outcrop midway between the Orontes and the Euphrates.

'Do you understand why my officers resent you?' Corbulo had asked, pinning the younger man with his uncompromising gaze.

Valerius held his stare. 'Because they think I am here to kill you?'

'No, because they think you are here to replace me. Are you?'

Valerius laughed at the thought. 'The truth is that I have no idea why I was sent here apart from to prepare a report I wanted nothing to do with.' He didn't reveal that he had already decided what the report would say. The eastern command of Gnaeus Domitius Corbulo was as efficient, well trained and disciplined as any in the Empire. Its soldiers and officers were loyal to its general and its general loyal to Rome. He would have done his duty, Olivia would be safe and Paulinus could do with it what he would. 'I have some experience of command, but not enough to justify appointing me your deputy. You, of course, already know that, which is why you have given me command of the auxiliary cavalry, a position which is largely meaningless because of the experience of my subordinates. It also, conveniently, keeps me away from your headquarters until I am summoned, unarmed and always watched by the two guards who are never more than ten paces from your side. If I am not qualified for the job I have been sent to do, what makes you believe I would want to take on a command which will always be beyond my capability and my rank?'

Corbulo sat back and gradually a smile broke the harsh lines of his face. 'I have been asking myself the same question. Perhaps together we can come up with an answer?'

193

But the question was never raised again and gradually Valerius felt he was being taken into Corbulo's trust. Now he would be asked his thoughts on the day's dispositions, his opinions on the qualities of the commanders of his cavalry *alae*, the tactics he would use in this situation or that.

One night the subject of Khamsin came up. 'It was against my better judgement to give you such a horse, but . . .' He didn't finish the sentence and Valerius now knew for certain that the Akhal-Teke mare had been Domitia's gift, not her father's. 'I might as well have tied a millstone round your neck and ordered you to swim the river out there.' Valerius opened his mouth to protest, but Corbulo insisted on finishing his argument. 'Let me explain. On the one hand, a cavalryman without his horse is nothing, and your Khamsin makes you a formidable warrior against any enemy, even the Parthians, who ride as if they have sucked a mare's tit since birth. Yet there is a paradox, because a cavalry trooper's horse should mean nothing to him. It is his transport into the fight, a platform for his weapons, even his last meal if need be. He must be prepared to ride it to death, or ride it on to the very spear points of his foe, as long as it advances his commander's strategy. I have seen you look at her, and unless you are a man without a soul you will hesitate when the time comes. And when you hesitate, you may cost a man's life, perhaps cost your commander a battle.'

At first Valerius was uncertain how to reply, but then it came to him. He said: *'There will be a day when your soldiers are mere coins to be spent. What will you do then, when you know you must order them into the abyss?'* Corbulo raised an imperious eyebrow. 'Marcus Livius Drusus, legate of the Twentieth legion, asked me that in the September of the consulship of Titus Sextius Africanus,' Valerius explained. 'By the following July, Britain was in flames and as Boudicca of the Iceni turned her warriors on Colonia I had to ask myself the same question.'

'And?'

'I did not hesitate to sacrifice my friends. I will not hesitate to sacrifice my horse, or myself, if the need arises.'

Corbulo had nodded and Valerius understood that their relationship had altered once more. No, not altered – developed.

XXVIII

Every man in Gnaeus Domitius Corbulo's army suffered the trial of heat and dust that was the endless trek from Zeugma. The Tenth Fretensis were in the van, the place of honour behind the general they had served so well, and they suffered least, because they did not have to eat the fine dust of those who had travelled before them. Those behind, the seven full cohorts of the Fifteenth Apollinaris and their attached auxiliary light infantry, marched in a thick brown fog for hour upon hour, never knowing how far they had tramped, only aware that every step was recorded in the pains in their aching legs and another mouthful of dirt. At first they had moved with their heads high, singing their obscene marching songs, but by the fifth day they had been worn down by the relentless sterility of their surroundings. Their eyes stared out of dust-brown faces like those of men peering into a blizzard, and they walked with their shoulders hunched and their heads thrust forward as if they were trekking through a storm. But they were Roman soldiers. Legionaries. Hard as the stones that formed the grey hills which surrounded them. For twelve long years they had marched behind this man. What was another mile? Or another ten? Or another hundred? They hefted their sixty-pound loads on shoulders forged of iron and baked in their armour and never complained. They would endure. And he would give them victory.

Behind each unit came their pack animals, mules and camels, with the extra spears and the water that sustained man and beast. Next in line, the baggage carts that carried their eight-man tents with their rations and the other equipment they would need for camp each night. To right and left, ahead and in the rear ranged Valerius's cavalry patrols, alert for any sign of Parthian attack. Each night the individual units created a defensive perimeter using what materials they could. No easily cut sods for the men of the Syrian legions, just dry stone and the earth they could chop from the iron-hard ground with their picks and mattocks. Every man knew his place and his duty, whether it was pitching tents, setting up kitchens or digging latrines. Every man who didn't have sentry watch ate his meal, gulped down his ration of water and collapsed in his bedroll, trying not to dream of the next day's ordeal.

Valerius spent his days in the saddle and his evenings with his commander. Only one man knew their eventual destination and with every mile they came closer his stature and his energy seemed to grow. In Antioch, Corbulo had been a tireless administrator and accomplished diplomat, a hounder of the incompetent and the criminal, a respected judge who tempered justice with compassion, if not mercy; a proconsul, with the power, though men could only whisper it, of an Emperor. In the field, Valerius saw a different Corbulo. Here was a leader the legionaries of Rome would follow to the very ends of the earth. On the march, he suffered their every privation, roaming the columns with his aides, encouraging and cajoling. He never seemed to tire. 'Just one more mile, and then another ten,' he would shout, and they cheered him through cracked lips from throats choked with Armenian dirt. He seemed to know every soldier in an army of twenty thousand men. If he recognized a legionary he had decorated, he would dismount and walk with the man and discuss their old campaigns. If he saw a man whose hob-nailed sandals were falling apart, he would reprimand his centurion for failing to have them replaced before the campaign began. He even supervised the placement and the provisioning of the supply depots set at three-day intervals which would provide rations, fodder and water for the army on its return. But there was another

196

Corbulo still, a Corbulo honed to an edge that Valerius doubted even his daughter would recognize.

It happened early one evening, on the fourth day after they had crossed the Euphrates, as the Tenth Fretensis prepared their defensive rampart for the night. The previous day Corbulo had noticed the men discarding their weapons before they began work. With increasing signs of Parthian activity he had issued an order that all legionaries should wear their swords while digging. The commander, as always, inspected the defences while they were being dug, making recommendations for improvement and giving praise where it was due. When he reached the foundations of the northern perimeter he came across a soldier working naked, apart from a sword belt. Valerius heard later what followed.

'You are improperly dressed, soldier.'

'No, sir.' The legionary, a veteran of twenty years, who had spent half his life in the legion and half of that fighting for the man addressing him, grinned. 'The general specified that we should wear our swords while digging and I'm wearing my sword, sir.' His companions laughed and Corbulo had returned the man's smile. That night the soldier was charged with disobeying a direct order, found guilty and sentenced to death.

'You think I am being overly harsh?' the governor asked when Valerius made his evening visit to the command pavilion. 'Corbulo the man can be mocked, but not Corbulo the commander. Corbulo the commander must be obeyed.' Valerius could have argued that the legionary might have misinterpreted the order, but he knew that wasn't the point. 'Discipline is what makes us what we are. The finest fighting soldiers in the world. Discipline is what allows me to lead a force of twenty thousand against an army of fifty, sixty or seventy and still know I can win. Indiscipline is a sign of weakness. When that man challenged my authority he weakened his legion in the same way a coward weakens it when he runs from the battle line. I would be shirking my duty if I did not serve him in the same way I serve the coward. No, I am not harsh.' By now Valerius had realized that the governor was not trying to justify his actions to the tribune who shared his wine and his battles in Caesar's Tower, but to himself. 'By our code,

I would have been justified in having him beaten to death by his tent-mates, a long, painful and degrading end. Instead, he will die by the sword as he has lived by it, and men will say Corbulo has been not only just, but merciful. Discipline.'

It was only later that Valerius understood that when the general had uttered that final, fatal word, he was thinking not about the man who was about to die, but about the man who had stretched his Caesar's authority to the limit and beyond. And the price he might one day have to pay.

Corbulo ordered constant cavalry patrols to see off any Parthian scouts who threatened to approach the column. The general made it clear he thought Valerius a fool for sharing these duties with his troops. For his part, Valerius knew the only way he would learn to think like a cavalryman was to live most of his waking hours in the saddle, sharing their hardships and dangers. He spent much of his time with Hanno's Thracian auxiliaries, riding until every bone in his body ached, but he had yet to lay eyes on a Parthian warrior. In the last few days he had eaten more grit than army rations, and Hanno had been right: his tender backside was well on the way to being saddle-shaped and the texture of tanned leather.

No cities barred their way in this wilderness, but sometimes they would come across a huddle of mud-brick huts where they would be greeted by some bearded ancient expendable enough to the village to be sacrificed to dangerous Roman whim. As long as they posed no threat, Corbulo ordered these communities to be left unharmed and his quartermasters bought up every spare piece of Armenian clothing they could lay their hands on. Most cooperated, but occasionally one did not. Eventually Corbulo lost patience.

Valerius was walking Khamsin when he found Tiberius at his shoulder, bright-eyed with excitement. The young man had spent the past few days complaining that he didn't have enough responsibility. 'I am the most junior of junior tribunes,' the boy lamented. 'Of course, I would never criticize my senior officers. Legate Traianus is a fine soldier and knows his business. But . . . but it can be irksome to be told always to stand and be silent, to listen and learn. I do not have the slightest authority, even over the meanest new recruit. I try to do my duty and tell myself that I will be accepted for my diligence and commitment, but I long to be accepted. I have volunteered to take charge of those on guard duty, but I am refused even that. If there is anything . . .'

Valerius had spoken to the legate and Tiberius's face told him the situation had changed. The boy's blurted announcement confirmed it. 'I am to have my first independent command,' he boasted.

Valerius waited.

'Well,' Tiberius admitted, 'I am to be nominally in command, but I must heed the words of the centurion.'

Valerius smiled. 'And what is this epic mission?'

'Oh, it is nothing important. A few villagers drove off some of our horses and their enemies in the next hamlet claim they were sold to a Parthian patrol. I'm to lead four centuries of the fifth cohort. We are to teach them a lesson.'

The smile froze on Valerius's face. 'And do you know what form this lesson is to take?'

Tiberius shrugged. 'Burn a few huts, I suppose. I know it's not much . . .'

But Valerius had been on patrols where barbarian villages had been taught a lesson, and he feared that Tiberius might be about to learn a harsh lesson of his own.

'Look, Tiberius. It may be more than that. You may be asked to do things that seem distasteful to you.' The younger man looked mystified, but Valerius knew it was something he must discover for himself. 'Just remember that you have your orders and let the centurion take the lead. Do what you have to do, but always remember you do it for your legion and for Rome.'

He abandoned the next day's patrol so that he could be with the main column when Tiberius returned from the punitive expedition. The young tribune led his three hundred legionaries into the fort, but this was no triumphal entry. He rode straight-backed, as always, never looking right or left, but even from a distance Valerius could see the unnatural set of his mouth and the blood that stained his face and armour.

Later, he found Tiberius sitting alone in his tent staring at his hands. The boy didn't look up when Valerius entered. When he spoke his voice was as cold as an empty grave.

'They were women and children, mostly, and a few old men, but you knew that. It was what you tried to warn me about yesterday. The centurion took charge and told me to stay close. We surrounded the village, so not as much as a mouse could escape, and then we advanced. There had been no orders, but I realized later that the men had done this so often that they didn't need them. They herded the villagers into the centre – there must have been a hundred of them – and the centurion read out a decree from Traianus that the people could not understand. Women were weeping. No screaming, not then. There were children, too young to know what was going on, playing and laughing. A pretty little girl looked up at me and smiled. I . . . didn't understand what was happening at first. But then the centurion told me to draw my sword. It was orders, he said: no man could stand back from the dirty work. The legate wanted me blooded, and I would be blooded. Then we killed them. No, we butchered them. It didn't take long. Three hundred swords against a hundred unarmed women and children, it wouldn't, would it? The little girl was still smiling when I killed her. Then I killed her sister and mother. When we finished they were just a big pile of corpses in a spreading lake of blood. The centurion was pleased. Quick and clean, he said, and no opposition.' He shook his head. 'I can kill, Valerius, believe me when I say I am a very good killer. But I did not come here to slaughter women and children because their menfolk might have stolen a few horses.'

'You didn't kill them because they stole a few horses.' Valerius kept his voice harsh. He knew sympathy was the last thing Tiberius needed. 'You killed them because it was your duty. That was the lesson Traianus wanted you to learn. Duty is everything. A legionary must not only be disciplined. He must be hard. Remember what you said when I told you my plan on the ship? *You're as hard as the iron in that* gladius *you wear*. Well, this is the world we inhabit, Tiberius. Traianus decided an

200

example must be made and if an example is to be made there is no place for pity or mercy. What would happen if every village on our line of march believed they could steal our horses with impunity? That would only be the beginning. They'd start raiding the supply lines, killing our sentries, and because we weren't strong enough or hard enough to make a proper example the whole country would band together and believe they could defeat us. Then how many would we be forced to kill? Not a hundred, not even a thousand. Ten thousand, and the rest would be taken as slaves. Hundreds of your comrades would be dead. By doing your duty and killing those Armenian villagers, you saved Roman lives. Occasionally, you will be given an order you do not agree with, like today. But always remember, there is a greater purpose.' He clapped the younger man on the shoulder. 'This is the army, Tiberius. If your commander tells you to march off a cliff, all you can do is ask which spot would give him the most pleasure.'

'I will try to remember that. I wish . . .'

Valerius made a decision. 'Tomorrow I am taking out a patrol.' For the first time, Tiberius looked up and met his eyes. 'I doubt we will encounter any Parthians, but at least it will give you the chance to carry your sword against a proper enemy.'

XXIX

Rome, September AD 66

An almighty crash filled the room as the golden table and its contents smashed to the marble floor. The palace slaves froze in position, careful not to let their eyes stray to where the Emperor Nero Claudius Germanicus Caesar stood, chest heaving, his entire body shaking. Even Tigellinus stepped back from the white heat of his master's rage.

'You mean he is still alive?'

'We have yet to identify . . .'

'How many Gauls of senatorial rank can there be? A dozen? A hundred? Put them all to the question. Find this upstart. How can I rule if I do not have authority? How can I have authority when some rustic pig farmer undermines me at every turn? I have seen the reports. Secret meetings attended by hundreds in the very heart of Lugdunum. I know what he calls me . . . M-m-m-m . . .' Foam flecked Nero's lips and Tigellinus thought he might have a seizure. 'M-m-m-urd-d-derer. The spawn of H-h-hades says I debauched m-my own m-m-mother.' Nero's voice rose to a scream. 'I want him found! I want him dead!' The wild eyes flickered and in an instant the shaking subsided. A small boy's voice emerged from his mouth. 'I want him dead, Tigellinus. And the rest.'

'The rest, Caesar?' Tigellinus's voice sounded as if the noose was already tightening on his neck.

'I know you have been keeping it from me.'

The Praetorian prefect's heart seemed to stop. How much did he know? 'Caesar?'

Now the eyes were cold as a German winter and that was even more frightening than what had gone before.

'You thought it was for the best.'

Tigellinus struggled to keep control of his bladder.

'You wanted to protect me.'

'Of course, Caesar.'

'They are all in it. The German legions, Otho in Lusitania, Galba in Hispana, Maximus in Britannia . . .'

'We cannot be sure, Caesar. The German governors certainly, but between them they hold sway over four legions. We must not act until they have been neutralized.'

'You have a plan, Tigellinus? Of course, you have a plan.'

'We must make them think they are safe. Believe they are being considered for high honour. Summon them to some place far from their strength. Seize their families while they are on the road. Then strike.'

'Strike, yes.' The small porcine eyes were unnaturally bright. 'But where?'

Tigellinus pondered the question as if he had never considered it. 'Greece,' he said finally.

Nero's plump features broke into a dreamy smile as they always did when they talked about the home of the gods. The visit had been arranged for months. In exchange for an announcement of perpetual freedom from tribute the Greeks had agreed to hold the Olympic Games two years in advance so that he could take part. 'Of course, Greece. But can we wait so long?'

'Their treason is in its infancy, Caesar,' Tigellinus assured him. 'Your hold on the army is strong. They dare not act without the collusion of the others and the others are fearful. I would not have agreed to your absence if I had doubts. Your popularity with the people has never been greater. Telesinus and Paulinus, who will share the consulship, are among your most loyal supporters in the Senate, and in any case their every word and deed will be monitored. At the first sign of treasonous behaviour my agents have orders to act.'

'Vespasian is still our loyal servant?'

'None more so, Caesar.' Tigellinus was no longer so sure of that. Certain facts had come to his attention which cast doubt on the senator from Falacrinae. But the conversation had reached a point he had willed it to reach, and Vespasian could wait. He had other prey in mind.

For all Nero's fears about his German legates and the governors of Lusitania, Hispania and Britannia, Tigellinus knew that only one man posed the ultimate threat. The others might send their little notes and hold their little meetings, but they would never act on their own. Only Gnaeus Domitius Corbulo had the stature, the determination and the military strength to supplant his Emperor. But did he have the will? Offonius Tigellinus was not certain, but he had long ago decided that, for the sake of the Empire, Corbulo must die. Little by little, he had undermined Nero's steadfast faith in his most successful general. Now he heard the words he had hoped for.

'And Corbulo?'

Tigellinus reached into the document case he always carried and retrieved a dispatch which had arrived by fast courier earlier in the day. He watched with satisfaction as Nero absorbed the details, his face growing paler and his hands beginning to shake. 'I was keeping it for a more appropriate time, when I hoped to verify the detail. However, the broad outline seems indisputable.'

'He is acting against my specific orders.'

'I am sure he has his reasons, Caesar, but . . .'

'No!' The word emerged as a groan. 'His *imperium* gives him power within the boundaries of the Empire. This is an invasion of a sovereign state. A direct violation of my command to act defensively and in concert with the governor of Judaea. He has exceeded his authority and usurped his Emperor's. No. He is acting as if he *is* Emperor. You say you have an agent in place?'

Tigellinus nodded.

The broad nostrils flared and the pale eyes took on a reptilian look that sent a shiver through Tigellinus. 'Then something strange happened. The face seemed to collapse in upon itself, and tears streamed down the pink cheeks. 'Not Corbulo.'

'Yes.' Tigellinus found he could barely breathe. 'He has deceived and betrayed his Emperor.'

Nero looked up. 'Not betrayed. Not yet. I must have more before I condemn Rome's greatest general. I must have evidence of treason.'

Tigellinus bit back a scream of frustration. The final piece had been in place only for the game to be snatched away from him.

But Nero would have his evidence.

No matter what it cost.

XXX

Each night now was colder than the one which had preceded it and Valerius shivered in the familiar pre-dawn gloom as he waited for the men of his patrol to form up.

For the mission, he wore the uniform of a lowly auxiliary cavalry prefect. There was no point in advertising himself as a senior Roman officer and inviting capture by some eagle-eyed Parthian scout, along with whatever horrors would inevitably follow. He had convinced the Tenth's legate that it would be good experience for Tiberius to accompany a patrol and he watched as the young Roman swapped his plate armour for a coat of linked iron rings sewn on to a supple leather tunic, and his ornate polished helmet for the crude pot-shaped headgear favoured by the Thracians. Like all his comrades, over the ring-mail he wore a hooded cloak of fine linen which had once been white. The cloth would stop the iron mail becoming so hot during the long day in the sun that it would blister the skin of anyone who touched it. Tiberius couldn't shoot the short bow with any accuracy, so he and Valerius carried the long *spatha* swords and the light oval shield of the auxiliary cavalry.

As ranking officer, Valerius was theoretically in charge of the thirty-man patrol. In reality he was happy to cede authority to Caladus, a wiry decurion with a greying beard and twenty years' service in the saddle. His sleep-dulled mind sharpened with the passing minutes and he felt the tension grow as the men checked their equipment to the accompaniment of the usual murmur of subdued voices, the snicker of horses and the faint jingle of metal harness decorations. They had yet to meet any Parthian scouts, but other patrols had picked up traces of their presence: the unburied remains of a campfire in a narrow defile, horse tracks in the dust and scattered manure from more than one animal carelessly left in the lee of a hilltop where a man might watch for signs of the Roman column. It was only a matter of time.

As the men formed pairs, Caladus rode the line making a last inspection of their equipment. He drew up when he came to Valerius.

'She's a pretty little thing,' he indicated Khamsin. 'But she stands out like a *signifer* in a parade of vestal virgins. Better to take one of these ugly bastards.' He pointed to the stocky, long-haired ponies the Thracian troopers rode. 'They might not make as good eating, but you can ride them to Hades and back and they never complain.'

'I'll stay with what I have.' Valerius slapped the horse's shoulder. 'She's never let me down yet.'

'Suit yourself.' The decurion grinned wickedly. 'But don't come crying to me when you're running for your life holding on to somebody else's tail, with a hairy arse spouting shit into your face and the Parthians taking odds on who's going to have your balls for a wedding present.'

'You should have that man whipped for insubordination.' Tiberius scowled at Caladus's back as they left the security of the temporary camp. He had the usual high-born Roman's contempt for the lowly paid auxiliaries who made up half the army. He also had the resilience of the young. The events of the previous day had not been mentioned again. 'It would teach him to respect a Roman officer.'

'And make him less willing to fight for me,' Valerius pointed out. 'Half of these men are Thracians, Tiberius, and half are Syrians. They understand that no Roman general, even Domitius Corbulo, values an auxiliary's life at one tenth that of a Roman citizen. If they weren't cavalry they would spend their entire service in some fly-blown desert fort where no legionary would ever set foot. They know the Parthians and they know this land. Out there we will depend on them, because in a crisis we don't have the skills or the experience to survive. If anything happens, you could do much worse than stick closer to Caladus than a tick on a sheep's back.'

They rode northeast, at an angle to the rising sun, so they would not be blinded as it climbed over the far horizon. For the past two days the column had marched across a great undulating plain of dry red earth and black rocks. The ground was cut by the occasional narrow riverbed where thin streams of filthy water crept sluggishly through shallow pools over porous rock and evil-looking, rainbow-hued mud. Caladus knew from experience that no matter how slowly they rode, the patrol would inevitably kick up a cloud of dust that would alert every Parthian within five miles. His solution, when they were far enough from the column, was to take the bulk of the patrol into any likely watercourse that appeared to lead approximately east, but to leave a single rider to spot for dust on the plain above. The tactic slowed their progress, but made them invisible to the enemy while ensuring that no Parthian could cross the plain undetected within a radius of ten miles.

It was dull work, but it had allowed Valerius the opportunity to get to know, after a fashion, the men who served under him. The bulk were Thracians, horse warriors seduced from their native plains to serve the Empire on the promise of citizenship and a grant of land if they survived twenty-five years of brutal service. Tiberius Draco, the soldier riding at his side, was a veteran with three wooden teeth and a scar running diagonally across his lower face from the left side of his top lip to the right side of his jaw. In mumbled dog Latin Draco recited how he had been given the choice of enlistment or slavery when a patrol arrived at his farm on the Black Sea coast demanding payment of taxes. The young auxiliary on Valerius's left was more forthcoming. Like Hanno, the Third Thracian commander, Hassan was Syrian-born. White teeth shining like pearls through his black beard, the son of a Damascus trading family cheerfully told Valerius he had travelled to Rome and marvelled at the wonders he saw there. All he had desired since was to win Roman citizenship and return to make his fortune. He laughed off the dangers of his profession. 'If

I had stayed in Damascus counting my father's profits I would have died of boredom by now. Here, at least, I am honoured for my skills and my loyalty.'

Valerius remembered the young auxiliaries who had fought and died for him in Britain. Bela, the cavalry commander who had taken a spear point in the belly defending the fleeing refugees of Colonia, but who had stayed in the saddle and fought to the last as the city burned. And Matykas who had sacrificed himself and his troop to give the last remnant of Valerius's defeated force time to retreat to the Temple of Claudius. Warriors. Soldiers. Men who had died for a Rome he had once believed in and would gladly have died for himself. A Rome worthy of the men who fought for it. But did that Rome still exist? He was no republican, but in the years since he had returned, scarred and changed, from Britain, he had experienced a different Rome — Nero's Rome — and been repelled by the perfumed stink of degeneracy, degradation and corruption. He had come to realize that in the new Rome, the Emperor did not rule for his people, or for the Empire, but for himself and the small circle of self-serving acolytes who surrounded him. When he thought of Nero, he was reminded of a wriggling maggot growing fat on the putrefying flesh of a decomposing corpse. The pursuit of power and profit and advancement drove the new Rome. Fear and doubt and envy ruled it.

Tiberius rode up beside him and he put the treasonous notion back where it belonged. Right or wrong, Nero had been born to rule.

'I thought it would be more exciting,' the young tribune complained. 'This country is less appealing than the desert which almost killed me. All we've done is skulk like criminals along these open sewers as if we feared the Parthians.'

'You may be a warrior, Tiberius,' Valerius smiled, 'but you have a great deal to learn about war. War is five parts waiting, three parts marching, one part watching and the final part equally divided between fighting and dying. A soldier learns not to be in too much of a hurry to reach that final part. And you would be right to fear the Parthians. Have you read Herodotus?'

The young man shook his head. 'My father believed that books weakened a man's will to fight. That they made him spend too much time thinking when he should be exercising in arms.'

Valerius bit back the automatic response this folly deserved and said instead, 'Herodotus writes that when Xerxes the Great passed this way to fight the Greeks he brought with him an army of Persians, Medes, Assyrians, Cissians, Arians, Caspians, Indians, Utians, Arabians, Babylonians, Mycans and Ethiopians.'

'This Xerxes was a Parthian?'

'A Persian, but of the Parthian line. My point is that his army was so great that it covered the land like a great black stain and wherever it went it left behind only devastation and grief. So great that no one, not even the king, knew how great. At a place called Doriscus Xerxes decided to count the warriors under his command. He ordered ten thousand men to form tight together and a circle was drawn around them, which was then fenced. The circle was filled again, and again, until none was left uncounted. It's said they filled the circle one hundred and seventy times. They swept everything before them.'

'Yet the Greeks defeated the Persians?'

'Yes, but the Greeks had Alexander.'

'And we have General Corbulo.'

Valerius nodded.

'Does the general fear the Parthians?'

'No, but he respects them.'

'Then I will respect them, too.'

Ahead of them, Caladus called a halt. 'This is far enough if we're to return before dark. No excitement today.'

He led them up the bank of the gully and back on to the featureless plain.

XXXI

The patrol had ridden less than a mile after they emerged from the gully when they discovered that Caladus didn't have a monopoly on invisibility.

A desperate shout from the flank guard was choked off instantly by the arrow that skewered his throat. Parthian cavalry swarmed from a stream bed two hundred paces away and broke left and right in a movement that threatened to encircle the auxiliaries. Caladus roared at his men to form up and without looking to see who followed kicked his horse into a charge. Valerius was slower to react, and as the Thracian decurion passed to his front Caladus shouted a warning. 'Get out of here. I haven't enough men to protect you. Ride for it.'

For answer, Valerius nudged Khamsin so she spun on her hooves after the auxiliary commander. Within four strides they were flank to flank and Caladus turned to check who was with him.

'Fool,' he said, but his face split into a savage grin and the wild light of battle shone bright in his eyes.

Valerius matched his grin. 'We fight together and we die together.'

'Fuck dying.' Caladus broke off to shout orders to his men. 'They'll be a mix of archers and spearmen. You and the boy take the spearmen. That way you'll have a chance.' Valerius looked up and for the first time was able to study the enemy horsemen. He saw immediately that

211

Caladus was right. They might be outnumbered, but at least half of the force opposing them carried ten-foot-long, narrow-pointed spears which were only of use at close range. 'Their archers will want to take as many of us with the first volley as they can, and then trade us shot for shot. We have to make it difficult for them. They're here for information and plunder. They don't like dying for nothing. The answer is to kill them. *Kill them!*' the Thracian screamed. 'Kill every last one of the gutless bastards!'

In a confusion of dust raised by thundering hooves, Valerius hauled his sword clear of its scabbard and called out to Tiberius. A voice answered from his right and together they swerved towards a group of Parthians streaming across the flank who had been surprised by the speed of the Roman counter-attack. An arrow flicked off his pot-helmet with a metallic clatter and he instinctively hunched over Khamsin's neck to make himself a smaller target. The next pair of shafts lodged in the ash shield fixed to his walnut fist. He glanced to his left and there was Hassan, grinning through his beard, with the short recurved bow strung and an arrow nocked and ready to fly. More blows on the shield before something slammed him high in the chest with enough force to knock him backwards. He almost fell, but the little mare adjusted her stride beneath him and he managed to stay in the saddle. He waited for the pain to come. The shock of the blow had numbed his body, but the arrow must have bitten deep, the needle point buried in the flesh of his breast. But when he dared to look down he saw the wooden shaft dangling from the ringed mail beneath his cloak. The point had penetrated the iron, but the heavy leather tunic beneath had saved him from serious injury. A man cried out to his god and Khamsin swerved to avoid the fallen body beneath her hooves, but Valerius concentrated on the half-dozen galloping figures ahead of him, picking out a spearman in a bright green tunic. He heard the *ziiipp* of an arrow as Hassan fired from his side and a horse in the centre of the Parthian line reared up screaming with a shaft buried to the feathers in its chest. Why weren't the Parthian archers aiming for the horses? He remembered Hanno's words at the bridge. A *Parthian would sacrifice his wife before he would sacrifice his horse*. Caladus had said they were here for plunder. Of course, they would want to capture the Roman mounts if they could. Valerius felt the battle madness fill him. He had no thought of victory or defeat. All he wanted to do was kill. If the spearmen charged, they might blunt the Roman attack, but they seemed reluctant to move, preferring to allow the archers to do the work for them. In a few strides it would be too late. Now, at last, they were moving. A sharp cry from his left and he glanced aside in time to see Tiberius's look of astonishment as he was thrown clean over his mount's shoulder as the beast went down in a welter of dust and flailing hooves. His mind registered the fact, but they were gone in an instant, and his focus stayed fixed on the rider he had picked out. In that odd symmetry of battle the Parthian also seemed to have chosen Valerius as his prey. He was accompanied by a second horseman and together their spears came down so that they were lined up on the Roman's chest, wicked needle points gleaming in the dying light of the sun. Small details. Dark, glaring eyes and snarling mouths. A flash of gold on the right-hand rider's wrist. The decorative scarlet plume on a horse's forehead. Without conscious thought Valerius's mind calculated speed and distance, the angle of attack, which had forced them slightly to their left. Less than twenty strides now. He saw the second man drop back a little. Two spears, one to Valerius's right flank, the other to his left. The first to draw his shield and open up his defences. The second to skewer him. No amount of mail and leather would stop a point with the weight of man and horse behind it. He knew he was dead, but pride would not let him turn away. He was a soldier. This was how soldiers died. He screamed out loud, anticipating the moment. Counted the heartbeats. The second horse faltering, its rider catapulted from the saddle by an arrow that pierced his screaming mouth with such power that only the feathers were left visible. The merciless eyes of the first, unaware he was now alone, the spear held two-handed and angled across his body. Valerius took the point on his shield and forced it past his head, feeling the breath of the iron across his cheek. Safe inside the point, the long blade of Corbulo's sword was already slashing upwards in a backhand cut that raked the spearman's iron-clad chest before taking him below the chin in a terrible blow that split his face from bearded jaw to the rim of his iron helm, carving through bone and teeth and gristle and splitting his eye socket in two. Valerius had a momentary vision of horror and felt the splash of hot blood and then he was past, seeking out the archers who hadn't joined the charge.

But the archers were no longer there. He hauled Khamsin round and had a moment of breathless clarity. Hassan and the Thracians who had accompanied him were circling, seeking targets, but never staying still long enough to be targets themselves. Within the dust cloud of the battle, riders of both sides darted in and out of the fray. Valerius noticed a horse standing over a still figure with its head bowed and he remembered Tiberius's sickening fall. He started towards the little tableau, but the horse was a roan, and Tiberius had been riding a grey. Desperately, he searched the dust for his friend. A gust of dry wind cleared the murk for a second and at last he found him. Tiberius crouched behind his dead mount, with a shield in one hand and the jagged remnant of a sword in the other. The shield had been pierced by a dozen arrows, the points three inches through the layers of ash, and the body of the grey was thick with others. Parthians hovered like vultures to his front and flanks looking for the killer shot. Even as Valerius watched, Tiberius staggered and almost fell with an arrow through his right leg. But he was alive. For the moment.

'Hassan!' The Syrian turned at the shout and followed Valerius's pointing finger. Taking in the situation with a glance, he nodded and galloped towards Tiberius, calling his comrades with him. The enemy archers saw the danger and prudently retired to seek easier prey.

Tiberius looked up as Valerius rode towards him and raised a weary hand in salute.

Valerius was still fifty feet away when he sensed movement at the outer edge of his vision. In the next second the image crystallized into a charging Parthian spearman with his lance couched and the point aimed at the centre of Tiberius's back. He screamed a warning, but the young Roman either didn't hear him or was too shocked to react.

Valerius kicked Khamsin into a gallop. He knew he had no chance of reaching Tiberius in time, but he had to try. In desperation, he altered course to intercept the enemy spear. The Parthian only had eyes for his victim and he could already taste the joy of an easy kill. His first indication of danger was a flash of iron to his left, but as he dragged his ten-foot ash spear round to meet it, he was already too late. Khamsin smashed into the Parthian's flank, a thousand pounds of solid muscle at full gallop, sending horse and man tumbling with a crash fit to wake the gods. The impact threw Valerius from the saddle, the breath knocked out of him and his sword sent flying. He felt the skin of his right cheek tear as he skidded across the unyielding earth. Desperately, he struggled to his knees to find the Parthian staggering towards him. The man's spear had snapped in the collision, but he had recovered the final four feet with its gleaming spiked tip and now he held it in front of him like a sword. A big man, with a heavy beard, his nose had been smashed almost flat when he landed. But he was determined and he was dangerous and he only had one aim as he advanced towards the unarmed Roman.

Valerius let him come. His eyes flickered between those of his opponent and the point of the spear, searching for the moment of decision. In many ways it was easier to face a man with a spear. A sword could come at you from any angle, but a spear had only one focus of attack. The question was: high or low? The throat or the guts? Which would he choose? A gutter fighter might feint with his eyes or the spear point, but the Parthian's tentative approach suggested that he was more accustomed to fighting on horseback than man to man on foot. High or low? The eyes said low and the spear followed them. Valerius twisted in a desperate sidestep that allowed the point to crease his right side, then spun along the shaft to smash the spearman in front of the ear with a fist of solid walnut that had all his weight behind it. The impact should have crushed the weak point of his enemy's skull, but the blow was high and the rim of the Parthian's helmet sapped the force of it.

The big man roared like a bull elephant and his arms enveloped Valerius, who realized when a leg wrapped round his that he had underestimated his opponent. The Parthian might not be a gutter fighter, but someone had taught him to wrestle. Sensing his advantage, the spearman used his weight to unbalance Valerius and they fell, the Parthian's bulk pinning the Roman to the ground. Valerius bucked and wriggled for all he was worth, lashing out with both hands and kicking with his iron-shod feet, but he could make no headway against the implacable solidity of the man whose only aim was to kill him. The Parthian had recovered his spear and now he stabbed the point down at Valerius's face. Somehow, Valerius managed to get his left hand to the other man's wrist in time to check the plunging iron. At the same time he smashed at his enemy's face with the wooden fist, but the Parthian ignored the blows as if they came from a child. Slowly, a hair's breadth at a time, the needle tip drew closer, aimed unerringly for Valerius's right eyeball. Screaming with frustration and fear, the Roman used every desperate ounce of his strength to arrest the progress of that wicked iron spike. The Parthian's lips curled back from his yellowing teeth and his hand shook as he maintained the pressure, but the movement was unrelenting and Valerius let out an involuntary cry as he felt the point touch his eyelid. The cry was echoed by the Parthian, but it was no yell of victory. His eyes bulged and the pressure on Valerius's left hand eased at the same time as he heard an obscene crunching sound. With a last shuddering intake of breath the spearman fell to one side to reveal Tiberius, swaying on his feet and with the jagged stump of the sword bloody in his hand.

'I think we are level now,' the young tribune said, before his eyes rolled up in his head and he collapsed in a dead faint.

XXXII

Sweat ran in rivulets from Tiberius's forehead and he bit so hard into the strip of toughened leather that Valerius wondered his teeth didn't break. His eyes were screwed tight shut in a face set in a grimace of pure agony that twitched with every movement of the iron forceps.

Gaius Spurinna, Corbulo's personal physician, and a man with a wit as dry as the old bones he transported with him everywhere, kept up a cheerful running commentary as he worked. The bones had been collected for scientific study from the battlefield at Carrhae just south of their route, and he speculated that a particularly fine backbone might have belonged to Crassus himself.

'If you had been more fortunate the arrowhead would have continued through to pierce the other side of the leg and I would have been able to saw it off and withdraw the shaft as sweet as a prick from a silky virgin crack. Of course, you wouldn't have enjoyed the sawing. Then again, you could have bled out before your comrade here got you back to me, so we must be thankful for what we have.'

Tiberius didn't appear thankful. Despite the tincture of poppy Spurinna had administered his face had taken on the colour of grey parchment. As the physician worked, his head began to thrash from side to side in his delirium and Valerius was forced to push down hard on his shoulders to keep him still.

217

'The trick is to manoeuvre the grip of the forceps around the head of the arrow and therefore nullify the effect of the barb, whilst doing so without disturbing any of the major tubes which facilitate blood flow and killing the patient. As you can appreciate, it requires a combination of delicacy and strength which only a physician of my exceptional attributes has at his disposal. Hold still, damn you. A sip of wine, please.' Valerius placed the cup to his lips. 'In your case the operation is made more problematic by the fact that the arrowhead appears to be lodged in the complex group of bones which make up the knee. Fortunately, you are in the hands of no ordinary physician, but a man who knows his bones. In the hands of an ordinary physician you might be reduced to crawling on all fours like a dog. Yes!' Tiberius gave a low howl not unlike a dog. Gaius Spurinna grunted with effort and his muscles bulged as he worked the forceps free with an obscene sucking sound, slowly bringing the shaft of the arrow with them. When it was clear, he gave a huge sigh, drained his wine and refilled the cup before washing the point of the arrow clean in it.

'With a little good fortune, it won't have been poisoned – for barbarians the Parthians are relatively civilized – and it carried no cloth into the wound, so if my theory is correct the chances of mortification are reduced. You may thank me, my boy. It is possible you may yet live to die on the battlefield.'

He looked down at Tiberius, who was drifting in and out of consciousness, muttering to himself like a child in a dream.

'Ungrateful wretch.' Spurinna smiled benevolently. 'Come,' he said to Valerius. 'We will report to the general. He favours the boy, you know.'

Valerius was about to follow, but Tiberius's next words fetched him up short of the door.

'I cannot do it. I cannot.' There was something desperate in the way he spoke, as if he was pleading with someone only he could see. 'Honour. Duty. Discipline. Honour, duty . . .' The mantra faded as Valerius took the young man's hand in his. 'Yes!' Tiberius's eyes opened, but they were looking at something beyond the tent and Valerius made the sign against evil. 'Yes, I see. It is clear now. I have no choice.' The eyes closed again and his harsh breathing subsided.

Relieved, Valerius stood up to go, but a last whispered word froze him in place.

'Treason.'

The army of the Corbulo travelled steadily northeast, skirting a range of low, featureless hills and alert for darting raids by the now everpresent Parthian scouts. Valerius stayed with the column, regularly checking on Tiberius's progress in the two-wheeled cart that had been cleared for him.

Tiberius was still weary and talked of nothing but getting back into the saddle, but gradually Valerius steered the conversation round to what was concerning him.

'When you were under the poppy you still seemed troubled by what happened at the village.'

Jammed into the corner among sacks of grain to reduce the effect of iron-shod wheels jolting across the rocks, Tiberius shook his head. 'I can remember very little apart from Spurinna's gentle ministrations.' He smiled. 'Besides, I know you were right. A Roman soldier's job is to obey, and let others concern themselves with things like morality and justice.'

'There was something else. An unguarded word. A word that can never be spoken lightly. Treason.'

For a few moments Tiberius might have been made of stone; then his expression changed. 'It's just a word. I didn't know what I was saying.'

Valerius said steadily, 'If there is something you know, Tiberius, you must tell me. It is much more dangerous to keep the knowledge to yourself.'

Tiberius hesitated. 'There is talk.'

'Talk of what? There is always talk. Have you ever met a soldier who didn't have something to complain about? If they're not complaining about the food, it's the quality of their boots or the weight of their shields. A thousand years from now soldiers will still be grumbling about the same things.'

'This is different,' Tiberius insisted. 'This is the officers, not the men. They wonder why we are here. In Judaea, a Roman province is being torn apart and Roman soldiers are dying. An eagle has been lost and Rome's honour dragged through the dirt. Yet we are marching in the opposite direction.'

'We are here because Corbulo has led us here,' Valerius interrupted. 'And where the general leads we follow. Somewhere out there the Parthian army is marching north to invade Armenia. With their king in Rome, the Armenians will stay in their fortresses and try to wait out the storm, but the storm will inevitably overwhelm them. The only way to stop the Parthians is to intercept and destroy them.'

Tiberius answered, 'Do not mistake me, tribune; the Tenth worships the general. They do not fear what awaits them if they fail, only the consequences if they succeed.'

Valerius gave a sigh. This was exactly what Vespasian had feared and Paulinus had hinted at. But the die was cast. 'General Corbulo is proconsul of the east; the Emperor has granted him *imperium*. He sees the greater long-term threat from the Parthians and he has the authority to make his own decisions. Do not concern yourself with strategy, Tiberius,' he said more gently. 'We are soldiers, you and I, and it is a soldier's duty to obey. Our loyalty is to Rome and to the Emperor, just as the general's is.'

'But that is why I spoke out.' Tiberius lowered his voice to a whisper. 'If the general succeeds there is talk of proclaiming him Emperor in Nero's place.'

On the fourth day after the ambush they entered a broad, flat plain a day's march across, and Tiberius, aided by the healing powers of youth, was back in the saddle, though he winced with every step his horse took. Valerius knew he would have to report the young tribune's revelation at some point, but the time never seemed right. Corbulo's army had been on the march for thirteen consecutive days and Valerius sensed his general's confidence growing with every passing hour.

His suspicions were confirmed when the Roman commander summoned a conference of his senior officers. An elaborate sand table was set up in the headquarters tent and Corbulo stood over it, with the Tenth's legate Marcus Ulpius Traianus to his left and Aulus Marius Celsus, who commanded the contingent of the Fifteenth Apollinaris, to his right. Valerius waited with the commanders of the auxiliary detachments. In addition to Valerius's cavalry wings, Corbulo's legions were accompanied by ten cohorts of Syrian and Numidian infantry, equally split between spear- and bowmen, two cohorts of Cretan slingers who could take a man's eye out at fifty paces, and a cohort of mountain troops. The specialized skills of these wiry highlanders, recruited from distant Noricum, would be invaluable if Vologases decided to make directly for Artaxata through the mountain country east of the great inland sea which was marked on Corbulo's sand map by a large silver bowl. The general's aides had placed small banners on the table to show the relative positions of the Roman and Parthian armies. Between the column and the sea lay a great flat plain bounded by mountains to north and south.

Corbulo leaned over the sand table and Valerius had an image of a great eagle sweeping over the landscape and taking in everything below. At last, he raised his head and the grey eyes surveyed the men in the room as if he was seeking out some buried fear or weakness.

'Tigranocerta.' He pointed to a banner on the edge of the hills at the eastern end of the plain. 'Three days' march away, the strongest fortress in the kingdom and the key to southern Armenia. I believe King Vologases must take it if he is to advance on Artaxata with any prospect of success. The governor is a client of Rome's ally, King Tiridates, and he has sent word that while he cannot help us, neither will he hinder our passage. By now, Vologases' scouts will have informed him of our strength, our progress and our line of march. Given the disparity in our forces, he will expect us to march directly for Tigranocerta either to bolster its defences or to bring him to battle outside its walls where we will have the support,' he gave a thin smile, 'for what it is worth, of our Armenian allies. Either event will give him pause, but neither will stop him. If we fight from within Tigranocerta, he will be confident that he can bottle us up and starve us out. In open battle, he outnumbers us three to one and if we give him the opportunity he will destroy

221

us, winning eternal fame as the man who defeated Gnaeus Domitius Corbulo. I will not let that happen.' The final six words were rapped out with the unrelenting certainty of an executioner's axe.

'The main Parthian army is here.' He pointed to a group of flags positioned beyond the hills to the south of the plain and grouped by the side of a snaking line that must be the Tigris. 'They will follow the traditional invasion route along the river, which provides them with a guaranteed source of water for men and horses.' He frowned as his finger traced the winding route through the mountains. 'His is a mobile army, but they cannot travel faster than their supplies. The route is narrow. It will take time. More important, it will give us time. Gentlemen, I mean to meet Vologases and I mean to stop him. Here, north of Cepha.'

Every eye homed in on the pointing finger. The Tigris wound its way through the mountains and eventually entered a broad, steep-sided valley. So narrow it was barely visible, a second valley cut northwards through the hills which were the last natural barrier between the Parthians and Tigranocerta, creating an avenue to the plain. Valerius pictured it in his mind. The valley was a dagger in the heart of Corbulo's plans. Through here, Vologases' mighty army would stream in their regiments and their divisions to deploy on the flatlands ready for the final march on the fortress. But . . .

'We cannot afford to meet him in the open. Crassus made that mistake when he faced Surenas at Carrhae and the Parthians destroyed his army one piece at a time. When Paetus campaigned here not five years ago, Tiridates served him the same way. A hundred archers, charging to fire, then retreating before our own could reply. A thousand minor engagements, each one causing more casualties, more confusion and more uncertainty. No, it will not be that way.' He picked up the banner representing his army and placed it at the north end of the valley. 'We will draw Vologases deep into the valley and there we will hold him, like a stopper in the mouth of a wineskin.'

'With respect, general . . . ?' Corbulo nodded to Traianus to continue. 'How are we to do that with less than two legions and a few auxiliaries? The King of Kings is no fool. Is it not possible you are leading us into a trap of our own making? You are inviting the Parthians to do to us what they did to Crassus. Attack and retreat. Kill and kill again with impunity. Their archers will bleed us dry and when at last we are forced to withdraw, their armoured heavy cavalry will cut us to pieces on the open plain. Surely it is better to fight beneath the walls of Tigranocerta where we at least have a line of retreat?'

Corbulo smiled, but it was a smile that contained a warning. Traianus, who had served with his commander in the Armenian campaigns of three years earlier, saw the look and seemed to shrink inside his uniform.

'Brave words, Traianus, and prudent ones. It is a fortunate commander who has officers willing to risk all if they believe he is wrong.' Corbulo allowed his words to hang in the air until the tension was almost unbearable. 'But I do not believe I am wrong. Vologases is indeed no fool, but, like every Parthian ruler before him, he leads an army not of regiments but of war bands, each with its own warlord, and each with its own strengths . . . and weaknesses. Not all of those leaders are as enthusiastic about this enterprise as the King of Kings. They have been forced to strip their lands bare before the final harvest is in, and now their women must do the work of men and slaves. They believe the eyes of Rome are fixed upon Judaea and they have a free hand here. He has convinced them that they will meet little opposition and the Armenians will welcome them. The last thing they expect is to meet a Roman army. Unless he achieves a quick victory and the plunder he has promised them they will soon pine for the warmth of their own hearths. Time is my enemy's enemy, Traianus. If we can stop them and hurt them, Vologases will retreat back to Ctesiphon, Tiridates will return to his throne and Armenia will be a Roman province for generations to come.' The pale, intractable eyes fixed the other man. 'Put your faith in me, Traianus.'

Traianus hesitated, studying the sand table in front of him and frowning over the narrow cleft as if he was seeing the army's doom. Eventually, he looked up. 'Very well, we can stop them. But how do we hurt them badly enough to force Vologases to retire?'

Valerius had been as intent on the sand map as the Tenth's

commander and it was only gradually that he realized that every eye in the room was now fixed on him. He raised his head and found himself meeting Corbulo's implacable gaze.

'That will be the mission of my loyal commander of cavalry, Gaius Valerius Verrens.'

XXXIII

Valerius knew his general well enough by now to recognize the moment of drama on which the whole performance hinged. Corbulo had drawn them in. Played on their fears. Now he was about to reveal his genius. But that genius depended on the fighting powers of Valerius Verrens and his cavalry and Valerius wondered how he was expected to live up to his commander's hopes.

While Corbulo had outlined his strategy to Traianus, Valerius had been concentrating on the map, trying to understand how his cavalry would fit into the general's battle plans. No matter how hard he looked, he could not see it. He could visualize the valley, a mere slice in a ridge of sand on the map table, but in reality perhaps a mile wide, with steep, weathered sides. If he guessed correctly Corbulo would anchor the flanks of his army against the valley walls using his auxiliaries and line his heavy infantry three cohorts deep in the centre, where they would face Vologases' elite mounted archers and spearmen. The valley would contain the attacking potential of both armies within a narrow front which would reduce the mobility of the Parthian cavalry and favour Corbulo's defensive strategy. But Traianus was right: it would still allow the enemy to use their archers to inflict a steady stream of casualties on the Romans. It would be a battle of attrition. And in a battle of attrition the side with the greater numbers would always win. Vologases wouldn't just give up and turn back. Romans would stand, and they would die, and eventually the Parthian king must have his victory.

And while they were dying, the ten thousand auxiliary cavalry which Gnaeus Domitius Corbulo had insisted were his greatest strength against the Parthian horse would be stranded useless behind the Roman line.

It was the strategy of madness.

Until Corbulo revealed his master stroke.

Valerius listened to the general's plans with growing dismay, but his eyes were drawn back to the map and the narrow valley. He studied every particle of sand as if it would reveal the true detail of the terrain. It had never been done before. Not in his lifetime. It was unorthodox – no, it was beyond unorthodox, stranded somewhere in that fog between genius and madness. Could it be done?

'Can you do it?'

'If it can be done we will do it.'

'You understand the importance of the timing?'

'I must strike at the rising of the sun on the second day.'

'It will be difficult. You must curb your impatience and that of your men.'

'They will not gladly suffer hiding in the shadows while their comrades are dying.'

'But it must be done.'

'It will be done.'

'Then we are in agreement. Traianus, you are satisfied?'

The Tenth's legate nodded agreement with a tight smile, but Valerius knew he was imagining the hours his men would have to spend being flayed by the Parthian arrows.

'Very well, return to your units. If the gods are willing we will reach our destination in four days. Tribune Verrens, stay, please.'

The general called for an aide to bring wine and ushered Valerius through to his private quarters at the rear of the tent. When they were seated he gave the younger man a long look.

'I sense you are not convinced?'

Valerius drew a deep breath. Again he remembered Vespasian's words. A good officer must say what needs to be said.

'I think it is a good plan . . . provided everything goes well. But there are a thousand reasons why everything may not go well. Traianus was right to speak out. For my own life it does not matter, but you are risking the lives of more than twenty thousand men and the reputation you have won over thirty years.'

'All war is risk.' Corbulo glanced at the wooden hand and studied Valerius's scarred face. 'How many men did you lead against Boudicca at Colonia?'

'Three thousand veterans and a handful of legionaries.' Valerius felt the familiar mix of pride and sorrow that always accompanied mention of Colonia. He saw again the faces of Falco and Lunaris, Messor and Corvinus. Smelled the smoke and the salt-sweet scent of roasting flesh.

'Three thousand against fifty thousand.'

'Yes, three thousand against fifty thousand, but I did not gamble their lives, I spent them in the knowledge that Boudicca had to be stopped, or at least slowed.'

'And was she slowed, this rebel queen?'

Valerius shook his head. 'She waited a day to burn Colonia and then marched on Londinium. She would have done that whether we fought her or not.'

'Yet you still fought her. Why?'

The younger man hesitated. 'I have asked myself a thousand times. I could have fallen back on the Londinium road and used the militia to slow her progress with one ambush after another. We could have withdrawn to the woods and harassed her flanks and rear; cut off her supply lines. No one would have blamed me.'

'I repeat my question, then. Why did you fight her?'

'Pride.' Valerius met Corbulo's unyielding stare. 'And duty. Catus Decianus had tasked me to hold Colonia. I fulfilled my orders. To the last man.'

The general gave a grunt of satisfaction. 'To the last man. Yes. I can understand how a man like you would do that, Valerius.' He poured another drink for each of them and picked up his cup. 'I also understand duty. It is my duty to stop King Vologases from restoring Armenia to Parthian rule. Not my duty to the Emperor, who would rather I was back in Antioch shuffling my forces against an enemy who will never come. Do not mistake me, I understand that I am placing my career and perhaps my life in the Emperor's hands. He is my Emperor and I trust him as he must trust me to do as I think right. But my first duty is to Rome. And to my soldiers. The soldiers I have spent to ensure that Armenia remains loyal to Rome and acts as a counterbalance against Parthian ambition. There will be a further cost, no man knows that better than I. The Tenth, though Traianus commands it, is my creation and I know that I will have to watch the men of the Tenth die. But we will win, Gaius Valerius Verrens, do not ever doubt that.'

Valerius nodded. If he had ever doubted it, he did not doubt it now. 'And then?'

'Then I will return to Antioch, and support Vespasian as well as I am able.'

The only sound in the tent was the gentle rustle of cloth moving in the breeze and the flutter of insects flirting with the flames of the oil lamps. Valerius wondered if Corbulo's servants could hear their conversation. Nero would have his spies in the general's camp, that was certain. Yet Corbulo had spoken openly and without fear and that gave Valerius the courage to do likewise.

'Men speak of you as the next Emperor.'

Corbulo went very still and Valerius wondered if he had misread his man. 'Then give me the names of those men and I will have them executed in front of the whole camp tomorrow.'

'I have no names.'

'Have I misjudged you, Gaius Valerius Verrens? Have you been sent here to incriminate me?'

Could silence truly have an edge like a sword blade? Corbulo waited for his answer, but Valerius knew that if the general needed one, he might as well go back to his tent and cut his wrists. Eventually, the other man rose and walked to the Tower of Caesar. He studied the tokens which had been placed in exactly the same positions they had occupied when the two men had finished their game the previous evening. With a nod, he picked up the blue stone representing the Emperor.

'Rome is not perfect, Valerius. Nero is not perfect. But Rome is Rome and Nero is our Emperor. No man can usurp the Emperor without disturbing the delicate balance that is the Empire. Rome is full of ambitious politicians who would not stand idly by as another stole their power. The city would have to be fought for. Fought over. And we both understand exactly what that means. Fire and sword. Blood and sorrow. Think of this stone thrown into a still pond. Watch the rings expand until they reach every corner of the surface. That is how it would be. Every man, woman and child in the provinces we rule, even those we merely dominate, would have their lives thrown into turmoil.'

He replaced the counter. 'You are correct. Other men would urge me to act. I hear the whispers – the message you brought from General Vespasian was one *Whatever he decides, I will support him*. I honour Vespasian as a man, a soldier and a friend, but he mistakes me. If I march, he will march with me. But what happens in Syria and Judaea and Cappadocia when we are gone? Will Vologases politely stand by as the legions leave the frontiers open? Would the Balkan legions support me or oppose me? Or those of upper and lower Germania? Would you ask me to risk Roman fighting Roman? No, if Vespasian marched, I would have to stop him. We talked about duty. My first duty is to Rome and to my province, which it is my sacred purpose to protect. Another man might act in his own self-interest, Valerius, but that man is not Gnaeus Domitius Corbulo. We will speak of this no more.'

Valerius nodded, and the general returned to the game. 'You have improved remarkably over the past week. I fear you have me at bay.' Valerius was surprised when he began to remove the pieces and place them in their starting positions. Corbulo saw his look. 'We will not be finishing this game. Traianus was right. Vologases is no fool. He knows that time is his enemy as well as I do. Soon he will realize that we have turned away from Tigranocerta and he will wonder why. At some point he will send his light cavalry ahead to secure the Cepha gap. I intend that you will be there first. I want you to take four cavalry wings of archers and spearmen and enough fodder, rations and water for five days. You will ride ahead of the main column and avoid all combat until you reach the gap. Your orders are simple. Once there, you will defeat any enemy forces who confront you, form a defensive line and hold the position until you are annihilated, relieved or the main column arrives. Have you any questions?'

'None, sir.' Valerius risked a smile. 'As you say, my orders are simple.'

Corbulo came close and grasped the younger man by the arm, his grip firm. 'Win it for me and hold it for me, Valerius, and together we will inflict a defeat on the Parthians they will remember for a thousand years.'

XXXIV

Athens, Greece

His world seemed to be closing in on him, until it had been reduced to this tiny dungeon in the palace he had commandeered on the slopes below the Acropolis. It had all seemed so different this past week.

For a few days during the Games on Mount Olympus he had felt as if he was soaring with the gods themselves. The wonder of his songs and oratory had beguiled the greatest artists in Greece, the cradle of culture and civilization, and they had hailed him as an Olympian on the very mount that had given the Games their name. In those few glorious moments he had left behind the troubles and consternation of the Empire and been able to bask in the glory of his own genius, to bathe in the cheers of the multitude and to drink the ambrosia of Zeus, Artemis and Apollo.

He sighed.

And now Tigellinus had dragged him back to an earth which, even at its best, was tawdry by comparison. The smell of burning flesh reminded him of the Great Fire.

The two men hanging from the seven-foot iron triangles were brothers and until recently they had been the governors of the two Germanias, Superior and Inferior. Tigellinus had brought Rufus and

Proculus Sulpicius Scribonius to meet their Emperor on the pretext that they were to receive the triumphal regalia for their victories over the Chatti and the Cherusci, Germanic tribes who had plagued Rome's frontiers for centuries. But instead of honours, all they had received was pain.

Nero walked past the torturers and lifted the chin of the elder Scribonius, Proculus, so he could see into his eyes. He had been very brave. Had offered himself for the glowing iron and the knives and the pincers if it would only spare his brother the trial. Instead, Tigellinus had used his courage against him and had the younger brother trussed up first. Nero had watched Proculus throw himself against his bonds as they had placed the red-hot barbs in Rufus's flesh, torn his nipples out and removed his nose, all to the accompaniment of the torturers' chorus of shrieks and howls and agonized groans. Then he had ordered the older brother's legs broken, so he had to crawl to the triangle where he could bring an end to his brother's suffering by replacing him. Of course, that could not happen. Each was the other's weakness. They must witness the other's pain and mutilation while Tigellinus and his clerks recorded the names that must eventually be uttered through broken teeth and torn lips.

'You were my friend, Proculus. Why must all my friends betray me?'

It was astonishing the change that fire and iron could accomplish in such a short time. The brothers had been young men in the prime of life when they walked into the receiving room. In their senatorial robes, they had carried themselves like the patricians they were: dark, leonine heads held high, proud of their achievements and proud of each other. With their long noses and eyes that disdained all but their own kind, men like this had opposed him at every turn since the day he had donned the purple. They had blocked his improvements, refused him the money he needed to emulate his illustrious ancestors, laughed behind their hands at his performances and sneered at his pleasures. Yet he had taken the brothers Scribonius into his trust. Not for them the tender mercies of Tigellinus, the threat of the arena, the sequestration of their estates and property. Not even the seduction of their wives. He had rewarded them with advancement, not because they were worthy, but because they were too indolent to do harm.

In the hands of an able governor either of the two Germanias could swiftly become a threat on Rome's doorstep. The legions of the Rhine frontier were elite, battle-hardened soldiers, who protected the Empire from the eastern hordes. They complained constantly of poor pay and poor rations and poor accommodation. It made them fractious and difficult to control. And dangerous. No Corbulo would ever command in Germania while he was Emperor. It would be like handing a condemned man a sword. Instead, he had given command to wastrels like these, in the sure knowledge that they would spend their time gossiping and entertaining. But they had proved him wrong. For the brothers Scribonius had plotted.

'Names, Proculus,' he said softly. 'Give us names and places and dates and your brother will be spared.'

Through the lightning bolts of agony that tore his body, Proculus Sulpicius Scribonius heard the voice. He had called on all the courage of his ancestors to be able to bear his torment and he would have borne it until death. But his baby brother's shrieks had eroded his resolve until he could take no more. His delirious mind screamed at him to save Rufus. Whatever the cost.

He sobbed like a child and the names began as a trickle, grew into a stream, and finally became a torrent.

Nero turned to Tigellinus. 'When you are certain you have it all, they go to the fire.' He hesitated. 'No, they were once friends. I will be merciful. Have them take their own lives, if they are capable.'

For the next two hours, Tigellinus checked and double checked the names and the dates, taking the brothers to new levels of pain to ensure not a single conspirator, or conspirator's wife, or friend, or acquaintance, had been missed. By the end there was no need for either brother to go to the trouble of killing himself.

Left to his own devices, Tigellinus would have added another name to the list, whether it came from the vomit-stained lips or not. But the roll call of betrayal was recorded. If Corbulo's name was on the list, the Emperor would call in the clerks to confirm it and, if he bribed them, they might even reveal that Tigellinus had placed it there. He couldn't risk that. He would find another way. The man now shivering in terror in the dungeons below the Palatine would provide it.

Willing or not, Annius Vinicianus would condemn his father-in-law. And, if not, there was always the Egyptian.

XXXV

Valerius struggled to stay awake as the mare picked her way over dry, rolling pastureland that stretched into the distance. No shortage of fodder now – the land would provide – but water for man and horse continued to be strictly rationed. They had been in the saddle for two full days, riding by the light of the moon after the sun went down, with only a few short rest periods. Corbulo had said that time was his enemy's enemy, but Valerius knew that it was also his. He had spent the hours after the general's conference organizing, cajoling and chivvying to ensure that the four cavalry regiments he had chosen for the mission were ready to march at dawn. Hanno rode at his side. The Syrian's Third Thracians led the column, which contained a second wing of mounted archers, the Augusta Syriaca, plus two wings of light cavalry, the First Ulpia Dacorum, which Corbulo had drafted in from Cappadocia, and the Numidians of the First Praetoria, one of the general's veteran regiments. They were still a long day's ride from the Cepha gap, but Valerius was determined to reach his destination before nightfall. Away to his left, rippling in the heat from the fierce sun, lay the endless line of hills he recognized from Corbulo's sand table. Somewhere to the northeast stood Tigranocerta and he prayed that the general was right and the Armenian fortress's commander would stay where he was. If the Armenian broke his word and decided to change

235

his allegiance from Tiridates to his brother, Valerius's little force would be crushed between two armies like a grape in a wine press. Even now Vologases could already be crossing his front and Corbulo's plans would be smashed to dust along with the thousands of men he led.

'Do you think they are out there?'

Hanno turned wearily in the saddle. His eyes were just visible in the folds of the dust-caked cloth that covered his helmeted head and his shoulders, but Valerius sensed he was smiling. The Syrian shook his head. 'We would have seen signs. More activity ahead; cavalry patrols seeking out our spearhead.' He waved a hand behind them to where the other cavalry units were hidden in a plume of yellow. 'Dust.' Of course, an army as large as that of the Parthian King of Kings would perpetually carry with it a cloud that cloaked it like a ready-made shroud.

Hanno removed the cloth from his face and spat. He had a feel for this land that no man who wasn't born here would ever match. 'Every sign of movement we have seen has come from the south, and nothing since we moved into this valley.' Valerius had never thought of the grasslands they were crossing as a valley, but he supposed it was true. The hills to the north were matched by mountains to the south which had started as low foothills the previous morning, but now created the formidable barrier that stretched eastwards to the far horizon. Unbroken. Yet somewhere out there was Corbulo's gap. If it existed. He dashed the thought from his mind, remembering the specific instructions he had been given. Riding behind them beside Serpentius was an engineer who had been with Corbulo from the start. The man had created Corbulo's sand table and he brought with him a leather scroll case containing detailed maps: maps he had drawn during the general's expedition during the consulship of Petronius Lurco. The gap was there. All Valerius needed to do was reach it before the Parthians.

'And we're sure we packed the special equipment?'

Hanno laughed. It was the third time Valerius had asked the question. For answer he adjusted the unfamiliar heavy shield that hung behind him and cursed its awkward unwieldiness. Valerius tested the sword slung on his back in a harness designed by Serpentius so he could draw it over his right shoulder. The cavalry *spatha* Corbulo had given him was a fine weapon, but the Medusa-pommelled *gladius* he had carried since Boudicca's death was a talisman that had accompanied him this far and he would have felt naked without it.

When the sun dropped close to the western horizon he began to fear that they'd missed the valley entrance. The chances of finding it in darkness would be slim for the sharp-eyed Thracian scouts even with a three-quarter moon to aid them. Fortunately one of the patrols stumbled upon a shepherd and his two herder sons and Valerius set off with Hanno to their camp to question them.

The man and the younger boy sat by the fire that had alerted the Thracians to their presence. The elder son stood belligerently by the flock of about thirty skinny, ragged sheep daring any of Hanno's men to come near them.

The shepherd waved Valerius to the place of honour on the upwind side of the fire and Hanno crouched beside him and made the traditional salutations in his own language. Valerius's nostrils twitched at the rank animal smell emanating from his host, but he nodded as the man answered Hanno's questions, revealing a mouthful of blackened teeth.

'He says he has seen no Parthian patrols,' the Syrian translated. 'Or he would have driven his flock to the higher pastures on the hills yonder. The Parthians would take his sheep, unworthy though they are, and cheat him. He knows the Roma are honest men who would never deprive him of his livelihood and would be happy to negotiate a price.'

'Ask him if he knows of the Cepha gap.'

The shepherd shook his head, but Valerius saw a flash of understanding in the dark, liquid eyes of the boy, probably less than ten years old, sitting opposite him.

'Ask him again, but more forcefully.'

Hanno grinned, but when he spoke his voice contained a hard edge and the shepherd glanced nervously at Valerius before he replied.

'He says, yes, now he understands what you mean, but he knows it by a different name, the Road of Sorrow, for this is the way the kings of Parthia and Seleucia have ever ridden to milk the lands of Armenia.'

'Tell him he will be well rewarded if he takes us there.'

The smile didn't reach the shepherd's eyes and he gestured regretfully to his sheep.

'Alas,' Hanno translated, 'he says he and his family must stay with their sheep. Without them they will starve when winter comes, as the north wind says it soon must. And there are wolves from the mountains; you have doubtless seen their tracks. He honours you, but he must decline, though he will gladly provide you with directions.'

The shepherd nodded and smiled ingratiatingly.

'Then the boy will take us.' Valerius pointed to the younger son and two of Hanno's escort lifted him to his feet.

The father began to wail, but Hanno snarled at him and he lapsed into silence. 'Now he is willing.' The Syrian grinned at Valerius.

'No, the boy will take us. I do not trust the father. He would find some means of slipping away in the night. Bring him.'

They remounted, leaving the shepherd standing beside the fire with the older son, who had abandoned his charges.

'What will we do with them.' Valerius understood it was not a question, but a reminder. 'If we leave them behind and a Parthian patrol stumbles on them as we have . . .'

'I know, prefect.' The Roman's voice was harsher than he intended, but Hanno's expression didn't alter. 'Make sure they are fed first.'

The Syrian issued the order and as they galloped off Valerius could hear him laughing. 'Aye, a full belly will make a cut throat all the easier to bear.'

'They are here.'

Valerius cursed as he heard the scout's whisper to the Third Thracian commander. The column had reined in a few hundred paces from the northern entrance of the Cepha gap, in the shadow of the hills, while a patrol checked for the enemy.

'How many?' Hanno demanded.

'Perhaps seventy, a reinforced patrol.' Only now did Valerius recognize the voice of Hassan, the Damascus trader's son. 'The usual mix of archers and spearmen, if their mounts are to be believed.'

'Seventy? You are certain? And you weren't seen?'

'Does a vole see the hunting owl on the first pass? Does the hare see the eagle?' White teeth grinned in the darkness. 'They are camped in the centre of the valley, but their sentries are weary and have grown careless. Janos slipped past them and checked as far as the great river. Is that not so, Janos?'

'Seventy, my life on it,' agreed another voice.

'Aye, so be it,' Hanno said, 'When we charge them you will be the first to meet their spears.'

'Wait!' Hassan turned at the sound of Valerius's voice. 'If you slipped past them once, can you do it again, this time with twenty men?'

'If I may choose them. The valley is broad enough for it to be done.'

'Is it worth the risk of discovery?' Hanno sounded doubtful.

'If so much as a man escapes, Vologases will send every sword, spear and bow he can get into the saddle and they will be on us before day-break. Can we take that risk?'

For answer, the Syrian made his dispositions. 'Janos, pick out your men. Archers, eh? Hassan, position your scouts and be ready to take out the guards at the first sign of an alert. Tribune, I would beg the honour of allowing the Third Thracians to make the attack.'

'Very well.' Valerius nodded. 'But I want you here by my side. You are too valuable to lose to a stray arrow. We will deploy twelve squadrons.'

He saw Hanno's grin of acceptance, but he knew the Syrian would be disappointed to miss the battle, if it could be called a battle with a numerical superiority of six to one and the element of surprise in favour of the attackers. But he could take no chances. Not a man could be allowed to escape.

'We need to know the position of Vologases and his forces, so I want prisoners.'

Hanno nodded and went to issue his orders, leaving Valerius alone in the darkness, or so he thought.

'How long do you think we'll have to hold them?'

'Vologases will march at first light, Serpentius, and I doubt if he's more than two or three hours away. Even if he orders a forced march it's unlikely the general will reach us by the eighth hour. Six hours, maybe more.'

'Then let's hope the King of Kings enjoys a long breakfast.'

Valerius imagined the might of the Parthian army marching against his puny, lightly armoured force. 'Let's hope he chokes on it.'

But first there was a valley to win.

Cloaked in their white shrouds, the twelve squadrons of the Third Thracian cavalry *ala* appeared as ephemeral as ghosts in the silver moonlight. They approached at a walk, spread in formation across the valley, with their prefect and General Corbulo's cavalry commander on their right flank. Valerius knew the cloaks provided camouflage of a sort against the moonlit rocks and grass, but it couldn't be long now. If the guards didn't react, the attackers would break into the trot at two hundred paces and sweep through the camp peppering anything that moved with their arrows. When Hassan's scouts had dealt with the sentries they would move into the Parthian horse lines hamstringing and cutting throats. Any Parthian who escaped from the camp would be cut down by Janos and his screen of archers.

Valerius reined in and watched the troopers ride by and he heard Hanno's whispered curse as his gelding twitched and fidgeted demanding to be with its brethren. His nerves stretched like lyre strings as the silent minutes passed. Hassan must have done well, because there was no alarm cry or trumpet call as the first squadrons reached the trot and it wasn't until they could feel the quake of the ground beneath them that the Parthians began to react. He heard shouted orders and panicked cries, a scream that was cut off the instant it began. Then the silver horde was on the little circle of Parthian tents.

It was done.

'Congratulations, prefect.' Hanno grinned at him. 'Now the real work begins.'

'This is the narrowest and most defensible point of the valley?'

'It is, sir,' Corbulo's engineer, Petronius, an intense balding man, assured Valerius. 'It narrows a little more to the north, but the valley walls are less steep. This is where we have the best chance of holding them.'

'Very well.' Valerius marched forty paces ahead and called his cavalry commanders to form a circle around him. They crouched together as troopers enclosed them in a ring of cloaks and Serpentius lit an oil lamp in the centre. With his dagger, Valerius sketched out a rough drawing in a sandy patch he'd chosen. 'The narrowest part of the valley is here.' He pointed to the position the engineer had indicated. 'But we will make our defensive line at this point.' He laid the dagger across the valley approximately where they now stood. If he expected a protest, or at least a question, he was disappointed, but he realized it was a measure of the respect he had won from these hard men in the weeks he'd ridden with them. He felt a pulse of pride that he immediately suppressed. It was all very well to issue orders, but if he made a miscalculation every one of these soldiers would be dead before tomorrow's sunset.

'Marcus? The Augusta Syriaca will form a covering line, here. First Ulpia and First Practoria? I want staggered lines of camouflaged two-by-two pits dug across the neck of the valley behind the defence line. We don't have stakes to make them proper horse killers, but . . .' He produced a four-pronged iron spike from beneath his cloak. 'Caltrops. Every man in the column carried four of these. That's ten thousand of them; to be scattered between the pits. A killing field fifty paces deep. You'll be working in the dark, but this has to be done properly. The pits and caltrops must be set to create diagonal lanes which will allow the withdrawal or reinforcement of all units. That's the job of our engineer.' Petronius nodded gravely. 'He will supervise your work. Finally, prefect Hanno? The Third Thracians have done their work for the day and done it well. They will form a reserve ready to support Syriaca and provide patrols to locate and track the army of King Vologases. I need to know exactly where they are and in what numbers from first light at the latest. Do you have any questions?'

'Why don't we fight from behind the pit line from the start?' the Syriaca's commander asked softly. 'By fighting in front of it we accept greater casualties and deny ourselves the ability to hurt the Parthians.'

Valerius nodded. 'That's true, Marcus.' In the flickering yellow light of the oil lamp he looked each of them in the eye. 'We fight in front of the pit line, because the pit line has been dug for the main force. We will fight and we will die in front of the pit line and only if we are on the point of annihilation will we withdraw behind it. That decision will be taken either by myself or, if I am dead, by prefect Hanno. Is that understood? This is our ground and we will hold them here or die in the attempt.'

XXXVI

The last scouts rode in at the gallop as the first light of dawn coated the eastern mountains pink and gold. The Cepha gap was a three-and-a-half-mile-long gorge that slashed through an otherwise unbroken range of saw-toothed peaks. The valley's thousand-foot sheer flanks of fractured red sandstone were divided by a mile of dry grassland at its widest point, but in places it was much narrower. Valerius watched as a fast-moving squall of Parthian cavalry appeared from the dust behind his patrol, howling and yipping and loosing arrows from the saddle. With every eye on their prey it was a moment before the pursuers realized what they were seeing and drew their horses to a disbelieving halt in a shower of flying earth. From valley wall to valley wall a long line of Roman shields blocked their passage. An undernourished, patchy line, its ranks lacking the solidity that would be expected from the cream of Roman infantry, but the message carried by the big curved shields was clear: the legions were here and if King Vologases' army wanted to reach Tigranocerta it must first destroy them.

Valerius had always known that the only way to hold the gap against a serious assault was on foot. That was why he had insisted the lightly armed cavalry exchange their regular round shields for proper legionary *scuta* begged and borrowed from the Tenth and the Fifteenth with Corbulo's assistance. Now the emblems of the two elite eastern legions filled the valley with dismounted cavalry troopers behind them. At this point the gap measured a thousand paces wide as the engineer calculated it. Valerius had formed his men into five weakened cohorts in line abreast, each one hundred men wide and five deep, with a ten-pace division between each unit. To the riders watching from a few hundred paces away it must have appeared that an unbroken wall of shields had sprouted across the width of the valley. Yet it was a pitifully weak, poorly armed and unsupported line. He did not have enough men to both hold the ground and form a reserve. In time of danger each cohort must support its neighbour.

Two figures broke away from the group of riders and rode south. Couriers carrying the unwelcome news to Vologases, King of Kings, that a force of phantoms had materialized to bar his way. The remaining Parthian horse, perhaps a hundred strong, burst into movement, first circling, so that Valerius guessed they must be retreating to gather reinforcements, before advancing to ride across the face of the Roman line at a hundred paces distant. Unlike the earlier patrol Valerius had encountered this was composed entirely of archers; small men, unarmoured, on light horses and ideal for the hit and run tactics that Corbulo had warned him were the Parthian speciality. He waited for the inevitable flurry of arrows.

But the patrol's commander must have sensed something in the line of shields that smelled of weakness. Without warning he wheeled his horse and led his men directly for the gap between the two left hand formations. If he could breach the Roman defences it would give him a deadly advantage when the main Parthian force arrived. Valerius knew that if the Parthians found their way to the auxiliary horse lines in a gully two hundred paces behind the lines, disadvantage could turn to disaster. A hail of arrows, fired at short range from the gallop, smacked into the shields of the front ranks of the two cohorts with the sound of a hundred branches snapping. Valerius heard the auxiliaries draw a collective breath, but thankfully there was no cry for the medical orderlies. Within two strides the Parthians reached the marker stones that identified optimum javelin range. The defending cohorts were a mix of bowmen and javelin throwers, and with a single shouted order

244

a hundred javelins sailed out from the spearmen flanking the gap and converged on the galloping Parthians like a deadly summer shower. Men grunted, screamed and gasped as the light spears tore muscle and sinew, scraped bone and found heart or lung; a dozen horses crumpled in a single choreographed movement, impeding those not agile enough to avoid them. Two more strides and the survivors absorbed another perfectly timed cast. This time those left unscathed reeled away from the killing zone and turned back, accompanied by the jeers of the untouched Roman line.

'Quiet,' Valerius roared.

A single rider breached the gap. An archer in the final rank of the left hand cohort turned and loosed. His arrow took the Parthian in the base of the skull and the horse rode on with the rider dead in the saddle until it reached the pit line and went down in a cloud of dust screaming with the agony of a snapped foreleg.

Satisfied, Valerius waited until the surviving Parthians had gathered in a sullen group well out of bow range before he ordered the clean-up. Men from the second rank of the Roman line ran to where the Parthian injured lay stunned and groaning among the dead. The auxiliaries roamed among the carnage with brutal efficiency, cutting throats and providing the mercy stroke as they stripped men and horses of weapons and arrows and recovered bundles of javelins.

'I want their coats and helmets, too,' Valerius reminded them.

All through the long morning the men of Valerius's little command stood in the burning heat and watched with growing dread the build-up of King Vologases' forces. The Parthians were preceded by the sound of distant thunder that echoed from the valley walls, a deep, menacing throb that seemed to slowly work its way into a man's soul. Gradually, the defeated survivors of the Parthian charge were absorbed into the mass of the army's vanguard, the countless horde of light horse which swirled and flowed like the surface of a great river across Valerius's front seeking some way to break the Roman dam. At first it was insubstantial, a veil of individual squadrons and regiments that lightly dotted the land, but gradually the veil became a blanket and the blanket thickened to become a great multicoloured swathe of humanity that blocked out the coarse grassland. The feeling of enormous pressure building up behind the vanguard grew, but they never ventured closer than four hundred paces.

'Why don't they come?' Hanno demanded. 'It would be the work of a moment to sweep us aside.'

Valerius nodded silently. Such a horde could turn the sky black with arrows and force the Romans into the tortoise formation – the *testudo* – that made them invulnerable to missile attack, but, conversely, would leave them open to a charge by the heavy armoured cavalry that were somewhere out there in that great mass. The answer came to him. His ruse had worked better than he had believed possible.

'It is because they think we are a full Roman legion. Through his spies, Vologases will know that Corbulo has marched, if not exactly where. Perhaps he has informed his generals, perhaps not. But the tribal chiefs who lead those warrior bands have been told that Armenia is already won and they are but an escort to see Vologases to his throne. This was to be a progression. They might expect some opposition from roving bands of Armenian rebels, but not this. Whoever commands the vanguard will look at our shields and see the prospect of all-out war with Rome. He dare not make his move without consulting Vologases himself, and Vologases dare not move without gauging the strength which opposes him.'

'Then we have won?'

'If Corbulo comes.'

But the sun reached its zenith and still Corbulo did not come. Valerius ordered the last of the water distributed amongst the men behind the curved red shields and it was like nectar in their dust-caked throats. By now the cavalrymen were reeling on their feet and he wondered if they were even capable of meeting a Parthian charge, never mind repelling it. Yet when he marched along the ranks to inspect their dispositions they cheered him as if they had won a victory. He remembered Paulinus, the man he had to thank, for better or worse, for being here, and the stirring speech the then governor of Britain had made before Boudicca's last battle. Valerius fervently wished he had the same words to say to his soldiers, but somehow they would not come. Not that it mattered. They knew the situation as well as he did. If Corbulo didn't come, they were all dead.

Still Corbulo didn't come. But the King of Kings did.

An ominous ripple ran through the ranks of the great army facing the Roman line and every man tensed to meet the attack. Valerius mounted Khamsin and took his place in the rear with Hanno and Serpentius at his side. From the centre of the Parthian horde a single figure emerged holding not a lance or a bow, but a branch of green leaves.

'It seems the King of Kings wishes to talk,' Hanno murmured.

'Then let us not disappoint him.' Valerius nudged his horse between the ranks and on to the plain, where he waited until Hanno joined him with an escort of mounted spearmen. Together they rode to greet the Parthian emissary.

They met midway between the two mismatched forces and Hanno spoke to the Parthian in his own tongue.

'He says that Sasan, spear carrier to Vologases, King of Kings, over-lord of Armenia, conqueror of Elam, protector of the Medes, and lord of Babylon, Sagartia and Margiania wishes to discuss the terms of your surrender.'

'Tell him that we came here to fight, not to talk, but if this Sasan speaks with the authority of the King of Kings we are willing to hear what he has to say.'

Hanno spat out the translation and the warrior nodded. At a hidden signal the Parthian ranks opened and a dozen mounted men emerged at the trot, led by an astonishing figure who glittered with gold from the top of his helmeted head to the fringe of the chain mail trapper that covered his mount's head, back and chest and extended to its knees. The rider was an enormous man wearing a long tunic of fish-scale armour, complemented by metal armlets and leggings. His gleaming helmet was topped by a plume of red horsehair and a mail curtain hung from the rear to protect his neck. This Parthian warlord had a face the gods had designed to project hatred. Dark eyes glared out from beneath beetle brows and the narrow, bitter mouth was topped by an enormous hooked nose and twisted in what might have been a smile or a sneer. Sasan wore his beard clubbed and plaited with brightly coloured ribbons and his broad moustaches fell below his cheeks. His escort carried spears twice the height of a man, but their commander's only arms were a long sword hanging from a loop at his wrist and the curved dagger in his belt. Beside him rode a figure in an ornately embroidered tunic with a large drum hanging from either side of his saddle. Valerius remembered what he thought had been thunder earlier in the day and realized that the drums were the equivalent of the Roman trumpets which could carry signals across the noisiest battlefield. Vologases would know the outcome of the discussions before he and Hanno returned to the Roman lines. If they lived that long.

The leader's horse stood a head taller than Khamsin, and Valerius studied his enemy carefully as Sasan brought the beasts nose to nose, making the Akhal-Teke quiver and shift. Tall, savage and as pitiless as the harsh landscape that surrounded them, the Parthian returned his stare with contempt.

'For myself, I would cut off the arms and legs of every Roman who insults my people with their presence and impale them alive as examples of what awaits the next invader who passes this way, but the King of Kings graciously accepts your surrender.' The words were in precise Greek-accented Latin and uttered in a tone of bored irritation. 'He will allow you to leave this place unharmed and unmolested with your arms and your standards on condition that you go immediately and do not stop until you are beyond the Euphrates.'

Valerius frowned as if he was considering the offer.

'Did I hear an ass bray, or was it the sound of an elephant farting?' He directed the question at Hanno, but he noticed a glint of mild amusement in the Parthian's eye. 'We have travelled a long way and this legion is only one of many. They are weary and need rest. It would take several hours, perhaps days, to organize the march, so I must decline your king's generous offer. Besides, the only invaders I see are the ones before me.'

Sasan sniffed and spat in Valerius's general direction.

'Do not think your pathetic little army frightens me, Roman. When I destroyed the legions of General Paetus at Rhandea I learned to read their strength by their standards. I see beyond your tricks. A wall of legionary shields with auxiliaries shitting themselves behind them. But it does not matter. The King of Kings could destroy you with a snap of his fingers. The only thing that prevents him is a desire for peaceful progress. What you see is but a fraction of the multitude which escorts the King of Kings to inspect his brother's dominions. Do you deny him that right? You are like a mouse beneath a buffalo's hooves. If you will not go, then move aside lest it squash you into the dust.' His eyes noticed the walnut fist. 'You have been careless, it seems. It would be unfortunate were you to lose any further extremities. Will they replace thy head with a wooden one when I take it for a trophy?'

'My head will remain on my shoulders while your bones moulder in the dust, Parthian.' Valerius matched the other man's tone. 'We are here at King Tiridates' invitation and here we stay. Tell your King of Kings to go back the way he came and no harm will come to him. Tell him that if he attacks me, he attacks General Gnaeus Domitius Corbulo, and if he attacks Corbulo he attacks Rome. Rome does not forget her enemies, but she remembers her friends. If your king is wise he will remain Rome's friend.'

'So the mouse squeaks defiance?' Sasan laughed. 'Good. It has been many a month since my spear tasted blood. I told Vologases he should have unleashed his hounds the moment our scouts reported you were blocking the valley. The next time you look at the sun, you will not see it for arrows. The next time you look at my face you will be screaming for mercy. Those who fight will be slaughtered. Those who yield will become beasts of burden carrying shit to my farmers' fields. I will take your skull for a drinking bowl, your wooden hand for my dogs to chew and the fingers of the other to make a necklace for my wife.' He turned his horse away. 'You talk well, Roman. Now let us see how you fight.'

As they rode back to the Roman position Valerius exchanged glances with Hanno. 'That went better than I expected.'

'Aye,' the Syrian said. 'I suppose they might have cut our throats then and there instead of making us wait.'

'How do you kill a man like Sasan?'

'First you kill his horse.'

'All I saw of his horse was its eyes and its hooves.'

Hanno nodded. 'Fortunately, Sasan is one in ten thousand. The king's spear carrier holds a high position in his court, almost a king in his own right. No ordinary man could afford such armour for warrior and horse. Most of the Parthian cataphracts wear body armour, but their horses are unprotected. It means the man is hard to kill, but the horse is not. But it is not the cataphracts we must fear. It is their archers who will kill us.'

'How long?'

'An hour, perhaps less.'

'Then pray that Corbulo comes soon.'

XXXVII

The attack would be in overwhelming strength. Vologases would mass his archers and savage the Roman ranks with endless showers of arrows that would turn the sky black. Shields or no shields, Valerius knew his men would suffer casualties. In an hour, perhaps less, a thousand of these men would be dead or injured. Perhaps he would be dead himself. And when the Roman line was holed and leaking blood, the King of Kings would send in his Invincibles, the armoured cavalry led by mighty warriors like Sasan. It was a battle which could have only one ending.

But it takes time to position tens of thousands of archers, and time to organize the metal-clad spearmen who would follow them. Too much time.

Because a blast of horns announced that Corbulo had come.

'Legate Traianus sends his compliments and where would you like us, sir?'

Valerius turned to find a breathless Tiberius at his shoulder, grinning like a boy presented with his first toga. He clapped the younger man on the shoulder.

'Your ugly face has never been more welcome, tribune. Tell Traianus I suggest he places the Tenth Fretensis in front of the auxiliary line. Cohort formation, with his flanks anchored against the valley walls.

The cohorts of the Fifteenth and the auxiliary infantry will form the second line.'

The young man ran off and Valerius watched with Serpentius as, to the sound of the familiar trumpet calls, the legionary heavy infantry streamed through the gaps in the pit line and along the front of the relieved auxiliaries, effortlessly moving from column to cohort. The legion was formed of ten cohorts, the tactical fighting unit of the Roman army, nine of them made up of four hundred and eighty men organized into six centuries of eighty legionaries each, plus the elite first cohort, almost double that strength with eight hundred men. The first included the legion's *aquilifer*, who carried the eagle standard and took his place behind the line beside his legate. The cavalrymen began cheering and Hanno opened his mouth to stop them, but Valerius interrupted him.

'Leave them be. Ten minutes ago they thought they were dead. Let them celebrate.'

'If they had any sense they'd attack us now.' Serpentius pointed to where the enemy archers wheeled and circled in apparent confusion.

Valerius nodded. Even with reinforcements pouring into the valley the Roman position would never be more vulnerable than now, with the defensive line half formed and the men weary from the long march. But half a mile away Vologases waited – and did nothing.

'That's the trouble with having an enormous army.' The clatter of hooves announced Corbulo's arrival, along with his aides and signallers. 'It takes a long time for commands to be distributed. Any of Vologases' generals who acted without orders would face the strangling rope, even if his actions resulted in victory.'

Valerius studied him for any sign of irony, but clearly Corbulo didn't equate his own position with that of a Parthian general.

'What is your estimate of enemy numbers?'

'Anything between sixty and seventy thousand, plus the usual slaves, stockmen and baggage carriers . . .'

'. . . and King Vologases' harem.' Corbulo frowned at Hanno's intervention and Valerius could swear the Syrian blushed under his dark skin. 'He is said to have three hundred wives,' Hanno stumbled on, 'and will certainly have brought at least half with him.'

'Then you must be sure not to inconvenience them, Valerius.' Hanno looked mystified and Corbulo continued, 'Seventy thousand? Similar odds to those faced by my old friend Suetonius against your rebel queen.'

'Similar odds and a similar position,' Valerius confirmed. Suetonius Paulinus had lured Boudicca to the field of his choice. A long shallow slope bounded by trees and hills to left and right to ensure he wouldn't be outflanked. And on that slope the flower of Boudicca's army died. 'But not a similar enemy. Boudicca's warriors were brave, but they weren't organized. They knew how to fight as individuals and they died as individuals. Vologases' army knows how to kill Romans and they enjoy doing it.' He thought he might have gone too far, but Corbulo only nodded distractedly.

'Then we must ensure the same outcome despite that uncomfortable fact.'

Valerius didn't mention the other similarity in the position of the two armies. Suetonius had left himself nowhere to retreat. If the Roman line had been broken the legionaries would have been slaughtered to the last man.

'Withdraw your troops when the Tenth is in position,' the general said. 'Make sure they are rested, fed and watered. You've done well, Valerius. You have given us a chance. But there is more work to do. I'll give you two hours, and then you must be in the saddle. Leave me one cohort of light cavalry to keep King Vologases amused.'

Valerius saluted and left Hanno to organize his men. On the way back to the horses he and Serpentius met Tiberius as the tribune hurried back to his general.

Valerius hailed the young soldier. 'Fortuna be with you, Tiberius. I said you would have your chance to become a hero. Well, this is it.'

Tiberius's eyes darkened. 'I had hoped to fight at your side.'

Valerius smiled. 'There will be other times, Tiberius.'

'What . . . ?'

'You know better than to ask. A good soldier obeys orders and keeps his mouth shut. For Rome.'

The younger man looked incredibly vulnerable as he returned the salute. 'For Rome.'

Serpentius commented, 'The Parthians will eat him alive.'

'No.' Valerius studied the retreating back. 'I don't think they will.'

His unit commanders were waiting at the mouth of the valley, and he quizzed them on the readiness of each cohort until Hanno arrived. When he finally revealed their mission a few of them shook their heads in disbelief, but no one questioned the plan and they dispersed to alert their troops.

Two hours later Valerius rode north at the head of Corbulo's cavalry, leaving to their fate the two legions who would soon be facing the combined might of Vologases' archers and cataphracts. He could feel the confusion and disappointment in his men. They were soldiers, and conditioned to obey orders without question, but that didn't stop them wondering why they were riding away from a battle. Well, they would find out soon enough. In an hour he would turn east towards the mountains of ancient Mazandaran and the Great Sea; a land that had defeated even Alexander. Auxiliary units arriving with the rearguard of Corbulo's force stared unhappily as their cavalry deserted them. There were a few shouts of derision, but Valerius and his men ignored them. The squeak of wheels alerted him to the arrival of a line of heavily laden carts. He remembered his puzzlement when he had noticed them in the baggage train at Zeugma. Now he saw again the massed ranks of Parthian warriors packed into the valley and thought he understood. So that was what the old fox intended?

With a last look back to where Corbulo awaited the first Parthian attack, he urged Khamsin forward.

To whatever fate would bring.

At first the going was easy on the dry flatlands north of the mountains. Valerius was able to deploy his regiments three abreast across the plain and minimize the dust cloud by keeping them to a walk. Only when they were well away from the valley did he have his signaller sound the trot. At first, the entire force was contained within a square mile of grassland, but, gradually, the country became more broken and the troopers were forced back into column. Even riding eight abreast Valerius was dismayed to realize his force stretched back almost five miles. Petronius, the engineer who had accompanied Corbulo's expeditions, rode at Valerius's side, occasionally consulting one of his scrolls and studying his surroundings with fierce concentration.

'This is it,' he said when they reached a path leading up a valley identical to a dozen others they had passed.

Valerius thought he sensed doubt. 'Are you certain?'

'Certain.'

'How many times have you been this way?'

'Once. Eight years ago.'

'Once?'

Petronius nodded. 'Once.' He saw the look in Valerius's eye. 'But I'm certain.'

The ground rose gradually and the path became less distinct. To their front lay what appeared to be an impenetrable mountain range, but for now Valerius kept his concerns to himself. He and Petronius rode ahead of the column until they reached a small plateau. When Valerius looked back he felt his spirits quail. By now it was almost dusk. In the golden haze the dust raised by the line of cavalrymen stretched far into the distance, snaking along a track that was now only wide enough to accommodate two horses at a time. The men at the tail would still be far out on the plain. It was impossible.

'Can it be done?' He cursed the fear in his own voice. Not fear for his life, but fear that he would fail.

'I believe so,' the engineer said. 'With the gods' aid.'

Valerius heard the unspoken 'and if the commander can hold his nerve'.

'Then it will be done.' The words emerged as a snarl and Petronius flinched at the violence in them.

It was the numbers, Valerius thought. The numbers made it impossible. Perhaps if he sent half of his regiments back it could be done. But that would leave him with too few men to achieve what Corbulo demanded.

'Is there any reason why Vologases shouldn't do what we are doing?'

Petronius hesitated before answering. 'No, but . . . it is unlikely. He already has the alternative of continuing along the Tigris to outflank us in the west. It would cost him a week and General Corbulo has placed a token force there to block him, but it could be done.'

Valerius looked at the sky as the first riders began to pass him. 'It will be dark in an hour.' The engineer nodded. 'Order them to dismount and wrap their horses' hooves to deaden any sound.'

He was still on the plateau when Hanno rode up twenty minutes later. The Syrian's exhausted eyes mirrored Valerius's thoughts. 'It is impossible,' he said quietly.

Yes, it was impossible, but it had to be done.

Because if Valerius failed, Corbulo's army was doomed.

XXXVIII

Rome

They came for Annius Vinicianus in the ghost hour before dawn, when the spirit is at its lowest and the mind dulled. He had been proud of the way he'd held out against their repeated questioning and threats. There had been no violence so far, and though he was a Roman citizen who would soon take his seat in the Senate, that had surprised him. He was no fool; he knew of the horrors Nero had visited on his enemies. That he had been treated so gently he put down to the fact that he had commanded a legion before he was thirty, and, more so, to being the son-in-law of the illustrious Corbulo.

How he wished he had listened to his father-in-law. Who could have predicted a little drunken tittle-tattle among old friends would lead to a damp cell and an uncertain future?

Without warning the door smashed back and he huddled against the wall as six jailers burst in wielding clubs and screaming at him to get to his feet. Helpless and bewildered, he was dragged bodily through a series of tunnels, but his legs told him that he was descending with every step. The deeper they went, the darker his thoughts; he had imagined this moment, had steeled himself for it. In his imagination he had conducted himself with dignity. Now, he felt only a hopeless terror that manifested itself in a weakness in his bladder and a head bursting with panic. His nostrils filled with the thick stink of decay and putrefaction until it blocked his throat like something solid. Far above him the palaces were filled with light and perfume; down here the slime and filth of ages coated the walls, glinting green in the eerie glow of the torchlight. Somewhere ahead a man screamed, a shriek of mortal agony that froze his blood and anchored his feet to the ground. It was as if a signal had been given. His guards turned on him and he went down screaming under a hail of punches and kicks. A blow from a nailed sandal dazed him and he felt himself picked up and carried until they reached some kind of wooden door that creaked when they opened it. Inside, stairs descended ever more steeply into the hill, like the passage to the Underworld. His stunned mind registered the rattle of chains and he felt his tunic being ripped away. When he opened his eyes he was fettered to a wall by the arms in a wide room lit only by the low red glow of a brazier. In front of the brazier a table was arrayed with a butcher's selection of blades, hooks and irons that turned his bowels to liquid.

The guards left him without a word and his mind fought the horror of what was to come.

It was a few moments before he noticed the eyes. They glowed an unearthly red, like the eyes of a rat reflected in the light of a street torch, and they belonged to someone, some . . . thing hiding in the darkness on the far side of the brazier. As he watched, the eyes came closer and he saw that they belonged to a hairless, flesh-covered skeleton that rattled something across the bars that held it captive. The creature stared at him with the intensity of an executioner and for the first time Annius Vinicianus knew the true meaning of fear. Without taking its eyes from him, the filth-covered beast began to rub the human thigh bone it held on the stone floor of its cage, sharpening the end to a fine point. Annius felt each unhurried scrape of the bone like a nail across the inside of his skull.

'You have met our Egyptian, I see.'

He flinched at the unexpected voice from the doorway. Offonius Tigellinus, a short sword naked in his hand, walked unhurriedly into the centre of the room and took his place by the hot coals. Annius sensed someone else in the stair, but the Praetorian prefect waved a languid hand and they were left alone with the baleful creature in the cage. Tigellinus allowed the silence to stretch until the thin membrane inside the younger man's head that is the dividing line between insanity and madness was near breaking point.

'They caught him in Alexandria,' the Praetorian said presently. 'Some sort of merchant. Children and young girls had been disappearing and they eventually traced them to his door. It must have been quite distressing. All that meat hanging on hooks, dried and salted as if it was in some butcher's storehouse. He had a special liking for fresh liver, I believe. Astonishing that they didn't kill him there and then. The Emperor was visiting Egypt at the time and decided to keep him as a pet. And an entertainment.'

Annius's eyes were locked on the red craters that held him as a snake holds a mouse. He choked back the bile that filled his throat at the thought of the horrors that had occurred inside these walls, the screams of the victims unheard beneath thousands of tons of rock and marble.

'I am innocent of any crime.' He despised himself for the fear that was so apparent in his voice.

Tigellinus shook his head sadly, not because it was not true, but because the young man chained before him could be so naive. 'Everyone who comes here is innocent at first.' As he spoke, he stepped closer and his voice seemed to caress Annius's flesh. 'One name can spare you this.'

Annius stared at him. One name? What name? He drew himself up as well as he could in his chains. 'I am a Roman citizen,' he cried. 'I am innocent of any crime. I demand to be tried by a court of my peers.'

'Very well.' Tigellinus sighed wearily. Two men appeared from the doorway. Annius Vinicianus had never seen eyes so empty. 'Begin.'

After three hours Annius had delivered up to Tigellinus every name his pain-swamped brain could think of. As well as those with whom he'd discussed the possibility of removing Nero, he had implicated most of his family and friends, his father's acquaintances in the Senate, many of the officers in his legion, and all the slaves on the family estate.

It seemed even the honoured dead were among his co-conspirators. He lapsed in and out of consciousness, but whatever horrors were inflicted upon him he never spoke the name Tigellinus prayed to hear. Tigellinus was an experienced inquisitor, but more so a seasoned survivor. The clerks were here to record the list of the newly guilty. He knew he could not utter the name himself, because Nero would hear of it and that would weaken his position.

But if he could only get this young fool to say the name once of his own volition the last stone would be in place. The danger to the Empire would be nullified. The Emperor would be saved from his own weakness.

It was time.

'Take him down.' The torturers lifted Annius Vinicianus from the hook that held his chains and laid him on the filth-covered floor. 'Is he alive?' Tigellinus already knew the answer to his question, but he stooped, gripping the point on the young man's arm where the shattered ends of two bones protruded from the flesh, and forced them together. Annius let out a shriek of mortal agony and his eyes flickered open. Tigellinus waited until they had focused on him before kneeling and putting his mouth to what remained of an ear. 'One name, Annius, and it will all be over. One name.' He frowned with annoyance at the incomprehension he read in the haggard face. 'One name, Annius,' he repeated. *'The name that is dearest to you.'*

Every minute of Annius's torment had been accompanied by the rattle of the naked thigh bone across the bars of the Egyptian's cage. The inhuman red eyes had taken in every cut and every touch of the iron, the ears every scream and howl. Saliva drooled from his thin lips and the flat nose twitched at the scent of cooking meat. As the victim had been lowered from the wall the cannibal's excitement had grown beyond containment and he began to howl like a dog.

For the Egyptian knew what was coming.

'Very well, have done with him,' Tigellinus said.

Annius felt himself being lifted. As his head lolled towards the cage the bright red eyes entered his vision and he remembered.

'No!' From somewhere he found his voice.

The cannibal had not been fed for a week and the howl was replaced by an animal shriek as he saw the living flesh being brought to him.

'No.' Somewhere in his incomprehensible terror part of Annius Vinicianus's brain fought for survival. A name. His torturer wanted a name. What had Tigellinus said? *The name that is dearest to you.*

The name that is dearest to you.

He couldn't think for fear. He had already soiled himself and now he did so again as he heard the rattle of the barred door being opened and saw the thigh bone pushed out to touch his flesh.

The name that is dearest to you?

The name that is dearest to you?

The name that is dearest to you . . . !

'Corbulo!' His scream was so piercing that even the cannibal re-coiled from it. 'Corbulo! Corbulo! Corbulo!' The litany only ended when Tigellinus put a finger to his smashed lips. The Praetorian com-mander beckoned the clerks closer.

His voice was almost gentle. 'What was the name?'

'Corbulo,' Annius sobbed, the awfulness of his betrayal only just dawning. 'Gnaeus Domitius Corbulo, general of the east.'

Tigellinus kept his face solemn. 'Very well. Keep him safe for the Emperor, and remember, Annius Vinicianus: the Egyptian will always be waiting for you here.'

Left alone with only the whimpering cannibal for a companion, Tigellinus allowed himself a smile of pure triumph.

The game was won.

XXXIX

Tiberius winced as another Parthian arrow thudded into his shield with the sound of an axe biting into a tree trunk. It could only be a matter of time before one found a gap in his defences and he would join the growing number who crawled to the rear groaning in agony and coughing up blood. Two hours, and already the legion was bleeding to death.

Corbulo had deployed the Tenth Fretensis in a double line of cohorts, each eight men deep and with a front of sixty, which stretched across the valley. Behind them, ready to be rotated into the line, waited the seven full cohorts of the Fifteenth, plus the auxiliary spearmen, slingers and archers who had marched alongside them. He had spaced his forces at intervals to allow room between them for his cavalry to launch counter-attacks. It was a tactic that had worked since the time of Caesar and Pompey and he had used it to hurt the Parthians at Tigranocerta. He was gambling that Vologases would be wary of those cavalry who now raised a constant dust cloud in the valley at the rear of the Roman line. What the Parthian King of Kings did not know was that the dust was being created by a single *ala* of five hundred men, barely enough to provide patrols, scouts and couriers for Corbulo's force.

Tiberius had watched the auxiliary mountain troops from Noricum scale the precipitous valley walls to take their positions on the heights above. With them went a unit of signallers, and the hillmen's job was to protect them and ensure Corbulo's dispositions stayed secret from Vologases while the Parthian movements would be communicated to the Roman general by flag. It would give him a small advantage, but advantages were few and far between.

'Bastards. Bastards. Bastards.' The man crouched behind the next shield muttered his profane mantra to the rhythm of arrows which fell like hailstones on a drum. 'Just come a dozen yards closer and I'll stick this *pilum* so far up your arse . . .'

But Tiberius knew they wouldn't come close, because they didn't have to.

Instead, massed ranks of mounted archers charged to within bow-shot of the Roman line to loose their arrows before withdrawing like surf from a beach and disappearing into their own dust, only to be replaced by the next wave of howling barbarians. Again and again they came, flaying Corbulo's snarling, impotent legionaries with clouds of missiles from a seemingly never-ending supply. In the front rank of the left-hand cohort, Tiberius's suffocating world was reduced to the rear panels of his curved shield, the only thing that was keeping him alive, and the sweating contorted face of his neighbour, packed close enough to share the stink of their combined fear that vied with the reek of voided bowels from someone nearby. Behind him, Tiberius could feel the presence of the man in the next rank whose aching arm held aloft the shield that covered them both from the aerial threat. His belly ached and his throat was filled with dust; heat, thirst and hunger were his constant companions. All around, above the constant rattle of falling arrows, he could hear the cries of the wounded and the dying to the accompaniment of the continuous thunder of the Parthian drummers urging the next wave forward. Cocooned within the claustrophobic protection of the shields he fought a rising tide of anger. The composite bows of wood, bone and sinew outranged any javelin and the general had ordered his auxiliary archers to hoard their precious arrows until they were needed most. It meant the Parthian bowmen could do their work unhindered and unthreatened. He imagined he could hear them laughing and prayed for the moment

Corbulo would let loose his spearmen. A quick dash and a single volley of the heavily weighted *pila* would teach them to laugh at Rome. But Tiberius had seen what happened when a man broke ranks. Through a gap between the shields he had watched as a legionary tormented beyond reason had dropped his shield and run into the arrow-flayed no-man's-land screaming for a proper fight. In the time it had taken to draw his sword a hundred Parthian arrows had transformed him into a human porcupine. No, he must listen for the trumpet call that would signal Corbulo's next order. And endure.

'Shit.' Tiberius winced at the sting of splinters on his cheek as the barbed point of an arrow punched through three layers of seasoned ash to stop less than an inch from his nose. He struggled to control an involuntary loosening in his guts and exchanged a shamefaced grin with the legionary at his side. His neighbour grinned back, but in the same instant the grin became a teeth-baring grimace and an animal groan escaped from his throat. Tiberius looked down and saw that the legionary's sandalled foot had been pinned to the ground by an arrow, with only the flight and a few inches of shaft showing above the shattered bone and spurting scarlet. Careful to keep the shield level, he reached across with his right hand to try to pull the foot free and allow the soldier to stagger or crawl back to where the medical orderlies struggled to deal with a steady stream of casualties. The barbed Parthian arrows were almost impossible to remove without proper surgical tools and any attempt was likely to leave a gaping hole that would condemn the man to a slow death.

'No,' the legionary rasped through gritted teeth. 'Here I am and here I'll stay. Just let the bastards come.'

But the bastards would not come. Not until the Roman line was a shattered, reeling shadow of what it was now. Only when Corbulo's proud legions had been humbled would Vologases loose his champions, the armoured cataphracts led by men like Sasan, invulnerable to arrow, sling and spear and wielding the twelve-foot lance that could smash through a shield to pin a legionary like a cockroach. They would scythe through the thinned ranks the way he had once seen a runaway cart smash through a market crowd, leaving broken bodies in their wake for the Parthian infantry, the poorly armed dregs of Vologases' army, to finish off. Then the way would be open to Tigranocerta and Artaxata and the King of Kings would sit upon his brother's throne and dare Rome to evict him.

But Corbulo had not come here to lose, just as Tiberius had not come here only to fight and die.

Night must arrive soon, and with it respite, and somewhere out there in the darkness was Valerius with the Roman cavalry. Thoughts of Valerius made him ponder the nature of friendship. For a few blessed moments he allowed his mind to wander. Tiberius Claudius Crescens was a young man whose upbringing had made friendship difficult, if not impossible. Discipline had been beaten into him from the beginning and with discipline came responsibility. He was a personable child and people warmed to him, but whenever he became close to the men of his father's command, or the bastard children who swarmed the village outside the fort, something always seemed to happen. He would see a rusty sword which must be reported. A boy's mother might have stolen an egg or another woman's ragged blanket. He called it honesty. They called it betrayal. Gradually they had learned not to trust him, and eventually to avoid him entirely. Even his brother had not been his friend, for he had been engineered to exhibit the same qualities. Eventually he had doubted that he would ever know the true meaning of friendship. Yet when he had met Valerius he had felt an unexpected warmth for another human being that surprised him. It was not only admiration for the scarred tribune's fighting qualities and the battle honours he had won. From the first, Valerius had treated him with respect and an affection that was almost brotherly. He remembered the epic fight on the ship and the contest of minds that was as intense as that of the swords. Somehow there was a bond between them that transcended mere acquaintance. He knew he didn't lack courage, far from it, but sometimes the battlefield could be a lonely place and he wished more than anything that Valerius could be here by his side. A weary sigh escaped him. What would tomorrow bring? For the moment, he was beyond caring. All he knew as the great drums thundered, the arrows fell and the men died, was that he must endure. And survive.

From his position behind the Roman line Gnaeus Domitius Corbulo watched his soldiers suffer and die. This was his plan, his decision, and there was no place in his mind for uncertainty. Yes, he could feel pride, even compassion for the men under his command who were bleeding out on the plain, but wars could not be fought without casualties. These men were legionaries and sometimes it was a legionary's duty to suffer and die, just as it was a commander's duty to stand and watch them do so. He studied the ebb and flow of the attacks with intense concentration. Somewhere in the centre of that immense throng the King of Kings wrestled with his own version of Corbulo's Caesar. He could almost feel the other man's frustration. More than ever, he was certain time was the enemy of Vologases. The Parthian army was composed of a volatile mix of the followers of power-hungry warlords and petty kings from all over his empire. They were impatient men with estates to work and harvests to gather. Flattery and bribery were the only diplomacy they understood. The King of Kings had promised them swift success and all the plunder they could carry. He could not afford to be blocked for long. Vologases' dispositions opened up his mind to Corbulo as if he was reading a map. The Parthian needed a quick victory, but was wary of the heavy casualties it might require. So far there was nothing new, and despite the losses Corbulo was suffering he found that reassuring. Vologases' horse-archers came in their thousands all along the Roman line, and with each wave a hail of arrows poured down on the wall of shields. Many of those shields must now be twice as heavy as when the day started because of the sheer weight of arrows embedded in them. But some of the arrows found gaps. Men bled or died in their ranks or crawled away between their comrades' feet to be replaced by those to the rear.

Behind the archers waited the heavy cavalry so central to the Parthian war machine. Magnificently armoured warriors, the cream of the Parthian nobility, mounted on big horses bred to take their enormous weight. They would not be used until Vologases was certain of victory. Behind them and forming the great mass of the army were the infantry, peasant conscripts dragged reluctantly from their homes and farms by their overlords. Poorly equipped and poorly led, they were of use only once the enemy was broken and on the run. Against a determined legion they were little more than fodder for his men's swords, but their sheer numbers made them a threat and Corbulo knew he could not discount them from his plans. Furthest back, out of Corbulo's sight, would be the Parthian baggage train, from where the long lines of camels ambled forward to resupply the archers. There, far beyond his reach, lay the vast supplies required to keep an army of this size in the field.

He looked to the sky. Another hour before darkness. He doubted that Vologases would send his cataphracts now. Darkness was Rome's ally. It would give the soldiers of the Tenth Fretensis respite from the storm of arrows they had endured for most of the long afternoon. But respite did not mean rest.

It was not the Parthian way to attack at night, but that might not always be so. If he were Vologases he might risk a massed attack of heavy cavalry riding shoulder to shoulder beneath a sky filled with fire arrows. A guard must be set and a line maintained. He studied his battered cohorts. They had borne their torment well, perhaps too well. Tomorrow, timing would be everything. Vologases must be tempted by his enemy's weakness.

He called the commander of the Tenth Fretensis to him. The grey-haired legate's face was lined with exhaustion, but his salute was brisk. 'Are the screens ready, Traianus?'

'Another hour, I believe, sir.'

It would have to do. 'I want them in place as soon as darkness falls. Once it's done remove every second century behind the pit line. At first light they are to lie down behind the auxiliaries where the Parthians can't see their shields. The Fifteenth will also withdraw behind the pits and form a new defensive line there. Vologases must be enticed by our weakness, but we cannot be so weak that he thinks he is being drawn into a trap.'

'Then may I make a suggestion?'

Corbulo nodded. 'Of course.'

'Place the remaining cavalry *ala* in the front line in two wings protecting the flanks. Vologases will believe you have been forced to use every man to hold it.'

It was a sensible idea and Corbulo pondered it for a few moments before deciding against. 'Either we lose too many horses when we withdraw through the pits, or they take the diagonal paths and risk the enemy identifying them and using them as well. No, the shields will hold the line.'

So tomorrow the legionaries would again suffer and die beneath the arrow showers until they were reduced enough to invite the twelve-foot spears of Vologases' cataphracts to annihilate them.

And unless Gaius Valerius Verrens and his cavalry could do the impossible, the army of Corbulo would die with them.

XL

Under the dull light of an ochre moon, Valerius allowed himself to be pulled up the track holding tight to the tail of the horse in front while he led Khamsin by her harness. The path was so narrow and hemmed in by rocks that they had been forced into single file, but the engineer assured him that when they reached the top of the steep slope the column would be able to disperse. Valerius prayed that was true, because the last thing he needed was a fighting force scattered across ten miles of mountains. For the hundredth time he told himself that this was no place for horses and that Corbulo's plan was madness.

He was grateful for the moon, because no man liked darkness and a soldier's superstitions were multiplied by the night. Before the march his cavalrymen had hurriedly made their sacrifices to Mars or Mithras, but the gods, Roman or Syrian, could only placate the dead, not banish them, and their ghosts undoubtedly inhabited these fearsome hills. Valerius had learned not to fear the dead in Britain, where he had once spent the night surrounded by three thousand gutted corpses from the Ninth legion. The memory was with him still, but it was a memory of courage and sacrifice and a fight to the death with no thought of surrender. He tried to focus on Domitia, but her face was distorted as if he was seeing it through shattered green glass and only her eyes were distinct; eyes that did not carry the message he expected or hoped for. A stumble forced him to concentrate on the path. It followed the contours of the hills, which loomed above like broad-shouldered giants, and the men allowed the horses to pick their own way on cloth-wrapped hooves through gullies and across precipitous slopes where the track had been gouged from the earth. Often, Valerius found himself walking in dense blackness with a sense of an immense void a few feet to his right, but he had trusted in Khamsin and she never let him down.

He walked behind the engineer near the head of the snaking, endless line of men and horses and Petronius told him how he came to know this inaccessible wilderness.

'It was at the end of the second campaign, while Corbulo was negotiating the peace. He had heard of the Cepha gap and immediately recognized its strategic importance – he is like that, no detail is too unimportant to be ignored – and asked me to survey it and the surrounding area. I was here for two months dressed in Armenian rags in the dead of winter. I marked out the site for a fort, if ever one were needed, but I wanted to know if the fort could be outflanked to the east, and if truth be told these mountains have a certain fascination. Men have lived here for thousands of years. There are cave cities close to our route that I would like to have visited again, but I fear we will have other priorities . . .'

A ragged scream cut the darkness from somewhere behind, followed by the muted thunder of crashing rocks. Horse or man or both? Petronius hesitated, then shrugged his shoulders. There was nothing anyone could do. The gods only knew how many more had been lost among the forces behind. For a few oppressive moments they waited for the sound of violent reaction that would signal the column's discovery, but Valerius knew he could depend on the scouts who ranged ahead seeking any sign of a Parthian presence. The two men carried on until they reached a broad basin, almost a huge natural amphitheatre, and Valerius ordered the lead elements to halt and allow the tail of the column to catch up.

'Make the most of the next two or three miles,' Petronius advised. 'The worst comes when we leave the road and begin our descent towards the Tigris.'

'Road?' Serpentius laughed. 'Even in Asturia this wouldn't be called a road.'

'Well,' the engineer said, offended. 'You will see just how good a road this is before dawn.'

It was past midnight now. They had been in the hills for four hours and Petronius reckoned they had only covered half the distance they needed before dawn. The route had taken them in a great flanking arc from the Cepha gap, first to the east and then south, on a perilous, little-used smugglers' track. 'There is a dried-up watercourse to the west, below the road,' the engineer explained. 'I will know it when I see it, but that is difficult enough in daylight. It leads to a broad gully that will bring us to the river downstream of the Tigris crossing point. If we can gather there undetected and form up on the open plain north of the river we have a chance.'

He didn't have to say it was only a slim chance and that at the first shout of warning Valerius and his ten thousand would be facing the bulk of the King of Kings' seventy-thousand-strong army. But that was for the future. What mattered now was that they reach the gully before dawn.

Despite their slow progress, Petronius insisted it could be done, and done in time, but that was before the patrol returned and reported the lights. The scout was a wiry, dark-skinned Numidian and he made his report in the slang-ridden dog Latin that was the common tongue of auxiliary units across the Empire.

'We saw fires in the ground, lord . . .'

'He must mean the caves,' Petronius interrupted.

'We obeyed your order not to attack, only look. They were hid in the ground, so I had to go closer to count their numbers, lord.'

'How many were they?' Valerius asked.

The man raised his open hands twice in answer, then showed four fingers.

'And where?'

He gave a long complicated explanation and Petronius groaned aloud.

'I know this place. A mile ahead. Caves set into the base of a cliff wall in the next valley.'

271

His face gave Valerius his answer before he asked the question. 'Can we bypass them?'

Petronius shook his head. 'We need to go through the valley to reach the riverbed. We could never slip past unnoticed with this many men.'

Valerius could feel the weight of the cavalry units backing up behind. There could only be one decision. He called for Hanno. 'A hundred of your best. This man will guide you. Make it quick, but be sure none escapes.'

'I'll go,' Serpentius volunteered. Valerius opened his mouth to refuse, but Serpentius was like a ghost in the dark and as good a man with a knife as he'd ever known. The Spaniard had also acquired a pair of Sarmatian throwing axes with which he was now as proficient as their previous owner. Valerius nodded and Serpentius grinned in the darkness and started removing his armour and anything else that might make a noise that would alert the enemy.

Hanno clapped him on the shoulder. 'Caladus will lead, but he will be happy to have you with him.'

He called his men together and gave them their instructions.

Caladus and Serpentius stared down the valley at the almost imperceptible orange glow the Numidian had pointed out at the base of the cliff. It was so faint that only someone passing close by – or one with eyes that could see like the desert falcon of his Berber homelands – would have noticed it.

'They have been here all night and seen nothing,' Caladus guessed. 'Perhaps they have been here several nights. Their commander has allowed them a fire in an inner room where he believes it is well enough hidden.'

'Careless,' Serpentius said.

'So careless it will cost him his life,' Caladus agreed.

'But not so careless that they have not set guards,' the Numidian whispered. 'Do you see them?'

The Thracian and the Spaniard peered into the darkness, but they could see nothing but shadows and rocks.

'To the left of the entrance. A tall man who stinks like a *houri* and

272

then, across the valley where he thinks he is hidden, a second, fat as a pig, though he moves lightly. And the third, hardly more than a boy, but more alert than the others, stands by the horses in a hollow beyond the next bend. The others are all in the caves, sleeping or talking.'

Caladus pondered his options. 'The boy with the horses is the greatest danger. One shout and he will be gone. Serpentius? Do you think you can get past the guards to the horses without being seen?'

'Keep to the centre of the valley,' the Numidian advised. 'There is the shadow of an ancient stream bed. Stay low and silent as the hunting leopard, and you will do it easily. I will take the guard on the far side.'

Serpentius nodded.

'I'll give you to the count of two hundred. A single arrow will deal with the third sentry. Then we'll surround the caves and kill the rest.' Almost before Caladus had finished speaking, Serpentius was gone, disappearing into the darkness with the Numidian at his heels.

The Spaniard slithered down the valley on his belly like the snake he was named for, ignoring the dry stalks and sharp stones that stabbed his flesh and tore his tunic. He kept his face low to the ground and trusted to the Numidian's instinct that the slight fold in the sweet-smelling earth would cover his movements from the watchers on either side of the valley. Despite the dangers, his breathing was slow and easy. This was nothing new for Serpentius. It reminded him of the night raids of his youth against neighbouring villages. But that was before the Romans came, with their lust for gold, their lists and their order. Before they took him for a slave and turned him into an animal in a cage to be exhibited before the scum and the degenerates in the arena. For a moment his mind was consumed with a familiar hatred, and it was not hatred for the Parthian warrior he stalked. This was not his fight and the Romans were not his people. But he had pledged his life to Valerius and Valerius was the closest thing to a friend he had. So he would kill. He would kill with regret, but the Parthian was already in his grave.

He made swift progress along the shallow depression and he neither saw nor heard the guards as he passed the pale light among the rocks. A minute later he smelled the horses.

A mile away to the north, Valerius willed himself to stay calm. Every

273

minute was precious. Every minute they wasted here was another minute when the men of Corbulo's army must suffer the agony of the Parthian arrows. It would take time to get the column in motion again. Time to negotiate the gully that would bring them to the river. And time to form up his men for the attack. Too much time. All around him men and horses waited impatiently for the order to move.

A gentle whisper reached Serpentius as he lay face down in the rough grass ten paces from the tethered Parthian mounts. The count of two hundred had long come and gone, but he could not afford to hurry. He would have the chance for one strike and one only. The knife or the axe? The knife: quicker, cleaner and surer. The unwary Parthian sentry was talking quietly to his horses as they snickered nervously in their halters. They were upwind, if the gentle movement of the air could be called a wind, of the Roman column, but some instinct had alerted them to the presence of others of their kind. Their nervousness should have alerted the guard, but Serpentius guessed there would have been many such false alarms in hills roamed by the lion, the leopard and the wolf. If anything, it increased his chances of success. Even if the animals became aware of him, the sentry was unlikely to react swiftly enough.

Drawing his long knife, he crawled through the grass until he was on the edge of the group of horses: small, light-limbed beasts favoured by the Parthian archers. He raised his hand so the closest would catch his scent and the animal snickered gently, wary, but not frightened of this new human presence. Shielded by the herd, Serpentius rose smoothly to his feet and reassessed his situation. The Parthian had stopped whispering and it was impossible to see because the cliff above shielded the moon, but Serpentius searched the darkness until he found what he was looking for. Not a man shape, just something that might have been a rock, but wasn't. When the rock moved, he was certain.

No man could approach an armed warrior in the dark without feeling fear, but Serpentius had long since learned how to channel his fear and turn it into ice cold, iron hard resolution. Another man would have rushed the sentry, depending on the element of surprise, but all it would take was the glint of the knife or the sound of footsteps to turn

274

surprise into disaster. Instead, Serpentius dropped to his stomach again and slid through the jungle of moving legs and fresh horseshit until he was within touching distance of his target. Still shielded by the shifting horses, he waited for his moment.

The sentry was little more than a boy, unblooded and on his first campaign, and he was angry that he had to spend another night with the horses. Part of his mind was on the older men who had laughed at him when he had warned against lighting the fire. The other chewed on the battle he was missing and the brothers who were gaining all the glory. The last thing he saw was a slim shadow that stepped from among the horses. The last thing he felt was the sting of the knife that sliced across his throat severing tendon and windpipe to leave him drowning in his own blood. But he managed to cry out, and that one cry was enough. The second guard had been sitting to his left and now he launched himself, not at Serpentius, but at the nearest horse, loosing the knot that held it as he went. He was in the saddle and moving before Serpentius could stop him. The Spaniard reached for the axe at his belt . . .

Valerius waited impatiently as Caladus led the patrol back. He had to be certain before he made his next move. One by one the Thracians came to him and laid a round object at his feet. He counted the bearded, snarling heads until he reached twenty-three.

'Your Numidian said twenty-four.'

Caladus shrugged. 'The Spaniard never came back.'

'We don't have time for this . . .'

He was interrupted as a silent figure stepped from the dark. Serpentius dropped the two heads he carried with the others.

'Twenty-five.' He turned to Caladus. 'I would have word with the Numidian.'

The Thracian laughed. 'You could count yourself fortunate, indeed, for then you would be in Elysium. He was always too cocky for his own good. You can never underestimate a Parthian.'

Three men dead, an hour lost. But the way was clear.

*

The sun was well up when they reached the river and Valerius despaired of discovery by some wandering patrol or foraging party. Corbulo had said time was his enemy's enemy, but now it was Valerius's. He had promised the general he would be in position at dawn on the second day. Instead, his ten thousand cavalry were still straggling across two miles of path and he didn't dare move out on to the narrow strip of floodplain that separated the mountains from the river until he was ready.

Petronius explained their position. 'Yonder you see the river.' He pointed to a deep gorge half a mile distant. 'It is only crossable at one place in this area, and that is at Cepha a mile upstream. From Cepha it is another four miles to the gap. Vologases will undoubtedly have left a guard on the crossing place, but beyond it all that will be between you and his army is the baggage train. The plain below us is hidden from the bridge by rising ground, but it is possible we will be seen forming up from the far bank, so there is no time to lose.'

'Pass the word to put on the tunics.'

Every man had carried a rolled-up bundle behind his saddle as well as his weapons and rations. Now they unwrapped them to reveal the Armenian tunics Corbulo had ordered his quartermaster to requisition on the long march from Zeugma. Short and woven of light cloth, they had intricately embroidered facings of gold and blue and red, similar to those of the Parthians. The tunics were loose enough to be worn over mail and Valerius gambled that any observer who saw them from a distance would be lulled into thinking it was one of his own formations.

'It may seem unnecessary, even foolish,' Corbulo had told him. 'You may not convince them, but even if you confuse them for only a second, that could be the second that makes the difference between victory and defeat.'

A courier forced his way past the riders behind Valerius and announced that the rearguard was ready.

With his heart pounding, Valerius gave the order to advance out on to the plain. After the long hours in the mountains it felt very open and vulnerable. There was no turning back now. In truth, for all his doubts and fears on the long night march there had never been any turning back. Corbulo had chosen his man well. They had outflanked the Parthians.

Yet the mountain crossing had merely been the first hurdle. Now he must attack Vologases' army of seventy thousand men with barely a tenth that number. His cavalry troopers were exhausted and hungry. There was no hope of support if the attack faltered and no place to retreat if the Parthians prevailed. If he failed, every man here would die, along with the thousands of Romans fighting for their lives a bare five miles away.

They were late to the fight, but they were here. The only thing in their favour was surprise, but as the cavalry wings began to form up behind him, with Hanno and his Third Thracians in the centre, Valerius felt the first rising of that glorious sense of invulnerability that preceded battle and he sent a silent prayer to Fortuna, the goddess of good fortune.

'At the walk . . . advance.'

XLI

Tiberius knew this was his day to die.

In the first light of dawn he had snatched a mouthful of bread from his pouch and a hurried drink from one of the carriers who traversed the depleted Roman line with a dozen skins of brackish water hanging from his shoulder. It was clear he would not complete his mission now, but that did not matter. He had done his duty. Even his father would be proud.

The initial Parthian sorties had come not long after daylight and the hail of arrows rattling against the curved Roman shields had resumed. That had been two hours ago, and already the man on his right had changed twice. First the fool who replaced the legionary with the wounded foot inched his shield to the side to take a look at the enemy and received a shaft through the brain for his trouble. An hour later an arrow had found a weak spot in a *scutum* and burst through as if it was made of parchment to pierce the shield's owner through the heart.

Yet now there was an unlikely respite when the arrows stopped. For a few moments he wondered if the Roman gods he had been invoking all morning had prevailed over the Parthian deities.

But not for long.

Because the thunder of the Parthian drums heralded a new terror.

The King of Kings had summoned his Invincibles.

From his position to the right of the Roman defences, Gnaeus Domitius Corbulo, proconsul of Syria and Cappadocia, commander of the armies of the east and three times holder of the triumphal regalia, watched the valley fill with a long line of gleaming metal and glittering spear points, and fought the unfamiliar gut-wrenching ache of despair. He stared out beyond the gaily coloured pavilions at the centre of that vast army to the horizon beyond, but the sky was empty and the signs he was looking for existed only in his mind. Valerius had failed him.

He understood he was being too harsh. That he had expected too much. His great plan had depended on a combination of exact timing and good fortune that no sane man could have expected. He had taken the cooperation of the gods for granted and now they would have their revenge for his hubris. And down there, in the shattered cohorts of the Roman front line, were the brave men who would pay the price. For a moment his heart told him to take his staff and share their fate. But he was General Gnaeus Domitius Corbulo and Gnaeus Domitius Corbulo did not shirk his duty, even if his duty meant watching his men die and feeling every spear, arrow and sword as if it was entering his own body.

A quarter of a mile separated the mismatched armies, but he saw movement as the long strip of armour shimmered and snaked like a viper shedding its skin and he knew they were straightening the line for the advance. The drums went quiet and an awful silence settled over the field. The Parthian host lumbered into motion.

'Prepare for the signal.' The young *cornicen* at Corbulo's side licked his lips and put his mouth to the curved bronze trumpet.

For the first hundred paces the Parthian cataphracts advanced at the walk. Only a thousand men out of an army of seventy thousand would make the attack because less than one in a hundred could afford the prohibitively expensive armour of bronze and iron that could take a craftsman a year to make. A nobleman like Sasan might arm and horse ten retainers, and arm them well, but many were protected by helms and mail handed down through generations which showed the marks of repair and long service. Precious few could fully armour their horses, and that made the horses vulnerable. Those without trappers made up

279

the rear ranks of the five divisions bearing down on the hated Roman enemy. The van of the charge consisted of the most heavily armoured, and therefore the richest and most powerful, of Vologases' retainers.

By the time they reached halfway they had broken into a trot and Corbulo knew from experience that they would go no faster. Their sheer weight and the length of the twelve-foot lances they carried meant they did not need to. He tensed, ready to give the order.

Courage was something Tiberius Claudius Crescens took for granted. Fear was bewildering. Fear meant a mouth dry as any desert, legs you knew could not run fast enough and the feeling that ants were crawling all over you. As he stood behind his arrow-scarred shield in the front line, Tiberius watched the great horses come and felt the ground shaking beneath his feet. One part of him wanted to applaud the magnificence of that armoured host, in their polished mail and their gleaming plate armour, the horsehair plumes streaming out behind their helmets. The other watched the spears drop so that every leaf-shaped iron point as long as a legionary's *gladius* was directed at a Roman shield and knew that his body was about to be ground to dust beneath the giant hooves.

'Now,' Corbulo said quietly. 'Sound the withdrawal.'

The harsh call of the trumpet rang out across the valley.

'Withdraw!' Tiberius's shout was echoed in every cohort across the Roman line.

The rear ranks were already on the move, cutting diagonals through the escape corridors the Roman engineer had marked. The front rank jogged directly towards the rear, shielding the route of their comrades from curious eyes, watching the ground below their feet and praying that the Parthians were far enough away to allow them to make their escape.

A shriek from Tiberius's left was testament that one legionary had been too slow, or a Parthian too fast. The young tribune turned just in time to see the sword-like point of the long spear punch through iron, flesh and bone as if they were silk, spitting the screaming man like a roasting duck and carrying him off the ground. Another stride and the Parthian charger's front leg snapped like a rotten branch and her shoulder dropped to throw her helpless rider in the air. The heavily armoured nobleman sailed a dozen paces and landed helmet first in the earth with a metallic crash, while the horse somersaulted in a cloud of dust to lie screaming with a broken back and its ruined leg flapping. At last Tiberius was through to safety and into the first ranks of the new defence line. His senses reeling, he turned to witness a scene of utter carnage.

The Parthian warlords were so fixed on their targets and so certain of their invincibility that they entirely failed to see the cunningly disguised traps. Each pit had been covered with a woven lid of dried grass that exactly matched its surroundings. Between them were scattered hundreds of the hellish four pronged caltrops which would force four inches of iron into the tender flesh of a charging horse's hoof. The front ranks of the Parthian charge disintegrated into a chaos of tumbling horses and riders. All along the Roman line, the flower of the Parthian horse herds, the sires and dams of generations of champions to come went down in a welter of shattered bone and sudden death. The bodies of smashed horses and men created a barrier for those behind and the second line of cataphracts had the choice of leaping over their dead and dying predecessors or crashing into the fallen in front of them. Those who chose to leap found more pits and spikes and the screams of the horses seemed never-ending. Only a few survived to take the fight to the Romans, and they were quickly engulfed by legionaries and auxiliaries who swarmed over the armoured horses like ants to bring them down.

Tiberius watched as a Parthian nobleman, his bearded face a snarl of hatred, speared one legionary while a second hacked the legs of his horse from under him with a sword. Once he was down, his heavy armour pinned him like an upturned tortoise. The metal saved him from the frenzy of hacking blades that smashed into his torso, but not from the dagger that first took out his eyes before slitting his throat as he screamed defiance in a tongue his killers could not understand. The democracy of the dead had no respect for rank. Mighty Sasan, spear carrier to the King of Kings, was among the fallen a yard from the Roman line. He had been tossed from his mount's back like a sack of grain and the impact of his landing had broken half the bones in his body and smashed his internal organs to so much pulp. Now he lay paralysed and helpless, cursing the ambitions of kings with the taste of blood in his mouth, and praying for the killing stroke he knew could not be long in coming.

'Prisoners.' Tiberius belatedly remembered the order that had been given what seemed a lifetime ago. 'We need prisoners.'

Two hundred of the Parthian elite were down, but hundreds more riders milled uncertainly in the dust storm beyond the barrier of dead and injured horses and men. A growl went up from the legionary line and they surged forward with sword, shield and spear, the memories of their hours of trial by arrow still fresh.

'Hold your station.' A senior centurion of Tiberius's cohort lashed out with the vine stick of his office. 'You don't kill until I fucking say so. Spears, now, spears. Any who are down are already as good as dead. It's those bastards still in the saddle we want. Aim for the horses.'

Each legionary of the Tenth and the Fifteenth had been supplied with four of the heavily weighted *pila* javelins, and in the gaps between the cohorts now appeared hundreds of auxiliary slingers and archers. They advanced until they were among the pits and the caltrops and the screaming horses and dying men, and forty paces from the survivors of the Parthian attack.

'Ready!' The cry went up all along the line and five thousand arms drew back. The *cornicines'* trumpets blared. 'Throw!'

To penetrate plate or mail, a *pilum* must strike at the perfect angle, but the five thousand javelins which flew through the air with a prolonged sigh were not aimed at the armoured cataphracts of the Parthian third rank, but at their mounts. The *pilum* consisted of a length of ash tipped by a shaft of iron the length of a man's arm and a weighted pyramidal point designed to pierce shield and armour. Now those shafts tore through the flesh and muscle and bone of the Parthian warhorses and thickened the bloody barricade of dead and dying which separated the two forces. Animal screams of agony and terror rent the air. While the victims of the first throw were still falling a second volley of javelins descended, killing and maiming still more. It was enough. A Parthian drummer sounded a frantic, unfamiliar beat and the survivors of the javelin storm turned their horses and fled, leaving their dismounted companions to stagger after them as best they could in their heavy armour.

A cheer rippled along the Roman line and but for the commands of their centurions the legionaries would have bounded forward in their thirst for more blood. Instead, they were hustled back into their defensive cohorts and the dying began again.

Because the Parthian bowmen were back.

XLII

Valerius rode in the centre of the front rank, with the reassuring presence of Serpentius at his shoulder. At first the land sloped steeply from the mountains to the river, making it awkward for the cavalry wings to keep formation on the dry, stony ground, but gradually it flattened out and the going became easier for man and beast. They were in loose formation, as befitted their thin disguise as enemy cavalry, and kept tight to the hill side of the plain. Valerius gambled that the Parthian baggage train and the camp followers of Vologases' army would stay close to the river and a guaranteed supply of water.

The baggage train of a Roman army was a disciplined, tightly structured unit run by experienced quartermasters and designed to ensure the ready provision of food or weapons where they were needed at any given time. Corbulo had explained that what he would find in the Parthian rear would be very different.

'The King of Kings has his personal baggage train, perhaps a thousand wagons and several hundred pack camels, from which he will feed and supply himself and the royal forces, and which will lead the march after the fighting troops. It also carries Vologases' concubines and his war chest, so it will be protected by the elite of his palace guard. Each warlord or petty king will also have his own train and they will haggle for priority, making their own time. There will be few guards on the rearmost trains, because the Parthians believe they have nothing to fear.'

Scattered groups of camp followers were the first sign they were reaching the rear of the main force, and these had grown thicker by the time they came level with the Cepha bridge, which was a seething mass of frustrated humanity and nose to tail ox carts. Upstream of the bridge, on the heights overlooking the Tigris, an entire city of wagons and tents sprawled into the distance beneath a haze of smoke from hundreds of dung fires. The sun was high now, and although they drew complacent glances from the Parthians on the fringe of the temporary settlement no one challenged them. It was clear that Corbulo's ruse was working. A cavalry formation in the rear of the Parthian lines wearing recognizably Parthian clothing must be a friendly force.

That was about to change.

Valerius called forward the commanders of the cavalry wings of the left flank. Hanno with his thousand strong Third Thracians was the most senior, and Valerius had given him command of the attack on the Parthian supply lines, with the support of two further regiments of five hundred spearmen.

'You have your orders. When you hear my signal, burn the wagons and the supplies and scatter the horse herds. Leave them nothing. If you meet opposition in one camp, move on to the next, then the next. Remember, your job is not to kill, but to destroy.'

'What about the bridge? Do we burn that too?' Hanno asked.

Valerius shook his head. It was a tempting target, but Corbulo's orders had been clear. 'You've seen the size of this army. We can hurt Vologases and we can make his men go hungry, but we can't destroy him. If this turns into a battle of attrition there can be only one winner. We have to leave him an escape route.'

While the three cavalry units moved into position, Valerius led the remaining horsemen up the valley. He knew their luck couldn't hold much longer. The shelf between the river and the hills was beginning to narrow now and it was only a matter of time before they were challenged. To his left a circle of brightly coloured cloth pavilions dominated the most substantial of the Parthian camps and he guessed it must be home to members of Vologases' closest retinue. Even as he watched a group of red-plumed riders broke from the camp.

'Wait until they hail us before you kill them.'

Serpentius nodded and passed on the whispered order. Valerius ignored the approaching riders and concentrated on what lay ahead. A rumble which seemed to vibrate the air was now recognizable as the pounding of the Parthian signal drums. Yet it was almost drowned by an even more pervasive sound. A sound which made the hair stand up on the back of Valerius's neck. It was as if someone had disturbed a giant beehive with a stick. The low drone of a million beating wings. But he knew what he was hearing was no sound heard in nature. It was the sound of a multitude, certainly, but a multitude of men. The last time he had heard that sound was when Boudicca's mighty horde had breasted the ridge before Colonia, filling the slope like an incoming tide.

'Signaller?'

'Sir.' The man readied the *lituus*, the ornate trumpet used by the cavalry for relaying commands.

The sharp cry of a warning shout was answered by the thrum of bowstrings and followed by the screams of at least two men and the thud of falling bodies. Cries of consternation rang out from the camp to his left.

'Sound the charge.'

The two distinct notes from the brass horn were echoed among the advancing squadrons and from behind, where Valerius knew Hanno would be launching his attack on the lightly defended baggage camps. Beneath him Khamsin responded to the call without the urging of his heels, surging into the trot and snorting through her nostrils. He could feel her excitement and that of the men around him as he reached for the long cavalry *spatha* and felt its familiar weight in his left hand. His ears echoed with the thunder of hooves across the packed earth. To his right, Serpentius snarled a litany of what sounded like curses, but Valerius knew would be prayers to the Spaniard's native gods. A dozen more strides and the air was thick with the stench of human excrement as they passed over ground where Vologases' tens of thousands of infantry had camped the previous night. In the far distance, still a mile away, a dark stain covered the gold of the fields of dried grass in the southern neck of the Cepha gap. His heart almost failed him at the sight of that huge mass of men. It had always been a gamble, but now that gamble was exposed as suicidal. The first rule of war was that a commander should not attack unless he was aware of his enemy's dispositions. Valerius could only be guided by Gnaeus Domitius Corbulo's advice and his own intuition. That advice and intuition said that Vologases would mass his cavalry against the Roman line and continue to use it in successive waves until Corbulo's army was destroyed, or so weakened as to be helpless before a final Parthian charge. If the King of Kings held even a few hundred of his armoured cataphracts in reserve they were capable of blunting Valerius's charge and destroying its momentum.

He chanced a look over his shoulder and was rewarded with a sky filled with towering clouds of smoke; the funeral pyre for King Vologases' baggage train. Hanno had done his job well. If nothing else the Roman soldiers holding back this huge army would see it and know hope.

Half a mile now to the mouth of the valley. The first auxiliary cavalry were already sweeping through the gaping, stunned stragglers hurrying to join the Parthian army; swords slashed down and blood stained the golden grassland.

'Hold the line.' Valerius roared the order and the signaller echoed it with his trumpet.

A Parthian war drum answered the call with a frantic beat and Valerius saw movement in the ranks ahead, as what commanders there were frantically attempted to form a defensive line. But these were conscripts who had been waiting for two days while their cavalry fought to breach the Roman defences. They were farmers and peasants, townsmen and shopkeepers who had no option but to march behind their lord and no inclination for battle. If they expected to fight it was against a defeated enemy fleeing from the cataphracts' spears. Yet even that expectation had been blunted by the endless hours of waiting. They were listless and bored, lying in groups wondering how long it was until the next meal. Now their leaders screamed confused orders and the sky to the east was black with the smoke of their burning rations and thousands of strange cavalrymen were bearing down on them at a terrifying rate. A few managed to form the semblance of a defence, but they were small groups of widely spaced spearmen. Most froze in confusion and terror.

A cantering horse takes less than a minute to cover half a mile. By the time the Parthians had worked out whether they were facing friend or foe that distance had halved, then halved again. Eight of Valerius's auxiliary wings were made up of mounted archers and he had placed them in the front ranks. They loosed their first arrows at a hundred and fifty paces, darkening the sky with feathered shafts that arched gracefully before plummeting into the massed ranks of the Parthians. Before the first had landed, a second volley was on its way, instantly followed by a third. Twelve thousand arrows rained down on the Parthian spearmen in the space of twenty seconds. None of the defenders wore armour, few had helmets, and the wickedly barbed points pierced skull, shoulder and back as men crouched to avoid the rain of deadly missiles. Instinctively they sought shelter, pushing back into the unharmed mass behind them, but there was no shelter.

The archers turned away, using the same tactics which had tormented the Romans for the past two days, but they were immediately replaced by Numidian spearmen who added their light javelins to the horror, hurling them one after the other into the cringing mass of Parthians. By now the killed and wounded lay ten and fifteen deep along the length of the Parthian line, carpeting the valley in a twitching mantle of death. Still it was not enough, for the bowmen returned, giving the enemy no respite and firing again and again until their supply of arrows was spent, then turning away once more.

Valerius steeled himself against pity. The killing must go on, for when the Parthians stopped dying the agony of the Romans would begin. He waved the light cavalry forward once more. Their javelins were spent, but they were far from harmless. It was time for the swords.

There was little cohesion to the Roman line, but there did not need to be. Fear was as great a weapon as any blade. The Parthian foot soldiers on the fringes of the great mass that made up Vologases' rearguard were already demoralized by the carnage caused by the Roman spears and arrows. Now their only thought was to escape these phantoms who had appeared where no enemy had a right to appear. Many had already thrown away their spears in blind panic, and as Valerius's mounted cohorts urged their horses over the corpses of those already fallen they scrabbled to bury themselves deeper in the illusory safety of the crowd. But there was no escape from the swords.

This was not war. It was slaughter.

The *spathae* rose and fell with the relentless rhythm of a farmer's scythe and with similar effect. Valerius cut left and right, carving through terrified, shrieking faces and balding skulls, chopping torsos from shoulder to rib and removing hands and arms raised in desperate attempts to protect their owners. And all along the Roman line men did the same. Though he didn't realize it, he snarled and grunted and cursed with every blow he struck. He tried not to see the grey porridge of an opened skull, the splintered bone of shattered arms or the pink mess of a sword-slashed lung, but he knew the images would remain with him for ever. Within minutes his left arm was slick with other men's blood; it coated his armour and he could feel it on his face and taste it on his lips. The sheer scale of Vologases' army, allied to the narrowness of the valley, protected Valerius's men from counter-attack, because the Parthian war bands which had retained their cohesion and fighting spirit had to battle their way through the men trying to flee the butchery. Even so, amongst the dead, the dying and the defeated there were still men prepared to fight.

'To your left.'

Serpentius's snarled warning gave Valerius the heartbeat he needed to duck away from the spear point that would have taken out his throat. He slashed frantically at the shaft and kicked Khamsin through the cowering bodies towards his attacker, a bearded Parthian with dark eyes and a mouth that snarled hatred. Inside the point he knew he had little to fear from the spearman, but this easterner was no shopkeeper. The long ash shaft came round in a hammer blow to the cheekplate of Valerius's helmet, almost knocking him from the saddle. As he clung to Khamsin's side, the men he had been killing saw their opportunity and with a collective howl rose up to haul him from her back, hands tearing at him and gouging at his face. Pinned by four or five bodies he felt a sting in his ribs as a dagger point managed to pierce his mail and the leather tunic beneath. It was only a matter of time before its owner sought out his throat or his eyes. Roaring with fury and with the violence of despair, he lashed out at the men holding him, but they were too many. A man pinned his sword hand and the bearded spearman sat on his chest and spat in his face before drawing the knife that would kill him.

A glint of metal flashed in front of Valerius's face, swift as any lightning strike, and the spearman's head spun from his shoulders leaving his still upright body fountaining blood from the neck. Another man shrieked as a blade split him from throat to crotch, spilling intestines in long coils from his torn body. Valerius hauled the dead weight of the headless man from his chest as his attackers scattered from the ferocious assault of a whip-thin madman with a face that was a gory mask of horror.

'Here!' Serpentius reached down and with another trooper's help hauled Valerius to his feet. Miraculously Khamsin still stood over him and he pulled himself back into the saddle. He had lost Corbulo's *spatha*, but when he reached over his shoulder the familiar grip of the *gladius* moulded itself into his hand and he was armed again. His ears rang from the blow to his head and he could feel blood running down his ribs from where the dagger had struck, but he had no time to rest. He forced himself to concentrate on the cacophony of sounds around him and tried to sense the battle. From somewhere he found a moment of calm, though the breath rasped in his throat and his heart hammered as if it was trying to break free from his ribs. Oddly, it was the soft hiss of disturbed air that registered first, confirming that the mounted archers had returned with their quivers replenished from captured Parthian supply camels. That told him Hanno was in control of his operation and, for the moment, he could disregard his rear.

The slaughter of the spearmen continued. There was no let-up in the butcher's-block smack of edged metal cutting into flesh and bone, but he knew the situation could not continue indefinitely. More and more Parthians were fighting back, and Roman blood now mingled with that of the enemy. Eventually the arms of his auxiliary cavalrymen would tire, the arrows would run out and the attack would lose its momentum. When the killing stopped the Parthians would be able to draw breath, and when they did they would see how relatively few the Roman horsemen were. Panicked or not, someone would organize a counter-attack and that counter-attack could only have one outcome. But Valerius had made his pledge to Corbulo and that pledge was to fight to his last breath, and that of every man with him. The question was, what was happening on the far side of that great army where the Roman line had endured all this long day? It endured still, Valerius was certain of that, or the Parthian foot would have been able to withdraw and reorganize. Vologases was still trapped between two forces, even if those forces were vastly inferior to his own. But this was not Caesar; being trapped did not bring automatic victory. Somehow, the king's confidence must be destroyed and his vast army demoralized. That could only be achieved by one man.

Valerius raised his sword and urged Khamsin back into the carnage, praying not to any god, but to Gnaeus Domitius Corbulo.

XLIII

Corbulo's face betrayed no emotion as another shower of arrows fell on his bloodied cohorts, but inwardly he shuddered with revulsion. The Parthians had become braver and more confident, advancing to the very edge of the line of dead horses and dead men which were the only things now keeping the enemy at bay. Unlike the Romans below, the mountain troops on the crags were winning their battle and the signallers kept up a constant stream of information on Parthian movements which were otherwise invisible to their general. It seemed to Corbulo that Vologases' growing frustration was written clearly in the steady build-up of troops just behind the front ranks of cavalry. Vast numbers now waited for the final order to advance less than two hundred paces from the fragile line of legionaries.

Corbulo could imagine, or believed he could imagine, the scene in the imperial pavilion. Vologases still had his tens of thousands of mounted archers, and eventually those archers could win him victory. But archers were ten to the *as*. It was the cataphracts which were the symbol of Parthian power. The armoured might of the nation. The warrior elite who kept the King of Kings upon his gilded throne. Now he had lost three hundred and fifty of those petty kings, warlords and clan chieftains and their most trusted retainers in a single afternoon, drawn in by a trick any basilica conjuror would have seen through. Not only had he lost his armoured spearhead, he had lost his key military and political advisers and the confidence of those who remained. The hierarchy which kept him in power had been fatally disturbed. There would be no talk of quick, bloodless victories now. Yet he still had a mighty army and given the right leadership that mighty army could smash its way through the thin Roman line. Already Corbulo could see infantry among the leading horsemen and he knew what would happen next. The archers would keep the embattled legionaries at bay while the foot soldiers manhandled the dead men and horses which barred the Parthian advance clear and filled in the pits. What would stop them then?

Tiberius watched the general as he deliberated, marvelling at the calm of the man. The Parthians had launched a second armoured attack midway through the morning, but it had been a half-hearted affair with few of the horses even attempting to charge the Roman cohorts directly. The arrow storm had been the worst torment and he knew he had been fortunate to survive after so long in the front rank. Now he was at Corbulo's side, the most junior of aides, courtesy of an arrow fired with particular venom which had soared over the lines to impale his predecessor through the right eye. The sweetly sick scent of death was thick in his nostrils and nothing he had witnessed since daybreak had changed his opinion that his own decaying flesh would soon be adding to the stink of corruption. Until now.

He had to look twice before he realized what he was seeing. 'General!'

Every eye turned to the far horizon.

Smoke.

A great dark swirling pall hanging in the still air behind and to the east of Vologases' army.

Corbulo's stern features were split by a grim smile and he sent up a prayer of thanks, asking the gods to aid the endeavours of Gaius Valerius Verrens. He had stopped Vologases in his tracks, he had bloodied him and now he had confused him. But that was nothing to the horror Corbulo was about to unleash on the hemmed-in Parthian army.

'Gentlemen, take your positions.'

A ragged cheer went up from the Roman line. Tiberius could hear the shouts of the centurions demanding silence and he imagined the gnarled vine sticks cracking on backs. But the cheer had unsettled the Parthians and it was as if a collective shudder ran through that packed mass of humanity.

Corbulo saw it too. Now. Now was the time.

'Loose the screens and deploy the artillery.'

On both sides of the valley, invisible to the Parthians because of their cunning construction, woven screens made from the long golden stems of dried grass that carpeted the valley had hidden Corbulo's secret weapon: the siege artillery, carried at such great cost in time and manpower from Zeugma. Behind the screens Roman engineers had constructed two pairs of great catapults that now dominated the valley. Others had assembled the legion's light artillery of stone-throwing *ballistae* and their cousins, the smaller but horribly effective *scorpios*, which fired giant arrows with the enormous power that gave them their well-earned nickname: shield-splitters. Each of the seventeen cohorts was equipped with a single *ballista* and ten *scorpios* and now the cohorts moved into open formation to allow the deadly machines to be positioned across the valley. Almost two hundred artillery pieces over a width of less than a mile. One every six or seven paces.

But it was the big siege catapults that Corbulo trusted would shatter the already cracking Parthian resolve. Designed to smash wood and stone and cow the inhabitants of great cities, the massive constructions of wood and iron could throw a stone weighing as much as a small ox for up to half a mile. It had taken patience and fortitude not to use them. To watch his soldiers die without fighting back. But now the destructive power that could destroy a city wall would be turned against flesh and bone.

The eighteen-foot throwing arm had been hauled back on its thick rope of twisted oxhide in preparation for the first throw. The projectile, a roughly carved rock the size and shape of a large cauldron, was in its sling.

'Loose!'

Tiberius heard the order and his eye turned automatically to witness the launch. Released from the incredible tension that held it in place, the oak throwing arm lashed forward with a force that kicked through the wooden frame of the huge siege engine and would have thrown it into the air if the engineers hadn't pegged it to the ground. With a gigantic *whuuuup* of released energy the arm collided with the padded buffer of hay-filled cloth sacks and sent its enormous projectile towards the Parthians. Unlike many of his peers, Tiberius had taken time to study the intricacies of his profession and he knew that the catapult was notoriously inaccurate. But with a target almost a mile wide and three miles deep accuracy didn't matter.

A tremendous whooshing surge accompanied the low arcing flight of the stone and for a moment the whole battlefield seemed to fall silent. Tiberius followed the dark blur until it was absorbed into the mass of humanity below. The ground seemed to explode and men exploded with it. He imagined he could see the pink haze as Vologases' soldiers were pulverized when the giant missile ploughed through them, robbing men of limbs and heads and swatting the big Parthian horses aside as if they were house flies. The power and the speed of the rock was so tremendous that men outwith the epicentre of the landing would be pierced by flying shards of bone and bludgeoned with lumps of still warm flesh. And that was just the first impact. Six times the stone skipped through the massed ranks, and each time it struck it caused carnage and consternation until at last it rolled to a halt in front of a pale and trembling Parthian princeling who looked down at the flesh-smeared lump of rock and fainted dead away.

The first missile was followed in quick succession by a second, a third and a fourth, and each missile killed fifty men and maimed a hundred more. But each of Corbulo's giant death bringers took at least thirty minutes to reload, and in the interval the Parthian warlords urged their men forward in a desperate bid to break the Roman line before the next cast. There was no thought of strategy now, only of survival and revenge. Vologases had lost control of his army.

However, before they could reach Corbulo's defences the Parthians had to get past the hundreds of dead horses and men from the earlier attacks. In the aftermath of the first Parthian charge the legionaries had used the lull to drag the big armoured horses together to create an almost unbroken barrier of dead flesh. The respite had also given the Romans time to collect the remaining caltrops and scatter them beyond the new line, and to recover the spent *pila* from the flesh of the dead and the battleground to their immediate front.

Vologases' infantry, had they been brave, well led and disciplined, could have crossed the barricade of dead horses and men, but no horse would, and so, for the moment, it was the war bands of Parthian bowmen who were left to charge and countercharge, peppering the Roman line. But the hail of arrows had begun to thin as supplies from the camel trains dried up, and more and more Parthians looked fearfully to the rear where the smoke from their precious supplies wreathed the sky.

And as they wavered, the *ballistae* and the shield-splitters opened fire.

Twenty at a time, in steady, evenly spaced volleys, a hail of ten-pound stones and five-foot arrows raked the Parthian front line. The *ballistae* could fire a missile a quarter of a mile, but here they were being used at forty paces and the destruction they caused was terrible to behold. Archers were smashed from the saddle with their chests and skulls stove in. Horses shrieked in mortal agony as the heavy arrows of the *scorpios* tore great gaping holes in ribs and chest. The devastating power was such that if the bolt missed the cavalry it would streak through to take the infantry behind, spearing not just one man but two, three and even four. Lack of arrows and the carnage they were suffering at the hands of Corbulo's artillery persuaded the mounted bowmen to retire through the infantry. At last, Rome's greatest general saw the opportunity he had been waiting for.

'Signal the advance,' Corbulo ordered. As the trumpet blared, he turned to Tiberius. 'You may join your cohort, young man. It is swords which will bring victory now, not strategy. Tonight we will drink a toast to Victory. Lead them on. For Rome.'

Tiberius saluted with tears of joy in his eyes. He had never felt so proud to be a Roman. He had fought and he had endured and now he had no doubt at all that he would win. He sprinted the hundred yards to where his unit was forming line along with the men of the Fifteenth and the auxiliary cohorts who had made up the reserve.

'Advance.'

They had begun the battle twelve thousand strong. Now they were closer to ten, but they started off down the valley at the relentless, measured tread that had made the legions feared from the windswept moors of northern Britain to the sun-scorched deserts of Arabia, and from Africa to the Danuvius. Still in their ranks they clambered across the stinking barricade of horse flesh that had kept the enemy at bay since morning and re-formed on the Parthian side.

Tiberius dressed his men's ranks and the long line of big shields straightened. All along the line other officers did the same. Behind the shields the sweat-stained, dust-caked faces were fixed and unyielding. They had suffered and endured and watched their friends die. They were still outnumbered seven or eight to one, but now they were doing what they were trained to do. Not standing around as helpless targets. Attacking their enemy. For hour upon hour they had stood and died without complaint and now it was all they could do to stay in their ranks. They had made their sacrifice; now they demanded the blood price.

'Forward, at the trot.'

Instantly, they moved into that steady-paced jog that they practised day in and day out. Tiberius drew his sword, but his men's remained in their scabbards. Each of them carried a single *pilum* in his right hand.

A rush through the air above them heralded a new volley of boulders and arrows that tore gaps in the Parthian line ahead. At the same time, a great crash shook the earth and a terrible screaming to the front left announced the arrival of the latest missile from the catapults.

A hundred paces away the Parthian infantry waited in a great bustling crowd, uncertain which was the greatest danger they faced. Some looked fearfully to the skies, wondering when the next terrible bombardment would arrive. Their stomachs tightened at the thought of the missiles which were now relentlessly flailing their line, gutting, dismembering and smashing. Yet the most ominous sight was the implacable line of brightly painted shields that now rushed towards them. An hour earlier they had sat comfortably at the centre of a great army, listening to the clash of arms, awaiting victory and grumbling about being so far from home. Now they were in the front line and death was on every side.

Fifty paces. 'Ready.' A legionary learned to throw the *pilum* at the run almost as soon as he learned to march. A running man could throw further than a stationary one. The staggered ranks of cohorts and centuries stretched the width of the valley and each centurion would choose his moment to order the cast, when the enemy was close enough for the javelins to cause maximum casualties and far enough away to allow his men time to draw their swords before the two lines met.

Forty. Tiberius glanced nervously to his left, searching for the threat of a flanking movement by the now underemployed Parthian archers. Even if they had no arrows they still had their swords, and a legion was never more threatened than when it was attacked from the flank while forming up for an assault. But there would be no flank attack, because the front line of Parthian infantry jammed the valley from cliff to cliff and blocked off any opportunity for the cavalry to advance.

Thirty. 'Throw!' A hail of javelins slanted out from the Roman line and fresh screams rang out across the battlefield as the lethal iron spikes found throat and face and chest. The order was followed by the musical hiss of a thousand swords being drawn, and the sequence was repeated again and again by the ranks behind. Tiberius watched the *pila* arc through the warm air and plunge into the massed ranks ahead of him. He heard himself growling like a dog and his ears told him the sound was being repeated all along the line. Ahead, howls and screams, white terrified eyes; a feral combination of fear, determination and hate. A wall of spears, but spears that shook in their owners' hands. His eyes focused on a group of five or six bearded men, but as he closed with the Parthian line every ounce of his concentration was bent on keeping his shield locked with the man on his right, just as the man on his left did with him. A man's instinct was to either surge ahead and be a hero or hang back and survive, but in a Roman charge neither was possible, only discipline. Hold the line. Stay in rank. Shield to shield. Swords ready.

A glistening spear point clattered against the rim of his helmet, but he kept his head down and it glanced off and he knew he had won. The big wooden shield with its solid iron boss smashed into something yielding. At first he was surprised at the gentleness of the contact. Shield line meeting shield line meant a crash like thunder, a rippling and grinding of unstoppable force meeting unstoppable force. But the poorly armed Parthian foot soldiers, deserted by their cavalry, had no *scutum*. He punched the shield forward and heard a grunt of agony from beyond.

'Now!'

At the command, every legionary angled his big *scutum* to his left, creating a narrow gap between his shield and his neighbour's, and rammed his *gladius* into the gap. Tiberius felt the familiar thrill as the sword's point pierced first cloth, then flesh, the muscle sucking on the blade as it dared to violate deeper and deeper into the body. He heard a man scream, but his mind was already on the withdrawal: the pull, the simultaneous twist of the wrist, the grip on the blade weakening and the stink of blood and torn bowels. He slammed the shield forward again, the rhythm of the battlefield taking over his mind.

'Now!'

The Parthians smelled of blood and death and sweat and fear and strange spices he had never encountered before. From somewhere, a shower of arrows hailed down on the rear ranks of the Roman attack. It was not only the Parthians who were dying.

'Now!'

A felled enemy clawed at his legs, but the legionary behind hacked at the clutching hand and it fell free with the fingers still twitching. For the first time Tiberius wondered about Valerius on his fine horse. Was he alive or dead? Perhaps they would cut their way through to each other and meet on the threshold of Vologases' pavilion.

'Now!'

His sandal slipped on something slimy and he glanced down. Below his feet was a red smear and a shattered skull with half a face and he remembered the pink haze as the great boulder from the catapult made its first impact. A certain cadence in the screaming told him that the boulders and the rocks and the great barbed arrows were still doing their work among the ranks ahead, but otherwise his whole being was concentrated on the weight behind the shield, the thrust of his arm and the threat from above and below.

'Now!'

With every word of command, each man in the Roman line took a step forward as he pushed with his shield. And with every step the men in front of them howled and died. A Roman legion was a killing machine and this was the killing machine at its most efficient, against the unarmoured and the unled; warriors who individually might be champions but in the claustrophobic crush beyond the shields were reduced to mere cattle to be slaughtered. A tortured, bearded face appeared below Tiberius's shield and he smashed his iron-shod *caliga* down on it, smashing the teeth, turning the nose to pulp and crossing the eyes. Yet the force beyond the shield was becoming stronger, each step more difficult to take, even with the weight of the men behind him. Tiberius guessed that somewhere beyond the Parthian infantry cavalry were being used to stiffen the line, the weight of the horses and the threat of death if a man took another step back bolstering the resistance of men who did not want to fight. If that continued, the Roman line would stall, and logic and experience said that eventually, when strength failed, a stalled line became a retreating line and then men died, in their hundreds and their thousands. Corbulo's face came into his head, the features drooping with exhaustion, but the eyes hard and unyielding. The face created conflicting emotions inside him. He had come to the east with a very definite opinion of this man and a single-minded determination to do what needed to be done, yet proximity to greatness had eroded his certainty until he was confused and disorientated. He knew that somehow he must rediscover that certainty if he was to do what he had to do. The thought gave him a new surge of energy and he thrust forward and killed another man. How many? It did not matter, because Corbulo could not fail.

And suddenly it happened.

A drum beat a frantic rhythm. The weight behind the shield faded away. A horn sounded a familiar but unlikely call and the Roman line stopped, dazed and uncertain whether to hold their line or to charge after an enemy who had retreated a dozen steps and thrown down their spears.

An armoured warlord in a green cloak urged his horse through the centre of the gaping Parthians holding a green branch high.

Corbulo had won.

XLIV

From his position by the largest of the three grave mounds raised over the Parthian dead, Valerius marvelled again at the size of the force Gnaeus Domitius Corbulo had defeated. They were the last stragglers of Vologases' great army, but they streamed past in their thousands and tens of thousands, spears on their shoulders, heads down and shoulders drooping, sharing the King of Kings' ignominy. Ignominy, but not humiliation.

Corbulo had been insistent, on pain of death, that the contents of Vologases' personal baggage train, his wardrobe, his library, his vast treasures of gold, silver and precious stones and his travelling harem of two hundred concubines, must be left untouched.

While the stink of death still hung heavy over the battlefield, the King of Kings had sat upon his lion throne of pure gold and his painted face had remained impassive as Corbulo dictated his terms. But those terms had been surprisingly lenient. The Parthian army could withdraw with its arms and its banners and its honour intact. There was no shame in having been defeated by a force with superior firepower and territorial advantage, the general stressed. This had been an unfortunate misunderstanding and they must give thanks to the gods that the casualties had been so light. Vologases' scorpion eyebrows had twitched at this description of a battle which had cost him the flower of the Parthian aristocracy, including some of his most important political allies. The ten thousand peasant levies who died were of less consequence. Corbulo would exact no tribute, beyond the expenses of the campaign, but he would take hostages from the great Parthian families, Gev, Suren and Karin. His only demand was that Vologases withdraw immediately beyond the Tigris and take his army back to Ctesiphon. The Roman forces would remain in place until the withdrawal was complete. There would be no repercussions from Rome, Corbulo assured him, and the hostages would be released the moment King Tiridates returned to Artaxata, the Armenian capital.

Valerius had listened to his general with increasing admiration. Corbulo had explained his strategy when they had met in the shocked aftermath of the truce. 'Better a wounded enemy who walks away than a trapped one with nothing to lose. If you cannot destroy your enemy, Valerius, you must leave him with a way out. His generals did not want this fight in the first place; now all they want to do is return to their estates and their wives' beds. But Vologases is a king and a proud man. If I humiliate him, or push him too hard, he may feel that the only way to regain his honour is to continue the fight.'

The King of Kings' interpreter had whispered the terms in Vologases' ear and after a moment's hesitation the Parthian ruler had accepted with the slightest incline of his broad head. Only the dark eyes betrayed the loathing he felt for the man who had thwarted him three times in his bid to extend his empire to the north.

After a mostly sleepless night, when it had felt as if he was camped beneath a giant boulder in a thunderstorm, Valerius had woken to find the Parthians already breaking camp and Vologases' armoured vanguard crossing the bridge of boats across the Tigris which had brought them here. The Romans waited another week while Hanno and his scouts shadowed the retreating forces. When he was certain they were gone for good, Corbulo paraded the remnants of his army around him in a great hollow square. They had started the campaign twenty thousand strong; now, with the battle fought, the dead buried and the wounded already on the way back to Zeugma, they counted fewer than sixteen thousand. They were bloodied and bruised, but they knew they had made history and they held their standards high.

'Soon we will be going home.' Corbulo's shouted words were greeted with a ragged cheer. 'You have fought, and you have fought well, as I knew you would. You have never let me down. I hope that, in turn, I have never failed you. Behind us we will leave the graves of the men who will not be returning with us. You have all heard the stories. Of men like Claudius Hassan, newly promoted decurion of the Third Thracian *ala*' – Valerius had a vision of the dark smiling face telling of his ambition to carve a life in Rome – 'who gave his life rescuing his comrade from the Parthian host.' Hassan had taken a spear point in the armpit, but stayed in the saddle long enough to get wooden-toothed Draco to safety. 'If he had lived he would have had the silver spear of valour. Instead, all he has is our thanks, and the knowledge that his deed will never be forgotten. As long as there is a Tenth Fretensis or a Fifteenth Apollinaris, none of their deeds will ever be forgotten. They are the honoured dead. I honour you as the valorous living . . . and I promise that you too will be honoured. I have sent couriers to Antioch with word of your deeds to be forwarded to Rome.' He read out a long list of names and Valerius suppressed a grin as he saw Tiberius, in the front rank of the Tenth, straighten to his full height at the news that he had been recommended for a gold torc. 'I know that *phalerae* and gold crowns mean much to you, but I also understand that the lack of plunder from our expedition will disappoint you.' A groan went up from the assembly and Corbulo smiled. 'You would not be human if it did not. However, forgoing Vologases' gold was as crucial a part of our victory as the sacrifice of our friends.' He allowed a long silence as the legionaries contemplated the personal cost of defeating the Parthians. 'Yet I have decided you cannot go unrewarded. Every man who fought will receive from my own funds a payment amounting to one tenth of his annual wage.'

The roar that greeted the announcement split the hills and sundered the skies and Valerius knew that if Corbulo had asked these men to follow him through the gates of Hades and over the Styx they would have fought their way into the Otherworld with their bare hands for him. He held his breath, because it would have taken just one cry of 'Corbulo for Emperor' to unleash a wave of popular support that would carry him all the way to the threshold of Rome. But these were Corbulo's soldiers and the iron discipline of their commander had been bred and beaten into them. There was no shout.

On the return march, with the Parthian threat reduced, Valerius spent less time in the saddle and often walked with Tiberius and the men of Corbulo's personal guard who were now under the young tribune's command. It amazed him how quickly the common soldiers were able to put the terrors of the battle behind them. When they weren't talking about women and wine and what they would spend Corbulo's bonus on, they sang traditional marching songs like the obscene 'March of Marius', which had more than twenty verses and chronicled the sexual exploits of a legionary from one end of the Empire to the other.

Tiberius was more subdued, the childlike exuberance overwhelmed by what he had seen and endured during the long hours of the Parthian arrow storm. The boy had become a man. Valerius knew only too well the horrors that visited in the night after a battle. The half-remembered glimpses of a human slaughterhouse: splinters of white bone against raw red meat, the obscene pink blue sheen of spilled entrails, or the fool's grin on the face of a severed head. The hair's-breadth escapes from death that hinged on the glint of a sword blade or an enemy spear point. The dead men who demanded why he had lived and they had not. These, as much as his wounds, were a soldier's baggage of war.

As they marched together he tried to lighten the mood by talking of anything but the campaign, but Tiberius seemed obsessed by the notion of duty.

'I felt sorry for the Parthian horses,' he said, in a voice that was flat and emotionless. 'But I knew I had to kill them. Some of them were beautiful and reminded me of Khamsin, but they died just the same, because it was my duty.'

'If you hadn't killed their horses, the Parthians would have killed you,' Valerius pointed out. 'War is about finding the enemy's weakness and using it against them. The foot soldiers Serpentius and I faced didn't want to fight us, but they had to be made to fear us or we would still be fighting yet, or more likely scattered across the plain with our guts hanging out.'

'So you did your duty.'

'As you did yours, Tiberius, and I will lose no sleep over it.' He covered the lie with a smile.

'But what if you were given an order you knew was wrong?'

'I thought we had already discussed that? There is no right or wrong, only discipline. Discipline is what makes us what we are, Tiberius, Roman soldiers. That was what your father taught you, was it not? He might have been harsh, but he was right. Only discipline and your example kept your men in line as they died under the Parthian arrows. Without discipline we would all be dead and Vologases would be on his way to Artaxata and Armenia would be lost to Rome for a hundred years.'

The young man still looked pensive. 'But what if there was a conflict between duty and loyalty?'

Valerius was bone weary and the question made even less sense than what had gone before. 'No order is given without a purpose, Tiberius.' The words came out more harshly than he intended. 'Hesitation only kills the men you fight beside. Disobedience means your own death. If you are given an order, don't think about it. Only obey.'

Tiberius darted an agonized glance at him, but Valerius's gaze was fixed on the horizon. If he had looked, he would have seen the firm jaw set and the young tribune nod.

So be it. He was a soldier. He would do his duty no matter how wrong it felt or how distasteful that duty would be.

XLV

The next day the army of Corbulo reached one of the great supply dumps their general had prepared for the return march. For the first time in two weeks food and water were plentiful and the men not on guard duty were given an unprecedented two days without drill or training. The grateful satrap of Tigranocerta had sent two thousand *amphorae* of fine wine in thanks for his deliverance. Corbulo ordered a ration to be served to every man, but the legionaries and auxiliaries found the sweet Armenian brew less to their taste than the leaded tavern vinegar they were more accustomed to.

Valerius spent the evening with the general, but Corbulo was a disappointing companion compared to the man who had approached the battle with such mercurial energy. It was as if victory had stolen something from him, or diminished him in some way. Even the diabolical challenge of Caesar's Tower couldn't energize him and eventually he shook his head and with a tired smile suggested that Valerius should seek some better company. Valerius returned to his tent, but he found sleep difficult to come by. A chill wind from the north cut through the worn leather and made his missing hand ache. For a while he lay and endured the ghosts of the past, but when Domitia's face reminded him that there were some things even courage and resolve could not make attainable, he rose and wrapped himself in a thick woollen cloak.

The moment he left the tent, Serpentius fell into step by his side. Valerius looked at him a certain way, but the Spaniard only shrugged.

'Just because you've covered yourself in glory doesn't mean your enemies will suddenly disappear. Everything's too relaxed for my liking.' He cocked an ear and Valerius made out the shouts of laughter from around the camp. Nearby, a legionary fashioned a melancholy tune on a whistle and someone crooned a love song. An argument flared and faded away in a few seconds. Normally the centurions and decurions would be moving among the men demanding silence, but clearly they had been lulled by the same post-battle euphoria as their troops. 'I've seen it often enough in the arena. A fighter is celebrating victory over one opponent and forgets the man behind who's about to put a spear through his backbone. It isn't pretty.'

They walked through the lines of tents to where Khamsin was tethered among the officers' mounts and the mare snickered with pleasure when she caught their scent. Serpentius scratched her forehead and grinned. The Spaniard was the least tender of men, but like everyone else he had been captivated by Khamsin's moist dark eyes, her ready intelligence and her courage. Valerius untied her and led her by the rope, taking comfort in her presence and the bittersweet scent she gave off. He marvelled at the good fortune that had brought her through the battle unscathed when so many other horses had died. Four or five times she might have been hurt or killed and he suspected it was only the Parthian love of good horseflesh that had saved her from harm. Their way took them round the camp perimeter in the cleared space between the lines of eight-man tents and the walls of piled stone. Despite the darkness, Valerius's footsteps never wavered. A legionary marching camp was as familiar to him as the forum in Rome, every one as identical as the contours of the landscape would allow and built in the few hours between finishing the march for the day and darkness. Every eight-man tent – ten of them to a century – occupied the same space its section, the *contubernium*, would inhabit in their permanent barracks. The fifty-acre area within the walls was cut widthways by the Via Principalis, which they were now approaching and which ran between gates set into the longer sides of the rectangle. Another road, the Via Praetoria, divided the southern portion of the camp, running north to south and forming a junction with the Principalis near Corbulo's living quarters in the *praetorium*. As they turned into the wide street, Valerius could see the flames of the twin torches which burned throughout the night at the entrance of the general's quarters. Everything seemed normal, but as they got closer he felt a warning tickle at the base of his neck and Serpentius stiffened at his side. They stopped thirty paces short of the cloth pavilion and the Spaniard sniffed the air as if it carried the scent of trouble.

Valerius kept his eyes on the entrance, waiting for a return to normality. What was missing was the reassuring twinkle of torchlight on polished armour. A member of Corbulo's personal guard should have stood alert at each the side of the doorway, but there was none. Six more would usually be positioned in pairs on each side of the tent, guarding against illicit entry. He searched the darkness for any sign of them.

'Buggers must be pissed somewhere,' Serpentius muttered, but he had his hand on his sword.

'Check out the rear of the pavilion. If they're not there *find them* and fetch . . . Tiberius.'

Slowly a terrible realization began to take shape in Valerius's mind. One at a time the pieces dropped into place. Tiberius was commander of Corbulo's personal guard, at Valerius's bidding. He remembered the ready smile, the interest in every detail of his past, the almost desperate desire to impress. *Perhaps you might commend me to General Corbulo and I have volunteered to take charge of those on guard duty.* The odd reaction when he discovered they were marching, not to Judaea's aid, but into Armenia. Just before the attempt to kill Corbulo. And that last anguished interrogation about duty and loyalty. He dropped Khamsin's halter and started running.

He slowed as he approached the pool of dancing torchlight outside the tent. Logic told him there must be a harmless explanation for the missing guard, but the instinct that had kept him alive so often on the battlefield screamed at him to act. He kept his hand on his sword hilt. He wouldn't draw it yet. To walk into the general's quarters with a naked blade might invite the same accusations his racing mind was levelling at Tiberius.

The earlier laughter had died away to be replaced by the low mutter that was the normal background noise of the camp at night as five thousand men talked softly in the darkness before sleep. But Corbulo's tent was utterly silent apart from the soft flutter of the torches in the light breeze.

With infinite care, he reached for the tent flap and drew it back an inch. Corbulo's command tent was divided into four compartments by internal cloth partitions and the first was the general's office. A dull orange glow painted the sparsely furnished space. Here was Corbulo's campaign desk, light and portable, where he issued his orders and read the constant flow of status reports from the two legions and their attached auxiliary units. Behind it a collapsible chair. To one side a couch where the great man could ease the aching bones which were so obvious to Valerius, but he would mention to no one, not even his physician. Satisfied, he moved softly across the carpeted floor and checked the second room, where the remains of a meal of bread and olives and a flask of wine lay on a table and Caesar's Tower stood as they'd left it two hours earlier. He became aware of a sort of grunting snore, like a pig shuffling in mud, and his heart slowed as he smiled to himself. Fool that he was to start at shadows. He would give those guards such a roasting tomorrow that they would think their arses were on fire. And Tiberius. How could the little bastard have let this happen?

Valerius turned to leave. He'd wait outside until the guard re-appeared. But something made him hesitate. No point in being here if he wasn't going to check. He only hoped that Corbulo wouldn't wake from his noisy slumbers to find him sneaking about his sleeping quarters.

Very gently, he pulled back the curtain that divided the two rooms. The snuffling sound was louder now, but the room was so dark it took time for his eyes to adjust. This was a small sleeping space, with the general's personal latrine curtained off at one end and his bed in the centre. Gradually, Valerius made out a dark hump where Corbulo's head should be and his tired mind worked out that the hump appeared to be squirming.

His sword was out of the scabbard before he had taken his first step, but the hooded man crouched over Corbulo had been alerted by the song of the blade and was already turning. Valerius went in low and fast, determined to drive his enemy away from the general. For all he knew Corbulo was already dead, or dying, his throat cut or a dagger through his heart, but he couldn't take that chance. Yet nothing could have prepared him for his enemy's astonishing speed of reaction. From nowhere, a heavy flour-filled sack slammed into his chest and slowed his attack. Tiberius. Only Tiberius was that quick. Even as his racing mind confirmed the assassin's identity the sack was followed by the general's gold-embossed helmet. The world went black and his skull seemed to explode as the heavy iron helm took him directly in the face. He was vaguely aware that his nose was broken as his legs gave way beneath him. Blinded by tears and with his head reeling he swung aimlessly with his sword until someone kicked it from his hand, leaving him helpless. He was dead. Tiberius would kill him and then finish what he had started. But if he was going to die he would die trying. With a snarl, Valerius shook his head and attempted to struggle back to his feet only to feel the sting of a sword point against the notch at the base of his throat. One push was all it would take. One push and the iron blade would pierce his windpipe and he would choke on his own blood until the moment the point was forced down to cut through his still beating heart. He raised his head to look into the face of his killer: Tiberius, wide-eyed and twitching, one hand on the grip and the other on the pommel, and both of them shaking.

'Bastard,' Valerius spat. 'Traitor.'

He sensed the moment of decision. The slightest shift in weight that preceded the thrust. It didn't come. Tiberius opened his mouth to speak, but before he could say anything Corbulo staggered to his feet with a roar.

'Guards! Call out the guard.'

Tiberius brought his knee into Valerius's face and smashed him backwards to be engulfed by the cloth of the tent wall. By the time he struggled free the young assassin was gone and Corbulo was on his knees retching. Valerius left the general and staggered through the tent and into the open. When he reached the doorway Tiberius was already halfway along the Via Principalis running towards the east gate. No escape there. The gate would be guarded and he couldn't leave the fort without a pass. But Valerius knew his man. Tiberius would not have made his attempt without planning his escape route. That meant a bolt hole and he was far enough ahead to lose himself among the tents and wait for his chance. But he had reckoned without Khamsin. Somehow Valerius made the leap on to the mare's back at the first attempt and kicked her into motion. Belatedly, he realized his sword was still lying in Corbulo's tent. But he had no choice. If he didn't catch Tiberius now he would be gone for good. For a moment he almost checked. What was he thinking? He knew what would happen to the young tribune if he was taken. But he was Gaius Valerius Verrens and he was as trapped in the twin coils of duty and discipline as Tiberius himself. He had given his loyalty to Corbulo and that meant that if his killer could be taken, he would be taken.

Tiberius heard the sound of hooves behind him and swerved between two lines of tents. For a few vital moments Valerius thought he'd lost him, but Khamsin made the turn in a single smooth movement and he picked out the dark figure a hundred paces ahead. Sleepy, astonished soldiers appeared in the tent doorways demanding to know what was going on, but Valerius didn't check as he closed with his target. He understood how dangerous Tiberius was. On foot or not the boy was quick enough and good enough to kill him. Would Khamsin run him down, or would she baulk? He couldn't take the chance. He would have to take him from the saddle. Thirty paces. Twenty. Valerius poised to make the leap. Then the cloak whirled and his quarry was gone, darting into the space between two tents. Too late to follow, but there was a junction ahead and he urged Khamsin on until the mare could turn and run parallel with the fleeing assassin. A set of *pilum* targets stored between the tents loomed out of the darkness like a legionary shield wall. Another horse might have hesitated, but

Khamsin made the jump without altering her stride. Her hind legs smashed into the wood and she landed awkwardly, but she never missed a step. Desperately, Valerius scanned the tent lines for Tiberius, almost missing the telltale movement as the dark-clad figure ran across their front. He shouted a challenge and Tiberius hesitated. Stumbled to a halt. Now he had him.

The young tribune stood, head bowed and chest heaving. Valerius slowed Khamsin to a walk, alert for any movement. Beneath the hood he sensed a prolonged sigh. An acceptance of the gods' will. He was wrong. When it came it was faster than anything he had ever witnessed. Faster even than Serpentius. Tiberius's hand reached out and the arm drew back with the fist gripped round the javelin from a rack that had been hidden by one of the tents. It whipped forward and the weighted spear sailed unerringly towards Valerius's heart. His mind watched the spear come, but the invisible strings that controlled his reactions couldn't keep pace with the gleaming metal point. He braced himself for the strike and Khamsin must have felt his unease because she reared up on her hind legs. He heard the wet slap of forged iron entering flesh, but surprisingly he felt no pain. It was only when Khamsin collapsed on her forelegs with a terrible scream, throwing him forward over her shoulder, that he realized what had happened. A rage as terrible as any he had ever experienced consumed him then, and he rolled to his feet and charged, screaming at his enemy.

'Stop or I'll have to kill you.'

The familiar voice touched the outer surface of his mind, but couldn't penetrate the killing fury. Valerius had no thought that he was unarmed and Tiberius had a sword that could chop him down in an instant. No concern that he might not survive. He crashed into Tiberius's chest and knocked him backwards, drawing back his wooden fist to smash it into the defenceless face. Then the mist that clouded his vision cleared and he found himself looking down into the steady grey eyes he knew so well. His hand dropped.

'Tiberius, what have you done?'

'My duty,' the boy said. 'Why did you not do yours? Better that you would have killed me.'

313

The sound of running footsteps forestalled any answer. 'Shit,' Serpentius whispered.

'Take him away.' A centurion's voice cut the silence. 'The general will wish to question him.'

As the young tribune was hauled to his feet and dragged off, Valerius walked slowly to where Khamsin lay on her side, the wooden shaft of the *pilum* protruding from her pale breast and the metal point buried deep in her heart. She still lived, the breath snorting gently in her nostrils, but the dark, intelligent eyes were already growing dull and as he watched she gave one last shudder and was still.

'Tiberius Claudius Crescens, you are found guilty of conspiracy to murder, attempted murder, neglecting your duty and failing to maintain a proper watch.' The senior tribune of the Tenth announced the tribunal's verdict in a voice devoid of emotion. 'Have you anything to say before sentence is passed?'

Valerius forced himself to look at the man who had been his friend. They had not been gentle with Tiberius. He stood between two guards still in the torn, bloodstained tunic he had worn the night before and barely recognizable as the boyish tribune from the *Golden Cygnet*. He looked at his tormentors through eyes that were mere slits in a face swollen like an over-ripe melon and bruised to the point where there was barely an inch of unmarked skin. A mumble escaped his cracked lips.

'Speak up, man.'

The young tribune spat in the dust on the floor of the tent. 'Duty. I was doing my duty,' he slurred. 'This court has no authority over me. I am in the personal service of the Emperor.'

'And what service would that be?' The speaker was Traianus, legate of the Tenth, who headed the tribunal while Corbulo looked on with cold eyes from a seat to the side.

'I am his agent in matters of imperial security.'

'And you have proof of this position? Some letter? A seal, perhaps.'

Traianus didn't hide the mockery in his voice, and Valerius knew that if a letter had ever existed it no longer did.

'In my tent. Sewn into the lining of my cloak.'

The legate shook his head sadly. 'Your tent was searched most thoroughly and no such letter was found.'

Tiberius began, 'You have no right . . .'

'Silence.' In the hush that followed Valerius could hear the buzz of insects trapped under the tent roof. 'You are sentenced to death by *fustuarium.*' Tiberius's face twisted as if a knife had been plunged into his back. *Fustuarium* was the most terrible of legionary punishments, when a man would be beaten to death by his tent-mates. 'The sentence to be carried out by the men of the governor's personal guard whose careers you have destroyed by your disloyalty. You are a disgrace to your legion, your uniform and your family. You have betrayed your legate, your comrades, your friends and your Emperor.'

'Never my Emperor.' Traianus flinched at the savagery of the words that escaped the condemned man's lips. 'Only one man here has betrayed his Emperor.' The whole room gasped as Tiberius pointed an accusing finger at the man whose evidence had condemned him. 'Gnaeus Domitius Corbulo overstepped his *imperium.* Gnaeus Domitius Corbulo disobeyed a direct order from his Caesar and set himself up as Emperor of the east. It is our *duty,*' Valerius felt the wild eyes on him, but he could not meet them, 'to execute the traitor Gnaeus Domitius Corbulo.'

Traianus glanced fearfully at Corbulo, but the general only shook his head.

'The ramblings of a madman. Let the sentence be carried out.'

The eight guards Tiberius had tricked into deserting Corbulo lined up naked and shamefaced at the centre of an enormous open square made up of the massed ranks of the two legions that formed Corbulo's army. Wiry and lean, their white torsos were a startling contrast to the dark brown of their faces, arms and legs. Each man's eyes flicked nervously to where a horizontal bar had been fixed between two eight-foot wooden posts like a miniature gallows. Tiberius had convinced his men that Corbulo had sent them wine gifted by the Armenians and relieved them from duty for the night. They were hung-over, terrified and shivering, and they knew a single word from their general could condemn them.

Now they watched fearfully as Tiberius was stripped and dragged in chains to the bar, where his hands were manacled so that he hung with his toes just touching the ground.

Valerius had pleaded for the leniency of a quick death for the man who had been his friend, reminding Corbulo of Tiberius's heroics in the battle. The general had stared at him with eyes as merciless as a hunting leopard's. Only now did Valerius discover just how merciless.

Corbulo marched out into the square and stood before the shivering, naked men, the sun glittering on the polished metal of his sculpted breastplate and the golden decoration of his plumed helmet. Valerius took his place at the general's side with Traianus and the other senior officers.

When Corbulo spoke, it was to the eight men facing him and the one hanging by the wrists from the makeshift gallows.

'You have failed me . . . the question I ask myself is: have you betrayed me?' The naked men shuffled and squirmed, but they had the sense to stay quiet as Corbulo's diamond eyes roamed across them. 'If I believed the answer was yes, you would be hanging beside the traitor.'

'I am no . . . ugh!' Tiberius cried out as the centurion standing to his right smashed a vine stick across his chest leaving a bright red welt. Corbulo continued.

'Now you will have your opportunity to show your loyalty and make amends for your lapse. This man,' he pointed to the hanging figure, 'attempted to kill your commander. This man betrayed his legion. He betrayed me and he betrayed Rome. But most of all he betrayed you. He deserves no mercy and he will have none.' He stooped to pick up the wooden stave that lay at the first man's feet and hefted it in his hand. It was a stout piece of ash – the handle of a *dolabra* pickaxe such as every second legionary carried – two inches thick, the length of a man's arm and worn smooth by constant use. 'You know what you have to do.' Valerius studied the faces and saw a mixture of fury, determination and in one case thinly disguised horror at what was about to happen. These men were veterans of Corbulo's wars, their features harshened by years

316

of hardship and campaigning, lines etched deep in skin weathered to the texture of leather. Horror or not, there would be no holding back from a blow. But Corbulo was not finished with them. 'You will strike to break bone.' A shiver of revulsion ran through Valerius at the simple recital of fact. 'You will strike to inflict pain. But you will *not* strike to kill.' He paused to allow this truth to filter into minds which had been steeling themselves to do just that. 'If Tiberius Claudius Crescens dies before nightfall, whoever delivers the final blow will take his place – there.' He pointed again at Tiberius. An already diminished Tiberius, the bruised face not the face of a temporarily damaged young man, but of a day-old corpse. A Tiberius who had clearly heard every word, judging from the yellow stream on his inner thigh and the damp patch in the dust below his scrabbling toes. 'And that will not be the end of it,' Corbulo continued. 'You will die, one after the other, unless that man lives until night.'

The sourness in Valerius's belly, like a shoal of tiny fish eating something dead in there, had expanded into a living, bubbling thing that made him fear for his bowels. Hero of Rome. The thought was a snarl; a rallying cry. You are a Hero of Rome. You will not vomit. You will not shit. You will not weep. For a moment, he wasn't certain who the thoughts – the inner shouts – were directed towards, himself or poor doomed Tiberius. You know death. You have seen death in every form. You understand that death can be a friend. But that was the awfulness of it. There would be no friend to escort Tiberius Claudius Crescens into the darkness.

At last Corbulo raised his voice, so that it echoed round the square of staring, armour-clad men sweating in the late-morning sun. 'This man would have murdered your general. This man would have brought dishonour to your legions. But worse, this man claimed that Gnaeus Domitius Corbulo, proconsul of Syria, wished to set himself up as Emperor.' He waited, daring any man to cheer, but there was only silence, a dull blanket of fear that weighed down on the entire assembly, man and beast. 'This man lied. I swear to you, the legions of Rome, upon my own life, that I am loyal to Nero Claudius Caesar Germanicus and if any among you believes otherwise you may step forward and plunge your spear into my breast. Gnaeus Domitius Corbulo wishes only to serve. To serve his Empire. To serve his Caesar. And to serve you.' He paused again, allowing his gaze to roam across the long lines of silent men. 'Sometimes serving can be harsh; difficult. As it is today. A lesson must be given and a lesson learned. We march in step or we march not at all. Let the sentence be carried out.'

XLVI

Tiberius had been mumbling incoherently to himself, but now as his executioners picked up their axe handles he began to shout, the strength in his voice growing with every word.

'I name Gnaeus Domitius Corbulo a traitor to Rome and his Emperor. I name Marcus Ulpius Traianus a traitor to Rome and his Emperor. I name Gaius Valerius . . .'

Valerius winced as the first wooden baton smashed into Tiberius's face, pulverizing his already broken nose and smashing teeth and bone in a spray of bright blood. It was a tentative prelude to what was to come; a half-struck, panicked swipe that sought Corbulo's approval and was intended to silence rather than maim. The decurion of the guard, a tall wiry Cantabrian with wolf's eyes in a feral child's face, was a decurion no more, and he more than any of them was determined to exact his revenge. He snarled at the man who had struck first to step back and organized the former guards into a circle. In the pause that followed, a soft, throaty murmur of anticipation or dread emerged from the surrounding soldiers but it was swiftly stifled by the growls of the centurions. The Cantabrian brought his axe handle round in a sweeping arc that landed across Tiberius's left shin with the sharp crack of a branch snapping in the wind.

The agony as the bone snapped made Tiberius give out a full-blooded shriek. He had resolved to be brave; to die with honour. But the coldness of Corbulo's words and the knowledge that whatever torment he suffered would have no end had unmanned him. His leg felt as if someone had pushed a red hot poker into an arrow wound. In his mind he cried out for his father, but he knew he would find no comfort there. When the next blow came, and then the next, his whole body dissolved into a mass of pain. His mind retreated from the horror that was being done to his flesh, but there was no escape even there. He felt himself broken one piece at a time and cried out for the stray blow that would end his agony. But the batons rose and fell, never landing a hit that might give him the oblivion he pleaded for. A hundred swords stabbed his chest as his ribs snapped one by one. His legs were smashed until they hung loose like sacks of blood and bone. He noted from somewhere above the brutalized body that was his own a sharp-edged sliver of white which appeared from an arm already broken in four or five places. Still the executioners kept up their terrible relentless rhythm.

A child's voice cried out. 'No more. Please, no more.'

From a dozen paces away, Valerius bit his lip until he could taste blood.

It is easy to beat a man to death, but to beat a man to within an inch of death when your own life depends on it is more difficult. The guards swung until the sweat ran off them in rivers and they could barely hold the slippery axe handles. Gradually, it became obvious they were cushioning their blows and avoiding areas of the dying man's body where a slightly overzealous swing could result in his, and their, early demise.

'Stop.' Corbulo called a halt as Tiberius's head slumped forward. The executioners stepped back, breathing hard and casting fearful eyes towards their commander. Accompanied by his physician, Corbulo walked forward to stand before the dying man. He took Tiberius's chin in his fingers and lifted it to look into the smashed, unrecognizable face. A thick streamer of clotted blood fell on to his hand and he flicked it away in disgust.

'Revive him.'

Gaius Spurinna had served Corbulo for ten years and had seen enough horror to last him a lifetime, but he hesitated to touch the obscenely hanging sack of battered flesh and broken bone that twenty minutes earlier had been a young man. 'Revive him,' Corbulo snapped again. Reluctantly, the physician reached towards Tiberius's shattered pelvis where two broken bones could be made to grind together, and as the condemned man gave a little shriek of agony, followed by an animal howl, the general addressed his former guards.

'You may think me cruel. You may think he has suffered enough. But the sentence must be carried out exactly as I ordered. Now continue, and the first man to hold back a blow will join him.'

So the pick handles rose and fell and the screams resumed until Tiberius Claudius Crescens, tribune of Rome, hovered somewhere between the living and the dead, and even Gaius Spurinna's reluctant ministrations could not revive him. Another man would have long since succumbed to his injuries, but there was a core of molten iron at the heart of the young tribune which would not be extinguished.

'Enough.'

Corbulo marched from the square and the legions were dismissed, the dust from their marching feet wreathing the execution frame, until only Valerius was left staring at the man who had been his friend. He heard someone come to his side.

'Poor bastard. You should have killed him when you had the chance.'

Valerius didn't take his eyes from the broken horror that was now Tiberius, but he shook his head.

'It would have been cleaner, Serpentius, but then you or I might have been hanging there instead.' He heard the Spaniard's grunt of surprise. 'That was the plan all along. Tiberius has always been Nero's man, Nero or Tigellinus. All this, the command and the investigation I was supposed to carry out into Corbulo's headquarters, was nothing but a cover. My job was to bring Tiberius here and place him in a position where he could get within a sword swing of Corbulo. You and I were decoys to divert attention from him as he did his work and to be sacrificed when we were no longer needed. If he had succeeded in

321

smothering the general last night no one would have been looking for Tiberius Claudius Crescens, the lowly tribune. They would have come for us.'

'He was a good soldier.'

'He was a professional assassin, so he should be. Growing up with that bastard of a father would have been the perfect training. His whole life was lived as a lie. The only thing I don't understand is why he didn't kill me.'

Serpentius turned to him, surprised that he didn't know. 'Because you were his friend.'

It was still three hours until sundown. Valerius stayed another hour. He was about to leave when Tiberius began calling out to his father in a tortured, almost indiscernible whimper. He listened to the young man appeal for love, beg not to be beaten and promise not to fail again. Then it changed.

'Mother?'

He winced. He had never before heard Tiberius mention his mother.

'Mother, please don't leave me.'

'Why don't you die?' Valerius whispered.

'Mother. I'm thirsty. Water.'

He came to a decision. 'Get me some water and a cloth.'

When Serpentius returned Valerius was still staring at the hanging figure between the two guards Corbulo had set. He took the cloth and with his left hand stuffed it into the fist of his right. Then he picked up the pitcher and approached the frame.

'No one is allowed near him, tribune. General's orders,' warned the senior of the guards, a veteran centurion of the Tenth.

Valerius shrugged. 'Rather you than me when you try to explain to the general how you let him die of thirst before the deadline.'

He turned to walk away, but he knew he had planted a seed of indecision.

'Wait.'

He stopped.

'All right, give him some water.'

Valerius had the pitcher in his left hand and he poured it over the cloth in the walnut fist, saturating it with water. When he was satisfied he used the damp cloth to moisten Tiberius's lips.

Through his pain, Tiberius somehow sensed the human contact. The feel of the liquid on his smashed lips took him back to the desert where he had suffered and almost died for his friends. For a moment he was back there, and out of the glare walked the long dead woman who had provided the only warmth of his childhood. She had come to take him home.

'Thank you, Mother.'

Valerius brought his left hand to the younger man's cheek in what appeared to be a caress. Neither of the guards saw the narrow, needle-pointed knife that he pushed up into the hollow below the younger man's right ear and into his brain. Valerius felt Tiberius stiffen and blood flowed warm over his hand to drip on to the already gore-stained sand below. At last, the life force left Tiberius Claudius Crescens, tribune of the Tenth, and, freed of his pain, his body sagged into the arms of the man who had been his friend.

XLVII

'Mmmmhh!' Valerius's eyes snapped open as a callused hand clamped over his mouth. Others pinned his arms and hauled him to his knees. As he grew accustomed to the darkness he realized that the tent was filled with legionaries in full armour including the centurion who had been guarding Tiberius who now stood over him with his sword drawn and a look of unfettered savagery on his face. There was a moment when he knew the man wanted to kill him, but it passed and he was hauled into the open and dragged through the camp towards the *praetorium*. The slim figure of Serpentius appeared from between two tents by the side of the roadway. Their eyes met and Valerius knew that all it needed was a signal. But that would mean death. Death for at least some of these men and certain death for the two men who opposed them when the centurion called up the reinforcements he undoubtedly had close by. Valerius had seen enough death for one night. He gave an almost imperceptible shake of his head and the Spaniard stepped back into the shadows.

The legionaries hustled him through the flaps and into the big tent where Corbulo sat behind his campaign desk with Traianus to his right and Celsus to his left. The three generals were in full uniform and Valerius suppressed a shiver as he stood before them, naked apart from a loincloth. This was the same tribunal which had sentenced Tiberius to his terrible end. Corbulo's narrowed eyes were the colour of the leaden seas which lapped Britain in winter, and just as cold. The room felt too small to contain the power of his anger. When he spoke, the words emerged through clenched teeth.

'You gave the traitor a merciful death against my express orders?'

Valerius saw no point in denying the obvious. 'The manner of his death shamed you. He was a soldier who fought for you and fought well.'

'An assassin.'

'A Roman officer doing his duty as he saw it.'

'A betrayer. Of his general, his legion and his comrades. A betrayer of his friends.'

Valerius bit his tongue at this incontestable truth. Hadn't it been he who had unleashed Tiberius at Corbulo like a launched *pilum* with his pompous exhortations to mindless duty? *If you are given an order, don't think about it. Only obey.* If he had listened more closely, perhaps he could have persuaded the boy from his fateful path. Perhaps Tiberius would still have been alive. But he knew it wasn't true. Even if Tiberius had turned his back on Nero and pledged his loyalty to Corbulo, how could the Emperor's most faithful general leave him alive without himself being guilty of disloyalty?

'And now we have a new betrayer,' Corbulo continued. 'I took Gaius Valerius Verrens into my trust. I gave him command and gave him my hand in friendship, yet he has deliberately flouted my authority.'

'Prolonging his agony achieved nothing,' Valerius met the cold stare without flinching, 'except to sully your reputation. It was not discipline you displayed, it was wanton cruelty. Tiberius saved your daughter when she was dying of thirst. You owed him a life, just as you owed me a life.'

With a snarl the general rose from his seat, almost overturning the desk. 'You dare preach at me? Gnaeus Domitius Corbulo is proconsul of Asia, conqueror of Armenia and three times holder of the triumphal regalia; more important, he is your general. I said once you were too soft. I was wrong. You are weak. A general cannot afford to have weakness at the heart of his command. A general cannot be seen to condone indiscipline, just as he cannot afford to ignore disloyalty. You leave me no choice. You say I owe you a life? Then I give you the life of your friend Tiberius Crescens, to whom you granted an undeserved mercy. But by disobeying my direct order you forfeit your own.' Traianus gasped and Valerius felt as if he'd been doused in ice water. He had known what he was risking when he helped Tiberius into the afterlife, but in his mind it had never come to this.

He listened to Corbulo continue. 'You will be taken from here at dawn to be beheaded before the assembled army. I give you a soldier's death. Be grateful.'

'I am a Roman citizen.'

Corbulo flinched as if he had been struck.

'I am a Roman citizen,' Valerius repeated. 'I demand the rights accorded by my status and my class.'

'You are a Roman soldier and subject to military justice,' the general said with finality.

'My orders came direct from the Emperor. Only the Emperor can pass judgement on me.'

Corbulo's face reddened and Valerius waited for the order for his immediate execution, but Traianus whispered something in the general's ear and he subsided into his seat.

'Very well, but you would have been wiser to accept my mercy, because when the Emperor confirms my sentence there will be none. Gaius Valerius Verrens, you are hereby declared incorrigible. You will be fed and watered, but no man will speak to you on pain of death. You will lose all privileges and be held in chains until confirmation arrives from Rome.'

The trek back to Antioch was a month-long torment of pain, filth and numbing boredom for Valerius. Each day his guards placed him in chains in one of the supply carts at the rear of the column and for hour upon hour he would shift from one painful position to another until his entire body became a mass of bruised flesh. At the halt, he would be lifted from the cart barely able to move and placed in an unfurnished tent at the centre of the Tenth Fretensis's marching camp.

The centurion followed Corbulo's orders to feed him – a bowl of rough porridge and a goatskin of water were thrust through the tent flaps each night – but, whether through neglect or purpose, he was not allowed to wash or shave. After the first week he was ashamed of his stink; by the end of the second he no longer noticed, apart from the sweet scent of decay from the leather socket covering the stump of his amputated right hand. The worst of it was the silence. His guard, well warned of the consequences, never exchanged a word with him, conveying their orders with rough pushes and thumps of the wooden staves they carried. At first, the slaves of the baggage train treated the high-born prisoner with curiosity, but after the first man to get too close had his jaw broken they kept their distance. Only once, on the eighteenth day, did Valerius have the comfort of conversing with another human being. How he distracted the guards Valerius would never know, but somehow Serpentius was able to reach the tent wall and whisper a greeting.

'Your friends have not forgotten you.'

'Tell my friends I thank them,' Valerius smiled for the first time in weeks, 'but that is precisely what they must do.'

But Serpentius would not be deterred. 'Tomorrow at noon Caladus and twenty men of his squadron will approach the baggage train for supplies. I will be with them. It will be the work of a moment to disable the guards and put you on a horse. We would be gone before anyone could react.'

'And then?'

'Armenia, or Cappadocia.'

'To be outlaws.'

'You would be alive.'

Valerius sighed. 'I brought this upon myself, Serpentius, and I knew what the consequences could be. Tell Caladus and his men that I honour them, but I will not let them sacrifice themselves for me. As for my friend Serpentius, though he has the disposition of a bad-tempered hyena, he should know that I will never forget his companionship and that buried in the corner of my quarters in Antioch he will find a leather bag containing fifty gold *aurei*, which should be some compensation for all the misery I have brought him.' Serpentius gave a low whistle at the size of the amount, which was equal to a legionary's retirement bonus for twenty years' service. 'He should use it to toast my memory and then return to the wretched mountains he came from, there to live as a king, or a bandit, as he pleases.'

'I will use it to toast your freedom.'

'No, Serpentius. I don't believe it will come to that. Gaius Valerius Verrens is a Hero of Rome, and he will meet his fate as a soldier.'

'Then I will use it to finish what Tiberius started.'

'You would kill my friend?'

He heard the Spaniard's snort of disbelief. 'General Corbulo has just sentenced you to death. How can he be your friend?'

'Corbulo is only doing what he sees as his duty as a commander,' Valerius explained patiently. 'Just as Tiberius was doing his and just as I was doing mine when I led three thousand men to their deaths at Colonia. He is a strong leader and a strong leader does not flinch from hard decisions. His anger is as much because I have forced him to this as it is about giving Tiberius a quick death. He thinks I am a fool and I believe he would rather I didn't die, but . . .'

'So you won't come?'

'No, Serpentius. I have walked in the shadows for so long that I do not fear what is to come. Sometimes I am tired of life and tired of living.'

'Then at least take this.' The tent rustled as something was pushed under the leather. 'Remember what they did to Tiberius and do not let it come to that.'

Valerius reached down with his left hand and fumbled for the object. His fingers closed over a small knife, such as a lady might use to peel her fruit. Or a man to open his own veins. He loosened the ties on the leather socket over his right arm and pushed the knife down until it was completely hidden before tightening them again.

'Thank you,' he whispered. But he might as well have been talking to the wind.

They placed him in a damp, windowless cell beneath the proconsul's palace at Antioch and he counted the days by the food his jailers provided. Stoicism had been ingrained since his days on Corsica studying under Seneca, and he searched the many texts he had learned by heart to find some positives in his predicament. But, gradually, captivity and solitude took their toll and wore away at his defences. The rattle of the plate heralding each new day was a constant reminder that each might be his last. Like a drowning man clinging to a branch he took to using every moment to go over his life and asking himself what he might have changed. Not his time with Maeve, or the cost each of them paid for it, because some things are as inevitable as the next day's dawn and their fate had been to meet at a time and a place that invited tragedy. Could he have been more of a son to his father, who had estranged himself from the family for so long? Only by sacrificing the respect that had finally brought them together at the very end, so, again, no. His life, it seemed, had been a series of perpetual dilemmas, and he had followed the only path open to the man who was Gaius Valerius Verrens. Perhaps every man's life was the same. It meant he could die without regret, if die he must.

He worked the little knife free from the leather socket. He had told Serpentius that Corbulo was his friend, but was that completely true? Could a man so iron-willed ever be said to have friends? Yet there had been nights, as they contemplated the tokens on Caesar's Tower in comfortable silence, when he had felt an innocent pleasure in another man's company he had never known before. The mists cleared and finally he realized what it was, this thing that had been gnawing at him. No, he couldn't have altered the relationship with his father, but he could regret that he had never been able to share the same companionable bond that came so naturally with Corbulo. Strange that he should have more in common with Tiberius, the man he had befriended and killed, than anyone alive.

The sound of the bolt snapping back brought him back to the present. Was this the time? He had the little knife in his hand and now he resolved to use it, not to kill himself, but to force his captors to kill him. Better that than being led docilely to the block like a white bull to slaughter on the temple steps. He gripped it in his fist, ready to take the first man who entered. The door swung back and a hooded figure entered, gasping as he rose up in front of her with the knife in his hand.

'What have they done to you?' Domitia Longina Corbulo drew back the hood and stared at the matted beard and straggling hair. The stench in the tiny room made her gag. 'I came as soon as I could. They discharged Serpentius on the first day. I think some would have had him killed, but my father refused. He took lodgings in the town and found a way to reach me.'

'You shouldn't be here. It's not safe. Did no one tell you that to speak to me was to die?'

Domitia bristled. 'Of course they told me. Do you really believe that Domitia Longina Corbulo would be dictated to by fools?'

'It was your father's order.'

'Then he is a fool, and I will tell him so. To think that my own father would kill his bravest and best for something as simple as an act of mercy. But you should not have provoked him, Valerius. He means to execute you.'

Valerius nodded. 'Yes, there will be no pardon from the Emperor.'

'If I could . . .'

'No,' he said solemnly, reaching out to touch her face. 'Not even if the outcome was certain.'

A tear ran down the velvet of her cheek. 'Then I will do what I can, even if it is with little hope of success. Sometimes I think he is a monster.'

'Not a monster. Only a soldier.'

XLVIII

Every head turned as Valerius was escorted into the room where Corbulo had issued his orders for the Parthian expedition. He struggled to maintain his bearing despite his filthy, dishevelled condition and the chains that weighed down his arms and feet. One by one he met their eyes. The general himself, pale as ever Valerius had seen him, his skin mottled like unset plaster. The familiar features of Marcus Ulpius Traianus, almost uninterested, as if his mind was on other things. A look of outrage from Gaius Pompeius Collega of the Fifteenth Apollinaris. Aurelius Fulvus, commanding Third Gallica. One surprising absence; he would have expected Mucianus to be here to see him condemned. And two unlikely additions. What had made Corbulo invite his daughter and Serpentius to the tribunal?

'Did no one think to clean him up?'

He felt his guards stiffen at the general's demand. The one on the left opened and closed his mouth like a dying flounder. Corbulo shook his head.

'No matter. Unchain him and bring him a seat.'

Valerius tried to hide his surprise as the guards removed his fetters and a padded bench was brought for him. He looked for some message in the faces of Serpentius and Domitia, but all he could read was suspicion on one and puzzlement on the other.

'Gaius Valerius Verrens, Hero of Rome, all rights and privileges of your rank and position are hereby restored.' The words spun in his head like a whirlpool and his mind struggled to grasp their true meaning. He hadn't expected to leave this room alive. Now, it was as if the past weeks had never happened. Corbulo continued: 'Do not expect an apology. You deserved death; be happy that you have my pardon.' He stopped abruptly, as if he was out of breath. When he spoke again, Valerius saw a new Corbulo, hesitant, even fearful. 'I offer no apology, but I do ask for your loyalty . . . and your help.'

Valerius studied the man who would have had him killed. A long moment passed before he answered. 'You have it.'

Corbulo nodded slowly and turned away, staring down at an open scroll on his desk. His shoulders sagged and he seemed to shrink into himself, before taking a deep breath and straightening again. When he faced his audience his voice had regained its composure.

'I have brought you here because you are all affected by what is written in the message I have just received. It is written in a code known only to myself and the Emperor. You are all aware of the reasons for my campaign against Vologases. I weighed the risks, political and military, and I made my decision. That decision, I do not deny, was partly influenced by pride. The pride of the Empire. Pride in my legions and their achievements in the last ten years. And, of course, my own pride. I would not countenance a repeat of what happened on the Rhenus. I have no regrets. I believe our victory has assured peace on this frontier for generations to come. But I knew there could be consequences.'

He turned to face Traianus and Collega. 'There will be no battle honours for the Tenth Fretensis or the Fifteenth, no gold crowns of valour, no *phalerae*, no torcs, no silver standards.' Traianus opened his mouth to interrupt, but Corbulo raised a weary hand. 'I know, Marcus, none better, how your men stood and suffered and died, and how in those last vital moments they took the fight to the Parthians, though defeat was more likely than victory. And no general could have asked for more faithful troops than the Fifteenth, Gaius. The reason . . .' He faltered and licked his lips and Valerius was looking at an old man.

332

'The reason there will be no honours is because, in the Emperor's opinion, there was no battle.' Traianus growled and Collega's nostrils flared like an attack dog's, but Corbulo waved for silence. 'The battle for the Cepha gap will be erased from history.'

'No.'

'Yes. Because it was never fought. There was no campaign. There was no victory. There were no heroes and there were no casualties. General Gnaeus Domitius Corbulo did not stir from Antioch. His soldiers stayed in their barracks.'

Valerius shook his head. How was this possible? He looked to Domitia, but all he saw was his own shock mirrored on her face.

'But . . .'

'There are no buts, tribune. I have been relieved from my command immediately, to be replaced by General Mucianus.' His face darkened at the personal betrayal the appointment hinted at. 'I am to attend the Emperor in Greece.' He produced a bitter smile. 'It seems I have other charges to answer than that of over-enthusiasm.'

The revelation and the consequences it implied were followed by a moment of silence before the room erupted. Domitia let out a sharp cry. All three generals were shouting at once. Valerius found his head filled with a vision of the future that had never previously seemed possible. He rose from his seat and went down on one knee in front of his general. 'Command us and we will follow you to the gates of Rome and beyond. To the Senate and the Palatine itself.'

Traianus, Corbulo's long-serving and faithful general, looked to his fellow legates for affirmation. They had discussed this individually when they were certain they would not be heard, but had never expected the day to come. Collega nodded at once, but Fulvus, whose troops were far away on the Judaean border, hesitated before giving his agreement.

'A single word from you and there would be a new Emperor,' Valerius continued. 'Mucianus poses no threat as long as we act together. We know Vespasian's views. You have already blunted the Parthian threat. A single legion each to contain Judaea and maintain order in Syria and you could march east with an army. You already have Asia. The

Danuvius legions would not stand in your way. Those on the Rhenus are in disarray, already on the brink of mutiny. Galba in Spain is too timid and the British legions too far away to react. The door is open to Rome. Nero has betrayed his people. He no longer deserves to be Emperor, perhaps he never did. Act now and the Empire will have the Emperor it has always deserved.'

'It is true, Father.' Domitia buried her head in Corbulo's chest. 'You must, or . . .'

Corbulo laid his hand upon her head and ran his fingers through her dark hair. For the first time Valerius saw him as a father; loving, compassionate and caring. When he looked around at the men in the room his eyes were filled with an infinite sadness and Valerius knew immediately that they were defeated before they had even begun. 'Have you forgotten, daughter, what I always taught you? That a Corbulo does not have the luxury of choice . . . only duty.'

Accompanied by the sound of Domitia's sobbing, he addressed Valerius directly.

'I need give you no reason for keeping faith with my Emperor, but your loyalty to me as a commander and a soldier deserves that I should. On the day of the tribune Tiberius Crescens's execution,' the grey eyes met Valerius's and he would always believe he saw regret there, 'I swore on my life in front of my soldiers that I would serve the Emperor, but even if it were not so I would never use what power I have to start a civil war that would ravage this Empire and bring its people nothing but sorrow. No man will ever be able to say that Gnaeus Domitius Corbulo was responsible for pitching Roman against Roman. All it would take is for a single commander to stand against me and the flames of war would be lit. Nero is no fool. If we reached the gates of Rome without conflict, he would bar them against us. He still has the support of the Guard and the mob. Perhaps they would throw down their swords and their cudgels and shout "Corbulo for the purple", but even if I knew it to be so I would not march.' He pressed his lips against Domitia's dark tresses. 'Because a Corbulo does not have the luxury of choice . . . only duty.' He turned to his generals. 'Return to your legions and continue as normal. This conversation is forgotten.

I pray you give General Mucianus the same loyalty you have always given me. Leave us now.'

Traianus would have argued, but Collega took him by the arm. Fulvus walked out with his head bowed. Valerius rose to follow them.

'Stay, Valerius. Spaniard? Arrange fresh clothes, food and a bath for your master on my authority, while I still have it. Take my daughter with you.' Domitia reluctantly prised herself from her father and with a tear-stained glance at Valerius obediently left the room.

Corbulo sighed and slumped into his chair. 'I have failed her. If only she had been a son   ' He gestured. 'Pour us some wine.'

Valerius went to the table and poured from a jug into two cups. He handed one to the general, but before the other man could drink he took a sip from his own. Corbulo laughed. 'Still loyal after all you have suffered, Valerius? Perhaps it would be better for us both if it was poisoned.'

Caesar's Tower stood on the table beside the jug and he picked up the small blue token, rubbing it thoughtfully between his fingers. As he did so, he studied the younger man; despite the filthy, stained tunic, matted beard and hair that looked as if it had been cut with a blunt sword, he still somehow managed to retain his nobility and his authority. The carved wooden hand which defined him an enhancement rather than a diminution.

'He has me between two stones.' He set the blue token between a pair of the larger whites. 'On the one hand he knows, despite everything, that he has my loyalty. He fears me, yet he still trusts me to do his bidding. On the other, he holds my family, my estates and the future of the name Corbulo in his grasp. He understands that I will not jeopardize them. He calls me to Athens because he cannot afford to have me in Rome, for fear of a popular uprising which neither he nor I would have the power to stop.' He shook his head and his voice filled with exasperation and anger. 'Can he not understand that by ridding himself of me he risks starting the very thing he is trying to avoid? As long as he had my loyalty and my legions no man dared act against him, because they knew that, wherever they struck from, Corbulo would act, and act decisively. They knew that the very name

Corbulo would dismay their soldiers and that one legion of Corbulo's was a match for any two others. He may rejoice when he hears of my passing, though I doubt it, for I feel Tigellinus's hand in this, but he will be wrong. For with my downfall the sands of time begin to run out for Nero Augustus Germanicus Caesar. What general is safe if Corbulo is not? What advantage in staying loyal when the next courier may carry your death warrant? Already there are stirrings in Gaul. The Rhenus legions will stay loyal to whoever pays them, but what will they do when they discover a *denarius* is barely worth three *sestertii* because of his excesses? Even a doddering fool like Galba in Hispana thinks it is safe to talk of the "need for change", while the degenerate Otho whispers encouragement in his ear. While I live Vespasian will heed my advice; when I am gone his ambitions may overcome his judgement. The fleet he prepares for the subjugation of Judaea could as well land on the beaches at Ostia. Nero is no soldier. He is barely a man; poorly advised and easily led. I pity him when he looks from his window and sees Rome burning and cries, "Where is my Corbulo?"'

'Then act,' Valerius pleaded. 'It is still not too late. Recall Traianus and gather the legions.'

Corbulo smiled sadly. 'Would you have me break my promise to the soldiers who put their faith in me? Would you have me betray the memory of young Crescens over whose dying body I made it? What kind of man would that make me? Not the man I wish to be remembered as.' He held Valerius's gaze. 'There is another message in the letter. A suggestion that if I take a certain course of action I need not fear for my family or my reputation.'

The room seemed steeped in shadow with the two men at its centre and the darkness closing in. Valerius said nothing. They both knew what the suggestion was. His mind filled with an image of Seneca. He'd heard that the old man had slowly bled to death in his bath still dictating modifications to his books.

'You should know that is the course I intend to take.' Valerius opened his mouth to protest, but Corbulo raised a hand. 'I will not go to Greece to grovel before that man. And that is why I need your aid, Valerius. Nero gives assurances that no harm will come to Domitia. I believe he is in earnest, for with all his faults he is not cruel, but I do not trust Mucianus. I fear that in his zeal the commander of the Sixth might wish to rid his province of a potential irritant, a focus for discontent. You must carry Domitia to safety. Before you decide, you should know that the dispatch from Rome contained a second command. One which fatally affects the future of Gaius Valerius Verrens. I have served Rome all my life and have never deviated from a direct order, but I choose not to see this one. It . . .'

'. . . does not matter what it says. I will escort the lady Domitia wherever you wish and keep her safe if it costs me my life.'

The general nodded. 'I am glad I have not mistaken you. Mucianus would have had you dead on that first day, for reasons which are clear now. But a man does not become a Hero of Rome by playing the spy, and there was another reason why you were spared. I recognized the regard in which my daughter held you.' His words were followed by a momentary silence while Valerius weighed their true implications. 'You pledged yourself to me then. Now I must ask another promise. Domitia is betrothed to a young man of good prospects and good character. Promise me you will do nothing to jeopardize that betrothal.' So he had known. Of course he had known. 'This is not a general's orders, but a father's entreaty. I must know that not only her life but her future is safe.'

'I promise it.' Did the words really emerge as a choked snarl?

Corbulo lowered his head, so Valerius couldn't read his eyes. 'You may leave me now. I have work to complete, but return in one hour. The guards have orders to allow you entry. I have arranged passage under false names on a galley for Alexandria and drafted a letter to General Vespasian outlining the situation. He will know what to do. Now, send Domitia to me.'

Valerius spent the next hour with Serpentius explaining the general's arrangements while he bathed, dressed in a fresh tunic and shaved. He and Domitia would travel as man and wife, with Serpentius as their servant. 'We'll be merchants, reasonably well off, but not rich enough to attract attention, and we travel light. The lady may be accompanied by her slave girl, but she can take enough baggage only for a single pack horse; tell her I suggest money and jewels, anything that is small, portable and valuable. She can replace her wardrobe in Alexandria.'

The Spaniard winced. 'Tell her?'

'All right, I'll tell her myself. Mucianus will track us down and it's possible that even Vespasian won't be able to protect us. We have to be prepared for that. We may have to run again.' He sent Serpentius into the city to buy appropriate clothes and food for the sea voyage. Then he went back to Corbulo.

Domitia was leaving the general's room when he reached it. She was clutching a piece of parchment, but as he held out a hand to her she looked at him with a mixture of anguish and disbelief and he was forced to watch her retreating back as she fled to her quarters.

He found Corbulo at his desk, dressed in a senator's toga with its broad purple stripe. The general's eyes were fixed on the *gladius* that lay on the worn desktop as if the gleaming iron had hypnotized him. At first Valerius thought it was a simple soldier's sword, with a leather-wrapped wooden grip and an iron blade the length of a man's forearm. Then he noticed the familiar silver pommel with the Medusa head. The triangular point was bright from recent sharpening. Still, for all its pedigree it was the weapon that had won Rome control of the world. A killing weapon.

Corbulo saw his look. 'Yes. A sword that has never been dishonoured. Is it not fitting?' He closed his eyes. 'I can remember the first man I killed. A tribesman on the Rhenus who objected to my cohort burning his village. It seems a long time ago. A lifetime.' His voice was flat and arid, like the desert wind hissing across a billion grains of sand. 'You understand why I have brought you here?'

The atmosphere in the room was suffocating, the last moments before a thunderstorm; the very air crackled with energy. Valerius found he had lost the capacity for speech, but the choked sound that emerged from his throat was confirmation enough.

'I will not die like some geriatric in a warm bath. But I do not wish to die alone.' Corbulo looked up sharply. 'It is not fear. I have come to value your . . . companionship. A soldier's companionship.'

He moved to pick up the sword, but it was as if it had just emerged from a furnace and his hands recoiled from the heat. Valerius noticed them shaking and looked away, but a whispered word brought him back to the man at the desk.

'Failure.' Rome's greatest general raised his eyes to meet his gaze and the bleakness there tore Valerius's heart. 'I have been a failure. A dozen battles, a thousand skirmishes, ten thousand dead, and for what? A general has his day in the sun. An Emperor bathes in his glory. Nothing. The same terms we had been offered by the Armenians and the Parthians ten years ago. The only true victory was the last battle against Vologases and Nero intends to wipe . . . it . . . from . . . history. No honours for the brave, living or dead, just a sandy grave and a secret order that no man who fought at Cepha should ever be allowed to return to Rome.' His features contorted as if he could already feel the iron in his heart. 'A failure and a coward. I was too afraid to lose my honour to do what was right. A Corbulo does not have the luxury of choice? A Corbulo is only a man and every man has a choice.'

'It is not too late.' Valerius was never sure whether he spoke the words, but, in any case, Corbulo ignored them.

"They would have followed me, but I failed them. I should have stood before my legions and accepted their acclamation and marched on Rome. You were right. Vespasian would have covered my rear, the eagles would have flocked to my standard and I would have been Emperor before Nero ended his final performance in Greece.'

'It is not too late.'

Corbulo looked up and said, 'It is time.' Now the hand that picked up the *gladius* was steady. He moved to a padded couch by the window, where he lay back, his eyes fixed on the ornate ceiling. Valerius could hear birds singing. He wanted to scream at them to stop.

'Strange how the world has never seemed so bright.' The general laid the sword aside and pulled back the folds of the toga to reveal a pale expanse of skin. 'Here?'

'No,' Valerius said gently, pulling the folds lower. 'Here.'

Corbulo picked up the sword again and placed the point against his stomach, just below the breastbone, and angled it up towards his heart.

Valerius turned his head, not wanting to see. He waited, but nothing happened for a few moments until the silence was broken by a whisper.

'I am not sure whether I have the strength.'

Valerius took a deep breath and turned to find Corbulo's eyes on him. He shook his head. Do not ask it.

'Would you deny me the mercy you showed my assassin?'

He didn't answer because there was no answer.

'Place your hand over mine.' In a dream he sat on the edge of the couch and wrapped his fingers around the shaking hands that held the sword hilt. They were bony and cold, an old man's hands. Instinctively, Valerius adjusted the angle of the sword a little and Corbulo muttered a quiet 'thank you'. 'On the count of three.'

Valerius looked into his general's face and saw a mixture of gratitude and apprehension. Sweat dimpled his brow, but there was no fear. He had followed this man to the very heart of war and he would have followed him to the grave if he had only asked.

'One.'

He closed his eyes and took a breath.

'Two.'

The hands beneath his fingers tightened their grip.

'THREE.'

With all their combined strength they forced the sword into Corbulo's resisting body. Valerius felt the moment the point sliced through the outer layers of flesh and into the sucking grip of the muscles just below the surface, then the moment of freedom before it found the beating heart. Corbulo gasped and let out a long agonized groan as the iron entered the very centre of his being. His whole body shuddered, but still the hands beneath Valerius's fingers forced the sword ever deeper into the pulsing muscle that held his soul. The shuddering intensified, and then, with a final sigh, he was free. It happened so quickly, that irreversible journey from life to death, that Valerius barely registered it. A towering beacon extinguished for ever in a single moment. Rome's greatest general, her greatest hope, was gone, sacrificed on the altar of her Emperor's paranoia.

He tried to stand, but his shaking legs wouldn't hold him, so he sat, motionless, filled with a terrible emptiness. His mind screamed at him that time was running out; he must get to the galley with Domitia before Mucianus or one of his agents learned of Corbulo's death. Still his body would not obey. He was conscious of the still figure at his side, but he couldn't accept it for what it was. The mighty intellect. The indomitable character. Gnaeus Domitius Corbulo had seemed indestructible. It didn't seem possible that he was dead. In that moment he made a promise to himself that was more binding than any oath. If he had to travel to the ends of the earth or walk through fire, if it made him a traitor to Rome or an outcast of the Empire, he would avenge this man. Somehow, Nero would die. When the room eventually stilled and he was able to rise, he discovered that his fingers were still locked around the dead hands on the sword hilt. He used the wooden fist of his right to prise them free and walked towards the door knowing what it was to be old.

As he reached it, a thought occurred to him and he turned to the cabinet holding Caesar's Tower. He studied the pieces for a few moments, his mind automatically memorizing their positions. When he was satisfied, he picked up the small blue token Corbulo had favoured and tucked it into the pouch at his belt.

Historical Note

If Cnaeus Domitius Corbulo did fight a last battle, it has indeed been erased from history. Yet, as AD 66 drew to a close, all the elements were in place for it to happen. With his brother Tiridates in Rome embracing Nero's dubious friendship, King Vologases of Parthia had one final opportunity to gain what he had struggled for more than a decade to achieve. The bulk of Roman forces in the east were entangled in a savage and bloody rebellion in Judaea that had forced Corbulo to strip the Syrian frontier of the legions which defended it. The road to Tigranocerta and Artaxata was open.

The question I set out to answer in this book was why Nero, at a time when he was beset by conspiracies and with Judaea in flames, should have ordered his most loyal and respected general to commit suicide. There are suggestions in the histories that Corbulo had been implicated by his son-in-law in one of the plots against the Emperor, but this seems to be backed up by little in the way of evidence and certainly not enough to condemn him. Nevertheless, Nero gave the order, even though he must have known that by doing so he not only weakened his armies in Syria, Cappadocia and Judaea, but also risked turning the legions against him. If Corbulo wasn't safe, who among his commanders was? Corbulo was, above all, a fighting general; his campaigns in Armenia are textbook examples of a soldier at the peak of his powers. Unfortunately those campaigns took place over several years and before Valerius would have been available to witness them. I needed a battle which encapsulated Corbulo the man and the soldier, and, let's be honest, an opportunity for Valerius to do what he does best. Fight.

The Cepha gap exists, though not by that name, and provided the perfect place for an outnumbered army to stop a superior Parthian invasion force in its tracks. Tragically, the road which leads to it from the Tigris crossing at Hasankeyf will soon, along with the city and the many historical sites associated with it, be submerged by a new and controversial dam project. Titus Flavius Vespasian, the future Emperor, probably did not reach Egypt to take over the Judaean campaign until later in AD 67, although his son Titus was there. History records that Corbulo travelled to Greece before he died, but for narrative reasons I have him take his life in Antioch and I hope I'll be forgiven for that rewriting of history.

Glossary

Ala milliaria – A reinforced auxiliary cavalry wing, normally in the east a mix of spearmen and archers, between 700 and 1,000 strong. In Britain and the west the units would be a mix of cavalry and infantry.

Ala quingenaria – Auxiliary cavalry wing normally composed of 500 auxiliary horsemen.

Aquilifer – The standard bearer who carried the eagle of the legion.

As – A small copper coin worth approximately one fifth of a **sestertius**.

Aureus (pl. Aurei) – Valuable gold coin worth twenty-five **denarii**.

Auxiliary – Non-citizen soldiers recruited from the provinces as light infantry or for specialist tasks, e.g. cavalry, slingers, archers.

Ballista (pl. Ballistae) – Artillery for throwing heavy missiles of varying size and type. The smaller machines were called scorpions or onagers.

Beneficiarius – A legion's record keeper or scribe.

Caligae Sturdily constructed, reinforced leather sandals worn by Roman soldiers. Normally with iron-studded sole.

Century – Smallest tactical unit of the legion, numbering eighty men.

Cohort – Tactical fighting unit of the legion. Normally contained six centuries, apart from the elite First cohort, which had five double-strength centuries (800 men).

Consul – One of two annually elected chief magistrates of Rome, normally appointed by the people and ratified by the Senate.

Contubernium – Unit of eight soldiers who shared a tent or barracks.

Cornicen (pl. Cornicines) – Legionary signal trumpeter who used an instrument called a *cornu*.

Decurion – A junior officer in a century, or a troop commander in a cavalry unit.

Denarius (pl. Denarii) – A silver coin.

Domus – The house of a wealthy Roman, e.g. Nero's Domus Aurea (Golden House).

Duplicarius – Literally 'double pay man'. A senior legionary with a trade, or an NCO.

Equestrian – Roman knightly class.

Fortuna – The goddess of luck and good fortune.

Frumentarii – Messengers who carried out secret duties for the Emperor, possibly including spying and assassination.

Fustuarium – Brutal legionary punishment where a soldier is beaten to death by his comrades.

Gladius (pl. Gladii) – The short sword of the legionary. A lethal killing weapon at close quarters.

Governor – Citizen of senatorial rank given charge of a province. Would normally have a military background (see **Proconsul**).

Jupiter – Most powerful of the Roman gods, often referred to as **Optimus Maximus** (greatest and best).

Legate – The general in charge of a legion. A man of senatorial rank.

Legion – Unit of approximately 5,000 men, all of whom would be Roman citizens.

Lictor – Bodyguard of a Roman magistrate. There were strict limits on the numbers of lictors associated with different ranks.

Lituus – Curved trumpet used to transmit cavalry commands.

Magister navis – A ship's captain.

Manumission – The act of freeing a slave.

Mars – The Roman god of war.

Mithras – An Eastern religion popular among Roman soldiers.

Phalera (pl. Phalerae) – Awards won in battle worn on a legionary's chest harness.

Pilum (pl. Pila) – Heavy spear carried by a Roman legionary.

Prefect – Auxiliary cavalry commander.

Primus Pilus – 'First File'. The senior centurion of a legion.

Principia – Legionary headquarters building.

Proconsul – Governor of a Roman province, such as Spain or Syria, and of consular rank.

Procurator – Civilian administrator subordinate to a governor.

Proscaenium – The area where plays were staged in a Roman theatre.

Quaestor – Civilian administrator in charge of finance.

Scorpio – Bolt-firing Roman light artillery piece.

Scutum (pl. Scuta) – The big, richly decorated curved shield carried by a legionary.

Sestertius (pl. Sestertii) – Roman brass coin worth a quarter of a **denarius**.

Signifer – Standard bearer who carried the emblem of a cohort or century.

Testudo – Literally 'tortoise'. A unit of soldiers with shields interlocked for protection.

Tribune – One of six senior officers acting as aides to a legate. Often, but not always, on short commissions of six months upwards.

Tribunus laticlavius – Literally 'broad stripe tribune'. The most senior of a legion's military tribunes.

Victory – Roman goddess equivalent to the Greek Nike.

Acknowledgements

Thanks once again to my editor Simon and his wonderful team at Transworld, my agent Stan at the Jenny Brown Agency and most of all to my wife Alison and my children, Kara, Nikki and Gregor, for their unfailing support.

ABOUT THE AUTHOR

Douglas Jackson is rapidly developing a reputation as one of the best historical novelists writing today. He turned a lifelong fascination with Rome and the Romans into his first two novels, *Caligula* and *Claudius*. *Avenger of Rome* is the third title in his series featuring Gaius Valerius Verrens; the first two, *Hero of Rome* and *Defender of Rome*, are available in Bantam Press hardcover and Corgi paperback.